I0545752

Aidan's Love
Twelve Dancing Princesses Book Twelve

Christine Young

Published by Rogue Phoenix Press, LLP
Copyright © 2019

Names, characters and incidents depicted in this book are products of the author's imagination or are used fictitiously. Any resemblance to actual events, locales, organizations, or persons, living or dead, is entirely coincidental and beyond the intent of the author or the publisher. No part of this book may be reproduced or transmitted in any form or by any means, electronic or mechanical, including photocopying, recording, or by any information storage and retrieval system, without permission in writing from the publisher.

ISBN: 978-1-62420-473-9

Credits
Cover Artist: Designs by Ms G
Editor: Christie L. Kraemer

Chapter One

Baltimore 1822

Aidan saw Blade leaning lazily on the light post across the street. With no doubt in her mind, he watched her. Her heart thundering in her chest, she picked up her skirts and increased her pace, fleeing from him and the real threat to her peace of mind he created. She knew he would catch up to her if that was his intention, yet she continued without looking back.

Before he spoke, she felt his presence looming beside her. Tilting her head a bit, she kept going, trying desperately to ignore him. Acknowledging his presence after he embarrassed her and humiliated her then had the gall to depart Baltimore for parts unknown without leaving a message meant he didn't deserve to be recognized. She would make him explain himself but not before she took a moment to rebuff him.

"You can't out walk or out run me, so why don't you slow down a mite before you swoon from exhaustion or fall flat on your face?" His voice was gruff sounding as well as impatient with her.

Her pride wouldn't allow her to give in to his request. Where she was concerned, he had no rights; none at all. She meant to fight him the only ways she could. Keeping her sights set on her home, she continued, her breathing coming now in short gulps. Damn and blast, she shouldn't have worn the corset. She rarely did so why today? Didn't know why she had Lilly help lace it this morning. There was no one in Baltimore she cared to impress.

Except Blade.

"Foolish woman, this isn't good for you. I understand you're just trying to make a point. I'll acknowledge that point. I've not been a gentleman to you, but I mean to change that. Slow down, I'm not going anywhere." His hand rested on her shoulder as if he meant to stop her midstride. Automatically, she brushed it off.

Foolish woman, she had a few choice words to say to him about that, but not until he apologized at least a thousand times. First, for what he did to her in London before her cousin's wedding and second, for leaving town without telling her where he was headed or when he'd return.

Chin held high, she resisted the temptation to stop and give him a piece of her mind. It seemed he fell back a step, still shadowing her but understanding she wasn't about to talk to him in the middle of the street or acknowledge his existence.

A gust of wind caught her skirts, tangling them between her legs. She fought for balance but knew when the struggle was over. Whirling her arms, she felt his hands at her waist, keeping her upright, pulling her against his hard body. She felt his entire length against her, every muscle.

Then, "Bloody hell." He caught her in his arms and holding her close, he carried her down the street to her home.

"I don't need your help, Blade," she protested, beating his chest with her fists even while she wanted to melt into him and enjoy whatever he might want to give.

"Appears to me, you do, Little Fire." He chuckled softly, seeming to appreciate her discomfort, while cradling her protectively in his arms.

"I can walk by myself." She gave up hitting the stubborn man. He'd do exactly what he wanted and there was nothing she could do about it.

"If I hadn't come to your rescue, you'd be sitting on your sweet little backside in the middle of the road," he told her, pleasantly grinning from ear to ear. "I don't want to see you hurt; only want to see to your pleasure," he paused seeming to think, "now that you're a woman grown."

Her breath caught in the back of her throat. She knew exactly the pleasure he spoke of. He'd treated her to the delicious sexual fulfillment before he vanished, and without a note she reminded herself.

When they finally reached the porch, he set her down to open the door. Still not wishing to talk to him, she strode inside, pulling her hat from her head along with a few pins that left her hair in wild strands before setting it on the coat tree. She blew the errant pieces of hair from her eyes.

"I didn't invite you in." Ignoring him further she left for the kitchen, needing a cup of tea laced with whisky, knowing all the while he'd follow her. Lilly always kept a pot of hot water on the stove and tea leaves close by.

"Smells good. Lilly must have baked cookies this afternoon. I believe I hear my stomach rumbling." He stood behind her now. If she turned, she knew he'd have his feet spread and hands on his hips looking as if he owned her.

"Help yourself." She poured her drink before taking it into the parlor knowing he would trail after her. If she didn't talk to him now, he would stay forever. Damn and blast, with the permission of her cousin's husband, he moved in months ago. All his clothes were here. It's just that he hadn't been here.

In the parlor, he relaxed, sipping his whiskey, studying her. A few cookie crumbs had fallen into the stubble on his chin. She tried to focus on anything but Blade, his broad shoulders and steel blue eyes, the way his muscles flexed when he moved. Tried to concentrate on anything but the way his hands had touched her, every part of her, aroused her in ways she didn't comprehend.

Rattled by enchanting memories of the time he seduced her, she ran her tongue across her lips while a searing heat rushed through her, reminding her of things she'd rather not think about. Against her will, he could do that to her; create a tempest swirling inside she was hard pressed to deny.

At times she didn't want to reject any advances he might make. If she gave in to his ploys, she would find herself in his arms and his bed before she could blink. After all, she'd been in love with him since she was thirteen, nine long years ago.

Inhaling a long deep breath and setting her cup on the table beside her, she asked and with a patience that was rarely a part of her character, "Where were you? All this time..."

"Ach lass, I was enjoying the silence." He rose and poured himself more whiskey. Returning, he sat next to her. Placing a hand on hers, he watched her carefully, his muscles tense.

"You don't want me to talk? Fine. I won't then. Be that way if you enjoy the sound of silence rather than my voice." She wanted to bait him, needed to erase the all-knowing smirk off his face. This isn't at all what she expected when and if he returned.

"Why are you so angry with me? I don't believe I've done anything to deserve your wrath." He brought her hand to his lips, placing a kiss on the palm of her hand, allowing his tongue to glide across her skin.

"Where were you?" she repeated with a little more force this time, tugging her hand to no avail while he drew circles on the underside of her wrist with his thumb. He wasn't going to seduce her so easily, she determined. She could and would resist him.

He lifted his shoulders, before nonchalantly speaking, "I left you a note. You should have read it. Then you would comprehend where I went and why along with the gravity of the situation. Truth be told, leaving you was the very last thing I wanted."

"It's been three months and I had no idea if you were even alive." She succeeded in pulling her hand from him then she crossed her arms over her chest, trying to calm her escalating nerves. Lord, but he could bring her to anger just as quickly as he could create a storm of desire she couldn't control.

He picked up her hand again, brought it to his lips. Gazing into her eyes before kissing the tips of each finger, he continued to explore the palm of her hand then her wrist. When he stopped, "I told you in the note I left on that table." He motioned to the one by the door.

Thinking, breathing, even sitting straight was nearly impossible when he brought his lips away. "A-a note?" she whispered, enraged at the masculine smile on his face and the way she melted with a tiny kiss on her hand. The man knew what he did to her. For a second time, she pulled her hand away.

Instead of conceding defeat and withdrawing, he picked up her other hand and sucked each finger into his mouth, his teeth nibbling on each tip. This time he continued his path of discovery and exploration up

4

her arm, kissing, biting. His tongue was warm and created its own magic against her flesh.

When he paused, "Yes, a note. Over there. It explained everything. Where and why. The gravity."

"I never saw a note." She stood, intending to show him there was nothing there. Before she reached the table, she faced him, and in a huff clearly confused by his seduction, "Regardless, you could have answered my question. You didn't have to—have to..."

"Make you breathless with passion and desire? We could go upstairs. No one is home."

"You did no such thing and no we can't. Lilly will be in the kitchen fixing dinner any time now."

"Make you breathless or write a note? I can assure you; I wrote one." Still his voice was too calm, too sure of himself, his smile self-assured.

It didn't appear that he believed she didn't see a note. Even if she didn't find one, it didn't mean he lied. Bending over and on all fours, she searched the floor below the table then tried to reach behind the nearby chair, stretching, moving her hand along the floor. She sneezed from the dust.

"I can't find anything."

His hand settled on top her back. "Let me help."

His mouth was close to her lips when she turned her head to reply. The warmth from his hand sent a whirling dervish of sensations spiraling to places he awakened a few months ago. A tiny whimper she had no control over made his grin broader.

She moistened her lips. "I don't want your help." Any more assistance from him and she'd drag him against her and make him give her those wonderful sensation he called a woman's pleasure. *Ninny, he would never let you take control.* Yet perhaps he would.

"But you can't reach as far as I can." His lips brushed softly against hers then in a blink they vanished.

"You're doing that on purpose." She closed her eyes, reveling in the touch of his hand as he slid it up her back then down to caress her bottom.

"Looking for the note I left you? I need redemption. Of course, I'm doing it on purpose."

"Then stop touching me and look for the bloody note so you can be vindicated. Or better yet just tell me where and why and I'll take you for your word." If he didn't stop soon, she'd end up a mindless, spineless puddle on the floor.

"I like touching you, hearing those tiny mews of pleasure and the soft flush that stains your cheeks when I do. Why should I settle for anything less?"

She'd wanted this for so long and now she tried to rebuff the potent attraction between them. Trying to move away, his body stopped her as he reached farther behind the chair.

"There it is." When he loosened his hold, she scurried away and standing, smoothed her skirts brushing off a few dust motes in the process. With a broad grin on his too handsome features, he held the object of her search high. "I believe this is what you were looking for."

"So, you found it. Care to tell me what it says?" As he stood and stepped toward her, she backed up, needing the physical distance between them before she did something stupid like throw herself into his arms.

It seemed he didn't mean to remain separated from her. Closing the distance, he read, "It says, my sister's youngest child was ill and she needed help, more than her husband could give her." He shrugged broad, masculine shoulders, "Since I was so close to Boston, I decided to visit another sister also. There you have it, proof of my sad tale as well as my vindication." He held it out for her to take as if he still wanted her to read it.

"I'm sorry I doubted you." There it was; she wanted an apology from him and she was doing the apologizing. Of course, she was. Women always apologized when it seemed the man should be doing that very thing, begging forgiveness.

"Come here." He stepped toward her again and when she moved back, her knees buckled as she hit the back of the chair.

"Stay where you are." She held her hands out, a tactical mistake he took advantage of.

"I need a proper welcoming kiss from the woman I'm now

officially courting." He held her hands and bringing her to a standing position, wrapped her arms around his neck while his hands bracketed her face.

"Hardly courting..." She tried to say more but his lips found hers, his hands at the small of her back pulling her closer, so close she felt the hard angles and planes of his body against hers, the raw energy of his strength, of the man.

The slow hot kiss reminded her once more of all he could do to her, all he made her feel when he touched her in certain intimate places. Yet she responded, letting him pull her tongue into his mouth, allowing him the freedom of exploring her body, with his mouth and hands.

Suddenly, he pulled away, a grim look on his face and with a soft almost regretful sounding sigh, "We should stop."

Stop? If he didn't hold her up, she would slide to the floor, melt in a pool around his feet. Her head fell against his chest while he ran his hands up and down her back, a soothing motion that calmed her nerves and eased the tension in her body but did nothing to eliminate the heat pounding through her.

"You can't do that," she whispered, barely able to speak.

"What." He grinned as if he knew what she meant to tell him.

With her hands fisted at her sides, "Make me feel all hot and wanting you then tell me to stop as if the kiss meant nothing to you."

He crossed his arms over his chest, studying her, meeting her gaze with the steel blue of his. "Would you rather I tossed your skirts and taught you a few new things about lovemaking here on the living room floor."

"That's a horrible thing to say." Yet she did remember the first lesson, the one where he confirmed to himself she was truly a woman grown, no longer a child. If she'd thought for a minute the size of her breasts would have established her womanhood, she might have padded her dresses.

"But so true."

"You haven't the willpower to stop before you ravish me?" She had no idea the effect of her words on Blade. A moment of apprehension swept through her when his eyes darkened.

"Where you and your sweet little body are concerned, I have no restraint. I used up all my patience where you're concerned years ago. With just that kiss, I was tempted to sweep you into my arms and take you to my room. If I did that, you would no longer be a virgin. Don't temp me, Aidan, unless you're serious." His threat was clear.

"I didn't know," she murmured, turning away from him and his piercing gaze. Yet she was thrilled he wanted her and even more thrilled he didn't revert to the excuses he used in the past, claiming she was still a little girl.

"Should we prepare dinner?" He led the way into the kitchen where Lilly had what appeared to be a meal simmering on the stove.

"You're back, Mr. MacPherson. Did you have a nice trip and visit in New York? Your sister must have been very pleased to have more help around the house and with the children," Lilly asked as she bent over to take something from the oven before setting the pan on the table.

"You knew where Blade was and you didn't tell me?" She couldn't believe what she just heard. "Lilly."

With spoon in hand and continuing to stir while looking over her shoulder, "Mr. MacPherson told me his plans before he left. I didn't mean to keep anything from you. He told me he left you a note. I thought you knew."

"I believed he got what he wanted from me so he disappeared." Aidan covered her mouth with her hands, appalled at what she just said when she saw the disapproving look in Blade's eyes.

"Excuse us, Lilly. Aidan and I need to talk privately before she embarrasses herself again. Is there a good place close by?"

"Walk down the path to the lake. It's part of the Andrew and Hepburn property and few go there. You should be alone," Lilly told them as if she surely knew his purpose. "I'll keep dinner warm for you."

"Many thanks," Blade spoke to Lilly then turned to Aidan, holding out his hand. "Come, Little Fire."

"Do I have a choice?" Mortified, she wanted to hide in her room, not go for a walk with him and what seemed to include a forthcoming lecture.

"I'm not going to hurt you or ravish you as you put it. We need to speak of something your innocence precludes you from understanding."

It was true, what he just mentioned. This courting stuff, if what Blade said was true was beyond her scope of knowledge or experience. She always had a way of blurting out her thoughts. This situation was no different.

She placed her hand in his before following him out the door. A cool wind blew in from the ocean. She shivered, wishing he could find someplace warm to talk to her.

"Wait here," he said and quickly disappeared. A few seconds later, he returned with a shawl for her to wrap around her shoulders.

They walked in silence until the lake appeared, her nerves unraveling one fine strand at a time until her body shook. So much had happened in the last hour. "Did you know my bathing suit is at the bottom of the lake?" She didn't know why she told him that.

His voice, dark and gruff as well as disapproving, he asked, "Just how did it get there?"

She sat down on a rock, picking up pebbles in her hand and letting them slide to the ground one at a time. "The logistics of its fall to the bottom aren't known to me."

He sat next to her, placing her hand in his. It always amazed her how small her hand appeared inside his. Lazily, he traced small circles on the underside of her wrist. She inhaled a long swift breath. He was doing it again, making her hot and breathless.

"Did you have an affair last summer before I got here? Edwin perhaps or was it that Hooley fellow?" His accusatory words shook her to the core.

"Why on earth would you think something so despicable of me? I've never? Edwin? Baxter? Goodness no—never." She tried to tug her hand away, but he didn't allow it.

"An absence of swimwear denotes nakedness. If you were naked in that lake with me, I would make love to you." His low husky growl sent a shiver down her spine.

"Are you jealous or angry?" She'd done nothing like he implied and never would unless it was with him.

"Both."

"I haven't done what you said." He brought the back of her hand to his lips for a quick kiss.

"Thank God. I'd have to kill the bloke."

"You don't mean that."

He didn't answer. "How?"

"How what?" She'd forgotten the question somewhere between his kiss and the words, *kill the bloke.*

With seeming patience, he repeated, "How did your swimsuit find its way to the bottom of the lake?"

"I wasn't wearing it." There, she silently patted herself on her back, having finally put an end to this story that seemed to anger him beyond anything she'd seen from him before.

"You think to make me feel better, woman," he growled. "If you weren't wearing it, you were naked."

"What? I wasn't. Not in the water." The tempo of her words increased. She spoke so fast she barely understood what she said. "Tira was swimming with Jamie and she nearly drowned because she'd been working so hard at the shipyard. She was so tired all her muscles cramped and she couldn't get to shore." She stopped a second to inhale a deep lungful of air. "Jamie had to pull her from the depths to keep her from drowning and the suit was so heavy he had to cut it off her. If he hadn't done that, she wouldn't be alive today."

Blade let a roar of laughter rumble from his belly. "Take another breath, Little Fire. I believe I've got the gist of what happened. Don't ever go swimming in this lake unless it's with me," he warned, pulling her close and giving her a quick hug. "Promise."

"Promise what?" She meant to be obstinate, didn't like the way he laughed at her.

"You won't go swimming naked in this lake, hell, any lake unless you're swimming with me. Promise." His hands rested on her shoulders, giving her a tiny shake. "I need to hear you say the word."

"I promise but Blade, I don't think I want to swim naked with you." She'd be so vulnerable.

"I hope to change that notion." He smiled, tenderly brushing a stray lock of hair from her face. "Now we have something else to discuss.

The reason why we're sitting here in the growing darkness talking about dead swimsuits."

"So, why did you drag me out here?" She knew it was because of the words she spoke in front of Lilly, but what she didn't understand was why he seemed so displeased.

He slowly repeated the words she told him, "I believed he got what he wanted from me so he disappeared."

"I know what I said but what I don't know is why you have to talk to me about what I said."

Looking away from her, he ran his hands through his hair. "This innocent stuff is killing me."

She straightened her back. "I'm not innocent. You gave me a woman's pleasure, or so you told me. So, you know I'm not naïve."

"I haven't made love to you yet." He paused in thought, running a fingertip along her arm. "What you said implied as much, however."

"I did? I made Lilly think that? She wouldn't care." She felt as baffled as she supposed she looked.

"You implied I made love to you then left you to deal with any unwanted results. It will tarnish your reputation if you repeat such things in front of gossips. You're right about Lilly though. She would never spread gossip."

"Lilly won't say anything." She agreed with him still puzzled. "What unwanted result?"

"No, she won't but now every time she looks at you, she'll think we've been intimate. And if you think about it, you'll figure it out."

"Why can't you just tell me what you mean? Why do I have to think? I'm sure I don't know what you mean," she asked, fed up with the guessing games and needing honesty from him.

He sighed deeply then seemed to agree with her. "From what we did, you're not going to be with child. But if I had my way with you, you might be carrying my child as we speak."

"I can't think of anything much more intimate than the way you touched my body, the places, the sensations..."

"Hush." He placed a finger on her lips.

The wanton inside her leapt free. She licked it then pulled his finger into her mouth. She heard a groan emanate from deep inside him. She smiled, realizing she held some power over his big body. "Did you like that?"

"Too much." He groaned again.

Too much, what did that mean? "I like the way you taste, not just your finger but your tongue and I want to taste other parts of you."

"Bloody hell." He couldn't help himself. He pulled her into his arms, giving her a slow deep kiss that had her panting for more. When he finished, he set her aside, "We have to get back."

"Are you hungry?" She ran a finger along his chin. "Because I'm not, at least not for food."

"Famished for you, that's why we should go eat."

~ * ~

"Your dinner is in the warming tray on the stove. Let me know if there is anything else you'll need. Enjoy," Lilly smiled at them as she walked from the room.

"Is that your stomach growling?" Blade asked as he dished up the plates of venison stew and set out the biscuits. "I thought you said you weren't hungry?"

"I guess all my blood was pumping to a different part of my body." She took the plate from him, setting it on the table, gracing him with a precocious Aidan smile. "Something you did to me."

Pure male laughter echoed in the room. While he knew Aidan McLellan would never bore him, had known that fact for many years, he'd never expected sexually laced comments from her, but did she know what she eluded to? "You can always say what comes into your head when you're with me, but you do need to curb your impulsiveness when you're around others."

"Impulsive? Don't know why you say that. If anything, I'm never impulsive."

"Sometime I'll show you, but I'm not about to explain anything while we're at the dinner table." The sooner he made her his wife the sooner life would be so much easier. Trouble was he was sure she was making him pay for past indiscretions. He'd pay whatever price she extracted from him to make up for his callous behavior over the years. Truth be told though, even as a thirteen-year-old, she overwhelmed him. From the beginning he'd understood denying her anything would always be difficult.

"Then we should move to the parlor," she said, picking up her plate, her hips swaying as she walked away.

He stopped her, "Not the parlor either. Would you like wine?"

"Why not? And yes, I'm going to the parlor. You can come if you'd like. Or not." She shrugged her small, delicate shoulders. "Your choice."

"Why not wine? Or why wine? It tastes good, relaxes, might...no never mind." He loved the myriad of expressions flitting across her face and the way her eyebrows narrowed when she was trying to figure something out. She pretended to know so many things but he was learning she was more innocent than he'd ever believed.

She stopped in the doorway. "Why not the parlor? There you go again making everything more difficult than it has to be."

"Wine?"

"Yes, and you're deflecting."

Of course, he was avoiding answering. He'd rather show her, pick her up and carry her to his big bed. Showing her would be so much easier. "Are you finished with dinner?"

He heard her huge sigh of frustration, he assumed, and watched as her eyes crossed for a second. "I'm done. Wasn't really very hungry." She brought her plate back to the kitchen and to the sink.

"Let's take the wine into the parlor. You can sit on my lap and I can enjoy watching you purse your lips when you say something outrageous and I won't explain it to you." He grinned at the expression he adored, having only seen it a few times as she was growing up. During those years he kept his distance, hoping some day she would still have feelings for him. Some day was here now and he intended to relish every precious moment with her.

"I'm not sitting on your lap." She picked up her wine and flounced from the kitchen, her hips swaying and provocatively enticing him.

"Suit yourself." He grabbed the bottle as well as the crystal holding his wine before following her.

In the parlor and sitting in a single chair, she held her glass out for him. He obliged by filling it. "What do you want to talk about now?"

"Us." The entire night, if he could have it his way would be about them. "What did you do while I was gone? Go out with Edwin? Or was it Hooley?" He didn't know why he brought up the odious man, but his gut tightened at the thought of her keeping the man company.

"I went to church and prayed that some demon would rise from the sea and swallow you whole." She peered at him over the rim of her glass, seeming to watch for a reaction.

His laughter rolled from deep in his belly. Of course, he understood. From her perspective he deserved that and more. "Anything else? You didn't spend seven days a week praying in church for my demise."

She sipped more wine, her eyes closing momentarily and when she opened them, they seemed to cross, her dark sooty lashes fluttering on alabaster cheeks. That gave him pause to think. Her lashes should be the color of her hair. When she opened them, their crystal blue depths never ceased to take his breath away, "No, I didn't. I spent the other six praying at home for your termination."

"I don't believe you." He stood in front of her. "Come, you don't have to sit on my lap, but I'd like you close to me. By the way, how did you make your lashes black?"

"As you've said any number of times, that might not be the wisest course of action." It seemed she ignored the last question and was thinking about where he was about to sit.

He picked up her wine and set it on the end table by the sofa then returned, "If I have to carry you to the sofa, I'll keep hold of you."

She didn't move, her breasts heaving as he sensed her panic. One moment she challenged him with sexual innuendos she didn't understand and the next, her eyes looked like those of a frightened deer.

"Give me a second to catch my breath."

"One."

"That wasn't nice." But she pushed herself from the chair and with what appeared to be wobbly legs, she made her way to the sofa. Sitting down, she drank the contents of her glass.

Taking his place beside her, he filled her glass again. "What are you, we, going to do tomorrow?" He wanted to spend the entire day with her, watching her and waiting for her to say something shocking she didn't understand.

"It's Sunday," she said, looking at her wine and frowning before twirling the contents around in circles.

"So, if you intend to pray, you're going to have make that sea demon something else." He put his arm around her, his hand on her shoulder, his fingers resting on bare skin. Pulling her to him, he made sure his chest was pressed against the soft curve of her breast.

"You're home now and all is forgiven. It's a church social and you will have to bid on my basket. Of course, you'll have to bring a lot of money because Sam always buys it, and he makes sure he can outbid everyone else there."

"I have to bid on your basket?" He wasn't sure what she spoke of, having not attended church in years or a church social ever.

"Of course, you do if you want to share it with me. The basket goes to the highest bidder. If you want my company, you have to spend the most money." She tilted her head provocatively, smiling. "All the money goes back to the church, who uses it for good causes."

"If I don't then Sam will win it and you will spend lunch with him. Not a chance in hell. Still..." Given what he knew about Sam, he understood the man was no threat to Aidan or winning her hand, so he didn't understand the wave of jealousy he was experiencing.

"I spend every Sunday with him. I do believe he's sweet on me." She turned in his arms, smiling sweetly at him.

"He's just protecting you from other suitors you might not want. Sam prefers men." Now it seemed he was absorbing Aidan's habit of blurting what he thought.

"What does that mean? Prefers men?" Lines creased her brow as she concentrated. "I don't understand."

This was not what he expected or wanted. Leaning toward her, he ran his hands through her beautiful red hair, extracting the pins, hearing them clatter to the floor. The length fell around her shoulders. Then he kissed her, long and slow, exploring her, tasting the essence of Aidan. He could never get enough. For him it was a drugging kiss. When he finished, "We should go to bed."

"Together?"

"Do you remember the time when you stood naked in front of me in my solar? You offered yourself to me." The image had been etched in his head for all eternity. She had been slender, coltish. Her breasts barely beginning to grow, it had taken a will of iron not to toss her on the bed and make love to her. He'd understood then, if he waited for her to grow into a woman, sex with her would be heaven sent.

Slowly, she nodded. He placed a finger under her chin, keeping her gaze focused on him. "That was a long time ago. I guess you thought I was a little girl."

"Not a little girl, but a young woman just coming into her own and you still had a lot of life to live. I couldn't take advantage of you although God knew I wanted to place you on my bed and have you then and there."

"But you didn't."

"I waited and now I'd like to do that very thing." *Bury myself deep inside your warmth and give you a woman's pleasure.*

"Tonight?"

"If you want." Bloody hell why was he provoking her? "I wouldn't refuse you but by the look on your face, you're terrified. I'll walk you upstairs and we can go to our separate bedrooms."

"You don't want to talk anymore?"

"Are you relieved? It's late and I know you're an early riser. We can talk tomorrow after I buy your basket."

"Alright."

At her bedroom door Blade pulled her into his arms for another kiss. The passion she responded with left him grinning, knowing when they finally did make love, she would give all of herself to him. "Goodnight, Little Fire. See you bright and early in the morning."

When the door closed behind her, he stood in the hall for a few seconds before walking to his room. Spending the night with Aidan in his arms would be paradise, but not tonight.

In his room he slipped out of his shirt, folding it neatly and placing it on a chair. He unfastened his buckskins in an attempt for comfort. After splashing water on his face, he lay down on his bed, his hands behind his head, thinking about Aidan.

Tomorrow the social, and in a couple of days, he intended to take Aidan with him to deliver Andrews' horses to his farm. Sam had been keeping them safe in the stable behind his blacksmith shop while he was gone.

He heard the knock on the door but didn't rise from the bed. When he saw her face peeking around the door, he smiled, knowing all along what she needed from him.

"Can I come in?"

"If you dare."

She stepped inside, closing the door behind her. Hands clasped in front of her, she looked at the floor then met his smiling gaze. Her hair fell in tangled disarray to her waist. He'd never realized how long it was.

"Are you going to make this hard for me?"

"I've no idea what you're talking about, and I don't want to make anything awkward. You're in my room, remember?" His gut tightened as he slowly rose from the bed, stepping toward her.

"I can't get my dress off. Lilly usually helps me but she's gone to bed, and I really don't want to sleep in it."

"Let me understand completely. I don't want to misunderstand you. You want me to take your dress off." The look of complete mortification on her beautiful face left him very nearly speechless.

"Yes, well no. I want you to unfasten the back then unlace my corset. As you can see." She moved so her back was to him, "I could only undo a few."

"I believe you've come to the right person." His nimble fingers worked their magic on the fasteners. As each one came undone, he couldn't help but leave an impression of his lips everywhere he saw naked flesh. Unlacing her corset, he helped the garment slip to the floor beneath her dress. For some reason she'd not donned a shift, and while she hugged the bodice of her dress to her breasts, she was naked all the way to her sweetly rounded derrière.

In his arms, he turned her, allowing his hands to slide down her back until he cupped her bottom in his hands, pulling her belly so she was positioned next to his pulsing rod. Only a thin layer of fabric separated them. Lord, but he gritted his teeth trying to stop himself. She could tempt a saint and he certainly was no candidate for sainthood.

"Thank you," she whispered, her breath wafting across his chest. The backs of her hands touched him, moved across him until she touched the hard buds of his nipples. "I like touching you. I like looking at you without clothes on too."

Holding her dress with one hand, she spread her fingers then moving lower stopped at the top of his waistband. He wanted to push his buckskins to the floor and let her wrap those slender very female fingers around him. He sucked in air, fighting the lust that was rapidly taking over his conscious mind and body.

"You're unfastened." His lips met hers in a gentle kiss. "Go back to your room before I do something I might come to regret."

She gazed at him, confusion in her eyes. "I thought..."

"That if you offered yourself to me, I would take advantage of the situation. You need to be sure sex is what you want before you give yourself to me. You must be sure the gift you're giving your first lover, well, that he's the person you want to give your virginity to. I'm not turning you away because I want to humiliate or embarrass you, or because I don't want you, but because I'm not sure you're ready."

"How will I know, how will you know if I'm sure? If I'm ready?" Her lips trembled slightly.

"Come, let's get you to your room." Blade walked the short distance to her room, behind her and made sure the door was closed tightly before he strode to his room.

Lying on his bed, Blade almost regretted sending her away. He didn't think he could sleep unless he found release. There were ways but he opted for a swim; exercise helped as well as the cold water. His Little Fire had no idea how difficult his actions this evening had been.

A few minutes later, with towel in hand, he strode down the dark path to the lake. He brought a lantern with him to light the way. For the end of April it was a warm evening. A sliver of a moon could be seen between a few strips of clouds and a slight breeze filtered through the trees. The croak of frogs and the hoot of an owl brightened the night.

Stripping to his small clothes he waded in until the water reached his waist. Then, inhaling a deep breath he dove. Swimming under water until his lungs felt as if they would burst, he finally surfaced. Sure, strong strokes propelled him to the waterfall that caught his interest. He found a path circling around the water and into a small cove behind it.

Trying desperately to think of anything except Aidan, he lost the battle. When he saw the secluded spot, all he could think of was Aidan and holding her skin to skin. He ran his hands through his hair, wondering if there would be any release for him tonight or ever, imagining a life in constant arousal.

He dove through the water into the lake. Making a list of things he needed to accomplish before he took Damian's thoroughbreds overland to the Andrews' farm, his mind strayed from the woman in the bedroom next to his.

They would meet Damian's men before the first evening. Camping out in the forest would be safer, so he'd timed everything with Andrews. If both parties left on the same day, they should meet shortly before six o'clock that evening. Nothing could go wrong.

When Aidan was involved anything could happen. *Clear your mind, Blade. Keep thinking of horses and the food you need to bring with you.* He needed good strong coffee, but Aidan liked her tea.

This wasn't working. Striding from the water, he found his towel. The lantern still burned. He tugged off his wet clothes and pulled his buckskins on then slipped his moccasins on his feet.

"Master MacPherson?"

"Yes." Blade reached for the pistol he usually wore.

"It's Joshua, Lilly's husband. But I suppose you know that. Saw you leave the house and head down the path. It's not always safe out here. Thought I'd stand guard for a few minutes. Figured you was havin' woman trouble the way you plunged into that lake. Not the right time of year for a swim, if you get my drift. It's mighty cold in there."

"Much obliged." Cold was what he needed. Blade towel dried his hair, looking to the house. No lights shown from the window of her room.

"We're too far away from both the main house and my cottage. You can't see lights. Sometimes drunken men from the bars stumble down here. I'll walk back with you."

"I wasn't thinking when I left the house." Well, he was but with the wrong part of his anatomy. "Left without my pistol or my knife. Had to get out of the house before I did something foolish."

With the silence of the night pervading his soul, he walked with Joshua "Take care and thank you again."

When he opened the door to his room, he stopped, traumatized by the site in front of him. Aidan lay on his bed, her wonderful red hair spilled across his pillow. She was curled up in a tight ball.

The vision of her was unparalleled. In his entire life he couldn't remember seeing anyone so beautiful, especially asleep on his bed. His gut tightened and the effect of the midnight swim in the frigid lake vanished.

"Aidan," he whispered, walking toward her.

The sound of her name in the silence seemed to wake her. She sat up, brushing hair from her face. "You're back. Where did you go?"

Once again, he was nearly naked. He needed to rid himself of the damp buckskins but didn't dare. Not for one second did he believe she was ready to see him naked and fully aroused.

"Why are you here?" That sounded too harsh. "Aidan, you should be asleep in your room. Where you're safe."

She shrugged, pushing the sheet and blankets to her waist, her red hair falling in wild disarray around her shoulders. "I heard a noise and I was frightened. I was looking for you. I searched the house but didn't find anyone so I came back here. Somehow I felt safer in your room."

"I'm glad of that. Would you turn around? I'm going to take my pants off." He walked to his wardrobe and rummaging inside found another pair of buckskins.

When he looked to see if she did as he instructed, he found a set of wide blue eyes staring at him. "I mean it, Aidan. Unless you want to see me buck naked, you need to turn around and close your eyes right now." At the moment he wasn't sure how he felt.

"You've seen me buck naked."

20

"True. Well almost. I never removed your clothing, but I did see certain parts of you." How could he refute something that was so accurate? Bloody hell, how could trying to be a gentleman and do the right thing be so fucking hard?

"No. You can't make me. I want to see you, all of you. I've never seen a naked man and I'm curious."

His breath caught in his throat. She sounded like a little girl at the beginnings of a temper tantrum that made him want to laugh. He wondered if they would have a girl, one who looked just like Aidan. He groaned knowing he was overstepping his bounds.

He had no words. Instead, he turned his back on her and slipped from his damp clothes then changing his mind, he pulled on a dry pair of underclothes and strode to the bed. "Do you want me to walk you back to your room or do you want to go by yourself."

"Neither." She patted the spot beside her. Aidan's angelic smile didn't fool him.

Two could play this game. He walked around the bed, settling in beside her and pulling her to him so her head rested against his chest. Her hand rose to caress him, and he prayed she didn't explore below his waist. He thought to scare her to her room, but he had the sinking sensation that tonight he would never frighten her away. Besides, if he were honest with himself, he wanted her in his bed and beside him for the rest of his life.

He closed his eyes, even while he kept his hands fisted tightly. A smile curved his lips while he thought of his first site of her this evening. In a virgin nightdress, she came to his bed to seduce or truly because she felt safer, he would never know. The gown was white and long, probably covering her beyond her toes.

He envisioned her in a filmy negligee, one he could see all her curves through, one he could...

She was asleep. The feel of her breasts against his chest, moving slowly with her breathing, caused such a wave of bliss to run the length of him. He would protect her always with his life. She was his through eternity and beyond.

She was asleep. He didn't dare wake her. This was something he never thought of before. His soon to be wife sleeping beside him and in his arms, the sensations more potent than sex and more enduring.

~ * ~

Laird MacPherson, Blade's father, sat up in bed willing his body to heal. He needed to stay alive until Blade returned with his bride, Aidan McLellan. It was too bad Blade scared her away, clear to the United States. If he died before Blade returned, there would be fighting over the land, MacPherson land. Blade's younger brother had always coveted this ancestral home for himself.

"Sir? You called for me?"

"I did, Angus, come in and help me dress. It's what I pay you good money to do. Besides I crave someone to talk to, a person I can trust. Then I need to have you help me downstairs. I must put in an appearance so the entire clan will know I'm alive and prospering. We must present a united front, you and I. Don't know how long it will be until Blade returns with his bride."

"You have a letter, sir. It's from your son."

"Ah, yes, it's about time. No, it's past time I heard from him. I pray this missive will tell me he's on his way home." The laird rose from his bed, extending his hand for the envelope. Quickly opening, he read.

Father,

I pray this letter will find you well and improving daily. As summer creeps closer, I'm sure the weather will heal what ails you. Take some time to sit in the sun and soak up the warmth of its rays.

As you know, I visited my sisters so my return will be delayed a month or two. I'm now back in Baltimore, courting the lady I mean to make my wife and hoping to return before the end of the summer. I vow I will be home by the end of August if not before.

I've promised Damian Andrews I would escort the horses he purchased from the Graham's to his home inland. By that time, I do hope I've also convinced Aidan to become my wife. As a last resort we will handfast so my homecoming will be eminent. When that happens, I'll sail for home. Nothing will get in my way.

Stay well,

Your son,
Blade

The MacPherson sat down, head in hands, moisture clogging his throat. Truly he didn't know if he could hold on until the end of the summer. Pretending good health was taking its toll on his body as well as his mind. He looked at his valet and confident as if his old friend could give him the advice and strength, he needed to do what Blade suggested.

"Help me dress. Something simple and I'll sit in the solar for a while before going downstairs to make my presence known. I need to regain their confidence and the only way that will happen is if they see me. Perhaps with the appearance of warm weather, my health will improve."

"Good, Sir, you must present a strong front for your son. You cannot show any signs of weakness. None of us at the keep want his younger brother taking over. Blade must get home soon if his brother's rise to power is not to happen and you must get well."

He coughed then cleared his throat. He really did feel better this week as the warmth of spring seemed to permeate his soul, giving health to his body. Winters here in this land were always harsh and difficult to endure.

Washed and dressed, with the help of his manservant, he sat in the solar, soaking up the warmth of the sun. Funny how this tiny bit of sunshine made him feel better. A dish of eggs and bread sat in front of him. His stomach rumbled. It was a good sign.

As soon as he finished eating, he'd go downstairs and visit with his people. They would relay the message to the second son that he was healthy and working. Yet the sooner Blade returned the easier this would be. He wouldn't have to spend the days looking over his shoulder for an enemy.

"Are you ready to make your appearance?" Angus asked.

The MacPherson groaned, understanding the importance of making his presence known. Each day he needed to go downstairs, mingle with his people, give them confidence. If he didn't, it would only be a matter of time before Blade's brother rode into the keep, demanding he step down.

Damn it, but this was his first son's birthright. He would not let anyone take it away from Blade, especially not his younger sibling. His fist pounded on the table, unwilling to give in to this malady possessing his body.

Chapter Two

Blade watched, frown lines creasing his forehead as Aidan walked away with Sam and the picnic basket that was supposed to be his. Aidan had been sure Blade would outbid Sam but he unexpectedly stopped bidding. She was also sure, Sam knew Blade was sweet on her, so why did he keep bidding when it was clear Blade had stopped.

For that matter why did Blade stop? Did he believe she wasn't worth that much money? A simmering doubt formed within. She'd been so sure she'd spend the afternoon with Blade. Now she was with Sam and Blade told her the man preferred men. Just what the bloody hell did that mean? Blade would tell her someday when he felt like it. Maybe Sam would explain if she asked.

"This looks like a nice spot." Sam stopped, turning he seemed to watch her. His boyish grin spread across his face. "Are you angry I outbid your lover? I can find him and make amends if you like."

"He's not my lover." But she hoped he would be soon. "I don't know why he stopped bidding but no, don't try to make amends. That's up to Blade."

"Only reason I can figure is that he ran out of money. No other baskets went for this amount. I like your fried chicken too much to let Blade get it without putting up a fight. Seems he going to be gettin' a whole lot more of it in the future." Sam grinned at her as if he knew something she didn't.

"Blade said you prefer men. What does that mean?" She watched his face redden and wondered if she should have asked the question, not meaning to intrude on anything personal.

"I'll tell you later." Blade stepped between the pair. "Should have told you when the question first came up then you wouldn't be putting Sam on the spot and making him uncomfortable. Who he likes or doesn't like is truly not our business." Turning to Sam, "my apologies for Aidan's question and for intruding on your picnic. Didn't think you'd mind too much. Aidan is an innocent and has no idea about the ways of the world."

"Don't mind unless you eat all the chicken and potato salad," Sam said grinning. "Make sure you explain everything to your little lady. Innocence can get a beautiful woman into a pack of trouble."

"The pair of you are talking in riddles and as if I'm not here. Don't know why you can't tell me right now or why I put up with either of you." Indignant at the pair, she was tempted to take her basket and walk away. Let the two of them fend for themselves. They could go hungry for all she cared. She didn't because Blade would find the food at home and Sam would get nothing.

Sam chuckled, seeming to enjoy her lack of knowledge at her expense. "In a way we already have and you'll figure it out if you think about it."

"Doubt it," she mumbled, looking for the perfect spot to have the picnic and hoping to change the subject. "Let's stop here." She spread a blanket beneath a large oak tree.

The men sat down and Sam opened the basket. "Wine and two glasses." He handed one to Blade then one to Aidan. After opening it, he poured. "Came for the main course not the wine. After that I'll leave you two lovebirds to do whatever you want."

"You don't have to wait on us, Sam. You did purchase the basket." Aidan watched as he heaped two plates with food before grabbing a chicken leg for himself and biting into it. With the serving spoon he dipped into the container of potato salad. "Lilly makes the best."

Blade had been watching with seeming fascination. "Thank you," he told Sam. "You can leave anytime now that you've had a taste of what you bought."

Sam roared with laughter. "Always to the point. The type of man I like but I'm going to finish my leg and maybe a wing then the rest of the potatoes. As I said a few seconds ago, then I'll be happy to leave the pair of you alone to do whatever lovers do." His grin broadened as if he knew exactly what Blade planned.

"You don't have to go. You're welcome company and I enjoy talking with both of you." Aidan looked from one man to the other baffled by their exchange.

"Sam understands he's a third wheel. Don't you Sam?" Blade twirled his wine, watching its contents even while he kept his gaze centered on Sam.

"But I enjoy watching the two of you. Seems the tension is so thick I couldn't cut it with a knife."

Aidan pushed her food around on her plate, her stomach churning. Men. At the moment there were two sitting nearby and she didn't want to acknowledge their existence let alone eat with them. She set her plate down but holding her wine glass, she strode downhill toward the water's edge. Sitting on a rock she watched the water rush past her.

"Thinking about me?" Blade sat down beside her, wrapping an arm around her and pulling her close.

"Don't you dare try to kiss me. I'm not liking you a lot right now." She tried to keep the sensations he so easily created from sweeping through her.

"You shouldn't issue a challenge like that when you know you want me to kiss you. Perhaps I'll do as you bid and keep my hands to myself the rest of the day." Blade had pushed the tendrils of her hair she'd artfully arranged away from her face. When he spoke, his lips brushed her earlobe, sending shivers of desire throughout.

She stood quickly, slipping on a small rock. He caught her before she fell, her burgundy splashing from the glass. "Oh, my..."

He pulled her close, sipping the droplets of wine from her cheeks and just above her breasts. His lips against her flesh were hot, compelling her to wish for more. All too well she remembered the heat of his lips as he tugged her nipples into his mouth, laving them with his tongue. She let her head fall back, giving him full access to her neck unable to push him away.

"You two need to remember where you are." Sam stood beside them, grinning like a fool. "Finished the potato salad and the rest of the chicken. The two of you might want to eat before the bugs get your food."

Heat spread through her. The palms of her hands against her cheeks burned. Sam had been watching and he was right. Mortified she rose and marched back to the picnic basket and blanket. She refilled her glass and sat down, trying not to pout.

Sam and Blade spoke for a few minutes before Sam left and Blade returned to the picnic. "I'm sorry you were embarrassed but I enjoyed the kisses. Want more but first we've got things to talk about."

"Like what? How you can find ways to shock and embarrass me in front of my friends?"

"No, we need to talk about tomorrow." He ran a finger up her arm watching her reaction.

She pulled away not wanting to give in to his sweet and very delicious seduction while they were in the open where obviously anyone could interrupt them. She'd let that happen before. "What's happening Monday?"

"I'm leaving town, but I hope we're both going to your cousin's ranch. I'm taking the horses I brought from Storm."

"You want me to go with you?" She wasn't at all sure about a trip like that. She hated creepy crawly things. Didn't like riding horses either. But she wanted to spend more time with Blade.

"Think of it as an adventure. I'm sure Amorica and Ravyn will enjoy seeing you and the same in reverse."

He looked so confident and sure of himself as if he knew her answer even before she did. A year ago she challenged herself when she sailed to Baltimore. What was one more challenge? "I suppose."

"That was enthusiastic." He laughed. "Maybe you could act a little happier about the prospect of spending so much time in my company."

"I've never done anything like that. How would we travel? Doesn't it take more than one day?" She imagined sleeping on the ground in the cold. "I'll freeze. What if it rains?"

He gave her a lazy smile, one that was hard to resist. "All good questions. We'll travel by horse and yes, it takes two days but I promise you, you won't be cold. I'll keep you warm."

"What if it rains?" He had an answer for everything.

"Damian is sending men to meet us at the half way mark. They will have a tent for us to sleep inside, a cart and food. All we have to do is get the horses to that point which should be easy. As we move into the less inhabited part of the state, we'll have bodyguards."

"I don't ride very well. No, that's an understatement." She avoided all four-legged beasts especially horses at all cost. She was petrified of horses. Of all her cousins she was sure she was the only one who didn't ride as if they were born to do it.

"Sam told me as much. He promised two gentle mares for you to interchange during the day. The last day of the journey you can ride in the wagon Damian is sending with provisions."

"You've thought of everything." She sounded sarcastic to herself. She would be alone with him and wasn't that exactly what she wanted?

"I hope so." He played with the lock of hair that had not been caught up in the bun on top of her head. She batted his hand away but he didn't take the hint. His fingers roved down her neck.

"Promise you won't laugh at me."

"Promise. My little fire, I would never laugh at you only with you."

"I'm afraid." The thought of traveling out of the city terrified her. The land was foreign to her. "There are Indians you know."

"I won't let anything happen to you. It's much safer now than when your cousins first homesteaded."

"I know. Amorica was captured and Damien had to fight a pirate for her. He could have died. We might not have ever seen her again." She shuddered at the thought, feeling ashamed of her fears.

"This land is much more civilized now. Nothing like that will happen and we will have at least ten men to guard us through the last phase of our journey. I don't want you to worry."

She couldn't think of anything to say. It seemed he had a response for every question and all her concerns. "I would like to be with you and I want to see my cousins. Sometimes years go by before we can get together."

"Good, then we'll finish this picnic. After that we'll go home and pack lightly. Only what will fit in a saddle bag."

"How big is that?"

"You can put in a dress and something to wear at night. Wear warm stockings and a good coat. Don't wear a corset. We don't know what kind of weather is around the corner and you want to be comfortable."

Mentally she mulled over her wardrobe and decided on a few things. "My nerves feel stretched thin. You'll have to look at what I pick."

"Don't worry. It'll be fun and this journey will get you ready for the trip to MacPherson land when we return to England. My family's land is farther north than yours, and the winters are harsh. We will, however, ride in a carriage."

"What makes you think I'll go with you when you return home?" She didn't like the presumptive air he assumed yet if he asked and didn't tell her what she was doing she'd agree to just about anything he requested of her.

"You'll look fantastic in the MacPherson plaid." He grinned at her all smiles.

"Be serious."

"By then you'll be my wife and all wives travel with their man. Don't they? Or did I miss something about marriage?"

Lord, but he sounded so sure of himself. His wife—that was the title she'd coveted since she was thirteen. Now she balked at the dream, fear keeping her from fully committing. It seemed he sensed that hesitation too.

"You're so sure of yourself." She bit out, angrily yet she didn't understand the emotions swirling within, didn't comprehend the frustration or hesitation.

"Not really. I wish I could be that confident but you're always sending me scurrying in one direction or another. I want you and I've waited for you but if you don't want me, tell me now. I don't want to spend any more time pursuing you if you can't commit," he told her sounding almost as frustrated as she felt.

"You know I do. It's just that..." She had no words. Now that he wasn't running from her, she didn't know what was expected. She slept with him every night now and he barely touched her.

"Just what?" He traced the line of her jaw with a calloused

fingertip. "What idea has you shaking?"

She moistened her lips then sucking the lower one into her mouth. Turning from his gaze she stared at the river as it made its way to the sea.

He touched her chin and drew it back so he looked into her eyes. His were shimmering yet challenging her to answer. "What has you trembling? I always thought you fearless."

"You."

"Me?"

She nodded, "You. I chased you most of my life. Now, suddenly you want me. I'm terrified I won't live up to your expectations."

"Bloody eyes." He drew her into his arms, holding her close, his hand on the back of her head.

She heard the strong steady beat of his heart. Felt the slow rise and fall of his chest. Unbidden tears slipped from her eyes. "I don't want to disappoint you."

"Once again, you unman me. You could never disappoint me. My only expectations are for you to stay by my side for the rest our lives and if God wills bear my children, as many or as few as you'd like."

"Nothing more?"

"Nay, what do you expect from me, Little Fire? I wouldn't want to disappoint you."

"All I want is your love."

"Well lass, I'm not at all sure love exists, but I need you more than I need to breathe. If you don't become my wife, my heart will cease to beat." He kissed her gently, slowly not with the fervor of his other kisses, but still sending a deep heat through her as well as a feeling of security and confidence.

"I've felt that way forever. I always believed those feelings to be love, yet it's not the way I feel about my father and cousins and I know I love them. I need to figure all this out."

"You're still so young. My feelings are pure and they don't exist for anyone else but you so what does a word such as love matter?"

"I suppose it doesn't." She let out a breathy little sigh.

"Today Lilly has promised us baked bread for the trip. She will put together a lunch and Damien's men will bring the evening fare. All we really need to do is pack and rest for tomorrows journey." Once more he took her mouth in his, seemingly enchanted by the tiny sounds she made when he kissed her. He pulled away. "I can't seem to resist your lips."

"I like yours too. They're soft and warm. They make me feel so strange inside." She wanted to feel more self-assured, needed to accept the fact he wanted her now after all the years of pushing her away.

"Are you going to sleep with me tonight?" His finger traveled across the top of her bodice, dipping slightly at her cleavage. She remembered other times when he touched her more intimately.

"If you'll have me. I don't like sleeping alone anymore. Don't want to if I don't have to." She rested her hand on his cheek enjoying the feel of his stubble against her palm.

"Every night from this day forward," he sighed softly his breath so close to her she felt warmth glide against her. "I need you beside me every night. Yet I'm sure your cousin will put us in separate rooms. Will you come to me when the house is quiet?"

"If you want me to, I will."

"Even risking Amorica's anger?" He smiled at her, waiting for her to answer.

He drew away, ending the gentle seduction and began packing the food. Aidan rose reluctantly and folded the blanket. A few minutes later they rode in the buggy back to the home they shared.

She wondered at the comfortable silence existing between them, not feeling the need to fill the time with conversation. Even though he assured her the trip would be safe, she still had fears. She certainly didn't want to fall off her horse and humiliate herself.

"We're here," he stopped in front of the stable and waited for the stable boy to come out. He hopped from the driver's side then striding around the back, he helped her down.

It didn't seem to Aidan he could resist. He held her against him for a few seconds, her feet dangling off the ground and her hands around his neck.

"Blade."

"What?"

She laughed at the look in his eyes. "You need to put me down."

"Do I?" He grinned while he cupped her bottom in his hands, squeezing. "I can barely wait until you're ready for me to make love to you. Every curve you possess entices me. I want to fill my eyes with every naked inch of you."

She swallowed hard, a shiver of anticipation sweeping inside. "I want you to do that to me, make love to me. I want to see you naked too."

"What Little Fire? What do you want me to do to you or more accurately with you?" He still held her off the ground.

"You must be getting tired."

"Hardly. You're as light as a feather. I should make sure you eat more so there's more to hold onto."

"I eat as much as I can," she shot back wondering if he liked her body the way she was. "Do you want me to get fat?"

"I like you just the way you are."

"You mean that?" she asked suddenly feeling more self-conscious than she had in a long time.

"You didn't answer my question. What do you want me to do to you?" He kissed her eyes closed then her cheeks, along her chin. "Just tell me so I can make sure everything is covered."

She couldn't think, could barely breathe. "I—I don't remember. You have to set me down."

"No, not until you answer my questions."

"What was the question?" She felt him pulse against her, his body hard and wanting her she assumed, and she felt an urgent need to discover that part of him she'd just become poignantly aware of.

"What do you want me to do to you? I need to know."

"Make love to me. Come inside me. I want to be as one with you." Her voice trembled while she spoke the word then she realized how much she wanted all of this to happen.

Against him she felt the thunder of his heartbeat. "I want that too, Little Fire. As soon as you're ready to commit to something more than a dalliance between us, I'll make love to you. I've no reason that I can think of to wait until we are wed. You need to understand that when you give yourself to me, there will be no regrets and no changing of your mind. I need to know the truth. Even if there is no marriage for a time, we'll be handfasted and any child we create will be legitimate."

"How will you know when I'm ready?" She was still so very puzzled by his words.

"I'm not sure. I think I'll know by your actions and reaction, by the way you look at me. Right now, you hold a part of yourself back. When we're wed, I won't allow that."

"I don't know how to give you more than I already do."

He laughed softly. "That I suppose is your innocence talking. One minute it seems you want to give all of yourself and next you pull away. You've put a tiny wall between us and it needs to come down first."

What he said was true but she didn't know how to tear it down. "I think I understand." It was, she thought, fear of the unknown.

"Good, then we are one step closer. Perhaps if you know what I'm talking about we can rectify this little problem." He let her slide to the ground. "Go pack. I'll check in with Lilly and see how preparations are coming for the next day. We need to eat and get to bed as soon as possible. Starting early tomorrow is necessary."

An hour later they sat at the table eating dinner. She folded her hands on top of the table. "I'm still anxious about tomorrow. You must know I hate bugs and crawly things."

"Nothing to worry av bout. Just wait, the journey will be fun and you'll get to see where your cousins live." He placed his hand over hers. "As soon as you're finished here you should retire."

With crystal clear blue eyes, she studied him. "Can I sleep in your bed tonight as I have been?"

~ * ~

It seemed to Blade, every night she slept with him was longer than the last. With her head resting on his chest and her body snuggled against him, he spent the night counting sheep but failing to sleep. Yet he wouldn't have it any other way. He craved this intimacy and closeness more than anything.

The next morning was cloudy and cold and a stiff breeze blew from the east. The sun hid from view. Standing by the horses, Aidan at his side and ready to leave, Blade pushed his hat back. "Are you excited?"

"About riding? No. About seeing Amorica and Ravyn? Yes. I wish the sun was shining. I'd feel a lot better if the weather didn't threaten rain."

"Me too." He didn't want to think about a deluge of water or the possibility of a storm hitting them. Damian assured him in a letter days ago that he'd make sure tents were available for them so they wouldn't get wet if the weather failed them. He laughed at the thought of two tents. They would sleep in one and the second be damned. A shelter tonight wouldn't keep the rain from them during the ride.

She smiled at him, but he was sure it was forced, "Shall we go? No reason to stand around staring at the clouds. I want this first day to go by quickly, need to get this over with."

Helping her onto her horse, it was the first time he had misgivings about bringing her with him. He turned to her, fear for her paramount in his thoughts. "Perhaps you should stay home."

"Without you? Never. Even though I don't like horses I'm not some frail or delicate woman. I'm stronger than you think. I can do this with my eyes closed." She urged the horse forward giving him no option except to mount his and follow.

He pushed forward until he rode next to her, misgivings still in his mind. "Are you angry?"

She didn't look at him or speak.

"Aidan, talk to me. The weather...I had this feeling and I try not to ignore my gut instincts."

"And you think a pampered little Scottish lass can't live through a rain storm?" she asked indignantly, gazing at him critically. "You know first-hand better than that. I can handle myself. It's the horse I might have trouble with and that won't change whether the sun is shining or not."

"I stand reassured as well as corrected. There's not a fragile bone in your tiny curvaceous body." He laughed at himself, realizing she could handle herself in most any situation. "I'm glad you decided to come with me. I would have missed you in my bed. I've grown accustomed to your body pressed next to mine during the night."

"Really?"

"Oh, yes, I'm looking forward to holding your hot body next to mine tonight and keeping me warm."

"Under the stars?" she asked and he noticed the shudder of her shoulders.

"Beneath a tent and yes under the stars," he told her chuckling trying to gage her reaction.

"I believe I like that. A tent. Will there be as many bugs inside as outside."

He didn't want to tell her bugs and other creatures would like the warmth and shelter just as she did. Then, trying to reassure her, "No bugs allowed inside."

For most of the day she didn't ask any more questions. She barely spoke and from time to time he watched her stretch her back and adjust herself in the saddle. He knew she was uncomfortable. It was a long time to sit a horse for someone not used to riding.

"We should stop and rest," he said watching the grimace on her face as the horse moved to one side.

"Not on my account," she shot back, slanting him a look he wasn't sure how to categorize but knew it wasn't complimentary.

"I need to stretch my legs."

"In that case we should stop." She pulled on the reins and he was sure he caught a look of relief cross her face.

Now he wasn't sure if she dismounted, she would be able to get back on her horse. She might not be able to walk. He never intended pain and had never really thought this far ahead. Quickly dismounting and dropping the reins, he strode to her. Lifting his arms to help, "Slide your leg over the saddle and I'll make sure you land on your feet.

"Blade..."

He saw her grimace of pain then she leaned forward. He caught her by the waist and pulled her away from the horse, keeping her from landing on the ground face down. For a moment she rested against him. "Can you stand?"

She pushed away slightly, "Of course I can." But when he loosened his grip her legs began to crumble.

Without asking another question, he pulled her into his arms and strode to grassy spot where he could set her down. "Stay put. I'll see to the horses."

She didn't say anything as he walked away and at this point, he was pretty sure she couldn't get back on the horse. He would have to make sure she walked a little to ease the strained muscles. If she couldn't go any farther, he hoped Drake's men would figure it out and send help.

From his saddle, he pulled out a couple slices of bread. He should have stopped an hour ago to eat but they were behind schedule and he unthinkingly pushed on. "Here, are you hungry?"

"I don't know." Her voice sounded strained.

"Where do you hurt?" He wanted to massage her muscles, ease the pain for her.

Her chin tilted upward a notch, "Don't hurt at all. We need to move on. Just let me rest a minute and I promise I won't hold you back."

"Promise me you'll tell me if any part of you is aching or if you need to rest. I know you aren't used to riding. Will you give me your word?" He watched as her back stiffened and he understood she was mulling over his words.

She shuttered her expression before looking away, her bottom lip caught beneath her teeth. When she looked at him, "I will tell you if I can't continue but that won't happen."

He waited, holding her hands in his gazing into her eyes. "I'm waiting."

"For what?" she asked to quickly.

"There are crease lines on your face that can be only caused by pain and the strain of riding for hours must have your legs crying out to stop the torment." He paused, hoping she would tell him how she felt. sep

"I don't want you to think I'm weak. I'm a McLellan."

"Soon to be a MacPherson and you're stronger than I think."

"I won't slow you down."

"It's alright to tell me how you feel. I won't think you're weak."

A few more seconds passed, then, "Blade I hurt everywhere. I even think my hair is in agony."

If her face wasn't so strained and her speech so honest, he might have laughed at the notion her hair was in pain. "I've never heard of anyone's hair hurting. We'll rest here and try to eat something. We've only about an hour more of riding then you can rest for the night. As I told you earlier, tomorrow you won't have to ride. I know Damian sent a cart with supplies."

"Thank God, I don't think I could sit on this horse another day. You would have to leave me here." She let her head fall back to rest on the tree behind her, her dark lashes lowering to fan against her cheeks.

"Eat this." He held out the chunk of bread. "I'll get the cheese Lilly packed."

"Thank you," she told him, closing her eyes.

When he returned, she was asleep the bread still in her hand. He decided he could let her sleep a few minutes but their speed had been slow and he needed to get to the rendezvous before dark.

Pacing, he didn't know what to do.

Thirty minutes later, he sat beside her, taking her hand in his. "Aidan, time to wake up." He kissed the back of her hand, trailed light kisses along her chin. "Aidan, wake up. We have about an hour more to ride. We can't stay here for the night. It's not safe."

A shiver of fear for Aidan snaked down his spine. His selfishness as well as his failure to take her needs into his concern clearly put Aidan's life in jeopardy.

She moaned softly, a tiny mew of pleasure as he kissed her lips. "Time to get up and I want you to eat. I've cheese to go with the bread then we need to walk to ease your muscles. They've probably tightened up while you took your nap."

"I fell asleep? We have to go. I didn't mean to let you down." She tried to rise but he stopped her placing a hand on her shoulder to keep her still.

"You haven't let me down. You're not used to riding and I pushed too hard. Now, no arguments, eat."

She nodded while she bit into the bread and cheese. He handed her a canteen of water to wash it down. "That's good. Hungrier than I thought."

He sat back, watching her drink. "Finish that and we'll take a walk. I know the last place you want to be is on that horse, but as far as I can tell it's the only way we're going to meet up with Damian's men."

"I want to do that. Don't want to be here in the dark, even with you beside me." She finished then held her hand out for him to help her up.

"Good girl." He smiled at her, wishing she wasn't hurting. He should have stopped more often.

When her legs felt all of her weight they seemed to crumble just as they had when she got off the horse. "Blade."

"You'll be fine," he gave reassurance he wasn't sure of himself. He wrapped his arm around her waist before encouraging her to walk. "One step at a time."

She groaned softly then tried to move forward. "One step at a time," she repeated out loud.

"Let's walk to that tree and back."

He felt her inhale a long breath and smiled at her determination. Not one word from her to give up. "I can do it. I feel better already."

Little liar, yet he admired her determination. At the tree they stopped. She leaned into him. "As soon as you're strong enough we'll retrace our steps."

"Nothing hurts like it did when you got me off that horse. We need to leave soon. I understand darkness will be upon us all too fast." She started to walk, stronger than before, seemingly more determined too.

The neigh of a horse and the lumbering sound of a cart caught his attention. "Blade MacPherson?"

"Aye."

"We reached the meeting spot. Andrews told us the little lady accompanying you wasn't use to horses in fact she didn't like them at all. Told us if you weren't there, we should set up camp and take the cart until we found you. So here we are. You ready to get to the camp?"

"Thank god, Amorica knew her cousin so well," Blade murmured. The worry of riding in the dark vanished in an instant. Even if the sun were to set, they would have men at their back.

"I could have done it," Aidan persisted.

"But now you don't have to." He helped Aidan to the cart then assisted the men to gather the horses and tie the reins to the back of the wagon. "You get to ride the rest of the way and I know you could have made it on the horse. You don't have to prove anything to me." He kissed her on the forehead. "I'll drive. I need to rest too."

"Of course, you don't, but I'd rather have you sitting beside me than anyone else."

The hour passed quickly even though Aidan used the time to lean against him and sleep. He kept an arm around her, securing her so she wouldn't fall. If there had been blankets, he might have made a bed in the back of the cart. Although, he was positive, she'd refuse telling him she wasn't tired.

As the sky began to darken a mist began to fall. Rain threatened and he still needed to set up the tent. When they pulled into camp, Damian's men had several campfires blazing and the scent of roasted meat filled the air. His stomach rumbled.

"We're here," he whispered close to her ear hoping she would wake up. "Time to eat and go to bed. I can't think of anything better right now."

He laughed as she woke up, stretching. "You know I was asleep."

"And I'm sure you won't have any trouble sleeping in a few hours after you've eaten. It seems Damian's men have set up two tents side by side but you're sleeping with me. We've little to do now, except enjoy the night, look at the evening stars if there weren't clouds covering them."

"I didn't do very well, did I?" She pushed flyaway strands of hair from her face.

He wanted to release the silken fire from the pins and run his fingers through the soft strands. "You were amazing. I was surprised when I saw the men coming to help but pleased as well. Tomorrow you can ride the entire distance in the wagon."

"I don't like horses."

"I know, Little Fire, but you were amazing and I couldn't ask for anything more from you. You gave all of yourself. I'm going to help you down and we'll see if you can walk." He wasn't going to tell her, but he was worried. After sitting in the cart for an hour her muscles might have ceased up.

"You have this strange expression on your face. Don't worry about me. Makes no difference right now, I'll be fine," she paused, smiling for the first time in hours, "You'll make sure I get everything I need."

"Will I?" he chuckled softly. "You have that much confidence in me?" More than he wanted to admit he appreciated her words. "Then let's see how you fared the last hour."

"No better time than the present." She held out her arms to him after he leapt from the cart.

His hands around her waist, he lifted her into his arms. Holding her against him, he whispered close to her ear hoping to start something they could work on tonight. "Should I put you down?"

"I think I can walk, really, just give me a chance."

He kissed her cheek then set her on the ground. "I'm good. Just a little wobbly. If you support me, I can make it to that campfire and we can warm up."

"Are you cold?" This was another concern. He promised her she wouldn't be cold.

"Just a bit." She stepped forward then another step. "I'm good, but don't let go of me."

"Everything all right, Sir?" The man who rescued them with the cart an hour back stood by them.

"She'll be fine as soon as she works out some of the aches and pains," Blade said.

"Good then, your tents are over there." He pointed to a semi-secluded spot with a small campfire burning in front. "My men will keep the fire burning all night so you don't get cold. Thought the two of you might want some privacy."

"Did Damian think of everything?" Blade wondered at how the man could have every scenario planned out. Of course two tents was not his idea of private but what Damian didn't know...

"Probably Sir, he does have a wife and they do travel this road on occasion. I'm sure he's learned over time what his wife likes and perhaps needs. There is one more thing," he paused for breath.

"What more could we want?"

"Besides some food in your bellies some liniment for the sore muscles she might have."

"Liniment? That might be nice." His body tightened as he thought of massaging her muscles, touching parts of her he'd ignored for longer than he cared to admit.

"I'll have men bring two plates of food. Damian did have his cook pack a bottle of Bordeaux for the two of you. Logan Maxwell keeps them supplied from his wineries in France and Italy, Chianti and Bordeaux. Enjoy and if there is anything more I can get you let me know. I'm set up across the camp from the two of you."

We must be getting the royal treatment.

"For camping out, I doubt if one could get better accommodations," he laughed pulling her close. "You're not going to be cold on my watch."

"Let go of me, please. I want to see how far I can walk. Promise I'll stop before I fall on my face. That wouldn't do my ego any favors."

"I'm going to trust your judgment."

When she gazed at him, lines creased her forehead. "Good."

"That's what I want to hear, but, Little Fire," he paused, "I always want to trust your judgment too. If you say you can do something, I need to be damn sure you're telling me the truth." Thoughts of the harsh winters near his home and dangers brought him back to his point.

Despite his fear, he let his hands drop to his side and watched as she moved forward on wobbling legs. Following closely, he tried to keep a small distance without intimidating and he kept telling himself the worst that could happen would be that she would fall and embarrass herself.

Half way to their tent she turned. "I'd love to have you wrap your arm around me. Right now." She gave him a half smile that went straight to his heart.

"Aw, Little Fire I've been waiting all day to hear those words of love." He was beside her and sweeping her into his arms, he carried her the remaining distance. A small blanket had been set outside the door to the tent. "Your throne."

He set her down on the blanket before he backed up a few steps watching her then turned to help with the meal but he was too late. One of Damian's men approached with the promised dinner, bottle of wine and two cups for the wine.

"I'm impressed," Blade laughed memorizing everything Damian provided for future reference to his travels with Aidan. His first priority was to pamper her and it seemed Andrews knew exactly how to pamper Amorica.

"I'm famished," Aidan said excepting a plate of food and glass of wine after it was poured for her. "I think this will put me to sleep. I've done next to nothing all day and I'm more exhausted than hungry even though my stomach feels as if it could eat a bear."

"Not until you eat the entire plate of food." He set her glass on a nearby flat surface.

"I can't eat all this food but I'll do my best. This looks like a man's plate of food." She sighed softly taking a small bite of the stew. "Do you know what this is?"

"Something delicious and coming from Damian's cook rest assured it's not snake. Although I've heard snake is very good." He laughed at her look of dismay. "No, don't put your fork down. If it came from your cousin, it's very respectable food, nothing strange."

She sipped the wine and ate the food then turning to Blade, "I can't keep my eyes open. Sorry." She set the half-eaten plate of food on a rock beside her then finished her wine. "Is there some place private I can go?"

Truly, Blade had not thought that far ahead. During the day, she'd made the best of awkward situations and now, in the midst of men, she needed her privacy. "I'll make sure you get what you need."

Minutes later they were back to the tent. Half the bottle of wine, waiting for them. "If we drink that I might not be able to get up tomorrow morning."

"They'll wait for us. Besides it's early and I want you to relax. We can watch the night stars through the trees, listen to the sounds and enjoy all that is new. Come here." He pulled her into his arms, offering her more to drink. "Relax now. When you finish, I'm going to give you a massage that will make your muscles feel much better."

"I'd like that although they're just a bit sore now. I believe I'll be fine in the morning."

He felt her relax against him, her head nestled on his shoulder, hand on his leg. Despite what he just told her no stars twinkled through the branches of the trees and the clouds yet the forest was alive with sounds. One of Damian's men stoked the fire, embers rising into the blackness.

"Are you comfortable?" Blade asked expecting her to be sleeping she was so very still in his arms.

"Very. More wine?" she asked holding out her glass for a refill. "It seems that after some food I've more energy. Not enough to go riding, just enough to appreciate you, and the way you make me feel."

He poured the last drops from the bottle. Their saddlebags had been set near the tent. "I'm going to talk to Damian's man." He pulled her prim nightdress from her bags. "Get this on. I'll be right back."

She smiled at him, waving him away. "Go on."

He walked away thinking about the night and all he craved from her. He wanted to make love to her and somehow his gut told him she was ready. He had sought her with steady purpose, with the intention of gaining her forgiveness and convincing her to marry him. Now he was close to his dreams.

"Tomorrow?" He stopped in front of Damian's man. "You want to get an early start I assume. We can be ready anytime, just let me know."

"As soon as the sun rises if possible." He pushed his hat back, "but if the lady needs more sleep that will be fine too. Mr. Andrews knows how hard this trip can be. Just take your time in the morning."

"What's the road like from here?"

"Depends, sometimes you won't see a soul. At other times there's bandits and men heading west, trappers, traders, rough sort. That's why Mr. Andrews sent enough men to assure your safety as well as those horses he's breeding."

"That's why he sent an armed guard. I was curious about that."

"Absolutely, doesn't want to take any chances with his horses or his guests. Figured you could fend for yourself but that doesn't change the fact it's nice not to be alone in these parts."

Soft sporadic raindrops began to fall. "Probably should get back to the tent if I'm going to use that liniment before she falls asleep. Hope the roads will hold up from a drenching."

"They will. Only time we have trouble with ruts is if a hurricane or a nor'easter passes through and drops more than the ground can absorb. It's not the season for that. We should be fine tomorrow. You have a good night's sleep and don't worry about anything."

~ * ~

Guy heard about Blade MacPherson's pending nuptials. He'd coveted Aidan for as long as he could recall. When he failed to steal Allura away from Hunter Gray, his half-brother, he set his sights on the youngest sibling thinking she'd be easy prey, her wild impetuous ways and all. His plans ended when MacPherson stepped in to stop him.

Blade had always been in his way, protecting Aidan even though it didn't seem he wanted her for himself. When he tied her to the rock in the ocean near the island to keep MacPherson and Gray occupied, he almost couldn't go through with the deed. The tide had been rising and the girls would have perished. His ploy almost worked too except once again MacPherson rescued the McLellan girls.

Now he had a second chance with Aidan, a chance to have her for himself and collect on the revenge that was his due. Blade's brother wanted the MacPherson inheritance for himself and he'd come to help the man get what he wanted. In the process he planned on having the little redheaded spitfire in his bed. He just wasn't sure how he would get past MacPherson on his home soil.

Many nights he couldn't sleep while he thought about her lush body beneath his, a woman's body, filled out now that the years had passed. He groaned thinking about her while his rod pulsed.

"Good evening." The brother held out his hand in greeting. "Good to see we've a similar purpose and can help each other. The clan deserves a leader who will stay home and see to their best interest not someone who flits between London and America."

"You mean your best interests." Guy laughed, clapping him on the back, understanding all too well what Leod wanted, power and wealth, damn the clan.

"Of course, just as you know exactly what you want," the brother said. "We can both get what we crave."

"Not too sure what I can do to help your cause short of kidnapping the chit for you. Probably a difficult feat the way Blade guards her but I'm sure we can find her alone sometime and take advantage of her vulnerability."

"You can kill my brother and in doing so, you'll have the lady you covet," Leod said."

"And what will you do for me?" Guy asked pointedly. "I don't kill for free. Especially when the risks are so high."

"You're getting the woman. Isn't that enough?" Blade's brother shrugged nonchalantly as if killing was nothing.

"In part of course. I would like something else, a token of good faith perhaps." Guy stroked his chin in thought. "Something to bind our friendship in the future. At the moment we can think and negotiate. We have time, I've heard his return will not be until August."

"My father might die by then. In that case our task will become much simpler. I'll simply move in and take the castle and lands for myself. The people will accept my leadership and be loyal to me if that happens."

"You have something to hold over the heads of the more powerful in the clan I presume," Guy new how perfect that would be. The brother would hold his knowledge over each man's head.

"I do have some profitable information that will proof useful blackmail material. No one lives without their secrets."

"I will be in touch. Keep me posted and I'll be here for you when I'm needed," Guy sat back, his glass of ale filled to the brim. "Do you have anyone to keep me company this night? Someone who can satisfy me."

"You want a redhead I presume?"

"Of course, but if there is no one like that send me the fairest woman you can find," Guy's thoughts flitted from Aidan to Allura. Either fair or red, either would do. He grew hard thinking about the two women. "Perhaps you could send two ladies. I've powerful needs."

"We could share if you like. A foursome is always fun."

"Not if one is your wife." Fat cow that she was he didn't want anything to do with her.

Blade's brother let out a roar of laughter. "My wife doesn't want me in her bed. I meet my baser needs with other women and that makes her happy. I know exactly who to get for us. Go on to the master solar. I'll send for the ladies and meet you there."

"Things are looking up," Guy thought as he stood and made his way upstairs to the bedchamber.

Chapter Three

Sitting inside the tent, Aidan struggled with the nightdress, trying to slip it over her head. Purposefully she wore a dress that fastened in the front so she wouldn't need help undressing. When she finished, she snuggled beneath the covers, waiting for Blade to come to bed.

Rain pattered on the canvas overhead. The sound was somehow soothing. She closed her eyes, touching her breasts, remembering how it felt when Blade's large hands embraced her, explored, caressing her intimately and how she responded to him.

He'd told her he'd make love to her when she was ready. She wondered when that would be. Tonight maybe? But there was no privacy and she'd feel so vulnerable. Sighing softly, she closed her eyes, recalling so much that had happened between them.

"Hello."

"Blade?" She sat up, pushing her hair from her face and watching as he opened the tent. "You're back. I wasn't sure how long you'd be."

"You miss me." His laughter was soft, but she heard the confidence in his voice as well as the note of humor.

"Of course not." She smoothed the fabric of her nightdress trying to think of an appropriate comeback but couldn't.

"Liar," he whispered, slipping inside to sit next to her, placing the palm of his hand on her cheek. "Lie on your stomach. I'm going to see what I can do about those sore muscles to make them feel better."

She did as he bid, turning on to her stomach, felt the gentle slide of his hands as he pushed her gown above her waist, realizing he would be gazing at her naked body. She should want him to look at her, knew it was something married people did. And yet, "What are you doing?"

"Can't massage your muscles through fabric. That just wouldn't do," he laughed softly, "Lift your hips so I can push the material higher. I want to make every part of you feel better."

The first touch of his hands was on her feet, massaging the arch, her toes then moving higher. She moaned softly, growing hot and wet with each caress and realizing he was slowly seducing her. "That's." She swallowed, trying to turn to look at him.

"That's what?"

She felt the whisper of his breath across her legs.

"Little Fire, you need to relax. This won't do you any good if you're so tense."

"I don't know but it almost feels the same as when you touch my breasts and..." Her hips rose involuntarily to meet his hands.

"Try to relax and let your muscles heal. Don't tense up so," he told her as his fingers continued their tender pressure.

He moved up one leg all the way to the top, slowly, gently working his magic, delving into her intimately then withdrawing only to repeat the process before moving on. "I'm trying but you don't know how this makes me feel. Just like another time when you touched me like this."

"Wish I did," he murmured, caressing her intimately again then quickly moving on to the other leg. "Sorry, I couldn't help myself. You're so beautiful. You slick my fingers and I want to forego my purpose here which is to ease the muscles so you can walk tomorrow and move to more intimate delights."

"Can anything be more intimate than this? But Blade, I liked how you touched me." She moaned softly as his hands found more tender flesh, hot swollen flesh.

"If there was any privacy at all, I'd give you your pleasure tonight." A shadow passed by the tent. "His men patrol to keep us safe. I don't think you'd like it if they poked their head in to see why you were screaming."

"Sir, everything okay in there?"

"All is fine," Blade answered, swearing under his breath. "Just using that liniment, you gave me."

"Good then, the patrols are changing. Someone will come by in another hour. Thought you might like to know."

"Thanks."

"What did he mean by that?" Aidan asked, turning over so she could see his face, but the night was too dark.

"Just wanted to give me a timeline," Blade chuckled softly, "best get on with this massage or we'll never get to sleep tonight."

For several more minutes, Blade used liniment and the magic of his fingers to massage her legs then moved higher. A whisper of a sigh escaped her lips and he found tense muscles at the base of her spine. He squeezed her bottom, letting his hand glide lower touching her intimately again and sending a wave of desire through her. "Don't tease me, please. I don't think I can't take any more of this."

"Ach, pretty fire, I want you too much. I'll try my best for more control but it's underrated."

"What is? I forgot." She inhaled a long deep breath trying to ignore what his hands were doing.

"Control," he said, his voice deep and husky.

Then he gave attention to her shoulders and across her back. She didn't know when the touch changed from his hands to his lips. Trailing kisses across her shoulders he turned her. "I have none," he murmured, his mouth dancing across her body.

"I don't think I want you to have any. Please, Blade."

Her hands rose to his neck as his mouth found her nipples, tasting them, biting gently her hips rose to meet him, begging for more as the tempest swept through her. Somewhere between the first touch to her feet he'd slipped his shirt off, now he pulled her close so his chest was flush against her, tantalizing her, enchanting with a promise so far unfulfilled.

Now he settled inside the blankets, rising above her to sweep exploring kisses over all parts of her. "Blade, please I liked what you did before when you showed me..." Good lord but words escaped her.

"And you'll like it every time. I promise."

He touched her, kissed her, the whirlwind and the magic he generated sent her soaring to such pleasure. She couldn't contain herself. She cried out when the spasms swept within with such intensity. He covered her mouth with his, absorbing the cries of pleasure until her body calmed.

His frame settled between her legs and as he rose above her, she was sure he was grinning, seemingly pleased with himself.

"You did it again to me. I can barely breathe but you..." She could think of nothing to say.

"I will find a time that is right and so very private we will have hours to explore so many possibilities it will shock you to your very core. We need time to learn about each other and tonight is not the time. When we make love for the first time, I want to have you to myself for hours."

"Blade." she settled her hands on his chest, enjoying the play of his muscles. "I want to be shocked to my very core."

He kissed her mouth lightly before rolling off her and bringing her head to his chest. "I'm going to enjoy every moment but for now you need to rest. Tomorrow is going to be another long and tiring day."

"I want to find a way to shock you," she murmured her fingers tracing small circles on his chest, delighting in the groan emanating from his. "Do you like it when I touch you?"

"You can touch me anywhere you please and I'll love it, just not tonight when a dozen men stand guard only a few feet away."

He knew the moment she fell asleep. Her breathing changed and her body totally relaxed into his. He stroked the silken length of her hair, letting it wrap around his fingers, enjoying the sultry heat as it burned. It seemed the fire of her hair set an inferno blazing within.

She would make a fine wife. He reached into his pocket and pulled out a ring he'd been given by his grandmother. It had been passed down for generations. Needing to join with Aidan as soon as heavenly possible he meant to unite with her by the ancient Celtic laws. If they were joined even in this way, he knew Amorica and Damian would allow them to share a bed. Damian might not understand but Amorica would convince him.

Either she was awake or her hand... He'd unfastened his buckskins to give himself relief and without him realizing what she was doing, her hand rested on top of his shaft.

"Aidan?"

"Hmmm.... have I shocked you?"

She was awake. "Aidan you can't." He moved her hand away even though it was the last thing he wished for. He was not going to have his first time with her in this tiny cramped tent and if she kept that up, he wouldn't be able to stop himself. She'd find herself beneath him.

Then he thanked god, she was asleep once more. Even though he would ask her to wed him, handfast with him, the ceremony would be nonexistent if at all. He would give her the ring and he hoped they could wed again with Amorica and Ravyn as witnesses in a church near the ranch. Within the next few weeks he hoped she'd carry his child.

As the sun began to lighten the eastern sky, the rain stopped. During the night he dozed off from time to time. Aidan slept fitfully, turning in his arms before she would calm herself and enter into a deep sleep.

Her dreams must have been disturbing. Usually she slept easily and quietly. Or perhaps he slept more than he realized. Whichever the case, he hoped she would be strong enough to make the rest of the journey without incident.

"Aidan," he whispered close to her ear, wishing they were alone and had all the time in the world. "Time to wake up." He touched her chin, bending to give her a quick good morning kiss before running his hands through her wild red hair.

"So soon?"

"The sooner we get up, the sooner we'll get to the ranch." He kissed her again, this time on the nose and tossed the covers away, knowing the gesture would get a rise out of her.

"Burr... you told me you wouldn't let me get cold." She sounded indignant.

"I don't have the time to warm you up no matter how much I'd like to do just that." He pulled on his shirt before exiting then he poked his head inside. "When you're dressed, I'll take you where we went last night for some privacy. Then I have something I want to give you."

"Can you get me a dress from my saddlebags?"

"I can do better than that." He pointed to her saddlebag in the corner. With that he left, whistling and despite the lack of sleep, felt energized and ready to get on with the rest of his life. Delivering the horses, finding a church to say their vows then returning to Scotland, MacPherson land first on his list.

He strolled to the nearby creek and splashed water on his face. Bloody eyes but he could use a good dunking. Soon though he'd have relief from the constant arousal plaguing him. He meant to make love to his beautiful wife tonight. Well she wasn't his wife yet but would be soon.

He returned several minutes later and waited outside the tent until Aidan made an appearance. "You look beautiful this morning."

"You've lost your mind," she said, attempting to wind her wild hair into a bun. "I'm a mess."

"A wonderful, beautiful mess," he laughed taking the pins from her fingers and deftly securing her hair.

"You could be a lady's maid." She slanted him a smile that could have melted his heart if she hadn't already done that very thing.

"I'll do your bidding anytime, dress you, undress you. All you need do is ask. I do like the undress part the best."

"You're incorrigible," she laughed.

"What else do you like about me?"

"You promised me a surprise."

"I did, didn't I?"

"Well?"

"You my Little Fire have no patience what so ever." He placed her hands in his, his breath catching in his throat.

"What's wrong? You look so serious."

"This is serious lass and very important to me." He broke into a Scottish brogue that seemed natural to her.

"Thought it was a surprise."

"Aidan, I assume you know what handfast is since you're Scottish and have lived your entire life in the highlands. While I want to wed you in the church, for now and before that can happen, I need to make sure any offspring we have will be considered a legitimate heir. Will you handfast with me? Today? This morning? In front of Damian's men as witnesses?"

Her gaze was wide-eyed, innocent but worldly at the same time. It didn't seem she needed to give his question much thought. "Yes."

"Then, it's settled. Damian's man is Scottish. I will have him witness a small giving of a ring and the promise to be my wife."

Holding her hand, they strode to the man. Blade pulled him aside, speaking for a few seconds before he said. "Be glad to."

Then Blade was beside her once more holding her hand in his. "Aidan McLellan will you handfast with me and become my wife?"

"Yes," she said, wishing to say more.

Blade slipped his hand in his pocket and pulled out the ancient ring, the silver circle made of entwined branches decorated with leaves and one small butterfly resting on a leaf. After a few words, he put it on her finger.

"There we are wed," he told Aidan before turning to Damian's man, "and you will bear witness."

"You may kiss the bride," Damian's man said with a chuckle. "And love her forever."

"It's about time." Blade pulled Aidan into his arms, for a kiss that was far from chaste, their tongues dueling. When he was done, he was met by cheers from all the men in addition a blush painted Aidan's cheeks. "Our first kiss as man and wife. It's about time. I waited nine long years for this moment." His life and his dreams would be fulfilled now that Aidan was by his side.

"We have hot coffee and bacon before we start. We'll stop at noon for a bite to eat. Otherwise this is it." Damian's man spoke.

Finished eating, Blade helped Aidan into the cart. As the day wore on the clouds floated apart, the sun warming the earth. The afternoon grew hotter. Aidan peeled off a layer of clothing. That simple gesture sent his mind spinning to the next layer and just what he'd get a glimpse of.

Since last night he watched her with an urgent need to ravish her. He no longer needed to search his soul for restraint. Thank God she didn't understand that look. In the few sexual encounters they'd had it always seemed she knew more than he expected.

They stopped for a bite to eat.

"We made good time. We should be riding into the ranch in about two hours. You two have a good night last night?" Damian's man asked with a not so subtle grin on his face followed by a chuckle.

Blade pushed his hat back and after a deep breath. "Well, you ever been in bed with your woman surrounded by a passel of guards? Even with a schedule check that environment is not conducive to lovemaking. Didn't want to be interrupted or discovered."

The man laughed again. "Nope, never had the misfortune. You must be mighty ready for real privacy. Now that you're wed, you might get it tonight. Couple years back the missus had Damian build a small guesthouse. Seems Ravyn an Aric needed privacy from the prying eyes of their kids."

"Good to hear." Blade's day just improved by another notch. If the guesthouse didn't work, he'd find somewhere else to go so he could finally make love to his wife.

As the hours wore on, they drove through a small village dotted with shops, small homes and a church. He noted a shingle hanging from one of the doors denoting a doctor's residence.

Damian's man rode by, "Andrews' ranch is about three miles down the road. We'll be there in fifteen minutes or so. Hope you and the missus have a good night tonight."

"You excited to get off this rolling form of discomfort." Blade adjusted himself on the seat. "My backside hurts."

"You could have ridden part of the way. I wouldn't have minded." She smiled at him as he picked up her hand, kissing the back.

"And see another man sitting next to you? Not a chance." Breath caught in his throat at the thought. Normally, he wasn't the jealous type but now, thinking of anyone else sitting close to Aidan made his stomach churn.

"I wouldn't snuggle against his arm, promise," she told him, stiffening and with a hint of indignation. "You know I've never, ever, wanted or thought about anyone but you."

"I should hope not since I've felt the same way for the last few years. When are you going to tell your cousin, we're wed?" Once more his thoughts went to the guesthouse and the privacy he longed for.

"I thought you would tell them." She smoothed her skirts, smiling coquettishly and slowly lowering her lashes. "Thought you wanted a room in the guesthouse for some privacy."

"And you don't?" He watched the slow rise of heat stain her face. He loved the gentle color he could elicit with a subtle suggestion.

"I really don't know what all the fuss is about." She tilted her head slightly and smiled at him.

He slanted his head back and roared with laughter. "My little fiery minx, you shouldn't tease. I'll see that I tickle you until you're breathless and naked in my arms."

"I'm not ticklish." The soft blush of pink deepened.

"I know for a fact that isn't true, but if you want to tell me tall tales be my guest. I'll always find out the real truth. You know, sort the false from what is actually a fact." He leaned close, hoping to seduce a tiny bit as his breath caressed her neck then his lips followed.

"There it is their ranch." It seemed she needed distance from his sexual advances. "After all these years I finally get to see their home." She clapped her hands together as they rode beneath the arch proclaiming the name Andrews Ranch.

Damian's man rode up beside them. "Going to turn off now. My home is back in town. Some of the others will leave you here too and some bunk on the ranch so they'll follow you in. Enjoy the rest of your evening."

"You too. Thanks for coming to help. We would have been hard pressed to make it here without it." Blade watched as the man turned his horse around and headed for town.

The road into the main house was lined on both sides with birch trees. The sun rested just above the horizon and Blade guessed it was about four o'clock. Bloody eyes but he wanted to get off this cart and walk. He'd welcome a good hour of hard work.

As they pulled up in front of the house two children ran out to greet them. "You must be Aunty Aidan and you must be Blade. Mommy told us all about you," the little girl said, staring at him as if he just grew a set of horns.

"You must be Lyssa and you must be the little man, Jessie. Am I right?" Aidan said ruffling the little boy's dark head of hair.

"We are," Lyssa said, an angel of a smile on her face. Blade bet she'd easily learned that expression, finding she could get just about everything she wanted when she flaunted it. He hoped he'd have a little girl who he could give everything to.

"Lyssa, Jessie, leave them alone now. They must be tired." Amorica emerged from the front door wiping her hands on a dishtowel. "Didn't expect you so soon. You must have risen at the crack of dawn. Come on in and freshen up." Then she turned to Blade. "Damian's in the stables. You want to take him the objects of his obsessions."

"I thought you were my one and only obsession." Damian walked around the corner of the house, grinning. Taking the porch steps two at a time he pulled Amorica into his arms for a quick kiss. "You got the biscuits baking yet? Remember to make a triple batch. Want an entire batch for myself."

"Of course, I'm making enough but dinner won't be ready for another hour or more. So, you better behave yourself and wash up before you come into the house. Don't want half the stable in the kitchen."

"Don't I always?" He pulled her to him again, his hands on her rear, pressing her against him. "But I don't want to behave that wouldn't be any fun."

These two were just as infatuated with each other as any newly married couple. He prayed Aidan would act the same in seven years, in seventy years if they were lucky enough to live that long.

Damian set her down. "Blade, come help me with the new horses. If you sat on that cart all day, you must be itching to work out the kinks. Let Amorica and Aidan have some time for girl talk. There must be a passel of stuff they want to catch up on." Then he strode from the porch and back in the direction he'd come.

"Read my thoughts of a few minutes ago." He helped Aidan down, uncaring what her cousin and husband thought, he pulled Aidan into his arms for a long slow kiss. Showing them how he felt was imperative and letting them understand she was his. When he let go, he watched her walk cautiously up the steps.

"And I'm sure you're in need of a long hot bath. Come on inside, I'll get some help and we'll get it ready and you can soak as long as your heart desires," Amorica said.

Blade smiled his pulse thundering from the kiss. A hot bath was exactly what Aidan needed while he needed a cold dunk in a frigid lake. Perhaps Damian could point him in the direction of cold water.

"You waitin' for Christmas," Damian hollered at him. "We need to finish the chores and get back to the house before the ladies eat all the biscuits."

"No more than you are." In a few quick strides Blade was beside Damian, itching to work off some of his frustrations.

"We've a guesthouse on the other side of the main house. I know you'll do what you want but with the children and all we'd prefer if the two of you slept in different houses."

"Not a chance," Blade said slowly. "We're handfasted. Aidan's my wife and we plan on marrying in a church as soon as possible. I don't intend to let her sleep alone when I'm close by."

"Don't know how I feel about the pagan ceremony. Not sure I can justify it as a real wedding."

"It's not your place to feel one way or the other." Blade bristled at Damian's comment. "We both have strong Celtic roots so in our eyes the ceremony is legal and binding. At home there is a matter in dispute. My brother is waiting for my father to die while I'm away. He means to steal the land, if I'm not there to claim it. Either way I'm hoping for a legitimate heir. Handfasting is just as binding and legal in the highlands of Scotland as a church ceremony."

"I understand. I'll leave it up to Aidan to convince Amorica." Damian turned his back.

In the stables, they secured the new horses, wiping them down and treating them as if they were royalty.

"Sir, we've a hole in the fence in the southern section of the property." One of Damian's men stood at the entrance. "What do you want done?"

"Dinner for me at least will have to wait. We need to check it out. Have we lost any livestock?"

"I'm going along." Blade wiped sweat off his forehead, enjoying the hard work. "We've got cattle at home. So, I'm not a novice. Can do more good there than I can eatin' your biscuits."

"Thought you just ate sheep," Damian laughed.

"Another misunderstanding, Englishman." Blade joined in the laughter, hoping they would find common ground.

"Fresh horses are over there."

The two men joined the messenger and headed south.

~ * ~

"How are you littlest cousin?" Amorica asked as she directed the people bringing hot water into the bathing room. "I see you and Blade MacPherson are finally, after all these years, together. There were times I didn't believe the two of you would ever be able to reconcile."

Shrugging her shoulders, "I forgave him. What else could I do? After all I've loved him since I was thirteen." For the last year and a half she'd had such changing emotions where it concerned Blade. One moment she detested him and never wanted to see him again and the next she prayed he would appear around the next corner.

"I heard the two of you are handfasted. Rumors spread fast around here. I doubt if Damian will think of you as wed, but I understand completely. It's part of your heritage and an excepted ritual in the highlands. Why didn't he wed you? You don't have to answer, I'm just curious."

"Don't get all judgmental. I know you're as English as they come, but even in England if the ceremony took place, it was deemed as legal. He wants to have a church wedding as soon as possible." She did too and when she thought on what they'd done, she didn't understand why he couldn't have waited until a church ceremony.

"Then you and I will start making plans. The minister in our church will be pleased as well as his wife who will want to overdo everything. I'm sure the good lady will put together a veritable feast in your honor. Since it is spring, the flowers are beginning to bloom so we can put together some bouquets."

"I don't want extravagant." Yet part of her yearned for a real wedding gown accompanied with flowers. She would have liked her sisters to stand up for her. While it would be nice with her cousin, her father wouldn't be there to walk her down the aisle. Damian would have to be a best man. She could walk herself down the aisle or perhaps Amorica could do the honors.

"Listen sweetie, in this part of the country nothing is extravagant compared to what The Duchess would conjure up. She would tap her cane and the dressmaker would be on her doorstep with fashion plates and fabrics within a blink of an eye. The flowers would be ordered and the venue set." Amorica laughed, a faint smile on her lips. "Damian and I wed in a small country church on the way to his home in Dover. I didn't want to marry him, thought I hated him at the time. The night before I shot him. Thank goodness my aim wasn't very good."

"The handfasting just happened this morning. As to a wedding, I've no idea what he'd like or wouldn't like for that matter," she paused, thoughtfully tapping her chin, "I never heard about your wedding. You say you shot Damian. Why?"

Amorica smiled seeming to remember that moment, "I just found out he was a smuggler. You know how I felt about smugglers. My feelings for him changed from infatuation to hate in the blink of an eye."

"I can't imagine how the two of you overcame that obstacle." Yet she understood if love were involved just about anything could be overcome.

"I loved him. Now, about the wedding, you can talk to Blade later. I brought in your saddlebag and I think the first order of business for tomorrow is to shop for more clothing. Did Blade tell you to pack this light? He should be ashamed of himself. The cad."

"I had no idea what light packing meant and he approved the items I brought with me." She wasn't really sure if he looked at the articles. "He didn't tell me I could bring more though."

"Of course, he didn't. He's a man. He doesn't need anything except buckskins and a shirt. Now I'm going to leave you to your bath, enjoy the water and take as much time as you want. When you finish come into the kitchen and keep me company. I suppose the men won't be too much longer."

Undressed, Aidan slipped into the steaming water, relishing the sensual play of the hot liquid around her body. Closing her eyes, she rested her head on the lip of the tub. He told her he'd make love to her tonight. Aidan smiled at the thought. She'd wanted that for so long. When she saw Blade in Baltimore that first day, she found herself terrified of the thought. Hers was such a turnaround of emotions. She knew because he crossed the Atlantic to find her, he wasn't going to take no for an answer when he proposed or anything else. He meant to pursue her until he got what he wanted.

She found the soap and washrag. It smelled of roses. Amorica's favorite flower. Quickly washing herself she ducked beneath the water, soaped her hair, rinsed with the bucket Amorica left for her. The scent of freshly baked biscuits floated into the bathing room, making her stomach rumble.

She was hungry, having eaten very little at breakfast as well as the brief stop midafternoon.

A few minutes later she was dressed. In the kitchen Amorica greeted her with a sour expression.

"Whatever is wrong? You look as if you just ate a lemon."

"The men won't be here for dinner. They're rounding up cattle in the south pasture. I fed the children while you were bathing and hopefully, they'll play in their bedrooms until bedtime. We have the entire evening to ourselves."

"If we're lucky?" Aidan laughed, looking to see what smelled so good. "Do they always behave?"

"Who?"

"The children."

"And no, neither the children or the men behave unless coerced. It's the biscuits that keep Damian in line. I can't speak for Blade." Amorica volunteered before she could ask. "Damian wants me to bake them every night but I keep him guessing. As to the children, they are little hellions most of the day. But when bribed, they can be little cherubs."

"Your specialty I've heard. Until Lilly taught me, I didn't know how to cook anything. Now I have a myriad of stews at my repertoire. She still does most of the baking though. None of us eat very much."

"I'm sure you didn't need to learn to cook and I doubt in the MacPherson keep that it will be a necessary skill either. I suppose your duties will be far different than mine."

"How long do you think they'll be? I thought..." What did she think? He would finish the lovemaking they had begun several times. The men could be back after she went to bed, and he would wake her with kisses. *You're a foolish romantic Aidan McLellan and you know it. Aidan MacPherson,* she reminded herself.

"Could be a few hours or all night. No way to tell at this stage. If it's going to take too long, they'll stay the night in one of the little shacks we built for emergencies," Amorica said.

"All night?" My goodness but she didn't want to wait any longer. She felt as if her body had been ready the last few days.

"Let's dish up, break out one of Logan's special wines and enjoy the evening. He sends a couple crates every six months or so. We just need to make sure we don't eat three batches of biscuits. Damian could forgive me anything except leaving him with no biscuits."

Between bites of fried chicken and biscuits and a few spring greens they spoke of so much.

"Tira just returned from London about the time Blade did. He went to New York and Boston to visit his sisters. I didn't even know he had two sisters." She sighed heavily resting her chin on her hands. "We're husband and wife and I don't know anything about him."

"Did Jamie marry Tira in London?" Amorica's fist tightened around her fork. "I never liked the way he treated her. Acted as if she was his mistress. My little sister deserves better than that."

"They did get married. The wedding was at Ella's and Drake's estate. The Duchess was so happy. It was the third wedding she got to plan."

"Three out of twelve and the last it seems. Did it go off without a hitch? The other weddings did not end well except for the fact the couples were wed," Amorica said.

"Nothing untoward happened. Everything that would go wrong happened before the wedding. Tira was abducted by Mathew Dutton, the owner of the brothel in town and one in London. He drugged her with some kind of aphrodisiac. From what little Tira was willing to tell me she and Jamie spent the entire night just trying to rid her of the effects. Making love was the only source of relief. But Tira said it was horrible and she wouldn't go into details."

"I..." Amorica began.

"These biscuits are really good." Aidan changed the subject, wishing the men would be back soon but having a sinking sensation they would be gone all night.

"Try them with the strawberry preserves I made last summer." Amorica passed the jar.

"Mrs. Andrews." One of Damian's men poked his head inside the kitchen. "I knocked but no one answered so I let myself in. Hope you don't mind."

"What is it?" Amorica rose from the table, seemingly concerned about the man's unexpected appearance.

"Damian sends word that they won't be home till early tomorrow morning if then, but he'd like most of those biscuits if you don't mind."

Amorica laughed, "Of course," and put together a basket of food. "How many of you need to eat?"

"Only Damian and Blade and two more. We can make do. Won't be the first time any of us has spent the night without dinner."

"Nonsense. We've plenty here. I always fix more than we can eat at night. Damian likes the leftovers the next morning with his eggs and bacon." She wrapped up the food before handing the package to him. "Enjoy. Tell the men to take care and hurry home."

"Thank you and you two have a nice evening."

Amorica poured them each another glass of wine. "I'm going to put the children to bed. Take the wine into the parlor and I'll be down in a minute. Just have to explain why Daddy won't be in to kiss them goodnight and say prayers with them. "They'll be disappointed but it isn't something that hasn't happened before."

Aidan picked up the bottle along with her glass. Disappointed in the news she found a comfortable spot by the window. Where out there was he? Was he safe? Was he disappointed?

"You look sad." Amorica walked into the room. "Is that my wine?" She sat across from Aidan.

"Just worried a little but I know they can take care of themselves.

The children are in bed?" Thoughts of her future and a possible family, flitted through Aidan's head.

"The children are always exhausted after a day of play. When their eyes are closed, they have the most angelic expressions on their little faces. It would seem the devil of the day leaves them for the night angel."

"Mama?" Jessie stood at the door to the parlor. "I want a glass of water."

"So much for the angel," she murmured. "Of course, you do. I suppose you'll think of something else you need in a few minutes. Is your sister on her way?" Amorica left to get the water but stopped when Jessie spoke.

"Lyssa and I both want to play with Aunty. You didn't let us when she first got here and we didn't think that was fair."

Aidan pulled the little boy into her arms. "I wanted to play too and I promise you if you go to bed, I'll play tomorrow. Your mother and I haven't seen each other in so much time I can't count the years. We wanted to talk."

"Where's your friend? The big man?"

"He's with your papa fixing the fence. He'll be back tomorrow or later tonight." Aidan put this in prospective. She'd waited seven years for this night. She could wait one more.

"Do you have nightmares when you have to sleep without your friend? Mama does. Sometimes at night I hear her screaming. A long time ago some bad men kidnapped her and Papa had to rescue her."

"I know. She's afraid of smugglers as well as pirates." Aidan wondered how much she should say to the little boy but she supposed Amorica would have told them the truth.

"My papa's a smuggler. I don't think she's afraid of him."

"Was," she pointed out. "He isn't any longer." What else would Jessie say? This certainly wasn't a conversation she felt comfortable with.

"Mama shot him but he didn't get hurt. Papa said it was just a flesh, a flesh something."

"That's enough Jessie. Aunty knows all about that story." Amorica handed the little boy his glass of water. "Now off to bed with you, scoot."

"Mama, can I have a glass of water too?" Lyssa appeared in the doorway, her hands folded angelically in front of her.

Amorica groaned. "Did the two of you have this planned? You knew Papa wouldn't be here to chase you back to bed so you're taking advantage of the situation. Water then back to bed. Don't you dare come back down unless the house is on fire."

Lyssa smiled her eyes alight with mischief. "No Mama, we would never do anything so das, dast..."

"Dastardly? Of course, you would. Since you're both up and I doubt if you'll stay in bed, I'll make a bargain with you." Amorica took Lyssa to where Jessie sat with Aidan and kneeling, she gave each a hug.

"I like bargains," Jessie said. "Can we have some cookies and milk too?"

"No, I don't have cookies but there is some chocolate cake. I'll cut you each a piece, Aidan too if she wants one. Will that work. Let's go back to the kitchen."

"Oh, yes..." Lyssa clapped her hands together the smile telling everyone that she just got what she'd been after.

"I'll pass on the cake and finish my wine. Perhaps another biscuit would be in order." Aidan needed to laugh at the children's antics, but she covered her mouth with a hand.

"You two little urchins have to promise to go to bed when you're finished eating." Amorica pointed a finger at each of her children. It seemed to make her point. "If you don't, I'll tell Papa and you won't be able to go riding tomorrow."

With that said, both children nodded and said, "Promise."

"Good, then I'll hold you both to that agreement. Remember no riding tomorrow, no going anywhere unless it's to do chores if you don't go to bed the second you finish the treat."

"We didn't promise that," Lyssa said, indignantly crossing her arms over her chest.

"Doesn't matter, it's your mother's rules and you must abide by them." Amorica laughed then turning to Aidan. "When you have children, you'll need to be creative when it comes to punishment and because you're in charge you can change or add to the rules at any time."

Aidan enjoyed watching the exchange of words between parent and child until Jessie stood in front of her asking, "Do you sleep with your friend?"

"Naked like Mama and Papa," Lyssa added with what Aidan could have sworn to be a smirk.

Aidan looked to Amorica for help, heat rising to her cheeks. "I." She licked her lips, trying to think of a viable answer. "My friend is my husband. You can call him Uncle Blade." She hoped at least this night she'd escaped answering.

"I heard Papa talking to your friend and he said you weren't married, not really. I heard him say you were handfasted and Papa didn't like that very much. I could tell by the look on his face. His eyes get all dark and hard when he doesn't like something," Lyssa said.

"The two of you are far too curious about someone else's business. In Scotland, handfasting is recognized as a real marriage. It comes from an ancient Pagan ritual and since both of them are Scottish they are considered husband and wife," Amorica told them.

"What does Pagan mean?" Lyssa asked, chocolate covering her tiny little face. In time she'd be as beautiful as her mama.

"Eat up. Your father can explain tomorrow. The two of you have worn me out with all your questions."

With that interrogation put to rest, Lyssa turned back to Aidan. "You didn't answer my question. Do you and your friend, Uncle Blade, sleep without any clothes? Mama and Papa try to pull the blankets up when we come into the room, but we can tell and Papa always has a silly grin on his face."

Once again Aidan felt the heat of color rush to her face. "No, no we don't. I always wear a nightgown and Blade wears something."

"That doesn't sound right," Jessie said. "If you're married you shouldn't wear night clothes to bed."

"Well, it's the truth." Aidan suddenly felt the need to escape the children. "And we weren't married until this morning. I haven't been to bed with my husband yet," she spoke defensively then wondered how this child had so easily pulled the truth from her.

"Are you two finished with the cake and the questions?" Amorica asked, tapping her fingers on the table. "You've been inquisitive and I've always wanted you to ask about things. It's the way you learn but tonight you were rude to your aunt and you embarrassed her. She's not used to being married yet or being interrogated by children."

"No, I'm not done, will you and Uncle Blade take us to the lake tomorrow? We want to swim," Jessie asked.

"You both know it's too cold to swim and I think your aunt and uncle might want some privacy. Heaven knows they aren't getting it tonight."

"Is that because they want to have children like us?" Lyssa put the last bite of cake in her mouth."

Aidan put her head on the table, clearly out of thoughts to answer the children and wishing Blade was here to deflect the questions, something he was very good at.

"Children, while that is none of your business, it is probably true. Most married folks want privacy so they can have children." Amorica picked up the plates taking them to the sink.

"I don't know why they have to have privacy when everyone knows storks bring the babies," Jessie said.

"No, they don't. You're just a little boy," Lyssa chimed in. "You don't know anything."

"Who told you that?" Amorica stood in front of her child, hands on her hips.

"Elizabeth. She said both her mother and father told her, so it had to be true." Jessie stood his ground. "And I know a lot more than you do," he shot back to his sister. "I'm older and almost a man so of course I know more."

"Being a boy does not make you smarter," Amorica said.

"See," Lyssa chimed in.

"We can talk about it tomorrow. Now both of you go on. Go to bed. I'll tuck you in again, but remember your promise."

"Can we tell Papa you gave us cake?" It seemed Lyssa would do anything and pursue any line of conversation to stay up one more second.

"No. One more question and you'll be sequestered to this house and chores tomorrow." For the first time Amorica sounded angry and out of patience.

"What does..."

"Go!" Amorica pointed to their rooms and taking both by a hand led them from the kitchen.

"Good, God," Aidan muttered thinking that having children was most likely the most foolhardy idea she ever had.

Amorica returned, "So sorry about the interrogation. They are a handful at times. Like I told you earlier when their eyes close they are little angels."

"The question is whether a person can survive the day with them around." Aidan drank the last drop of her wine.

"You'll come to appreciate their honesty when you have a few children of your own. They are a breath of fresh air in a world where at times evil abounds. There is nothing like a child to keep you on your toes and aware of every word that comes out of your mouth. I swear I still haven't always learned to curb my thoughts."

"Perhaps I don't want children."

"Nonsense." Amorica waved her comment away with her hand. "Don't let my little hellions scare you. What they give back in return is priceless."

"Maybe, but I suppose I'll have to be with Blade long enough to find more than a moment of privacy if we are ever to have a child. "

"Don't be impatient. Blade will make time to consummate your marriage. He's a man after all. Indeed, I'm shocked he hasn't made love to you already."

"He wanted to wait until he thought I was ready. I think this morning he decided. That's why the handfasting."

"It only takes one time with a man," Amorica said. "If the timing is right."

"Where am I going to sleep? I'm exhausted and the wine seems to be making me yawn. Strange that I did nothing but sit all day and now I cannot keep my eyes open."

"Where are my manners? You can either sleep in our guesthouse or the spare bedroom. It's your choice."

"We, Blade and I, thought we would spend the night in the

guesthouse and privacy but it doesn't seem I'm in need of that special commodity tonight since he isn't returning. I don't want to spend the night alone in the guesthouse. If you don't mind, I'll stay here."

"Follow me." Amorica led the way. "Here you are. If you need anything don't hesitate to get it. I'll retire soon too. No sense waiting up for a man who is not coming home, now is there?"

"I don't suppose there is." Aidan looked at the bed, envisioning Blade lying on it, waiting for her with a wicked smile on his ruggedly handsome face, his eyes sparkling with passion.

This certainly wasn't what she expected, another chaste night.

~ * ~

"What month is it?" The MacPherson pushed himself from his bed with a groan, shuddering from the pain in his legs. The ragged breath escaping his lungs left him coughing.

"It's May milord. I'm sure Blade will be here soon. I've laid out clothes for you to wear. Do you want to go to the solar and eat your breakfast before you greet your people?"

"Have we heard from him?" The old man coughed again. This time blood stained his cloth.

"Not yet. We both know it takes a lot of time to send messages across the ocean then receive one back in return. Be strong. Your oldest son has never let you down and he won't now. He will come home with a wife and a possible child on the way by the end of summer as promised."

"Leod brother lurks in the shadows, waiting for me to die. I had word he joined with Guy, Hunter Gray's half-brother to steal the keep from Blade. I won't have it. Send men out to discover what it is that Guy wants. If we can do it, we'll offer him more rewards than Leod has access too."

"I believe we already know. He covets what Blade has, the woman your son has protected for seven years, Aidan McLellan. Blade foiled the evil man at every turn and now he joins forces with the younger brother to wreak more havoc on his clan. It is simply revenge."

"Doesn't Guy have a wife?" The MacPherson asked, wondering

what kind of evil existed in this man.

"Yes, and they have spent a lifetime seeking only what they want at any cost. She is as evil as Guy, perhaps more so. She has no conscious. Rumor has it they both take lovers and whenever possible blackmail them for money and power."

"I must stay strong." The MacPherson closed his eyes searching his frail body and muscles for strength. "Blade will be here as soon as heavenly possible."

"Here, let me help you up then we'll walk to the solar."

"My habits are watched daily by spies. I know this but still wish to sleep the day away. If you weren't aroun d to drag me from my bed..."

"Nay, ye canna."

"I know. I know," The MacPherson muttered eyeing the door as if it was a mile away. Groaning, his hand on his back, he used all he could muster to push himself from the bed. Pausing for a moment when he stood, to gain his strength.

His man helped with his clothes then on to the solar. He waved and smiled at the upstairs maids as they scurried around accomplishing their chores. They would curtsy and return the greeting as they passed by.

In the solar, he was met by one of Blade's closest childhood friends. The only man his son was closer to was Hunter Gray. He was the only man in residence the MacPherson knew he could trust with his life.

"Good morning." Liam sat next to him. "I hope this day brings you nothing but joy. Oh, I remember the days when you chased us with a stick when we'd done something naughty."

The MacPherson chortled. "And I remember when both you and Blade tossed the caber farther than I. That was the day I quit entering the contest. You and Blade grew up to be fine young men. I wish I could say the same about my other son. What did I do wrong with him?"

"Unfortunately, that is not why I'm here."

"Not to reminisce? I would love to talk about the past. It seems these days I remember my youth more easily than the present. In any case, what bad news do you bring today?"

"Don't have time to dwell on the past today, but another time I would love to hear the stories of your life. It's a shame you have no grandchildren to pass your tales down too."

"I hope to have grandchildren soon and I pray I live long enough to hold them in my arms. Blade needs to take care of that for me."

The MacPherson suddenly felt a wave of sadness and a bit of regret wash through him. His son was stubborn. He waited seven years for Aidan McLellan to become a woman. There were many women who would have swooned at the idea of becoming his wife. Thank God she had not been two years old when he met her.

"We need to talk about the business at hand," Liam reminded the MacPherson. "There is much to consider before I take my leave."

"And what is that?" He cringed at the thought of what his youngest son might be brewing in his mind.

"Money has changed hands. Some among the people who we felt would stay loyal to you are being forced to side with the younger son."

"What does he hold over their heads?"

"It seems he's gifted them with funds to repair their homes or even to feed their families. Now when he calls for the money with exorbitant interest attached the people cannot pay up. He is offering forgiveness of the debts in exchange for their help when the time comes."

The MacPherson drummed his nails on the table in front of him, grimacing. His breakfast left uneaten. "I wish you could find some magic cure for what ails me but you cannot."

"I can, however, if you approve, give these people the funds to repay the loans they've incurred and remind them all they need do is come to the laird for help in times of trouble. I would tell them you are aware of his perfidy and promise to keep the hold, one to be honored."

"How much do you speak of?"

"A paltry amount I believe. I spoke to the man who keeps your books. He has told me the funds needed would not amount to much in the scope of your holdings. He even explained the money could be paid back in a percent of their income from their harvests, what they are able to sell. There is no need for interest to factor into the equation."

"Then I charge you with the duties. I assume you've identified the families who need our help. Make sure everyone who lives within our protection knows we will see to their needs. Tell them not to go to my youngest son no matter what he offers them."

"I'll put your orders into action immediately. Good day sir." Liam left.

Chapter Four

Be careful what you wish for became Blade's mantra as they rode from the ranch house. He wanted to stretch his legs and work his muscles but he'd also wanted to be home with Aidan this evening. It appeared that would not happen. The sun sat above the horizon and he assumed it would be close to setting when they reached their destination. If Blade didn't know better, he would have guessed Damian created this just for his benefit and to keep him away from his new bride.

Damian rode as if he was born to sit a horse and Blade admired this. The horses he brought Damian were meant to race. From what he understood, the ranch didn't survive on the cattle or the crops they grew. Andrew's prosperity came from the horses he bred.

While he didn't race them, he bred and trained the horses. Foals from his mares brought a handsome price. And those special horses came from Ravyn's sister and those horses were direct descendants of Storm Graham's prize stallion, Fiacre.

At least an hour passed from the ranch house to the break in the fence. Damian pulled his horse to a stop when he reached the site. Two of his men stepped forward.

"About fifty cattle slipped through the open spot. We've rounded up at least a dozen and built a holding pen over there. The worst is that the wild horses we were going to break, some of them slipped through, including the stallion. Don't know if we'll be able get the big guy back unless we offer up some of his mares as bate."

Blade had never quite thought of things that way. The stud and his mares, he laughed at himself deciding to change his ways with Aidan. She had always believed she was his equal and he's always thought it a whim to indulge. Perhaps it wasn't. Maybe she was more than equal to him. He'd lusted after her for years but did he really know who she was and what her dreams were? They needed to get to know each other better. They had a lifetime. He meant to start as soon as possible.

He laughed again, realizing she'd lusted after him too, but he knew he needed more from their marriage than their infatuation for each other. Coveting a lifelong commitment meant there would be more to this relationship than sex.

The thought was new to him. Even after all these years, he had only thought of Aidan as his wife and a mother to his children. For so long it seemed she was constantly underfoot and even though he pretended to see her as an annoyance, she slowly inched her way into his heart.

He shook off his thoughts, needing to concentrate on the work at hand. "What can I do?"

Damian turned his horse, seeming to survey the landscape. "We've got about an hour of work time before it gets too dark to see. Go with Daniel and see how many cows you can herd over here to get corralled. Keep an eye out for the stallion. You can't miss him he's pure black, gorgeous and I think he knows it. If you see him, come back here."

Blade set off with Daniel, working the horse as he'd been trained and bringing animal after animal into a herd, they could take back to the makeshift holding pen. Hours passed and by his count forty of the fifty cows were now in a pen and the sky was now too dark to work.

Resting a forearm on his saddle horn, he watched Damian give final orders. Darkness prohibited work. There were two shacks. They would sleep in one and two other men would occupy the second. The rest of the men would return to their homes then come back at the crack of dawn.

Inside the shack, Damian put wood in the potbellied stove to keep the fire going. On a small table the food Amorica sent their way waited for them along with a pot of coffee that was made earlier.

"How do you feel?" Damian asked grinning. "You wanted to stretch your muscles. Did you get what you wanted?"

"Wipe that silly grin off your face. You know how I feel. I'm missing my wedding night. Thought I'd be someplace a lot different to sleep this evening." Blade wiped sweat from his forehead.

"You shouldn't bed her until you're legally married by a minister." Damian bit into a biscuit before offering Blade one. "I had to wait a couple months after I was legally married to bed Amorica. What's one night, since I know you're not going to take my suggestion."

"My life, my wife." Blade picked out a piece of chicken shrugging as he did so. "Will spend it the way I want."

"You can have one biscuit but I get the rest, just because you have to listen to my snoring all night." Damian still looked pleased with himself.

"Just one? You going to eat the other two dozen?" The last conversation Blade wanted with Damian was about his wife. Biscuits seemed a lot more palatable.

"Maybe for breakfast. This fare will have to serve as both. Which bunk, top or bottom?"

"You tell me. Would rather take the bottom. Don't cotton to falling out." Blade figured he'd end up on the top bed despite anything he'd say.

"Guess I shouldn't have asked. You take the top." Damian laughed, stuffing a third biscuit into his mouth. "Even cold these are mouthwatering."

Blade finished his coffee before hopping onto the bunk. "See you in the morning," Crossing his legs, he placed his hat over his eyes.

"Good night," Damian said. "Pleasant dreams."

Blade dozed but his thoughts went to his father and his waning health then to Aidan waiting for him in bed alone covered from head to toe by her prim little nightdress. Damian was right, one more day in the scheme of things made little difference. They would wed in the church. If Damian had his way the marriage would take place tomorrow but he understood Aidan wanted more.

Rain fell during the night but when the sun rose only a soft layer of mist floated from the grass. Outside, Damian's men were already hard at work, the hole mended and the cattle corralled.

"Well, I'll be damned. Looks like the stud came to his mares. It seems being jailed with his mares is more appealing than wondering around alone without them," Damian laughed, then turning to Blade, "Is that how you felt last night, jailed?"

"That was the truth." Blade realized again. Perhaps this time away from his Little Fire was good for both of them. Truth be told, he craved her more now than ever.

"Sir." Daniel approached. "Think we got all the cattle, the fence is mended and as you just saw, the stallion returned of his own accord."

"Could have spent the night at the ranch." Damian smiled at Blade.

"Looks like that's the truth." Blade wasn't going to let Damian goad him into anger. Ever since last night when Damian told him they would have to stay at the shed, he was sure his brother-in-law planned to keep him away from his new bride from the start of this adventure. But this was just one night. What would he come up with tonight and the next one?"

"We'll finish up here," Daniel said. "The two of you really didn't need to stay the night."

"Bonding," Damian said with a chuckle. "I needed to talk to my new relative by marriage and he needed to understand certain truths about this family and their women folk."

"So, you accept the handfasting." Blade studied the big man, understood his power and heard the story of how he rescued Amorica. He was not a man to toy with, but Blade never meant to do that.

"Never. Should we go back? If you're lucky the women will have risen. They'll be cooking breakfast for the both of us."

"My fantasies confirmed." Blade said, mounting the horse one of Damian's men brought to him.

Damian set out, a slow pace while Blade wanted to race his horse, needing to see Aidan as soon as possible. -Again, he swore to himself he wasn't going to let Damian under his skin. When the ranch came into view, his horse nickered softly eager for his stall. He felt the same, eager to see Aidan, maybe crawl into bed with her for a few minutes if she was still there.

"Looks like you're out of luck. No warm woman waiting in your bed." Damian pointed toward the ranch. Smoke billowed from the chimney.

"Just means Amorica is awake. Aidan could still be in bed, longing for her husband to come to her."

"And you mean to find out."

"Of course, wouldn't you?" Blade dismounted handing his reins to the man who strode out to greet them. Making his way to the guesthouse he opened the door searching for the bedroom. There were two on the first floor and Aidan was in neither. He supposed she might have slept in the main house. Knowing he wasn't returning she might have felt more comfortable there.

He walked to the main house realizing Damian was most likely right. He wasn't going to find Aidan still in bed. The scent of bacon and coffee wafted through the air. Funny thing was, he wasn't hungry for food just Aidan. His body hardened as he imagined Aidan in bed, red hair in wild disarray around her. He wanted to wrap the silken fire around him.

In the kitchen Damian held Amorica in his arms, his mouth molded on hers in a greeting that sent a wave of envy through Blade. Where the bloody hell was Aidan?

"Morning."

Amorica pushed away from her husband when she heard Blade's voice. "Down the hall second door on the right."

"You shouldn't have done that. I was enjoying his torment." Damian's mouth slanted over hers again.

Blade eagerly strode down the hall, opening the door before knocking. "Aidan? You still in bed?"

She turned, half dressed and stunning with her hair falling over her shoulders. "Blade, you're back already," she said opening her arms to him. "I missed you so much."

He swept her into his arms, carrying her to the bed. He fell upon it with Aidan on top of him, his lips joining with hers. His hand found her breast, needing the soft flesh. "God how I missed your sweet little body last night nestled against mine. When we left, I didn't know I would have to spend the night with Damian."

The knock on the door surprised and angered him, knowing it had to be Damian out there. "Bloody hell."

"Time for breakfast," Damian called through the door. "Best you get to the kitchen before I eat it all." The following laughter sent Blade's blood boiling. He rolled over an arm across his eyes. "That man could drive me insane before we are wed."

"What's wrong?" Aidan sat up beside him, running her fingertip along his arm. "I've never seen you look quite this disgruntled. How is he going to drive you crazy?"

"Nothing I won't fix after breakfast." Blade didn't want to tell Aidan all her brother-in-law did to make sure they spent the night apart. What possible scenario could Damian conjure to keep them a part another evening.

Didn't make a difference even in the name of being a good guest, he wouldn't fall for anything Damian dreamed up to keep him away from his wife.

"I need to finish dressing." She moved from the bed to her gown, which hung over a chair. Slipping it over her head, she put her back to Blade. "Can you fasten it up for me?"

"I'd rather take it off," he muttered knowing that would have to wait until another time.

"Really, Blade, we need to be considerate. Amorica will probably make everyone wait for breakfast until we get there."

Reluctantly, he rose from the bed and did Aidan's bidding. "There, are you satisfied?" But he couldn't resist a quick kiss on her neck before he wound her hair into a pile on top her head, securing it with the pins she offered.

"I am. What did you do last night? Is everything fine now?" she asked as she opened the door and waited for him.

"Everything is just fine and would have been even better if we returned. Damian wanted to make sure we didn't spend the night together. Will most likely dream up some new torment to keep us apart this evening."

"And you're angry with him."

"Truth be told, yes but we are going to find some place today where no one will disturb us and we're going to spend the entire day alone together." He would make sure his inquiries to such a place were with Amorica as well as a pledge for silence.

"I'd like that as long as we can be sure two children won't follow us. I did promise them I would play with them today and knowing that, they are going hold the hastily made promise over my head. You should know after spending some of the evening with those two I'm having second as well as third thoughts about having any children."

"We can sneak away and pretend we were planning our wedding. Which would hold a tiny bit of truth." He prayed, too, she would change her mind again. Children were more important to him than he cared to admit right now.

"Smells good," Blade said grinning as he stepped into the kitchen. "Hope there's some hot biscuits to go along with the rest of the meal."

"Where are the children?" Aidan asked, praying they wouldn't appear and ply her with more embarrassing questions. With Blade here, she could only imagine the possibilities.

"They ate earlier. Now they're outside playing. Are you relieved?" Amorica asked as she set platters of food on the kitchen table.

"Thank goodness, after last night's questioning I don't believe I can handle any more."

"Questions?" Blade asked wondering what he missed. "The children were up to some mischief? And I missed out on it. Would have loved to embarrass them right back. I've certainly had my run ins with little ones. Know just what to say to send them on their way."

"I'll tell you about them later." Aidan fiddled with the napkin, never, if a wish could come true.

"They're just curious little souls," Amorica said, laughing yet at the same time rolling her eyes to study the ceiling. "But I certainly understand why you want to avoid them," she said as she passed one of the platters of food around the table. "There are days that if I could avoid them I most certainly would."

"Can I help with the dishes?" Aidan asked when she finished eating. She carried her plate and Blade's to the counter.

"No, I'm ashamed of Damian and his ploy last night. If you head west, you'll come to a lake. There is one rowboat, so no little children can pop up unannounced. You'll have as much privacy as you'd like. If Damian starts asking, I'll find a way to distract him. As you must guess, distracting him is not difficult."

"Promise your husband won't show himself in order to rile me." Blade asked, thinking he just said too much.

"I riled you? Was afraid nothing I was doing would get under your skin. Glad to see something worked last night." Damian slapped Blade on the back, returning from outside where he checked on the children. "I'll wash the dishes then I've got some chores. Sure, you don't want to help out? Stretch some muscles?"

"Not a chance, I'll not fall into the ploy again."

"I've put together some food and of course a bottle of wine for your enjoyment." Amorica sent Damian a look that would have had Blade running in the opposite direction if she'd stared at him in that way.

"It's walking distance." Damian smiled twirling his knife around his fingers and glaring at him. "Might take you twenty minutes or so but the sun's shining and there's not a cloud in the sky."

Damian was damn good at the game he played. "You practicing up for when your little girl has her first beau. It's years away but I suppose a father can never get enough practice."

Damian paled for a second but seemed to recover quickly. "Guess I am. What can I do better?"

"Nothing. If I see you before Aidan and I return to the house from our excursion, I'm going to find a place in town to stay." Blade picked up the basket of food Amorica put together and took Aidan's hand in his other. "We'll see you all before dinner and not a moment before."

"You promise there is only one rowboat." Aidan turned.

"Promise." Amorica said smiling.

"Doesn't mean I can't build one." Damian called to their departing backs, laughing. "Maybe the children will have more luck pestering you two today than it appears I'm going to have. Amorica's got me on a short string."

"Finally, I'm going to have you alone. It's seems like a lifetime." Blade picked up the pace until he realized Aidan was hard pressed to keep up with him. "Sorry, I'll slow down."

"I could have stayed with you. It's just my skirts get wound around my legs," Aidan protested breathlessly.

"And you would have been exhausted before we found this paragon of privacy Amorica promised," he laughed, stopping briefly to pull her into his arms for a quick kiss. "Wouldn't want you to be exhausted."

"I think we're here."

The lake rippled with sunshine shimmering down upon it. He couldn't have asked for a better day for a private tryst on an island.

"This is beautiful." Aidan shielded her eyes with her hand. "I forgot my bonnet again. I'm going to have freckles."

"I adore your freckles." He kissed her on the nose then set the basket in the tiny boat. "I should have grabbed a blanket. Maybe that's why Damian was laughing as we left.

"Of course, you would like freckles. They've always been the bane of my existence. Everyone made fun of them along with my red hair." She pursed her lips.

"I'd like to kiss the pretty pout off your lips but I think I'll wait. Don't want to linger here where if anything can go wrong it most certainly will." He helped her into the boat then pushed off.

As he bent to rowing the boat the shoreline grew farther away. Aidan splashed water at him. "Keep that up and we'll both end up in the lake."

"I thought the cool water would feel good. Don't you like to take cold swims? I've heard you mention it more than once." she asked so innocently he groaned from the wayward thought her words conjured.

"Not today. I've other plans. I won't need a frigid swim if my ideas are fulfilled."

"You going to tell me about them?" More water hit him in the chest.

"What?" he asked innocently.

"Your plans," she said.

"You going to tell me what the children asked?" he countered.

She ran a finger around the collar of her gown. "It's hot sitting out here on the lake. Can you row faster?"

"You're eager to be in my arms?"

She looked away for a moment. When their gazes met it seemed they held a spark of raw uninhibited passion as well as fear.

"It's a beautiful day. I'm guessing that last night the children were more precocious than you imagined they'd be."

"They wanted to know if I slept naked with you like their mama and papa. Thankfully I could say no."

"Not for long," Blade laughed. No, not after tonight he told himself. She would never wear that prim white nightdress that hid her toes and every other part of her when they slept together.

"What does that mean?" She splashed him again.

He ignored the droplets admitting to himself they did feel good on his hot skin. "It means, my Little Fire, you and I will sleep naked every night. I don't want any type of cloth keeping me from touching any part of you." He laughed at the shocked expression on her face.

"We will?" She moistened her lips and he wondered just what her active little mind was mulling over.

"I don't know if I'll like that. What if I'm cold?"

"Trust me, I'll make sure you don't want to sleep any other way and when you're in my arms you'll never be cold."

"I do trust you but I'm really not too sure about what you're saying. Sleeping naked doesn't sound practical."

"It's very practical for what I have in mind." He couldn't help himself, he winked at her.

"Making love?" She let her hand rest on her chest, her eyes wide crystal pools of blue. "If you say so. You're the expert."

Her words made him laugh again. He hoped she'd stay just the way she was for the rest of her life, blunt and to the point, accompanied by a hint of innocence. She knew what he planned, even anticipated what was to come but she truly had no idea all he expected to give and to also receive.

The boat touched ground. He jumped from it, wading through the water to pull it ashore. "I could have done that. We used to take turns dragging our sailboats onto solid ground when we sailed to the island."

His gut tightened remembering the past as well as the hazards. "I know that island and all the danger. I've got to say we won't be living close enough to it so I won't have to worry about you sneaking out to go there. Now that you're my wife, you've no need to get your feet wet when I'm around."

"That place holds a lot of good memories. Perhaps you could go there with me sometime."

Blade moored the boat high on the ground. "And bad ones if I recall. I'll never forget the site of you and the fear in my belly when I found you tied to a rock in the ocean with the tide rising. You could have drowned." He shuddered at the thought, knowing he needed to think of more pleasant thoughts such as bedding his new bride.

"Well, that's true, but I refuse to dwell on what's bad and the things that happened in our past. You rescued me and I've been forever in your debt. You were my hero from that day forward."

"I wasn't your knight in shining armor before?" he chuckled, remembering the days when she followed him around.

"No, you avoided me as if I had the plague," she countered. "And I was jealous of every woman I saw you kissing because I knew you would be taking them to your bed."

After setting her on her feet he grabbed the basket. "Perhaps I can collect on some of that debt today. Looks like a path heading inland. Should we find out why Amorica sent us here?"

"I'm sure it's a paradise of Amorica and Damian's making?" she said stepping forward.

He grabbed her hand. "Stay with me. I know we are supposed to be alone here, but I'm going to remain cautious and alert. Even if there is only one rowboat, one never knows what's around the next bend in the road."

"And you should be vigilant. We don't know if Amorica's two little hellions don't have a way here that no one knows about, a log raft or something. I wouldn't put the feat past the two of them."

"They really affected you. I would have thought with so many siblings you would understand perfectly everything they do." He pushed overhanging brush aside, holding it away from Aidan.

"Do you forget so easily that I'm the youngest of all the cousins as well as my siblings? I have no experience with younger children. There was no one at the castle. Everyone always seemed so grown up."

"I do have experience, and most are horrible. With four siblings all of them younger I took part in some of the antics but was the victim of them more often than I care to remember. When we have children, I'll take the lead when it comes to discipline," he told her feeling smug.

"Really and I dare say if we have a little girl, she'll be able to get anything she wants from you."

"Only if she looks like you."

"I wouldn't wish red hair and freckles on my children." Aidan stopped in the middle of the trail arms crossed in front of her.

"Since there is red hair in my family, we're bound to get at least one." He grinned tugging on a lock that had escaped, wishing all of it would come tumbling down around her shoulders. He would take care of that tiny problem later, meaning to run the length through his fingers.

"And how many do you want, children that is?"

"At least a dozen," he told her and almost laughed at the expression on her face. She looked horrified.

"I don't think so, two or three should be more than enough to satisfy your male prowess."

"We can discuss the number of children later." He truly didn't want that many but he agreed with Aidan two or three would be nice.

"Look." Aidan stopped, pointing straight ahead. "That's incredible. I can't believe what I'm seeing."

"No wonder Damian didn't want us to come here. I heard him arguing with Amorica this morning, and I don't think now that it was just about your virtue and whether or not handfasting is a true marriage. He doesn't like sharing this little piece of paradise with anyone. Neither would I," he said.

"This is their private oasis and Amorica was willing to let us use it. She has left me speechless."

In front of them was a structure that was covered with curtains hanging from all sides. Inside a bed was the main piece of furniture, but there were tables and a few other chairs for sitting. Pillows adorned the furniture.

Blade set the basket on the ground and sweeping Aidan into his arms strode the distance to the bed and set her on it. "Don't move."

He left. returning in a moment with the basket, opening it and the bottle of wine he poured them each a glass.

"Isn't it too early for wine?"

"Has to be noon by now and if it isn't, I don't care. Drink and relax, I know you're nervous about today."

"Then, I don't care either." She sipped, watching him over the rim. "What are you going to do?"

"Relax and enjoy this moment, after we leave here, we won't have a moments peace until things are settled at my home in Scotland. I want to enjoy every second I'm with you. Are you hungry?" he asked famished for her not food.

"No." She looked at the wine glass she was holding in her lap. "I think I want you more than I need to eat. We've been waiting so long. Every second makes me more panicky."

He moved closer, running his fingertip along her neck, enjoying the tiny tremor he sent through her. "Then we should not wait one second longer."

~ * ~

She just wanted this first time to be over then she could be happy and she would have a better idea what he wanted from her. Moving away from him, she held out her trembling hand. "I can't stop shaking. I want you to do this quickly, make love to me but from everything you've said, I'm sure that's not what you want."

"You're right, lass. I want our lovemaking to go on forever. I never want you to tire of me or I of you. You are my life Aidan. I'm trying to understand your fears but soon you will have none. I promise you."

"You gave me a woman's pleasure weeks ago. Is there a man's pleasure too? Can I..." She moistened dry lips. "Touch you?" She knew how brazen her words sounded but she couldn't help herself.

He groaned. It was a low deep sound resonating from his chest, "Do you always think of others?"

"No, I'm always self-centered. At least that's what I've been told." She looked up gently stroking his chest, exploring parts of him so different from herself. "I need to see you naked. I've never seen one, a naked man and it's only fair. You ken it?"

"I'm certainly glad there have been no naked men in your life. You can see me after I've brought you pleasure." He touched her gently, caressed her neck then across her collarbone.

"I don't want to be the only one without clothes on this time. When you—when—last time, I wasn't naked but you looked at me, you saw everything, every part of me I'm supposed to keep private. The Duchess would have been shocked at what I let you do with my body. If she had been there, she would have rapped you on the back with her cane."

"I doubt anything can shock that woman," he muttered, his voice deep and gruff. "But, yes, she most likely would have told you that I was remiss. If she'd had her cane handy, she would have used it. I'm sure."

"She lectured us several times before I left for Baltimore. Never let a man touch you below the waist. Only kisses, that's all we were allowed to give. I allowed you so much more. I wanted everything you did. Couldn't think or breathe."

"Now, I'm your husband. I've every right to see you and I'm sure your siblings and cousins allowed more once they got to know the men who adored them enough to wed them. Simply put, it's the way of the world."

"You did look at all of me that time. You could have done more though. I don't think I would have protested or resisted," Aidan said, tracing a path down his chest to just above his waistband.

"I suppose you're right but I needed to prove something to myself first."

"So, do I. Don't I have the right to see you?" Her voice fell, and she inhaled a long deep breath, thinking about unfastening his buckskins before he could give her an answer. It seemed her fingers rested so close to them.

He took off his shirt and loosened his buckskins for her as if reading her mind. "Are you sure? I don't want to frighten you," he asked seeming to study her, a hint of reluctance in his expression.

He stopped short of removing his pants, "Now it's your turn. Do you need help with your dress? The back fastenings and the corset, it seemed you needed help this morning."

She turned, afraid to push this further. She wanted to see him naked and beautiful standing in front of her like the statues she'd seen in museums. His fingers busied themselves until the bodice fell away and he pulled the fabric down until the dress pooled on the floor beneath her feet.

"It seems you can see all of my top half and you're still covered," he laughed. Placing kisses across her shoulders "If we're playing this game of what's fair and what is not, this situation seems unfair to me. I wouldn't think you intend to discriminate."

"A piece of clothing for a piece of clothing." She sipped her wine, smiling and understanding at least for this moment he was doing what she asked. He meant to let her see all of him. She wanted to touch his chest, run her fingers across his stomach then lower to the part of him she knew to be amazingly different from herself.

"You still wear more clothes. How about a drink for a drink then an article of clothing at one's discretion?"

"Your buckskins then." she smiled, watching him over her wine glass, very pleased with herself and what she initiated.

It didn't seem he cared. He pulled them off, his small clothes remaining then settled next to her, smiling broadly. "Do you like what you see, my bonny lass?"

She swallowed, her mouth suddenly dry, parched. "Yes..." She touched the palm of her hands to the corded muscles of his chest then more boldly than she ever believed she could be settled her fingers on his upper thigh.

He inhaled sharply, and seeming to grit his teeth, "I'm certainly glad of that."

"You are very different but I want see more of you, and ken what makes you a man."

"I'm glad of that too but far more different when you see the rest of me."

She suddenly felt lighthearted and not nearly as afraid as she'd been a few moment ago. "And when will that be?"

"Soon, but first I get to remove a piece of your clothing." He paused, seeming to look at her from the tips of her toes upward. "Your underclothes I believe." His hands were under her skirts, tracing the length of her legs until he reached the waistband of her petticoats. Slowly he pulled them off.

"I thought I got to choose." She trembled, excited, eager, thrilled to finally see this man she'd loved and admired most of her life. She sipped wine again, feeling the potent liquid begin to relax her. "Your turn now and you will be naked."

"You'll have what you want but I'm not too sure this is a good idea. Perhaps we should wait until..." Yet he inhaled long and deep before removing the last article and sitting down beside her.

"Can I touch you?" She looked at him, her eyes wide, inspired by the awe she felt as she gazed upon him. She had never thought a man would look like he did. Her tongue swept across her lips as she reached forward, tracing a gentle path along him, mesmerized and unable to think of any words to describe what she was feeling.

Beneath her fingers he jerked, moved, and it seemed it had a life all its own. "Best be careful what you ask for." His voice was raw, throaty with what sounded like desire. "I don't know how much control I have."

"You want me to stop?" She bent close tasting the tip of him. "I don't want to do something wrong." Truly she needed to explore him, kiss him, give him pleasure like he gave her. *A man's pleasure.*

A primal growl whispered through the little sanctuary. "Never, yes...if you don't want me to explode, shocking you further."

"It doesn't look like the statues I've seen," She kissed the length wrapping her hand around him and squeezing gently.

Through gritted teeth, "It is my shaft or rod, my sex and so many more names take your pick." She looked at him then once again settled her mouth on the tip, taking his rod inside, sucking, enjoying the primal sounds he made and the way his fingers gripped her shoulders.

She couldn't help but lift her head and smile at him as she moved her hand along him, saw the strain on his face, around his eyes then the primal growl, which she hoped was pleasure. Suddenly he jerked in her hands liquid spurting from him.

"What did I do?" Panic swept through her. This had never been her intent. All she wanted was to touch and explore him as he did to her. She needed to give him the sweet pleasure he gave to her.

He lay back, pulling her into his arms. "Bloody eyes, did you have any idea what you were doing to me?"

"I..." She had no words. "Whatever it was, I promise I won't do it again." She was mortified that she'd done something horribly wrong.

"Hush, you touch me like that any time you want but given a choice I'd rather lose my seed inside you." He told her running his hand along her arm as his ragged breathing confused her more. "That was a heaven on earth I've never experienced before. I loved it when you closed your mouth over my sex."

"Thank god, I didn't hurt you. For a moment I thought..." She stroked his chest, let her fingers settle on his tiny nipples watching his hips jerk and his rod harden again.

"No, you could never hurt me. I wouldn't allow it."

"Is that?" She touched the liquid on his chest.

"Are you truly that innocent? Aidan you know I've never been chaste except the last two years but I've never bedded a virgin or anyone so completely innocent as it seems you are. That is my seed and when I'm deep inside you, it will join with you and make a child."

She was amazed, perhaps in awe. "I never knew."

Grabbing his shirt, he wiped the liquid off his chest. "Don't move a muscle." He set off down the path. When he returned the cloth was wet and he was wringing it out. "Wanted to wash it. Now, I'll hang it up here to dry." He set it on a peg.

"Tell me all you know about sex." He sat down next to her, his gaze focused on her lips.

She felt her eyes cross and blood rush to her face. "All I know is what you've done to me and what I've seen in the stables. Nothing more. No one has talked to me or given me advice."

"Your sisters didn't tell you what happens between a man and a woman? I know it's usually a mother's job but." He sounded frustrated as he ran both hands through his hair. "So, it is all up to me?"

"My sisters are all much older than I am and they've been away. Allura had other considerations than her little sister's education about what happens in the bedroom. I don't believe Eveleen knew any more than I did."

"Then, we are quite the pair. All I know about virgins are the jests between men who have seduced one." He stole a breath before gazing at her. "You are beautiful and scary now. I thought to—bloody hell, I don't know what I thought. This isn't at all what I expected. But then I know I wouldn't have it any other way. You are mine and always will be Aidan MacPherson."

"You don't want to make love to me now?" she asked, as moisture pooled in her eyes. "Because I'm a virgin? I thought that's what men wanted."

"I don't want to hurt you and now I'm afraid I might do just that. I don't know what I was thinking."

"That you wanted to make love to your wife?" She smiled wondering if he would finish this today or if he would put it off for some other time. The thing was, every time they delayed the inevitable, it made her a little more terrified and she did just want to get this over with so she could move on.

"I did. Bloody eyes, I still do."

She touched his cheek. "That's the thing. Everyone has a first time. All women were virgins at one time. But," she paused looking at his anatomy that had grown hard a second time. "I don't think your...rod...will fit inside me. You are huge, it is huge."

"No worries, you're tiny but I've confidence everything will fit just fine." He smiled tenderly running his hands through her hair loosening the pins until her hair fell around her, his handsome grin giving her courage. "Let's just start at the beginning. Pretend you didn't see me and you have no idea what will happen."

"I would disagree. We can't go back and no matter what you say, you're just too big." She gazed at him again reached out as if she meant to touch him then pulled back, closing her eyes.

With a low growl, he pulled her to a sitting position and tugged her shift over her head. Quickly he removed the rest of her clothing.

Gently touching each of her nipples with a fingertip.

"Are you ready?" He placed his hands on her shoulders then ran them down her arms until he held her hands in his. "Only pleasure, Little Fire. I won't hurt you. Just let me show you the way. I promise to take this slow and make everything perfect for you."

She looked at herself then at Blade. Sunlight filtered through the curtains and the foliage painted his body in dancing light and shadows. He was so hard, his muscles taut and bulging in his arms and legs, his waist and hips slim. His strength and size had always mesmerized her, drew her to him in ways she never imagined. She would have to trust him.

"I want to be but I have to reiterate, you are huge and..."

He set a fingertip against her lips, "Hush, remember how I touched you and kissed you? You were hot and swollen. You slicked my fingers with your cream when I caressed you intimately. Because of your passionate response to me, I will come inside you easily. Your body will stretch to accommodate me."

She nodded moistening her lips and reaching out to stroke him. He pulled her into his arms and gently laid her on the bed before spreading her legs and coming down on top of her.

His lips touched and explored while his teeth nibbled every inch he could find. Her body soared, reaching for him, testing each caress with one of her own. When his hands stroked her intimately, sounds from the back of her throat seemed to make him smile. Then he brought his fingers to trace her cheek, she felt the wetness he talked about and felt the heat as it seemed to rise to an inferno. Perhaps he was right.

The ache increased, as did the fire until the tiny cries she made startled and amazed her. His rod rested against her core as if waiting for her to accept him into her. "Please," she whispered. "I need you."

"Ach, lass do ye trust me now? Do you believe me?" He sucked a nipple into his mouth while his fingers danced attendance on the other one. Then he drew her tightly into his arms, and she was afraid he'd let her go.

"Aye."

He kissed her lips, stroking her back softly, and she felt the sensual dance of his fingers along her spine, igniting a fire within while his lips brought their liquid heat, down to the small of her back then over the rise of her hip. He paused watching her from above, enchanting and magical sensation sweeping through her in a staggering manner, so intense she could only sigh and feel her body shudder.

He held her in his arms once again. Her gaze met his. She knew an impending need. One she could not hold back nor did she wish to do such a thing.

"Your lips are so soft, delicious," She touched his mouth with a fingertip, "so very different from the rest of you."

"And you are soft everywhere," he laughed. "No one has ever called any part of me soft. This is a first."

"Well it is probably the only place," she told him indignantly.

"We're going to do this, you know." He told her, kissing her cheeks and nose then trailing kisses down her neck.

"I'm going to trust everything you've told me. You're not going to hurt me and you will fit."

"Those are the words I've craved to hear from you, Little Fire."

He captured her mouth and feeling the duel of his tongue with hers, once again an urgent raw hunger seared through her. His hand moved fervently over her breast, creating an inexorable ache within her. He kissed her, teasing her body. She felt as if there was nothing sweeter than the way his hands moved over her. On top of her he shifted, moving lower to massage a most sensitive spot, suckling upon her. Even as he did so, yearning gripped her and she moved against him, her hands traveling the length of his spine then resting on his buttocks.

He stroked her breast and she rose up against him and he whispered soft words into her mouth. "All you need is to trust me and believe in the magic and the enchantment of this day and this moment. I'm your husband and I will always give you pleasure. Feel my touch, Little Fire, here and here. Feel it become a heat you can't deny one that sets you on flame. The passion resides deep inside you." He stroked her upper thigh, set his leg over the apex of her thighs. "See," he whispered then slipped a finger deep inside her then two. "I will fill you with my shaft and your body will clench around me and accept all of me."

"Blade." Her body arched in response, begging for him. "I ache and burn. Please I can..."

"Little Fire." He breathed into her mouth, "Soon, you will feel me inside you, very soon, have patience. I'm going to do so much more."

She inhaled swift and deep, trembled against his caress then shifted remembering his touch and the sensations she was coming so close to experiencing once more. A tempest was running rampant within her and still he was teaching her memories she would not soon forget.

"You are mine, Aidan, as is your passion and the wild sweetness waiting for us to discover in each other's arms."

"Blade, are you mine too?" She wondered at that. Was it possible since they were wed?

"Yes, no one else's. And I want to give you everything you've ever desired then more. I want you to wonder at the sensations that are about to sweep through you." He rose above her and gently caressed her lips with just the breath of his own then drew a pattern between her breasts with his finger. Enticingly, he lowered himself against her once more. Wherever he caressed her he kissed her until he lay between her legs. Touching her parting her, stroking her kissing her.

A soft fervent cry escaped her. Her fingers tugged upon his hair. He caught her hands and held them within his own. Once more she was reminded of another time when he held her hands. She moaned softly. Her head began to toss, her body to writhe.

"Open your eyes, Little Fire. I want to see them." And she wanted so much more than she ever thought possible.

Beyond the tiny private oasis, the day cast shadows as light danced inside. The afternoon breeze stirred exquisitely against her flesh. In the light of the day he created all the magical enchantment, the storm inside her and it was all so much more than she could have ever imagined.

He grinned roguishly, finding the most sensitive spot within her folds the center of all her sensuality and toyed mercilessly upon it, laving, teasing, demanding with the caress of his lips and tongue. She began to tremble as he rose above her watching her with the silver gleam of his steel gray eyes. "Please," she whispered softly, "I need you now."

And she did indeed need him. The sensations coursing inside her seemed to grow until she arched wildly against him. Sounds of her rising passion filled the afternoon, frantic, breathless, desperation filling her. It seemed she spiraled out of control achingly sweet.

Then, he was atop her once more. His eyes glittering with desire, she could ask for no greater wonder. His rod slowly slid into her, filling her with the wonder and the fervent sensations. She felt her body clench around him, as he pushed deeper.

Then, she cried out in pain, trying to tug her hands free of his. Tears welled in her eyes. "Stop."

"Nay, lass, I cannot." Yet he held himself still and seemed to wait for her to accept him again.

"You promised." She tried to buck him off which only served to push him farther inside. Yet suddenly the wonder of this union took hold.

"I didn't know it would cause such pain but it changes nothing. I still would have filled you and waited for the hurt to vanish. I promise our union will never cause you pain again."

She breathed in deeply once again tugging at her hands. "Let my hands go. I want them to be free to explore you."

He did, and her fingers wound into his hair, pulled his mouth to meet hers while her hips lifted to take him farther inside. She shifted beneath him encouraging him. When he did, she gasped and arched to meet his thrust. Her gaze met his, locked as if he was her lifeline.

He moved demandingly. His huge arms held his body above hers as he thrust into hers then again and again. He moved faster and harder, his expression taut and strained as if he held back.

Then she cried out, unable to keep the pleasure inside her as her body sent waves of carnal pleasure within her while she arched to take more of him inside. Spasm of sweet pleasure began to ripple through her. Her fingers played along his shoulders, kneading, burrowing, gripping him. He thrust hard against her just as sensations seemed to split and explode within her.

She gasped, clinging to him as the force of her climax seemed to sear within her. So absorbed with the ecstasy, she didn't realize he was still poised above her, watching her and that the liquid heat spilling from his body was filling her.

She shuddered, staring at him, sudden tears warming her eyes. "I trust you," she whispered. "Even after that day when you said you gave me pleasure. I never realized the real heaven you were waiting to bring to me."

"Heaven?" He grinned appearing so much more than pleased with himself.

"Yes." She lowered her lashes, seeming suddenly shy.

He rolled off her, the sheen of sweat covering his body. "My wife," he whispered. "You've pleased me more than you could ever guess. Have I pleased you?"

"Blade! Aidan! You're about to have company. Don't know how long I can hold them off."

"It's Damian. What can he want?" For a moment she thought he was there to torment them both once again. He would never invade their privacy, not unless there was an emergency.

"Bloody hell, what does he want now. Cover yourself." He pulled on his buckskins and moccasins, striding down the path to the rowboat.

"You're never going to believe who just showed up," Damian called out from the far side of the lake.

Aidan hastily slipped her dress over her head and followed Blade. Who just showed up? Had to be Aric and Ravyn but their appearance wouldn't come as too much of a surprise.

When they reached the water's edge. Damian sat on his horse, negligently leaning on the saddle, a broad, all-knowing smirk on his face.

"Well?" Aidan asked. "You don't need to let the suspense continue."

"Everyone's favorite Duchess. She's on her way as we speak, wicked cane in hand and the Laird McLellan bringing up the rear."

"Good God," Aidan muttered. "You're joking. "Papa?"

"I've been calling out for the two of you for about fifteen minutes." He turned to look over his shoulder. "There they are."

"Papa." Aidan whirled, rushing up the path and trying to put all her clothes into a respectable order.

"Let me help. Remember there is only one rowboat and the vessel rests on our side of the lake." Blade followed and now stood beside her, sweeping the dress from her and handing her the rest of her clothes in the proper order, then finishing with her hair.

"How did I get so lucky to find a man who could put my unruly crimson hair into a bun?" she asked but inside terror swept through her. They were wed, she kept reminding herself. They had done nothing wrong.

He chuckled, kissing the nape of her neck then extending his arm for her to take. "Remember, we did nothing wrong. You are my wife and we've witnesses to prove it."

"Why do you think they are here?" Panic swept through her then fear that something happened to someone, anyone of her family then discounted it. Amazed her aunty traveled all the way to America, she decided to wait for answers before jumping to conclusions.

By the time they rowed across the lake Charlotte and David had arrived on the beach. The Duchess stood next to the McLellan, her cane in hand shaking it at Blade.

~ * ~

"Young man, how dare you seduce my niece under the guise of handfasting. I should give you the wrong end of the cane right where it would hurt the most." The Duchess waved her cane in the air.

"Now Charlotte, you can't do that no matter how much you'd like," the McLellan said, "but I can make my youngest daughter wear a chastity belt until they are legally wed."

"Papa, you would not. You practically encouraged Hunter to make love to Allura before the vows were said. How can you be so insensitive, hypocritical and, and..."

"I'm your father young lady and you'll do as I say." Then, he directed his attention to Blade. "Your people in the highlands might consider handfasting as legal and binding but rest assured in the lowlands they do not. It is a pagan ceremony with nothing based on God's will. You will wed my daughter the proper way, in a church. I don't want to hear any protests."

"I planned to do just that as soon as Amorica and Aidan can put it all in motion. There was never any doubt in Amorica or Damian's mind that a wedding was what we planned all along."

David felt his anger escalate, "You seduced my daughter in the guise of handfasting. Admit it."

"I made love to my wife." Blade persisted seemingly unwilling to give credence to anything his father-in-law said.

"I told him no one recognized handfasting any longer. Told him he should wait until they could be legal. Now any offspring could be bastards." Damian gave a huge sigh coupled with the shrug of his shoulders. "One just can't trust the youngsters these days to listen to sound advice."

"No matter," The Duchess gave a loud harrumph. "Aidan you will remain in town until the wedding, which is to take place in three days and she won't be found in bed with Blade MacPherson until after the marriage. If the minister won't agree to something so soon, I'll make it worth his while."

"You expect me to stay away from Aidan for three days?" He sounded incredulous and David wanted to laugh. He had fond memories of his youth as well as the mother of his children, Sadie who passed away years ago, but even now he didn't like to sleep without Charlotte by his side. He understood the young man's distress.

"Of course, we do." The Duchess rapped her cane on the grass. "I expect you to treat my niece with the respect she deserves. It was what was demanded of all grooms who wed my nieces in London."

David chuckled to himself. Without the benefit of hard wood beneath her cane the gesture lost its impact, but he didn't doubt for a moment that if Blade provoked her further, she would use the sword end on him. The thought struck him that she might have demanded his compliance but not one of her nieces obeyed her mandate. For that matter, neither did she.

"It's a foolish notion," Blade said an angry snarl in his voice.

The Duchess continued as if Blade said nothing. "And I expect you to respect the wishes of Aidan's family who do not consider handfasting a legal marriage." She pointed to Aidan's hand." Even though

I see you gave her a pagan ring, it is still not legal."

Damian rode up beside Blade the reins of a horse in hand. "Brought a horse for you Blade. You should thank me now. If I weren't so thoughtful, you'd be walking back to the house alone. Doubt if The Duchess will allow you to ride in the buggy with your beautiful fiancée."

"I'm riding with Blade. I'm sure that horse can take two of us for that short of a distance." Aidan spoke up looking defiantly at The Duchess and her father seemingly determined to put her interest in the forefront but was doing nothing of the kind.

"No, you're not young lady. You're riding in the buggy. Don't take this moment to defy me," the McLellan said.

"It's alright, Aidan. You go with your father and The Duchess. We need to do as they say for the time being. I don't need to rile everyone who is important to you." He gave her a quick kiss on the lips, which garnered him a ferocious scowl from The Duchess as well as Aidan's father.

Walking with her to the buggy, Blade helped her up, purposely letting his hands linger on her a few moments too long. It seemed he didn't really care if he goaded them just a bit.

"I'm not going to let them dictate to me what I can and can't do." She sat down crossing her arms in front of her then staring straight ahead. "I'm a grown woman after all."

The Duchess sat beside her, "You'll be glad we came, eventually. I know how smitten you've been with this man most of your life, but you've waited this long. You can wait three more days. Now, I get to plan a wedding for my youngest niece. She deserves one and I'm going to make sure it happens as early as possible. It's going to be the wedding of your dreams."

"Why are you here Aunty? Really?" She turned her anger towards the one woman who loved her more than life, very apparent. "It's not to see my wedding. I'm sure of that."

"I came to see what all the to do was about in America. Why Amorica and Raven won't move back to England. And," she paused. "I came to make sure the two of you had a wedding you'd never forget, hoping you were not already on a boat headed to London or MacPherson land. I have your best interests at heart, young lady. Someone has to make sure Sadie's youngest is not taken advantage of. I'm sure your beau doesn't believe that's what he is doing, but he's wrong. A handfasting in most minds doesn't make a legal marriage and any heir you birth will be questioned."

"I've said it before and I'll say it as many times as need be, I don't want anything extravagant. A justice of the peace or a traveling minister would suffice. You didn't have to come here to make sure I wasn't hurt by Blade. He only wants what is best for me. Amorica and I already started planning the wedding."

"He wants what's best for him, sex and your body. As for the wedding, I understand, not extravagant but beautiful, yes. James Macmurra allowed me to bring fabrics and fashion plates for you to look at even though they took up substantial room on his ship. Also varying shades of Belgian lace for the trimmings. I've some gorgeous ice blue fabric that will bring out the color of your eyes if that's the one you choose."

"She's incorrigible," David said, grinning and knowing now his youngest would be legally wed. He'd been listening to the conversation and enjoying Charlotte. Perhaps he'd been enjoying her a bit too much. They certainly weren't setting a good example for the children and grand nieces and nephews. A wave of guilt swept within. Perhaps he should ask her to marry him before everyone figured out they were spending their nights together behind closed door, and unwed.

"What the Bloody hell is that?" Blade, as was Aidan, were staring at the grounds around the ranch house.

Chapter Five

To Blade the grounds appeared to be a circus. Colorful tents adorned the area around the house. Men and women scurried between the canvas shelters and the house with various objects. He looked to The Duchess who had a broad grin on her face.

Once down from the buggy, she strode to the house where Amorica and Christel waited. "Come along, Aidan." Blade heard the words yet he was beyond his endurance. These events, orchestrated by The Duchess had taken on a life of their own.

"Christel." Aidan ran to her older sisters, arms wide for a hug. "You're here too. Why?"

Christel stepped back looking at her sister. "Ryder had an urge to wander, see another sunrise and see his best friends, Damian and Aric in the process. The Duchess hoped we'd be part of a wedding and here we are. I'm truly sorry they interrupted your tryst. If I could have put a stop to it, I would have. But they were a force no one could stop. You know The Duchess as well as anyone."

"You and Ryder had no interference in your relationship and that must have been bliss in so many ways. My heart fills though, when I see so much love for me and for Blade. We'll wait until the vows are said just to make Papa happy." Aidan seemed to speak from her heart.

Blade heard the words, grinning. Not if he could find a way into her bedroom. They would not wait, now that he'd tasted her, come to feel the passion her tiny form held, breathed in the essence that made Aidan so unique, he wasn't about to do without.

Amorica stepped from the house. "Come, I've spread the fabrics out in the parlor and the lace is close by. You've a lot of decisions to make this afternoon and before dinner. I've sent a man to town to retrieve the two seamstresses who live there. Luckily they both have daughters who can help so they will come with their mothers."

In the room, Charlotte sat near the freshly baked lemon bars, watching the scene unfold. "This is so much fun, don't you all think?" She smiled. The Duchess was always at her best when she was getting her way. Today was no different.

Aidan plopped down beside her. "The experience would be better if you and my father weren't so autocratic. I want some of that brandy and if I have enough so I can fall asleep I'll be much happier than I am now. I don't want to make decisions I just want to marry Blade so everyone will leave us alone. Someone else can decide what I should wear."

Blade followed the women into the room, insinuating himself in the proceedings. The urge to rattle The Duchess possessed him with a force he truly didn't understand but the fury he felt at the demolishment of his carefully constructed plans sent him on a path for revenge. This day he'd planned so carefully. They should still be ensconced in the island gazebo, sipping wine and enjoying each other's company.

He picked up Aidan's hand and placed a not so chaste kiss on the palm, lingering then gazing into her eyes. "I like that blue one." He pointed to Charlotte's favorite yardage, "and perhaps that lace. Do you approve of my taste?"

"I do like it. Perhaps we should cut this short and settle on the ice blue fabric. I'd like to take a walk with Blade."

"No, you don't," The Duchess spoke up. "The two of you know you're not to be alone until after the vows are said. Besides we still don't have a pattern for the fabric."

"I noticed you and the McLellan, well, your bags were all placed in the same room in the guest house. You two sleeping together?" Blade challenged Aidan's aunt and was pleased with the rush of color to Charlotte's cheeks. "Seems like the same rules should apply don't you think."

"That's none of your business, young man. What David and I do is between us." She tapped her cane on the floor her expression changing to something he couldn't quite figure out. This wasn't The Duchess,

Aunty Charlotte or Charlotte.

"Since you and David are making Aidan's and my sleeping arrangements your business, I see no reason not to insinuate myself into yours." He pulled Aidan on to his lap, his hand resting close to her breast. A slight slip and he would cover it, knowing the elders would berate him for his actions but willing to take whatever they doled out.

"Blade don't," Aidan whispered. "I don't want to be embarrassed," she pleaded.

"Don't hold you on my lap?" he asked his fingers pressing into her ribcage before sliding to her waist. He smiled when she squirmed and he grinned even wider when he saw the furrowing of The Duchess' brows.

"Blade, I swear."

"Aidan, can you help me in the kitchen?" Amorica asked seeming to take pity on her cousin and Blades' argument with The Duchess.

Aidan tried to stand but Blade held her still then reluctantly, he let her go before turning his attention back to Charlotte. "Perhaps there should be two weddings. Some of this fabric and lace might appeal to you too, Aunt Charlotte." Clearly, he taunted her but had not expected David to appear.

"I believe that's a splendid idea but I should talk it over with my girls. I mentioned the idea to Charlotte a few days ago but she's failed to give me an answer," David said. "What do you say, Charlotte? Shall we tie the knot with my youngest and her beau? We would certainly be setting a better example."

"It's a superb idea," Christel said smiling and pouring each a glass of brandy before settling in a chair beside her father. "You're certainly correct. You wouldn't want to set a bad example to the grandchildren and grandnieces, let alone your daughters."

"I dare say the Duke will approve. Before he died, he encouraged me to seek another man if something untoward happened to him. I did tell him, though, that I would never find anyone else to love. I feel as if I'm cheating on him."

"Whether you're wed or not," Christel said still smiling. "If you're sleeping together without benefit of marriage... well, I just don't think it's something you should do. A double wedding would be grand."

"It's not like we're living together," Charlotte said, folding her hands in her lap. "David still lives in Scotland and I in London. We only see each other every couple of months."

"That's only because neither of you are willing to permanently give up your homes. I think my father should move to London so the two of you can be together all of the time." Christel sipped her brandy, a smile of bliss on her face. "Allura and Hunter take care of everything at home anyway. You can come and visit anytime you like."

"I think that would be nice. You won't be so lonely," Aidan said.

"I've Scarlett. I'm not lonely dear, but thank you for your concern. When David is in the city it's wonderful, but I don't need him every day." It seemed Charlotte spoke defensively.

"You don't want to marry me? Why not?" David stood over Charlotte clearly displeased with what she said. "Am I not good enough for you?" His hands rested on her shoulders.

"I didn't say that. I don't want the youngsters to pressure you into something you might not want," Charlotte said.

Clearly enjoying himself, Blade grinned, loving the fact the tables had been turned. Blade said, "Charlotte, you cannot mean to sleep with David until the two of you are wed. The two of you must be celibate these next two nights. It will make the wedding night so much better."

Suddenly, there was a hush around the room as all turned to stare at the couple. "What do you say Charlotte?" David asked. "Shall we make this a double wedding and abide by our rules?"

Charlotte looked at the floor then the man standing in front of her waiting for an answer. "I think we should and if we won't allow the children to sleep together then I suppose I must stay in town with Aidan."

"Ach lass, and I was looking forward to you warming my bed tonight. I don't see how we have a choice, though. We don't want to be accused of saying one thing and doing another," David said, smiling and appearing very pleased with this new situation.

"All the girls will stay in town," Amorica said, "Don't you agree Christel? In fact, we shall pack our bags immediately and we won't see any of the men until the wedding. That way no one feels left out or picked on."

"We should take the crate of wine. The men can drink the Guinness we brought," Christel said.

Somehow the thought of all the men in the same situation as he found himself in, warmed Blade's soul.

"Are you proud of yourself?" Damian scowled at Blade as if this was his fault. He and Ryder just entered the parlor seeming to look for their wives when the end of the discussion was disclosed.

"No, but all seems fair here. The only couple who is not wed in some form or other are David and Charlotte. If I have to spend the remaining two nights in a cold bed then it seems right and fair the rest of you should do the same." Blade grinned, enjoying the fact that Damian was getting a small bit of what he dished out.

"There is really nothing to do about it. If we are to get two wedding dresses sewn in two days then we will all have to lend a hand and move into town," Amorica said.

"Oh, my, I don't think I remember how to sew a stitch," The Duchess moaned.

"And I never knew," Aidan said as Blade's hand found its way beneath her dress, hidden from the view of everyone in the room.

He traced a path along her outer thigh until he reached her belly, covering it with his hand, enjoying the way she responded to his touch and the fact everyone was so immersed in conversation about the wedding they didn't notice. He sought more intimate places.

At the sanctuary when they so hastily dressed, she'd not had the chance to put everything on. A significant part of her clothing was still on the floor in the gazebo. Now his fingers delved into her swollen feminine parts, caressing the tiny nub. It seemed she still craved his touch as much as he needed to be inside her.

"Blade..." she whispered. "You cannot mean. Not here."

"I can." He slipped a finger inside her and was able to do so because she opened her legs for him.

"You're a cad and what will you do if I scream out your name and climax here in front of everyone," her voice was so soft and low he could barely hear but he caught the gist and felt heat sore in his body.

"You will not." His voice was so low she leaned closer as if trying to hear. "I won't let you."

"So, you mean to torment me?"

"I suppose this is not well done of me," he told her, wishing he could carry her away to someplace private. He withdrew his hand only to touch her on the cheek where she could feel the dampness he'd just enjoyed.

"No, it is not."

"I dinna ken if I can wait two nights to possess you," Blade whispered.

"You will have to unless you can find a way into my chambers."

"Perhaps we, the men here, can join together. I'm sure none of them are looking forward to the next two nights alone and sleeping in cold beds."

"A united front?" she queried.

"When all are faced with what they wished on one person, the tide will change." Blade felt sure he would be able to see his bride before the vows were exchanged. "Yes, a united front."

"Damian is so bent on keeping you from me, I doubt that even to see Amorica he would change his mind."

"Perhaps if he couldn't get his biscuits, he would join with me against the McLellan," Blade said gazing over the room and understanding he would probably be chaste for the next few nights.

"You're crazy if you believe he likes biscuits more than his wife," Aidan said with a tiny huff.

"Come ladies, we need to get our bags onto the carts and head into town." Christel clapped her hands together herding the women into compliance.

"I'll come to you tonight," Ryder said to Christel.

"No, I think not. We will all be busy with wedding affairs. If we are to put this double ceremony together every moment of time will be directed that way," Christel said, making sure Ryder knew what was expected of him. "You and none of the others need make their way into town. We won't entertain you. Not even in secret. We will be up most if not all of both nights."

"Dinner is ready in an hour. If you men don't wish to let it burn, I suggest one of you take charge, Damian?" Amorica said. "You're in charge."

"I'm a decent cook." David stepped forward. "Don't like burnt food and I don't trust the rest of you."

In less than an hour the ladies were kissing their men goodbye. Blade watched the carts disappear over the horizon to the town beyond.

"See what you've done." Damian stood beside Blade scowling his displeasure and seeming to petulantly blame him for everything.

"What I've done?" Blade chuckled, truly knowing the agony Damian must feel. "Oh, you mean the biscuits?"

"Of course, not you big oaf. Now we're all going to go without our women folk until the wedding."

Blade shrugged, "Or we could join forces. Don't believe for a moment that if everyone is occupied, they'll care about what I'm doing."

"I'll care," the McLellan said, stepping up behind him. "And I'm going to charge all of the in-laws with guard duty. I stand firmly behind the fact ye are not wed to my daughter. I wasn't there for any of them except my oldest and I intend to make it up to them, all of them and now most of all my youngest."

"By tormenting me. How did I get so lucky?"

"By making the wedding night that much more memorable." David searched the faces in the room. "Will you all pledge to stay away from your wives and in the process keep Blade from leaving the ranch?"

Blade stifled a groan, understanding that he'd probably been beaten at least in this round.

"I've chores," Damian said, striding from the room, then over his shoulder, "Anyone have frustrations to work out can join me, scooping up manure."

Ryder and Blade followed to the stables. For an hour they shoveled manure and hay. Fed the animals and tried to keep their minds from their empty beds. When the dinner bell rang, they washed in the trough, the cold water assuaging some of the aches and pains the day brought but not the most potent agony.

When Blade closed his eyes, all he could envision was Aidan, stretched out before him naked and in the throes of her climax. His body hardened and he must have groaned.

"Thinking about what you're missing?" Damian clapped him on the shoulder. "Me too."

"You might say that. This certainly isn't how I envisioned tonight or the next one. But I suppose abstinence might make the next time better." He wasn't about to acknowledge a wedding night. In his mind he had that this afternoon in the private oasis supplied to them by Amorica and inadvertently Damian.

David brought a couple of cases of Guinness from one of the carts outside into the kitchen.

"Do you suppose we can drown our sorrows?" Ryder asked, joining the conversation.

And if the men were drowning their sorrows in beer, if he remained sober, he might be able to sneak into town.

"Don't even think about it," Damian whispered for his ears only. "I for one don't plan on getting soused this evening. And I received a message from Aric that he and Ravyn will arrive around ten. Sent one of my men out to meet them and apprise them of the situation here. He'll leave his wife in town."

"You've thought of everything," Blade said, feeling the ache in his groin. "Too bad you're so smart you might have out smarted yourself."

"I hope so. I've thought of everything. We've all agreed the most important thing these next two nights and days is to keep you here and away from Aidan. My guess is that you've only had one time with her."

Blade didn't answer, wasn't about to reveal anything intimate about his relationship with his wife. It was not Damian's or anyone else's business. Hands fisted, Blade strode from the stables and to the house. Inside David greeted each one with a cold beer. He sipped the heady brew, beginning to think the only way he'd survive would be drunk.

"We're going to eat in the kitchen," David said, seeming to search the faces of the men. "And there is enough beer to keep us through the night. What do you all say? Let's just enjoy this evening with no regrets. We can break out the cards."

In the parlor, "So, I've heard The Duchess has tried to keep all her charges separated from their beaus on the wedding night," Blade said.

"And was successful with no one."

"Not Amorica and myself," Damian said, restating the facts. "But then I wed Amorica before I made love to her."

"I married Ravyn in The Duchess' parlor," Aric stepped into the room. "Before either of us even thought about sex. Well, I suppose that's not true. From the moment I saw her that was all I could think about. For reasons most of you know she was terrified of the act. We had many cold nights before I finally consummated the marriage."

"I'll get you a beer." David rose from his seat and returned a little later.

"You didn't consummate the marriage until months later." Damian laughed. "I'll never forget how you chased after her when she left you."

"She asked me to go with her," Ryder said. "Being single at the time I knew if I took her back to Baltimore and the waiting ship, I was sure you'd kill me."

"Well, while that's true no one else needed to know," Aric said. "Some things are sacred between a man and his wife."

"The Duchess wasn't at the McLaren castle to keep me away from Christel," Ryder said. "But there were so many other obstacles to our marriage. She wanted to be a nun but they kicked her out of the Abby."

"So, all of you did just as you pleased but you seek to keep me from my wife," Blade said.

"You're not married," Damian reminded him.

"So, you think, but I am." Blade rose to refill his glass, realizing the forces tonight were against him. He decided he would try to relax and let whatever was meant to happen come to pass.

"The Duchess wasn't at my castle to stop me. I made love to Christel before we were wed. That fact negates nothing where you are concerned, Blade. A man should not have his wife before they are wed."

"Do you regret it?" Blade asked, pretty sure he knew the answer.

"Not for a moment," Ryder laughed. "More beer for everyone. Then a new round of reasons why we should keep Blade from his blushing bride."

"He's already sampled all she has to give," Damian interjected.

"I say, what Aidan and I have done in privacy is not something any of you are welcome to talk about. It is just that, private, and between Aidan and myself." Blade had tired of this discussion hours ago but understood it wasn't going to end any time soon.

Damian stepped in, with a slap on Blade's back. "He does have a point. What happens in the bedroom, or my private sanctuary is just that, private. Let's drink to Blade's coming nuptials and keeping him from riding into town."

"I never thought you would agree with me about anything," Blade said, wondering at Damian's words.

"I don't publicize my relationship with Amorica and I'm glad you feel the same about Aidan. Now that we're all in the same place, without our ladies, we should ban together."

"As long as David stays here with us, I won't try to see Aidan tonight or tomorrow. We're going to let the ladies plan these two weddings and be pleasantly surprised in two days," Blade said, watching the men in the room to see if they agreed.

"Is that a promise?" David asked, sampling the stew he made, or finished making. "Needs more salt," he mumbled.

"As long as everyone else makes the same vow, I will do the same," Blade said specifically watching Damian for his reaction even though he'd said as much a bit earlier. Blade didn't completely trust this man who had goaded him from the moment they met.

The others looked at each other clearly displeased with the conversation. Each one had a look of chagrin on their faces including the McLellan. Blade knew they weren't about to vow to stay away from their wives.

"Just as I thought. The moment the lights go out at the ranch each and every one of you intend to make their way into town and their wife's bed," Blade said. "Tell me the truth. Am I wrong?"

No one spoke. "Then we should all go together. No one should be left here, alone, including me."

"I can't allow that," David spoke up, "Aidan's my daughter and it's up to me to protect her."

"If everyone has gone into town, who's left to stop me?" Blade persisted. "Besides, it's up to me to protect her now."

"We could hog-tie you." Damian suggested, pleasantly, his smile anything but angelic.

The anger sweeping through Blade was unprecedented. He'd never felt this way before. He paced the room, searching the others for a tiny bit of shame and he saw none.

He downed the last of his beer, leaving the men talking. In the room assigned to him, he pulled off his shirt before kicking off his moccasins and unfastening his buckskins. The manipulation is what galled him. This was a game to these men who had never answered to anyone their entire lives.

He was close to their age and had lived life the way he chose, until this moment. Now they treated him as if his beliefs meant nothing, as if he was a child. He put an arm over his eyes, trying not to think. The clock ticked and the seconds seemed to pass at a turtle's pace. Through the open window he heard the soft sigh of the breeze and smelled the scent of Daphne.

Outside he heard the sound of horses' hooves as the men rode into town. He decided that despite what everyone else was about, he was going to be honorable and above board.

In two nights, his wife would be in his arms and no one could gainsay him. She was his forever and waiting would only make his first night with her even sweeter as The Duchess had implied. Keeping his in-laws, especially her father, happy was important.

This was what families were about. He wanted to keep the peace between everyone. Not much time had passed and he heard hoof beats of returning horses. He was curious, yes, but his mind rushed to the obvious conclusion. The women sent their men home. A chuckle rumbled from his chest

Ach, he would not be the only man here tonight who would be celibate. Outside the room, he heard the commiseration and the swearing. He grinned, laughing at the situation. Tempted to rise and confront Damian, he decided he'd wait until tomorrow morning.

Suddenly the door burst open and Damian stood in the frame. "You knew this would happen."

"Knew what would happen?" He grinned, wishing he could have seen the expression on his face when Amorica sent him packing.

"They would reject us." Damian ran both hands through his hair, the lines around his eyes more pronounced.

"You give me too much credit. It seems, however, the ladies understand what is fair and what is not. Besides they said as much. Told us they'd be working most of the night if not all."

"Maybe. They were too busy with your wedding to have anything to do with us."

"Yes? Priorities can bite you in the butt." Blade enjoyed himself, reveling in Damian's discomfort.

"They were hard at work sewing and planning the menu for the wedding day. Even the minister's wife was in the room working. She looked appalled when we showed up unannounced. What the devil takes that long to plan a wedding and sew a dress?"

"Like any good minister's wife would." Blade could barely contain his laughter. "The minister, bless his soul, is probably celibate tonight also. There is the ceremony called handfasting. We did make our vows to each other in just a few minutes."

"Amorica told me not to try tomorrow night either. They had too much to do to see to our carnal needs." Damian sat down in a chair, letting his legs stretch out in front of him. "Need a cold dip in the lake," he muttered.

"Now you understand how I feel."

"Even if we would have allowed you to spend time with Aidan, she would be busy also. Be sure, you won't see her until the wedding day."

~ * ~

The ladies settled into their rooms then met in a meeting room at the hotel. The hired seamstresses were present along with their daughters as Aidan and Charlotte mulled over the fashion plates.

"I'm going to use this ice blue fabric you suggested and this dress." She held up one of the plates. "It needs to be simple yet beautiful too."

"Do you want a veil?" Christel asked. "It would have to be something that would highlight the beautiful color of your hair."

"I recall when you made fun of the color of my hair and my freckles." Aidan vividly remembered the teasing. "The rest of you were all blessed with beautiful blond hair, Eveleen's with just a touch of red. I was always so jealous."

"I never made fun of your hair but your fabric choices. You were always wanting to choose colors that would make you look ghastly rather ones that would enhance your gorgeous coloring."

"That's not the way I felt. With freckles and flyaway red hair, I was always thinking how beautiful all of you were and finding myself lacking." That fact was so true and she always wanted to be older remembering how Blade would sneak away to find a woman to bed then return with a self-satisfied look on his handsome face. She'd always wanted to be the woman he snuck off to bed.

Christel hugged her tightly. "That was never our intent. When you picked out the scarlet color for Allura's wedding we all knew how horrible it would look on you. This ice blue is going to highlight your exquisite complexion and hair. Blade will think you're the most beautiful woman in the entire world."

"Really?" She still had reservations about her beauty and felt dowdy among her sisters.

"I promise you that you are going to be beautiful and Blade will fall even more in love with you than he is now," Christel said as she watched seamstresses cut the fabric.

Her heart stopped and she was unwilling to let her sister and cousins know that Blade didn't love her. He wanted her yes, but love was not something he felt. She decided then she would never tell him how much she loved him. She would never make herself vulnerable.

As the night wore on Aidan's dress began to come together. By morning the first fitting took place. The ladies had taken turns sleeping and sewing. Charlotte picked out a pale pink fabric the sleeves and neck lined with Belgian lace.

The minister's wife, Elsia baked a large wedding cake, standing four layers high. She began work on the potato salad and by morning three large bowls were assembled.

"Did you see the look on their faces when we turned them away," Amorica asked laughing. "Damian looked like a little boy who got his hand slapped when he reached into the candy bowl."

"They are not used to the word, no. We all spoil them so much," Christel said, laughing. "I wouldn't have it any other way."

"Aidan, try this on. Let's see where you need any nips and tucks." Amorica directed the seamstress and her cousin.

Carefully, Aidan slipped her arms through the sleeves, trying to avoid the pins.

"It's so beautiful." Ravyn sighed softly. "At times I regret not having a real wedding with a beautiful dress and all that goes with it."

"Me too." Amorica agreed with her cousin. "Damian is proud of the fact that we wed before we made love but as to the wedding, he really gave me no choice then he kept me in a secluded place near Dover where his mistress still lives. Only he kept denying the fact the woman was his lover."

"It was horrible of him and we were so worried about you. You did lose the wager, hands down," Ravyn said chuckling at the memory.

"That was so long ago, a lifetime it seems. I've forgotten. What exactly was the wager?" Amorica asked.

"Who could lose your suitor first," Christel said with hesitation, seeming to realize it was something she didn't want to remember. "You were the only one who cared about the man who sought to court you. The rest of them were fops and wastrels."

"I know, that was so funny, Aric and Ryder weren't our suitors," Ravyn said. "No, Aric was my protector. I lost my heart to him the first time I saw him lurking in the gardens. Still don't know what he was doing there."

"So true, they saved us," Christel mused, making as many tiny stitches as she could in the petticoat that went with Charlottes dress. "Ryder saved me in so many ways. He helped me find the child that was stolen from me before I even saw the little boy. And he raised him as his own."

"You found a good man," Amorica said thoughtfully. "It might have taken a while but he stayed with you and I admire that in him."

"We all married good men," Ravyn said. "I was so stupid and I almost lost Aric, would have if I hadn't dug down and found some of that Graham strength. I was so stubborn. He finally couldn't refuse me and after that he vowed to live in London even though I knew he'd be miserable."

"If I recall Aric thought you were too fragile to live in the west and be his wife," Amorica said. "He certainly didn't know you very well. Growing up you were always the toughest of all of us."

"I finally convinced him," Ravyn said. "Convinced him I couldn't live without him and I was tougher than he thought. Tougher than him I do believe."

"You and Damian left the ranch. You were going to go back to London without telling him. I'll never forget the look on Aric's face when he discovered you went away with my husband. He looked as if he could kill and I prayed it wasn't Damian he took out his wrath on."

"I was sure he meant to throttle me when he rode into the clearing that night. Damian had spent every moment slowing us down, finding some reason to stop. He knew Aric would come after me even when I did not," Ravyn said with a heavy sigh, "I really didn't think he would."

"Men," Aidan said recalling all the times Blade tormented her with the fact he thought she was a little girl. The worst time was before Ella's wedding and they were discovered in the gazebo, his hand up her skirts. She smiled at the thought. It seemed that was where his hands seemed to be whenever possible now.

"Men," the other ladies agreed.

"Come, it's nearly two A.M. now some of us should go to bed, some should wait up to ward off the men if they try anything," Amorica said, looking at Aidan. "All the men save Blade and David have shown up tonight. Do you suppose the other two are just biding their time until we let down our guard?"

"Blade doesn't want to rile his future father-in-law. I'm sure he's decided to wait as Papa wanted," Aidan said, wishing he would at least show up, letting her know how much he cared. "I can't say why David didn't come to see Aunty."

"He would play a role model to Blade," Charlotte said calmly. "They must have made a pact, dear. I'm thinking more and more good thoughts about your young man, Aidan. I believe my opinion of Blade is reversing. I'm starting to like that boy."

"Blade had been more than honorable over the last seven years. I would have given him anything he asked for and he knew it," Aidan said, realizing now just how much that control cost him. "Yet until recently, he hasn't asked for much." Just her body.

The work continued and the ladies made sure Charlotte and Aidan received enough sleep to be beautiful brides on their wedding day.

When Aidan woke that morning, two days later, a steaming bath was in her chamber and when she looked out the window a light fog blanketed the ground. If it rained they would have to move inside the hotel and there was not enough room for all of them and the congregation who Elisa invited. It seemed everyone in town was to be at the ceremony.

Aidan stretched, slipping out of her nightclothes before testing the water with a finger. In the tub she relaxed, thinking of tonight and being with Blade again. It seemed to her the two days had been tantamount to a lifetime. And she wondered at that.

After she fled to Baltimore, she'd spent months not even talking to him let alone sleeping with him. All it took was one time in his arms, giving her a woman's pleasure then that one time in the gazebo making love for her to realize how much she desired him, her passion for him raw and so very new.

What a difference a month had made in her life. Four weeks ago, had she thought she would be marrying Blade with more than half her family witnessing the ceremony, she would have called them crazy.

The door creaked open, "Don't spend all day in the tub. We still have your hair to fix and the dress for one last fitting. Although..."

"Tira! You are here too?"

Tira laughed, "Jamie and Annie are here also along with our baby. I hope he doesn't cry and interrupt your wedding. Can you believe Aunty is marrying your father?"

"No, not when I first heard about it. I thought of mother but realized she would want him to be happy. I fear there will be an encounter in heaven though," Aidan spoke, chuckling at the thought

"Between the Duke and your Papa," Tira said.

"It would be hard to figure out. Everyone loved each other so much. Kind of like us, siblings and cousins," Aidan said. "But neither one should live alone any longer."

"Not the other way, they were sisters after all. And Charlotte's first love will always be her Duke."

"And Sadie will be Papa's first love," Aidan said.

"Come finish your bath. I've brought a bucket of warm water to rinse your hair."

"Are you happy, Tira?" Aidan asked. "Is marriage to your Jamie all you dreamed it would be?"

"Jamie is my love and my life. The children are the only other beings who come close and the love I hold for them is different. I can't explain. You'll know when you have children. But I would give my life for my husband and my children if necessary. They are everything to me. So, yes, I am very happy. I couldn't wish for anything more."

"I'm glad you could say that. I think I feel the same but Blade's feelings toward me are all too new for me to say as much. I want him to love me but he's never said the words and I'm afraid he never will. He has implied, though, that he doesn't believe in love."

"Knock, knock." The door crept open. "You out of your bath yet?" Christel with the others behind her walked into the room. "Ah, I see you're not. We'll wait out here. I'm going to hang your dress up so it doesn't get wrinkled. Charlotte will be here in about ten minutes."

Girlish chatter filled the room, giving Aidan reason to smile. Wine bottles were uncorked in celebration and Elisa brought in a tray of little pastries to be enjoyed as pre-wedding fare.

Christel was beside her with the water, "You ready for the rinse?"

Aidan nodded thinking suddenly she might not be ready for the wedding though. "Yes."

With her hair washed she accepted the bath sheet Christel held out for her, wrapping it around her. "But I'm not sure I'm ready to be married. My stomach is churning and look." She held out her trembling hands.

"How does one get through these horrible nerves?"

"Pre-wedding jitters that's all. I had them too. I'm sure they will go away," Christel said. "Your underclothes are there." She pointed. "When you have them on come into the other room and we can talk about your nerves and lace your corset. You will be so beautiful you'll steal his breath."

What was it about this day that made her insecure and without confidence in herself? For so many years she chased Blade, gave him no room to pursue other relationships and when he dallied with another woman jealousy swept through her. At times, when she was younger, she strove to keep him away from other women, insinuating herself in the discussion and being as obnoxious as she could be.

Now Blade MacPherson was minutes away from becoming her husband and she felt the greatest urge to run away. She stood in front of the mirror, looking at herself, her flyaway red hair and freckles the center of her attention. What had ever made her think, he would want her. Yet he said he did. He called her his wife.

"Aidan?" Christel poked her head in the door again. "We're waiting for you. Do you need more help?"

"Oh." Her hand on her chest and swallowing the lump of fear in her throat, "I'm coming."

Christel strode toward her. "What you're feeling is normal. As soon as you see him at the end of the aisle, you'll know your heart. Men have a way of never telling their women they love them, but eventually they all come around. I don't know what it is that keeps them from saying the words. But I'm going to assure you, the way Blade looks at you, says everything. He doesn't just want you in his bed, he loves you and would lay down his life for you."

"You really think he looks at me like that?" She had never heard anything that sounded so absurd.

"I do."

"I remember telling Tira the exact same thing. Jamie's gaze followed her wherever she went and the expression on his face...I don't know how to describe it but I knew and everyone knew he loved her."

"See, it is the same with you and Blade. Come, cheer up, I've got a glass of Chianti waiting for you and we've brought presents."

In a daze, Aidan followed Christel and when she stepped into the room, Aunty Charlotte stood in the center, dressed all in pale pink and looking happier than Aidan had ever seen her holding two glasses of white wine.

"For you Aidan and one for me. To many years of our happiness." She handed the glass to Aidan.

"Yes, Aunty, to our happiness, and Papa's and all the years of love waiting for us. I know the two of you, in the absence of your first spouses; you will make each other happy. I just wish you would not have joined forces against me to keep me away from Blade."

"My dearest Aidan. You've always been a favorite of mine. You look just like your mother, red hair and all. Your disposition is so much like Sadie's. Every time I look at you, I see her. And something your father has never told you, your journey to love was much like Sadie's. She fell in love with David when she was very young and while he enjoyed her antics, he avoided her at all cost until he finally saw her as a beautiful young lady old enough to court and marry. Which he did as soon as possible, I might add."

"I never knew about their story and I barely knew my mother. She passed away when I was very young." Aidan missed her very much. She had so few memories of her mother to hold close to her heart.

"She could have helped you understand your feelings for Blade and perhaps slow your rush to become the woman he would court. But you did well by yourself. Your instincts served you in a good way. Now you're about to wed the man you've loved most of your life. Are you ready?"

"Oh, Auntie, I'm terrified, but what you just told me has given me more confidence. Yet there is so much for me to learn about my husband. I'm going to live in the highlands and we've always thought them uncivilized and rough. I only pray I can adjust."

"Do you believe Blade is uncivilized and rough?" Charlotte asked, smiling and taking Aidan's hand in her as if to reassure.

Aidan laughed feeling her spirits uplifted and once more eager for this ceremony and her life to follow. "He is rough around the edges sometimes but he's not uncivilized. Perhaps Hunter tamed him some, teaching him the ways of the English aristocracy. He is used to taking what he wants no matter the cost and I'm glad he wanted me and was willing to wait for me to come of age."

"All men are like that but he won't ever force you even if it's what he wants and I believe you know that," Charlotte told her with seeming knowledge of Blade MacPherson.

Aidan thought of all the times Blade treated her with such sweet gentleness going back all the years since she'd known him. She sensed his character even when she was thirteen and over the years, he'd never let her down. He'd been there for her in times of need. She tried to forget those instances when he humiliated her.

"Thank you, Aunty. I feel better now."

"So, drink up and have something to eat. It's going to be a very long day. The one thing you must do is not forget to eat. We are going to get you ready, now. You are so beautiful there is little to do."

"Aunty, you forgot the gifts," Christel said, her hands on her hips. "We must do that first."

"Oh, yes the gifts. My old age, sometimes I'm a bit forgetful. Now I have the first one. Your father wanted me to give this to you. It was your mothers." She held out a string of diamonds. "She wore these in her hair at her wedding. As I remember they were so beautiful and stood out against the beauty of her stunning red hair. Your father wants them to be yours and if you have a little girl with red hair to pass them on to, you must do just that."

"Thank you." Tears formed in her eyes and she was relieved she had nothing, no makeup, on her face that would smear. Everything would have been ruined. "You and Allura and Eveleen don't mind if I get them?" She didn't want to cause any hurt feelings.

"We don't. We've all received gifts from father. Allura the land we all grew up on. She has no reservations about any gift father might pass on to you. This was special for you," Christel said.

"And these diamonds were given to Sadie by her mother," Charlotte said, holding them out. "I'll let Christel arrange them. She is much better at that sort of thing than I am."

"Grandmother had red hair too, or so I've heard," Aidan laughed softly understanding how precious her family was. She would never escape the bane of her hair but if she had a little girl, she could help her understand how beautiful she was and unique as well.

"That's why they should belong to you and hopefully a little girl who has the same wonderful features," Christel said. "You must teach her how to choose fabrics that will enhance her beauty not make her appear sallow. I think some of the fabrics you did choose was to frustrate your older sisters."

"Have some wine, and food please. Bread, cheese, meat are all on the platter as well as pastries so first put something in your stomach. Then we will dress you. The sooner the vows are said the sooner..." Charlotte let that thought hang in air as if food for thought. "Well, we still have the reception to get through and I don't think Elisa will let anyone go home before she is satisfied enough has been eaten. She has prepared a feast in celebration and has said she expects all the food to be gone before anyone leaves."

"She must love you a lot, Amorica," Aidan said, paring a piece of cheese with bread. "Why would she go out of her way like this for two people she doesn't even know."

"I can't say but I'm thrilled she helped so much. Without her, there would be no food today," Christel said, sipping her wine then twirling in a circle. "Now, I brought you a necklace to borrow today. Diamonds and sapphires alternate on the piece. Ryder's mother owned the necklace. I've worn it a few times and I'll be honored if you wear it today. It will be your something blue because I think Tira has something borrowed for you."

"While this doesn't completely match the necklace, it will go with your hair piece." Tira held out a bracelet of diamonds. "Jamie gave this to me after we were wed but it was a gift to me when our son was born. You can borrow it."

"I have sapphire earrings to borrow also and they are also something blue. Of course, your dress has pale blue highlights. So, you are taken care of but we need to make sure Aunty Charlotte has something blue as well as something borrowed," Amorica said.

"Well." Christel jumped into the conversation again. "Papa

wanted to give her this dress plaid which is nearly all blue to drape over her shoulder during the wedding and wear afterward."

"And I will lend you, Aunty, this pink tourmaline necklace. Damian gave the choker to me when our second child was born. Something borrowed and something blue for both of you," Amorica said stepping back and looking at the two ladies with admiration in her eyes.

The finishing touches were made on each of the brides. Aidan wore light makeup but she made sure her lashes were darkened and a light blue tint put on her eyelids, highlighted her eyes as well as a light shade of pink on her lips to give them a gorgeous color.

While Charlotte protested to no avail, the girls made sure she darkened her lashes and her lips were tinted.

Since the McLellan was a groom at this wedding, Ryder escorted Aidan down the aisle and gave her away while Damian did the same for The Duchess. The minister kept the ceremony beautiful but brief. When the couples were united under the eyes of God, they kissed.

Aidan was shocked by Blade who let his tongue delve between her slightly parted lips and with his hands cupping her bottom pulled her so close she felt his rod against her belly.

"Blade," she whispered. "You cannot do this."

"I've waited two days and I'll be damned if I'm going to behave myself now," he whispered close to her ear, the heat sending a ripple of pleasure through her. "And I'm not going to let you more than a few inches away from me. I want to take you to our room and make love to you right now, the reception be damned."

Her heart leapt within her chest while her body responded to his words as well as his touch and the inferno his lips created. "I want the same thing, Blade, but we can't. You know that to be true. If we don't eat something, we won't have the strength to consummate the marriage."

"I have more than enough strength," he mumbled.

"Well I don't." She tried to sound indignant but she wanted exactly what he did, to leave and be alone with her husband.

"Doesn't mean I have to like it. Thank you," he responded to greeters he didn't know, shaking their hands and smiling politely.

"You made it two days." Damian slapped Blade on the back, his way of congratulating Blade.

"And how were your nights?" Blade pulled Aidan closer, his fingers squeezing her waist then drifting higher.

"Think you know the answer. The dancing has started are you going to let Aidan dance with anyone but you? The look in your eyes tells me the answer. But I do believe you're going to have to give her father a dance." Damian left, seeming to search for his wife who was now dishing up potato salad and fried chicken.

"Damian is right, this time. I want to dance with Papa but after that I'm all yours." Aidan smiled at Blade, very aware of his hand exploring places that weren't appropriate.

"When can we cut the cake and leave?" He shifted his hand so it was in a totally unsuitable place for these proceedings.

"Behave yourself, Blade. I swear, I'll make you wait another night if you embarrass me. There are certain polite society mandates we must adhere to today."

"Then dance with me and we'll find a secluded place where I can kiss you," Blade lifted an eyebrow and Aidan could guess his thoughts.

"I don't think any place like that exists here." Aidan did see the huge trees but they weren't secluded not like the balconies in the ballrooms in London. There was really no place to get or give a kiss.

He pulled her into his arms, holding her too close but it seemed no one cared what they did. "I'll find somewhere I can kiss you properly. I want to be inside you and if it's only my tongue I'll have to make that do for the time being."

"Like you did at the wedding." One eyebrow rose in speculation. "You should not have taken such liberties," she chastised him.

"That was chaste for what I have planned and after our interlude in the gazebo you're no longer an innocent. You know precisely what I want, plan to have before the night is over."

"Excuse me, the two of you need to eat." Christel stood beside her laughing and seeming to understand she interrupted something inappropriate. "You have time for that stuff later, much later. Everyone is waiting for the two of you to dish up before they can eat. Elisa says everything has to be eaten before anyone is allowed to find their beds."

"Christel is right," Aidan said standing on tiptoe to give him a chaste kiss but unable to reach him.

"Ach lass, you mean to torment me more." He helped her, pulling her against him and settled his mouth on hers, tracing the seam with his tongue and once more allowing his hands to wander upward.

Aidan wasn't at all sure if she should allow him what he wanted before the celebration was over. But the decision was taken from her hands, when Damian showed up with Aric and Ryder.

"We're hungry too, but the sooner you and Aidan get started here, the sooner we can all find our rooms and find what we've been denied for what seems like years," Damian said with agreement from his two friends.

"The three of you always stick together?" Blade asked.

"They have a point. Look Charlotte and David are waiting for us too," Aidan said, laughing inside. It seemed all the elements warred against Blade, but she also knew in a few hours all would be well. "You must have patience. Why if I hadn't known you for seven years, I'd think you were completely lacking in that department."

Linking her arm in Blade's, they walked to the serving line. Her stomach rumbled with hunger. Thinking back, she'd had very little to eat, just the bread and cheese and a small glass of wine early this morning.

"Thank you so much," Aidan spoke to Elisa. "This is so wonderful and Blade's favorite foods." She squeezed his arm, hoping he would take the hint and agree with her.

"Ach, the wee lass is right. They are among my favorites, fried chicken and potato salad. Thank you so much for your generous help."

"Help yourself," she said, beaming at them seeming pleased with his words. "There is plenty for seconds. But then," she paused, "You most likely have other plans for this evening."

Aidan and Blade with Charlotte and David behind them, dished up their meal before sitting at the head table to eat. Bagpipes warmed up nearby and Aidan's toes started tapping. She knew Blade wanted to find the bedroom as soon as possible but she needed to enjoy the day and talk to all the wonderful people who were here celebrating this special event with her. They were Amorica's and Damian's people and she wanted to show her respect.

123

Amorica poured wine then set a full bottle of Logan's Bordeaux on the table beside Aidan and Blade. Finally, with something in her stomach beside the cheese and bread from hours ago and an entire glass of wine, Aidan felt relaxed and sleepy-eyed.

Her nerves had been stretched taut for two days. She leaned into Blade, enjoying his warmth and strength before closing her eyes. When she first saw him so many years ago, the sight of him stole her breath. And the idea that after all the years of waiting, he was truly her husband, thrilled her.

"Don't fall asleep, Little Fire. I've got plans and you need to be wide awake if you're going to enjoy my attentions to your body."

She sat up, blinking, enjoying the moment. "I think I've only slept a few hours the last few nights. I hope I can stay awake."

"I plan on doing my best to make it happen," he chuckled, placing tiny kisses down her neck and sending shivers to every part of her. "See you are wide awake now and heating up for me." Beneath the table his hand found the bottom of her dress, slowly lifting it, she felt the tender glide of his fingers up her leg.

"I promise I won't fall asleep." She moved trying to dislodge his hand but managed to do the opposite. Before they were in their room, she didn't want him to discover her secret but if he kept on, he would know.

"Little Fire, I'm shocked, but pleased none the less. Do you have any more surprises for me?"

"It was Tira's idea. She told me Ella..." his fingers caressed her intimately. The ache and heat increasing as she moved to allow him deeper access.

"Had I known sooner, I might not have been left speechless. I do ken I wouldn't be here assuaging my hunger for you with food and wine. Always dress like this for me." Taking her hand, he placed it on his arousal.

"We still have a few hours to get through." She could barely speak. "You weren't supposed to know until later tonight. Now I don't know how I'm going to survive if you keep touching me."

"But I do know and you shouldn't have done something so outrageous if you didn't want me to respond to your actions with one of my choosing. You shouldn't spread your legs for me if you don't want me to seduce you right here and now, hear you cry out my name. Everyone would look at you, stunned by our brazenness."

"Everyone would look at you."

"You're wrong. You are so beautiful in the throes of your passions; they would stare at you."

~ * ~

MacPherson Castle, July

"This will all be mine as soon as you die, old man." Blade's brother sat down next to the MacPherson, laughing. While he coveted this place, he'd been patient seeking out the best way to steal it away. He'd wanted it for years just because Blade was the heir. Now he wanted it because he was in deep financial trouble. He'd gambled and lost his entire fortune.

"No." For the first time in months the MacPherson felt his health improve. "The will is clear and validated. Blade is to inherit and his sons and even daughters after that if he has no sons."

"Blade is not here to lay claim to his inheritance and that is half the battle. I'll be here when you die, old man, and once I own it, no one will take it from me, not even your favorite son. This is an easy keep to defend and with Guy's help, with his men, I'll have no trouble."

"In that you're wrong." Blade's dear brother, Hunter stepped from a hallway to confront the man he knew Blade had despised for most of his life. "I've brought men as has Logan Broon another Scottish friend. We've more men on the way to defend this keep until Blade's return. You've underestimated the friends Blade has. In marrying Aidan McLellan, he inherited the help and wealth from twelve braw men."

"You can try," Blade's brother muttered. "Guy is strong too and he's willing to do anything to gain what he wants."

"No, he is evil and ruthless but he is a very weak man. I know his tricks and will not be surprised by anything he tries," Hunter went on to say. "If life gets difficult, he'll turn tail and run."

"I'm not on my deathbed yet," the MacPherson said, understanding the gist of Hunter's words. "I'll be around long enough to see and hold my grandchildren. With the strain of trying to hold this keep taken from me, I feel my health returning."

"So, you should understand you have no claim here and no way to wrest this from the rightful heir," Hunter said, smiling.

"I don't believe anyone else would come here on Blade's behest. What has he done to warrant any loyalty save yours? He has been a mercenary nothing more."

"You're wrong. Blade has been a true friend to all of the McLellan clan and their relatives. While you have taken from everyone you've encountered. Where you are concerned there is no loyalty or trust."

Chapter Six

Blade smiled, when Aidan quickly clamped her legs together. Bending close to her ear, letting his tongue caress the tiny shell, then blowing softly inside. "You're playing with fire, and I'm willing to take the offense. I suppose that's why you're my Little Fire. By the time we finally find our room and our marriage bed you'll be begging me to tear off your clothes."

"I'm ready to beg right now." But she sat up straight and smiled at all the people just as if his hand wasn't resting on her inner thigh and exploring, moving higher, continuing his subtle seduction.

"More wine?" He poured with one hand while he caressed the muscles of her upper thigh. "Are you hot and wet? Do you want me inside you?" His whisper sent her body into tiny tremors, which he seemed to enjoy.

"Yes, please."

"To which one?" He teased her farther.

"Both." She gulped for air. "Maybe we should dance. I need to stand, need some distance from your roving fingers."

"Drink your wine first." He handed the glass to her, watching her drink until she finished the glass.

"Now we can dance." Pulling her into his arms they moved in time with the music. The Scottish tunes, ones she'd not heard for quite some time played to the haunting sounds of the bagpipes. Whirling her in circles then behind a tree, he stopped. "Now we can kiss and I can explore more of your sweetness."

He held her head with both hands, letting his mouth possess hers, sliding his tongue along her lips. When she responded to him, he slid his hand down the length of her leg, slowly pulling her skirts higher until he touched tender flesh and she hoped no one would find them until he was done. Until she could find release from the sweet agony he created.

"Are you sneaking away before the cakes are cut and claiming what you've missed out on the last few nights?"

She'd know Damian's voice anywhere and knew once more he'd goad Blade. "Go away and mind your own affairs," Blade snarled.

"Don't have to when you're so blatantly seducing Aidan in public. When you put the entire idea of chivalry to shame, I can say whatever I want and perhaps she needs my protection."

"Damian, leave them alone." Amorica tugged on his arms. "You cannot pretend Aidan needs protection from her husband. The marriage is now legal in everyone's eyes."

"Only if they come out from behind that tree." Damian's smug smirk left Blade with fisted hands and frown lines on his forehead.

The ringing of a bell caught everyone's attention. The Duchess stood at the table with the cakes, Elsia beside her. It seemed Charlotte was eager to be alone with David also.

"Time to cut the cakes," the minister's wife called out. "We want to celebrate these two beautiful couples then leave them to the privacy I suppose they crave. The rest of the guests need to stay, eat and enjoy the dancing."

"Too bad, old chap," Damian said, clapping him on the back. "Now you have to come out from behind that tree. "Oh, I'd just like you to know, thirty buttons. It'll seem like one hundred before the night even begins. Have fun with that."

"Good luck, after the cake is cut, I no longer have to stay here and pretend I'm having fun." Blade grinned at his tormentor.

Blade and Aidan cut the cake, placing the piece on a plate. Aidan lifted the slice for Blade to eat and took a small bite. When it was his turn, he managed to smear her lips with the icing. "Now I get to taste you and think about what is not under your wedding gown."

"Blade no." Aidan was reaching for a napkin to wipe away the icing when his lips descended and he slowly licked the sweet confection from around her mouth. Taking his time, she couldn't help but let out tiny sounds of pleasure.

"Perfect." Then holding her hand in his and raising both into the air, "We are retiring for the night. I hope you all enjoy the rest of the evening. We'll be leaving on the morrow so thank you all for everything you've done for us."

Unable to wait for Aidan, he swept her into his arms and without running, he quickly strode to their room, taking the steps two at a time. At the door, he struggled a moment with the knob. When it was finally opened, he carried her inside his mouth hungrily molded to hers then kicked the door shut.

"I've waited a lifetime for this night," Aidan said, tugging at his shirt, needing to run her hands along his body, feel his muscles constrict with pleasure.

"How am I ever going to get you out of this gown without ripping it? God I can't wait." Then remembering Aidan's lack of underclothes sat down on a chair and spreading her legs so she straddled him.

"Don't rip it, please." Her hands were on the fastenings of his pants, fumbling, but slowly getting the job done. "I don't think I can wait for you to undo all those tiny little buttons. It took Christel a long time to fasten them."

He sat up and slipped his clothing to the floor. Aidan ran her hands beneath his chest, touching him, exploring, learning him. He pulsed against her over heated core. "Bloody eyes, Aidan. You're ready for me." Then he remembered how slick she was when they kissed by the tree or tried to.

"You know I've been ready since you discovered my secret. Nay, since I saw you standing with David, waiting to say your vows. You could have had me then and there right in front of everyone and I don't know if I would have protested," she whispered seemingly barely able to speak.

He laughed, his hands around her waist, he lifted her until the tip of his rod touched her and he helped her take him inside her velvet heat. "Blade." Her head fell back and he couldn't resist the invitation, she couldn't help but give.

He touched her, kissed and nibbled and licked every bare piece of skin he could find while his fingers fumbled with the tiny buttons at the back of her dress.

"Bloody eyes, how do you undo these? They are so tiny. My fingers can't get them through the loopholes."

"Just do it please." She rose on him then as if unsure of what she should do she settled herself against him.

He groaned. "I cannot...one is undone. Thirty buttons." He suddenly realized what Damian had been laughing about.

While he struggled to rid her of the gown, she stroked his chest, letting her fingers play with every part of him. He growled, saying her name. "Aidan."

"Raise your arms." He did, leaving the itty-bitty fasteners alone for a moment so she could lift his shirt over his head. "I love the way you feel beneath my fingers." She nipped at his shoulder, then up his neck until she reached his ear.

"You're killing me, Little Fire. Indeed, if I can't get this dress off you, I swear I'll go up in flames," he murmured. "I've waited too long since we handfasted to taste your beauty again."

She leaned into him, giving him better access to the buttons on her dress. Her fingers winding into his hair, sifting through it then found his ear with her tongue. She swirled it around the shell then bit gently.

"Do you want me to sit still or..."

He wasn't too sure if she understood what she was asking. "Don't sit still. Ride me, move on me while I try to get you out of this dress."

She did move on him, slowly at first then faster, suddenly stopping to look at him, "do you like this?"

"If I liked it any better, there is little I could possibly enjoy more." He left the buttons alone so he could give his attention to her swollen bud of pleasure, massaging and seeming to relish this even though she was still wearing her dress.

It seemed, he delighted in the tiny mews of pleasure, the way her body melded with his and as she moved on him, he could barely control himself. Her nails slid across his shoulders.

"Blade, I..." He watched her as her breaths came rapid and so quickly, she could barely breathe.

"That's it, Little Fire, just relax and let it happen." Her breath entered within him as she reached her climax, crying out while tremors swept through her again and again. It seemed he felt every wave of pleasure she felt as he filled her and his seed entered into her.

"I've no bones." Her head lay against his shoulder. "Blade?" He was still deep inside her and in an instant fully aroused once more. "The buttons?"

"I can't undo them."

She pulled at her dress. "I've got to get out of this, now." He heard her words the sound of panic and the unleashed tension.

"My fingers are too large for the tiny holes. I think I've only opened three," Blade mumbled still trying to get them undone.

"I can't do this. I'm going to find someone who can do this for me, unbutton the bloody dress." She rose leaving him, headed for the door.

Quickly he pulled up his pants, following her, afraid she would disappear or worse... Hell he didn't know what worse could be.

When she knocked on a door, whispering Christel he felt a sudden surge of relief. He could imagine what Damian would say under this circumstance if she knocked on his door.

"Christel, Christel, are you in there. I need your help. I can't..."

When the door opened, Christel stepped forward. "Aidan, whatever is wrong? What can't you   do?" Then it seemed she knew.

Aidan turned and looking over her shoulder. "The buttons, he can't undo them without ripping. I've got to get out of the dress."

"Who is it?" Ryder asked.

"My sister. I'll be back in a moment. Sometimes he gets a little impatient. Just like your man I suppose," Christel giggled.

Blade didn't like it when Christel laughed but realized it was better than Damian knowing what had happened, that he couldn't bed his wife because he couldn't undress her.

A few minutes later Aidan returned, clutching the bodice of her wedding gown to her chest. "You watched?"

He didn't know what to say. "Of course, I made sure you were protected. I didn't want to let you out of my sight."

He pulled her into his arms, once again his lips finding hers as he backed his way into the room, closing the door behind him. He moved away. She still clutched her dress to her chest. Taking her hands in his, he watched as the gown fell to the floor. Then he kissed her hands, the backs, the palms then her fingertips.

"I'm so glad Christel's fingers could undo those god-awful fastenings. Now I'll make sure the corset and the rest are on the floor also." His nimble and very practiced fingers made easy work with that which he was familiar with.

Her hands were on the lacings of his pants again. She slid them to the floor. He groaned, needing to breathe with her, to stare into the clear blue eyes that always reflected his love for him.

God how he loved her, she was the very essence of what defined him. He couldn't resist her breasts but he craved to have her beneath him and to be between her legs, to feel the length of her responding to him.

"Wrap your legs around me." He whispered as his teeth made tiny forays down her neck and across her collarbone then lower. He needed to taste and explore all of her, know the essence of her as he slowly made his way down her body. She was the tempest igniting the fire within him. Her heat burned his soul, enchanting him to a point he would give up everything for one more moment to bask in her magnificent inferno.

He strode to the bed, laying her down, his body hard craving her, yet he wanted to take his time, to feel her writhe and arch beneath him. He needed to see into the beautiful depth of her eyes as they drew him into her, mesmerized all that he was. The primal dance between them heated to a firestorm that couldn't be refuted.

His hands ran through her hair, caught by the diamonds meant to decorate not hinder his attempt to make love with his wife. Again, he was afraid he would destroy something precious and he stopped, groaning in frustration. "Aidan, can you...we need to take the adornments from your hair. I need to wrap myself in its length and feel the silken fire emanating from it."

He was totally mesmerized by his wife, had never expected such a thing to happen. She was once an adorable impetuous child and now she was his wife, his love and he would move heaven and earth to shelter and defend her.

She sat up, her breasts a tantalizing delight to him. He had so little control. He watched as she tried to untangle the string of jewels from her hair, the beautiful white globes swaying provocatively crying out for his touch. "I'm sorry, my hair is my nemesis, always has been. It is always in tangles."

He ran his hands up her neck to entwine in her hair. "I love your hair. It's so much a part of who you are." He kissed the freckles on her cheeks.

"Well, I don't want to go to Christel to get this from my hair but I'm afraid the strand is hopelessly ensnared." With her sigh of frustration, the tips of her breasts brushed across his chest.

He never thought that while he was fully aroused, he would enjoy watching his naked wife try to disengage a strand of diamonds from her hair. But seeing her breasts as they moved with her efforts, he could only smile and enjoy. She was his life, his love.

Tempted to touch her nipples he held back, enjoying the foreplay and the anticipation. He didn't think he could have her enough tonight to satisfy all the years of waiting and he prayed she would carry his child soon if she didn't already.

Slowly, one tiny section at a time, she disengaged the diamonds from her wild red hair. Truly, he didn't think he could wait a moment longer for release. But she was his wife, his love...his love, perhaps he did love her. Nevertheless, tonight none of that mattered.

In a huff, and finally ridding her hair of her nemesis, she said, "you could have helped."

"No, I would have made a bigger mess and I was enjoying watching you." He touched her and enjoyed the rapid tightening of the hard, rosy bud and the swift intake of her breath.

"I'm so... Please Blade do something, I ache..."

He understood that burn but enjoyed the arousal and knew the release would be all the sweeter if he tantalized and enchanted stirring her more and more until the climax seized her.

"As do I. Touch me, like you did the other day in the gazebo." He let his fingers find new places to tantalize.

"You want my mouth on your..."

He grinned loving the play of emotions across her beautiful face. "I do. You can't imagine what it feels like to have you suck me inside your mouth and have your tongue slide along my length." He wanted to challenge her and release all her inhibitions so there would be nothing between them.

"Truthfully?"

"Truthfully, I do. I enjoyed it the first time more than I ever would have thought possible. No one else has touched me like that. I think now that you know the power you have over me, it will be even more tantalizing."

She gazed at him. "If that's what you want," she said before she slowly lowered her mouth to kiss and take his member within her mouth. His hips jerked when he felt the glide of her tongue and the heat of her lips.

His fingers wound into her hair, sifting through the glorious strands. When he knew he was almost at the limit of his control, "Come, kiss me." He pulled her up his length then lowering his mouth to meld with hers.

He lifted his lips from hers. Thought himself half crazy for waiting a moment longer to claim what they both yearned for. Her sky-blue eyes were focused on him. Her lips were moist from his caress, still so tempting, inadvertently inviting him to take what she offered.

He smiled at her, realizing how precious she was and the passion she held for him inside her, all for him, had always been for him. He was suddenly humbled, by the thought.

He ran a finger seductively around one areola to the other then back. Then flicked the hardened peak with a fingernail, watching the erotic rise and fall of her hips and the sway of her breasts.

She moaned softly, her hands resting on his chest, her nails scoring his flesh leaving tiny marks.

He whispered nonsense words lifting his lips just a fraction from hers. His voice was low, rich, deep. Demanding everything she had to give and he wanted all the passion she possessed.

He swept an arm around her, bringing her fully against him. The length of his body shuddered hard, shaking with determination to bring her the greatest possible pleasure. He found her lips again. Caught them, held them. Stroked the rim with his tongue, plunged between them.

To his delight, he heard a delicate mew tumbling in her throat than a soft purr. Her hand rested upon his shoulder, pausing then stilled. Her fingernails dug into his flesh, explored the breadth of his neck and shoulders.

"Please, Blade. I need you now. Need to feel you inside me." She told him yet her voice shook with desire.

"That's what I needed to hear."

He pulled her tightly into his arms, roiling her over so she lay atop him, unwilling to let her go for any reason. He kissed her lips, stroking her back gently, feeling the sensual curves and plane of her soft body.

He broke from her lips to touch her again, his tongue tracing the shape of her before slipping deeply into her mouth once again. He caressed the silken skin of her back, sweeping the length of her spine, creating erotic swirls at the base of her backbone with his fingertips, stroking the curve of her hip, the rise of her buttocks.

He had touched nearly every part of her. Yet he needed to taste more of the fiery passion she possessed turning her again. He trailed his kisses to her earlobe, along her throat. He lifted the mass of wild untamed red hair and kissed the nape of her neck. He shuddered, sighing deeply burying his face within the red silk and kissed her, the red cloud falling around her, enjoying the scent and feel of her hair. He moved her, shifting so she lay upon her stomach and lifting the length of red hair off her once more then pressing a kiss against her spine.

"You taste so good, bloody good," he whispered, "Just like I always knew you would, just like a woman should." Once again, he shifted her so he could more easily kiss her.

"I..." It seemed she didn't know what to say.

Laughing tenderly, he brushed hair from her eyes. He lavished her shoulders with his caress then moved lower to the rise of her breasts, down the valley between them. He paused, sensations surging through him in a staggering manner from the taste and feel of her as she suddenly sighed and shuddered against him, closing her eyes for a moment.

He held her in his arms wishing they could stay like this forever.

Her gaze met his; very wide, soft, dazed and enchanting magically working her wiles on him.

"Ah, my Fire," he murmured then continued the foreplay by capturing her mouth and enjoying the duel of her tongue with his own. An urgent hunger seared through him. His hand moved fervently over her breast, the peak pebble hard. He kissed her teasing the small tight bud in the swollen feminine folds, treasuring the sweetness and amazing scent of her, sucking upon the fullness before moving to her other breast.

She moved beneath him erotically enticing all of him. While she did so, desire gripped his loins, a fierce heat swept within and he moved against her, needing her in the most elemental of ways yet wanting to prolong this pleasure.

He had yearned to take this joining slow but her body wept for his. She was stretched out on her back. Her skin was moist with an exotic sheen, touched by the warm, golden candlelight. Her hair was a tangle. Her limbs were long and beautiful, and her breasts were rising and falling so very rapidly. Her eyes were soft, glazed as if he had taken her quite by surprise. He had not and they both knew it for the truth.

"You are mine, Aidan, as is your passion and the wild sweetness that is the very essence of you.

Anguish ripped through him. Enough waiting. She was wet, hot and swollen with need. He felt the bowstring quivering of her form, the fervent tempo of her hips. It was time to seize and hold her.

He found the swollen bud once more, caressed and massaged until the tiny sounds emanating from her ripped through his core. She trembled and the slender beam of light glowed against her flesh.

"Are you trying to torment me, Blade? Please, need you inside me."

And he understood the mounting urgency. The sensations inside her seemed to grow at a feverish pace until she arched wildly against him. Sounds of her rising desire filled his soul, soft, desperate, breathless. Noises he delighted in hearing and prayed would never cease when they joined. It seemed she whirled out of control and to Blade it was the sweetest sensation.

Then he was inside her. Her eyes shimmering with pleasure, her naked body lush and full, pleading for him. She cried out softly, closing her eyes for but a moment, for it seemed she wanted to see into his eyes. His shaft slid into her and he remembered their first time when he hurt her, no longer.

"Oh..." she sighed. "It does fit..."

And he laughed, "You know it does. We tested that fact once already."

He moved inside her demandingly. His arms held his body above hers. He thrust into her and into her again, until he reached her womb. He wanted his seed to take root inside her. His gaze locked with hers, absorbing all the desire he saw inside their beautiful blue depths. He saw the magic as well, calling to him. He moved faster and more demandingly, his body fraught with tension.

"Blade," she cried out, seemingly unable to keep the pleasure inside. Her fingers fell upon his shoulders, her nails raking across his skin. She pulled up to him, meeting his thrusts with a rhythmic arch of her own.

Her lips and teeth touched upon his shoulders. She covered them with zealous kisses and gentle nips. Her hands played upon his back but it seemed she tried to hold on to him as tightly as she could. The force of her nails digging into his skin.

She gasped pulling him hard against her as the ripples of her climax seemed to capture her. For a few seconds it seemed she was so absorbed with the ecstasy she didn't realize he remained above her, watching as his seed was spilling into her.

He fell to her side, slick with sweat and breathing hard. His happiness knew no bounds.

She shuddered, touching his chest even while she closed her eyes. "I feel as if I've run for hours and I can only lay here in a boneless mass. Sex with you seems to get better each time."

"I hope you can say that in twenty, or thirty years."

She let her fingertip glide against his lips, "I'm sure I will."

He laughed, tracing the taunt bud amazed and the instant rise to passion as his lips found hers again.

"We cannot stay up all night as much as I would like to do just that," he murmured as he stroked her again. It seemed this night of lovemaking would be endless.

He must have closed his eyes, must have slept for a few hours yet the pounding on the door came all too soon. Blade rolled over, looking out the window to see the sun had risen at least an hour ago. He'd made plans to leave at dawn but the night of lovemaking had changed those plans. Still they should reach the halfway point before dark.

Running his fingers along her arms, reveling in the little sigh of pleasure created by his touch. "Aidan."

"Hmm..." She rolled into his arms and he was hard pressed not to sweep her beneath him and make love to his wife one more time before they had to be on the road.

"Rise and shine, we are an hour late, Little Fire."

The pounding started again. "I'm afraid it's most likely Damian reminding me the wedding night has come to an end and lauding it over me."

"You up?"

"We'll be out shortly," Blade called out as he threw the covers off, standing beside the bed, admiring his wife. He could wait because he had tonight and the next one and all the nights and days if it pleased both of them after that.

Pulling his clothes on, "Dress in something simple and warm. Charlotte has allowed us to use her carriage to the halfway point. The last half, I'm afraid you'll have to ride."

She gazed at him, her sleepy eyes seeming to absorb what he told her. She'd let the covers remaining to her slip to her waist. He could never get his fill of looking at her. She pushed her hair away from her face her lush breasts enticing him further with every movement.

Then she nodded, "I'll get dressed."

"Meet me downstairs in the entrance."

"Will anyone else be up?" she asked as if she wondered if there would be anyone to say goodbye to.

"Probably not. I know you won't see some of your cousins for years. Perhaps now that their children are older, they will come to London."

Tears slid down her cheeks. Tenderly he brushed them away

realizing how much she was giving up by following him to the highlands. "You will see them again. I promise you."

~ * ~

The wedding night, for Charlotte, was all she ever expected. She and David had been seeing each other since the day after she left Eveleen at the port of Dover to challenge Logan to take her with him to Bordeaux.

Her only intention had been to tell David what happened between his daughter and her husband, well perhaps that wasn't her only thought. Now David was strong and virile and it seemed that after Hunter took over the running of the McLellan clan, he regained strength daily.

"Did I please you lass?" David asked, tenderly stroking her arm, then lower, to cup her breast and toy with the rosy bud and watch as it hardened. He played with it and heard his new wife's mew of pleasure. "Again?"

"You know you pleased me. Don't we have to get up," she gasped as his hands explored more of her, erotic, intimate places she never thought a man beside her duke would touch. She closed her eyes enjoying all that he gave.

"I want to please you even more."

Her fingers wound into his hair then she let her nails score his flesh, across his shoulders and down his chest. "I don't think that's possible." She sighed into his mouth as it molded over hers, this tongue slipping inside.

He rolled over, spreading her legs with his body before once again tasting a rosy pink nipple. "Ach lass you are so sweet."

Charlotte couldn't stop a chuckle. "No one has ever called me sweet, not even my duke."

"When you are beneath me, lass, you are the sweetest delicacy I've tasted in so very long, delicious," David whispered, his hand settling on her breast, teasing the tip before investigating lower to even more erotic spots.

She had never thought she'd miss this but now she knew heaven in his arms. "Again?"

"I don't want to stop, do you?"

"No, can we stay in bed forever?"

"Whatever you want lass."

Yet the incessant knocking on the door told a different story.

~ * ~

They stood together on board one of Jamie's ships watching London come into view. With her back resting against his chest, Blade's hands were settled on Aidan's slightly swollen belly. He knew how pleased he was about her pregnancy and truth be told she was too. The child would be born some time in February at the MacPherson castle.

He kissed the nape of her neck. "Are you happy to be home?"

"My home is with you. London has never been home to me. I was only here a few short months. McLellan land has always been the place I call home. So, I'm off to a new adventure with my husband. I'm sure MacPherson traditions will not be so different than that of the McLellan's even though they are highlanders."

"We'll take a carriage to the Montgomerie estate and discuss strategy. The Duchess told me how Drake and Logan set up a line of inheritance that could not be broken even if all the expected heirs died. We are going to add our names to the list. With all of your cousins, spouses and their children there is no way my brother could kill all of those people before dying himself."

"I..." She moistened her lips wishing life were simpler and that people didn't covet what others had. From what she knew Blade's brother once had a substantial amount of wealth.

"What is it?"

"Does anyone know were coming." She watched the city pass by, a small bit of nostalgia flitting through her head.

"They expect us sometime this month. The Duchess made sure Drake would know we would be seeing them and why before she left for her new adventure," Blade said, stroking her cheek.

"I would like to see Ella but I'm hoping that perhaps Eveleen is in the city. Could we stop at the Maxwell townhouse before we leave for the

Montgomerie estate?" She missed her sister and while she'd been pleased and surprised to see Christel at her wedding, she was closest to Eveleen.

"As soon as we dock, I'll send a message. I'm sure your aunt apprised all of your siblings of the approximate date of our arrival as well as why. I don't think it will be a coincidence if Logan and Eveleen are in town or even staying with Drake and Ella."

"You think she knew we would marry?" Aidan asked surprised.

"I told her my intentions before I left for America and I've sent her several messages to update her," Blade said.

She felt such a surge of relief. There were things she needed to talk about with her sister and while Ella would listen, she wasn't her sister.

The ship docked, the gangplank was lowered. They strolled toward the street and the line of carriages waiting for fares. After a short ride, they stopped at the Maxwell townhouse only to be told that Logan and wife were not at home.

Aidan felt a moment of disappointment but she quickly regained her composure knowing that Eveleen and Logan were most likely at their winery in Bordeaux or the one in Tuscany. It was, after all, summer and growing ever closer to harvest time. The crops would have to be overseen.

She was so tired now, the growing baby absorbing so much of her energy. She rested against Blade, his arm around her. "Are you feeling all right?" He sounded concerned and almost afraid. "You're not to overtax yourself. Promise me you'll tell me if you need anything."

"Just tired." She let her hand rest on his chest, knowing she wanted him desperately. Yet she just didn't have the energy in the evenings. Sometimes she fell asleep before he came to bed. He never woke her and every morning she vowed to try harder to stay awake. But the sickness she felt each day was growing harder to hide from him.

"It's the child?" he asked seeming concern for her and she knew he was.

"I've heard it gets better after the third month. And I believe that's when my feet are on solid ground again, I won't fall asleep before you come to bed." She looked at him, you know you can always wake me up."

"Be assured once you have the energy to see to all my needs as well as our child's I might take you up on your offer. Right now, you need all the sleep you can get," Blade said, wrapping an arm around her shoulders and pulling her close.

"Do you mind if I sleep now? It's at least an hour drive to the Montgomerie estate and a little nap would be wonderful. Perhaps I'll be able to stay awake tonight, visit with Ella as well as a short tryst with you."

He pulled her into his arms. "No, if you don't care if I try to keep you awake." His lips found her ear as he blew softly then whispered how beautiful she looked in her day dress of lavender. "I want to see your belly swelled with my child and when I place my hand there to feel the wee babe kick."

"I must admit I'm not really looking forward to waddling around, unable to see my feet."

"We've an hour with no one to intrude or find something else for me to take my mind off you." His teeth closed gently on her neck, while his hands travelled lower to rest on her stomach as if he thought he could feel the kick.

"No one has gainsaid you since Damian left us at the half way mark from his ranch to Baltimore. You've done exactly what you wanted with me, and I've enjoyed every moment."

"So, you don't care if I have my way with you here in the carriage?" he asked while his mouth explored what little exposed skin he could find.

"I'm not as agile as I used to be." She sucked a lip into her mouth. "I just don't know if..."

"Hush."

The hour passed more quickly than she could have ever expected and she somehow felt more energized when they arrived even though she had to adjust several layers of her clothing. Blade helped of course, doing more damage to her appearance, her hair flying wildly around her face. It seemed that he tried to tangle it more. He'd never had trouble arranging her hair in the past.

When they reached the front door of the estate, the home appeared as if it was empty. But a few moments later, Ella raced from the front door, Drake following slowly behind her.

"You're here." Ella wrapped her arms around her. "And look at you. You're finally married to Blade."

"It's true. He travelled to America just to marry me and bring me back to Scotland. We did create quite the commotion though and your sister's husband made life fairly miserable for Blade until the ceremony finally took place," Aidan said.

"Of course, he did. Would you have expected anything else from Damian? When he has visited, he's always been the one who instigates trouble," Ella said. "Come inside, you and Blade must be exhausted."

"Did you know Aunt Charlotte married my father?" Aidan was still surprised when she thought about the union yet she was happy for them.

"No." Ella covered her mouth with her hands in seeming shock. "You're going to have to tell me all about it."

"I will. It was really quite the thing. We had a double wedding."

"Let's go outside on the patio and talk. I'll have cook bring us tea and something to eat. Are you hungry?" Ella asked.

"Famished, we haven't eaten since this morning. Blade was in such a hurry to get here. We stopped at the Maxwell townhouse. I was hoping Eveleen would be there," Aidan said, still disappointed she'd missed her sister, having no idea when she might see her again.

"It looks as if they are going to talk business. You can catch me up on the wedding and my sisters," Ella said, leading the way to the patio.

Aidan sat on a cushioned chair that was shaded by a nearby tree. She stifled a yawn. "It feels good to sit even though I've been sitting for the last hour. You have to catch me up on all you've been doing, the orphanage and your need to give those children a better life."

"Stay there. I'll be right back. I'm going to find cook and have her bring refreshments. Then we can tell each other everything." Ella left without glancing back.

Aidan looked up when Ella returned. Inhaling a long deep breath, she wasn't sure how to tell her cousin she was pregnant. "Where are your children?"

"For the next hour or so, napping. You are in luck. They are little terrors when they aren't asleep," Ella said. "Ashcroft gets into more trouble daily and there are times he needs two baths."

"Just like Amorica's two wild ones." Aidan remembered the horrible questions the children Lyssa and Jessie asked. "Do they get those traits from their fathers? I certainly hope so."

Ella laughed, and with a wink, said, "Probably both. Don't you remember how incorrigible we were as children? Drake would tell you that trait still exists in me but only when I do something he doesn't agree with. Otherwise I'm always the most rational thinker."

"I have been with Blade what seems like a lifetime but we've been together for such a short span of time. He has called me incorrigible though. Among other things, such as child, which he has now disavowed." Aidan placed her hands on her belly, remembering the wonderful nights they spent over the last months.

"You're pregnant," Ella said, with a gasp of recognition then started grinning. "That's why you're asking about the children and I bet you want to know what my children will do."

"Amorica's children asked the most embarrassing questions. I had no idea what to say, how to tell you."

"You were tongue-tied?"

"I was. Jessie wanted to know if I slept with my friend naked. I had no idea a child would even think of something like that."

"They only parrot what they see or what they are told. Always keep that fact in mind."

Aidan nodded, trying to absorb all that Ella said, while her stomach churned.

"First off when are you due? You don't show at all so it's got to be this winter," Ella said tenderly. "And remember what I just told you, children will only ask about those things they've heard or seen first-hand."

"February, sometime in the middle of the month."

"Are you excited?" Ella asked.

"Excited, terrified, exhausted and so much more. Blade thinks I should eat everything he gives me and believe me it's three times what I used to eat. I don't know what to do with that man. I know his intentions are good but he's going to drive me crazy with all the shielding gestures that I don't need. Besides, it seems I can't keep anything down."

"He's overprotective?" Ella asked. "I'm not at all surprised. Drake is the worst."

"More than that. He wants to take care of me, do everything for me. He would button my shoes if I would let him," Aidan sighed.

"He doesn't believe you're capable of dressing yourself," Ella said. "Just wait, by the time you're almost due, you might need someone to help you with your shoes and anything that involves bending over."

"How did you know?" Aidan asked, suddenly perceiving the answer. "Drake was just the same."

"You just figured this out, and rather than wanting to undress me he had this incessant need to help me with my clothing." Ella laughed outright, "wait until it's time for the birth. He'll be a bit unhinged at first and he'll drive you completely crazy while he hovers over you in the guise of helping."

"They should have something for fathers, a book or something to read, to teach them how to behave," Aidan said, taking a bite of one of the little spice cakes cook brought outside.

Ella poured tea for them both then changing the subject. "Do you need to take a nap before   dinner?"

"I napped a short bit in the carriage and I don't want to sleep everyday away even though sometimes I can't keep my eyes open." Aidan stifled another yawn. "Truly, I don't want to take a nap."

"In another month or so you'll get your energy back. Enjoy it for the time you have because at the end you won't be able to walk normally and exhaustion will take over again," Ella said with a little laugh.

"I can hardly wait until I have more energy."

"Tell me about Aunty. Why did she marry David and when did that all come about? Nobody here even knew they were seeing each other."

"Apparently they kept their indiscretions hidden very well. Papa decided they should try to set a good example. They, Damian, Aunty, David all decided the handfasting ceremony we had wasn't good enough. All involved said we were setting a bad example for the young people."

"Really, you handfasted and your Papa didn't think that was good enough?" Ella asked, with a bit of a laugh.

"No, he didn't and I've no idea who figured out they were sleeping in the same room, probably Damian, but whoever it was challenged them to set an example too." Aidan shrugged a bit. "That's when we decided there should be a double wedding. After all Aunty needed a wedding too."

Ella doubled over in laughter, tears sliding down her cheeks. "That is just so precious. I wish I could have been there."

"Tira was. I was shocked to see her and Christel and Ryder came. All in all, I had a beautiful wedding and of course The Duchess made sure everything was perfect for both of us," Aidan said, recalling that day with fondness but also remembering the thirty buttons as well as the claustrophobia when Blade couldn't undo them.

"Tira was there. How I've missed her. I do get to see Tavia though and I'm glad of that," Ella said, sipping her tea. "Tira's wedding was nice too but the events preceding it were horrible. Tira and Jamie had so many misunderstandings.

"What's it like?"

"What?" The dreamy expression on Ella's face vanished.

"Having a baby? I don't have anyone to ask. When I'm at Blade's home, I'm not going to know anyone. I don't even know if they'll like me."

"I'm sure you won't be alone. There will be people, his people to help, to talk to and you're his wife. They'll feel the same way about you that they feel about him. I'm sure they love Blade."

"I don't know. How will I ever make friends?"

"I'm sure you'll find a way. You've never had trouble making friends before. I'm sure everyone will love you and be more than willing to talk to you, Blade's wife," Ella said with confidence.

"I understand that." Aidan tried to stifle the threatening tears. "I guess I'm afraid of everything I don't know."

"Mama, who is this?"

A little dark-haired boy barreled into the room. "I don't remember her." His little voice indignant while he pointed a finger at Aidan.

"Ashcroft, I want you to meet my cousin, Aidan MacPherson. She is another one of your Aunties and you don't remember her because you weren't born the last time she was in London."

"Aunty Aidan?" The little boy said her name very slowly, seeming to mull the idea over in his mind. "Do you have a present for me?"

"Ashcroft!" Ella's voice was stern. "That is rude."

"Then I don't like her. My aunties are supposed to bring me presents."

"I didn't know," Aidan said, shrugging her shoulders not sure if she cared if he liked her. "Perhaps if you're nice I'll bring you one next time I come to London."

"Yes, my little man, and you have to be very nice to her so she doesn't think you're a wild little hellion," Ella said, patting Ashcroft on the head.

"But I am a little hellion, Papa calls me that all of the time just before he tosses me in the air and it must be a good thing because he's always smiling," Ashcroft said.

Aidan groaned, her head in her hands then she looked up. "That's a huge name for such a little man. Do you think he'll grow into it?"

"Mama and Papa call me Ash," The little boy said, grinning and nodding his head. It seemed he already understood the world was his for the taking. "You can too."

"Very well, Ash, why does your papa call you a little hellion?" Aidan wasn't all that sure she wanted to know the answer but since the question was asked, she meant to muddle through.

He shrugged his little shoulders. "I dunna know. Maybe cause I am. What is a wild, little hellion?"

Aidan felt a wave of love sweep through her even though she barely knew this little boy. And she understood Charlotte's love and admiration for all her nieces. It was called family and family was everything.

"You are so very sweet and precious. Don't ever change," Aidan said, a shadow or a glimpse of a movement caught her attention, drawing her gaze to the patio door.

"Aidan, you're back." Eveleen walked into the room, untying her bonnet and setting it on the table. "I heard you finally married that big oaf whose name is Blade. It's about time he saw how special you are."

"Eveleen!" Aidan rushed to give her a hug. "I'm so glad you're here. They told us at the townhouse you weren't there, so I didn't expect to see you."

"Is that tea and cookies?" Eveleen stepped farther into the room, scooping up Ash to give him a hug. "How are you little man?" She handed him a toy boat, "don't fall into the lake when you play with it."

"See." Ash said as he studied the boat before setting his gaze on Aidan. "When can I go to the lake?"

"You're going to have to make do with the bathtub until your father has time for an outing. I'm not abandoning my cousins right now."

"Mama said I could have a cookie," Ash said, losing interest in the boat for the time being.

"When did I say that?" Ella asked, sending him a disapproving glance. "You know better than to make up stories."

"You would have." Ash said, his little face scrunched into lines. "You always let me have treats in the afternoon after naptime but you forgot."

"Yes, that's true. Help yourself to one cookie." It seemed Ella remembered to say one cookie just in time. Ash looked poised to grab the plate and run.

"So, what is new? Besides of course your marriage to Blade. I'm so happy for you," Eveleen said while she helped herself to a cup of tea.

Aidan told the story one more time while Eveleen gasped in surprise with each new revelation.

"Aunty has married Papa? Truly I had no idea about any of this," Eveleen said her eyes wide with surprise. "When have they even been together long enough to fall in love?

"It's all true," Aidan confirmed watching Ash play with the toys that had been set out on the patio the new sailing vessel included.

She was in love with this little boy and even more in love with the tiny child growing inside her. Boy or girl, it didn't matter. She knew Blade wanted an heir in order to secure his inheritance but if it weren't for that, she knew he'd love a little girl, and as he said, one who was just like her, red hair, freckles and everything else.

"What are the men talking about for so long?" Aidan asked, her stomach suddenly rolling. She rose from the chair then lost her breakfast on the patio bricks. "I'm so sorry. It seems I've been sick forever. It's increasingly hard to keep this part of my condition from Blade. Indeed, I haven't kept anything from him. I know it will pass but..."

"No need to apologize. I'll get someone to clean this up. Drink some tea it will make the nasty taste in your mouth go away," she said as she left to fetch a maid.

She returned quickly with a bucket just in case Aidan needed it, then, "You all know that Drake's brother abducted me and tried to sell me at auction in order to abscond with what he wished was his.

"No, I left for Baltimore before all that happened. It must have been awful," Aidan said, realizing that once Blade finally came to his senses and decided she was the woman for him, her life had been easy and filled with tender concern.

"Drake doesn't want anything like that to happen to any of us. His plan is to set up a line of inheritance that would stop any in-law from killing and taking what isn't theirs," Ella said. "At the moment the chain of inheritance includes everyone in our family and their children except Blade and Aidan. The wills are in constant change. Every time one of us has a child, all the wills must be updated." Ella informed Aidan.

"Makes sense. Blade's brother is trying to do just that. He's trying to find a way to have what he's always coveted, the MacPherson land." Aidan put her hands on her belly.

"How far along are you?" Eveleen asked seeming to know the answer before she asked.

Aidan nodded, "Almost two months maybe. I'm really not sure but Blade thinks I might be three months along and he doesn't want his brother to do anything to me or the baby."

"And you've been losing your meals for how long?" Ella asked.

"Most of that time," Aidan reluctantly admitted, "Blade doesn't think that's normal either even though I'm able to hide it from him most of the time. He doesn't know how bad it's been."

"Well, he's right it's probably not normal. A little sickness in the morning is one thing but constant sickness is serious. Your face is thin almost gaunt and now that I look at you there are dark circles under your eyes. You must get your rest," Ella said sternly.

"I am trying to do that while Blade hovers. Enough about me, what else is happening?" Aidan asked.

"Hunter is at the MacPherson castle as we speak to lend reinforcements." Eveleen said. "Because Hunter and Blade have been friends for years, and they stood by each other when they were mercenaries, he feels it's his duty to protect what is rightfully Blade's while he is away."

"Somehow I think there is something more going on here. Logan doesn't know what it is but both Drake and Logan have feelers out to try and find out who the other people involved are," Eveleen said, her words resonating in Aidan. "According to Logan, Blade's brother doesn't have the resources to do this on his own."

Aidan could never forget Guy and all he tried to do so many years ago and she'd never forget the ocean water as it nearly closed over her head. Guy had tied her to a rock in order to force Blade's hand. His ploy had very nearly worked.

"The spies are at work," Ella whispered then giggled. "In all seriousness this business scares me and Aidan is walking into the middle of it all."

"Yes, very serious, and I think I'm finally over the fact that Logan can kill as easily as he can breathe. He doesn't enjoy it nor does he abuse his skill." Eveleen grimaced. "He has only used this ability to defend himself or those he loves."

Ella inhaled a long deep breath, gazing at her two cousins. "I don't think this espionage thing will ever end for the two of them. It's in their blood even though they say they are no longer involved."

"Don't let Drake fool you," Eveleen spoke up. "Drake has never been out of the game. He directs people now, sends them on missions. I don't suppose it's something I should have told you, but there it is. Logan says neither of them are involved in anything dangerous."

"And we're expected to believe them?" The indignant tone in Ella's voice was easy to hear. "Nothing dangerous until they grow bored, I suppose. They did help Tavia when that killer was after her. So, I suppose there is good to come of this ability to spy."

Aidan had no idea how to answer something like that. She didn't think Blade would ever lie to her but she also knew he meant to protect her at all cost. Did that mean he would lie if he thought the lie would keep her safer? At the moment all she could do was run to the bucket in hopes of not disgusting anyone with her retching.

"You must be Aidan and can I assume you carry a child?" Addie poked her head in through the door.

When Aidan was finished and had a chance to sip more tea, she nodded smiling at the new arrival. "Yes, to both."

"Nice to meet you. You do know we've all been waiting for yours and Blade's arrival." She waved her hand in the air, smiling. "In any case they've banded together to help out." Addie walked onto the patio, joining the small group. "Hamilton and I are going to the McLellan castle to lend reinforcements and aid to Allura. There is something nefarious going on and Drake has heard that Guy has resurfaced and might try to take what he coveted seven years ago when Hunter won Allura's hand."

"No, Guy is involved? That can't be true." The tremor shooting down Aidan's spine unnerved her as well as the memories that had just resurfaced. Without even closing her eyes she could feel the frigid waters covering her and relief when Blade dove into the ocean and sliced the bindings, carrying her to the safety of the warm boat and his arms. Vividly she remembered how he held her and warmed her when she might have died.

"The fact hasn't been confirmed but both Drake and Logan believe it to be true and are taking precautions," Addie said. "May I?" she poured herself a cup of tea. "I suppose brandy would be medicinal at the moment."

~ * ~

"I've arranged for our solicitor to be here this afternoon. I know you're eager to continue your journey and you should set your affairs in motion now before you reach the MacPherson holdings and before you have a possible child who could be killed or kidnapped," Drake said. "You need to take every possible precaution regarding your inheritance and everything you've worked for."

"Appreciate all your help. The situation at home is dire. Hunter has brought some men to help defend the MacPherson keep but I'm worried about McLellan land. If Hunter is away, it makes the keep vulnerable to anyone who might covet it."

"Don't worry. Hunter has taken all of that under consideration. We have enough men among all of us to keep everyone safe," Drake said. "And I believe more are coming."

Logan strode confidently into the parlor where the men had settled, shaking hands and giving quick hugs in greeting. He sat down accepting a drink. "Good afternoon."

"What news?" Drake asked prowling the room, unable to sit. In any case, it seemed he did his best thinking on his feet.

"Before I came here, I visited the bureau. Word is Hunter's half-brother Guy has a substantial commitment invested in Blade's brother. My informant has told me he wants Aidan."

Blade inhaled a swift breath of air, his fists clenching. "My wife; he coveted her as a little girl. If I had let him get close to Aidan, he would have taken her then. But, it was only after he knew he couldn't have Aidan and I'm sure it was only because Aidan was interested in me. I was the closest person to Hunter who he could hurt. So now he continues his game of revenge, desiring what I hold dear and close to my heart."

"From what I've heard, Guy has not shown up at the MacPherson keep even though your brother is there, Blade," Logan said. "He is wisely keeping his distance in case of your brother's failure."

"He could be there and no one would ever know. He's a master at disguise. That's how he got into the McLellan keep before Allura and Hunter were married," Blade said remembering those days all too well and now Guy had his sights set on his wife.

"Hamilton, good of you to show up since you've no invested interest in us this time," Drake said striding forward to greet one of his retired spies. "We can use the help. I'm sure you're needing some adventure."

"Just thought I'd drop by. Addie wanted to see Ella and Eveleen and the kids, you know." He shrugged grinning. "Besides you're right of course I'm bored, think Addie is too. Neither one of us is used to spending so much time sitting in a parlor drinking tea. The baby just doesn't provide any excitement yet, even though we adore the little tyke. Spitting up on my jacket is the best he can do."

Drake laughed seeming to understand what his friend talked about but Blade thought he'd like some of that kind of excitement. He wanted to be home, in the highlands where he belonged building a family and watching them grow. He wanted lots of kids, as many as Aidan would like. In the last years, he'd spent very little time on MacPherson land and perhaps that's why his brother believed he could gain the inheritance. Blade meant to remedy that situation and once he was home he wasn't going to leave soon.

"Gavin sent the papers over to be signed a few days ago. He wanted to lend a hand at the MacPherson keep. We've sent quite a show of unity to the highlands. I really believe once your brother understands that even if he kills you and your offspring he will never inherit, he will look to some other person he can torment. Next time the other families are in town they will add your names to their wills and sign as well," Drake said striding to the desk to pick up the papers that needed signing.

Each man signed three copies. One for each of them, one to be kept in a safe in the bank of England and one for the next in line to inherit.

Blade felt the first vestiges of stress begin to leave his body since his father first told him of his brother's plan.

"Shall we go see what the ladies are doing?" Drake asked.

Blade stood, more than willing to see Aidan, hold her and make sure her fatigue and nausea was not overpowering her. Eager to see Aidan and impatient to be on his way home tomorrow morning, he led the way.

When Aidan saw him, she set her cup of tea on a table and strode to meet him with a hug and a kiss. He pulled her into his arms, molding his mouth on hers telling her how much he wanted her and relieved she didn't look more exhausted than this morning.

"How are you? Are you getting enough to eat?" Blade asked, looking at the tray of cookies.

"See what I told you." Aidan shot a look at Ella who was laughing.

Blade felt uncomfortable not knowing what they spoke of. In any case, "you need to eat and keep up your strength." He didn't want to mention her problems in keeping the food down when the others were in the room. "We leave for MacPherson land tomorrow morning as soon as we can get ready. The journey won't be an easy one even though we've the best carriage money can buy. You will be as comfortable as possible. We can stop anytime you ask."

"I know. I'm not looking forward to the trip though. We've already spent so much time traveling. I long for something permanent," Aidan said with a soft sigh that shot straight through Blade's heart.

"I should have thought more about you and your health. This would be so much easier if you didn't carry the child. We could have waited." Blade felt a wave of guilt sweep through him at his selfishness. As to the babe he'd only thought of his needs, having no idea what pregnancy would do to Aidan.

"Hush, Blade, I wanted you to make love to me. Don't blame yourself. You need an heir and I think we both wanted a child. We both know that."

"An heir could have waited and there is an easy way to keep my seed from going inside you. I could have done that but I was so filled with love and lust. I never thought once to withdraw before I spilled myself into you." His voice was low but he was sure everyone heard the interchange. Perhaps not the men who were involved greeting their wives. Strange, how a thirty-minute absence could have him longing for her company.

"Who's this Papa?" Ashcroft was in Drake's arms and he was tossing him in the air.

"A friend and Aunty Aidan's husband. So, I guess you can call him uncle." Drake tickled him and the little boy laughed and squirmed in Drake's arms.

"Are they going to have a baby so I can have someone to play with. You need to tell them to go to bed," Ashcroft said with grave seriousness. "You can't have a baby unless you're in bed and naked."

"That wouldn't be polite if I told them that," Drake told his son laughing and tickling him.

"But you tell Mama that all the time."

"Hush Ash, why don't you have another cookie?" Ella said in an effort to distract Blade from what her little boy just said.

"You never let me have two." It seemed he protested until he realized what his mother just said before he grabbed a cookie, biting into it in almost the same breath.

"The two of you should have brought your children," Ella said with a little smile. "They do play well together."

"I needed a break. Besides, our little man is not quite up to playing with Ash. He doesn't understand what Ash wants to do."

"And the baby, well, need I say she would only lie on her back and wave her arms in the air," Addie said.

"Who is staying for dinner?" Ella asked the small group. "I believe Cook is trying to tell us it's time to eat."

"A free meal? I never turn anything down that's free. What do you say Addie, we eat then go to bed for the chance at another child, a boy this time then were off to Scotland? Should we take tents and sleep on the ground?" Hamilton picked up Addie's hand kissing the palm.

"Bite your tongue, we're going to stay in the finest Inns and if I see one tent or sleeping bag, I'll divorce you without a second thought."

"I wouldn't let you." Hamilton grinned wickedly. "We both know I'd find you in my bed before I could count backwards from one hundred. You can't live without me."

"As are we traveling to Scotland," Blade said thinking the two had a different relationship. "Too bad we can't travel together."

Chapter Seven

"Stop," Blade tapped on the roof of the carriage to signal the driver.

Quickly helping Aidan from the vehicle, he rubbed her back while she lost what little breakfast she ate. Dark circles underlined her eyes and even though she was probably three months pregnant, she'd lost weight. He hadn't expected her to gain yet but not this.

"I'm sorry." She accepted the water he handed to her and sipped. "I thought I could eat. I should have known better."

"We'll rest here for a few minutes," Blade said, knowing she would throw up more than once. This had gone on for the last month. She'd been constantly sick. He knew he had to keep water in her and so he made sure there were a couple gallons in the carriage each day not that she ever drank that much.

"If we rest here, you might not make the MacPherson castle by sunset. We really need to keep going. I don't want to hold you back."

"A few minutes only. We can travel in the dark. This is my land and I know every twist and turn with my eyes closed. I sent a messenger this morning to tell them we'd be arriving. I can send another man to let them know they should send a few extra men to meet and to see us to the keep."

"I suppose that will have to do. I would like to rest somewhere the countryside isn't swaying." She sighed softly, "I just want this nausea to end."

Didn't people just have babies? He'd never guessed there could be so many problems and they'd barely begun this journey.

"Drink some more water."

"I'm going to drown if you make me take in one more drop." She sipped anyway, giving him a sideways glance. It seemed she understood, in this matter, it was better to comply with his wishes than to argue.

"You have to drink and I'm sorry if I keep persisting. I just know that from battles, the sick and injured, the ones who drank more water were more likely to survive," Blade said. "I can't tell you why just that they did."

"I believe you and trust you." She turned and lost the water she just sipped, letting out a tiny moan in the process.

He persisted, handing her the bottle of water again. She smiled weakly taking the water once more. "You will feel better. I promise." Yet he knew he couldn't make that promise.

"In six or seven months I presume." She smiled at him but it didn't reach her eyes.

He laughed but realized she wasn't laughing. "I'm sorry I did this to you." He sat down on a large rock and drew her onto his lap. His arms around her, he let her set her cheek on his chest.

"You won't be when the child is born." She looked into his eyes, touching his lips. "Don't say anything more to blame yourself. We will have more children. I won't let this dissuade me and I won't be traveling again. I'm promising myself and you that this won't keep happening."

"I understand what you're trying to tell me, Little Fire. We will be home tonight and you will sleep in your bed, our bed. You will feel better in the morning just knowing you are home. This is the real beginning of our lives together. So far, it's not been easy. I promise you I'll do everything in my power to make it better."

She kissed him on the lips, a long slow kiss, one where he let her control everything. Then, "I think we can travel again. There seems to be no rolling in my stomach, at least for now."

"You sure?" He smoothed wild strands of her hair away from her face, his hands on her cheeks, trying to see the truth in her eyes. "You wouldn't lie to me now would you, lass?"

"I might but I'm not lying this time. The sooner this carriage is put to rest with all of your carriages the happier I'll be. If I feel sick again, I'll tell you and promise I won't lose the contents of my stomach on you."

She tried to laugh but coughed instead, closing her eyes, seemingly exhausted to her bones.

He stiffened at her words, anger rushing to the forefront. "You might lie to me? I cannot have that, no, not at all. Never."

"Only if it wouldn't hurt you and if it would get me something, I needed more than sitting on the side of the road hearing the minutes tick by. I need to be home before the next day dawns."

"Those words don't make me feel any better," he told her wondering if he'd ever trust what she told him again.

"Let's continue the discussion in the carriage. I find I've suddenly a lot more energy." She smiled at him, standing and slowly making her way to the vehicle.

He was beside her, his arm around her waist supporting her, still wondering if she'd always told him the truth. "We will continue this in a more appropriate setting and when you feel better." His voice grew low and harsh.

"Blade, lying isn't part of my nature."

"I'm sorry." His voice gentled. This wasn't the time to bring more stress on her frail health and he knew that fact. Not for a moment did he think this pregnancy was normal. There was something wrong and true enough they needed to be at the keep. She needed real rest, something that had been lacking for her since they'd been wed. The rough roads and nights at inns, a different bed every evening had wrought its toll on her.

"Can you give me a few minutes to close my eyes and possibly sleep?" Her hand rested on her abdomen and he had a sudden flash of fear.

"Are you cramping?" He didn't want to believe his rush to get home would put her and the child in jeopardy.

"No." She closed her eyes. "I'm not. It's just that I'm a bit dizzy. The world is spinning around me and I'm afraid I might faint."

"Are you lying to me? Aidan, I really need to know. Look at me so I can read the truth in your eyes. There are things that can be done if you are having pains." He held his breath, his muscles tensed beyond anything he'd felt before, even when his life and Hunter's was on the line, he had never felt this terrifying tension.

"No. I promise you and I shouldn't have said I might lie. Really, I wouldn't. The truth solves more problems than lies, even if the falsehood is said with all sincerity to protect someone. The ground does seem to be moving though. Can you stop it?" She chuckled softly, leaning into him seeming to rely on his strength. She rested her head on his chest as his arms pulled her close warming her.

He needed to let his power and strength sweep into her. "Tell me if there is any change in your body or how you feel." His concern reached levels he never experienced before. He'd never had a wife and a child on the way. "Promise me."

"Yes, I promise because I want you to smile at me every time I see you." She had looked at him. Once again, she settled her head against his chest, closing her eyes. "You never smile anymore."

He listened while her breaths slowed and reached an even cadence. Dear God what had he done? He should have left her in London with Ella and Drake until the child was born instead of dragging her miles and miles in a carriage over rough terrain and in hot weather. Someone should shoot him.

The carriage bumped and rolled along the rutted road. She groaned, as they hit a deep hole. This was not good for her and the child but there was nothing to do about it. He was a bloody fool. He couldn't lose her now that he just claimed her as his own. He didn't want to lose the child either. His fists tightened, anger at himself and his stupidity growing.

Looking out the small window he understood she'd slept most of the morning and into the afternoon. The sun would set in about an hour. He realized he must have slept also. Trying not to wake her he stretched an arm then a leg. They were both numb. It was a meager price to pay for her minimal comfort.

"Sir?"

Startled, he looked out the window. "Liam? I'm glad you came after my message, someone I can trust. It seems we are in need of an escort."

"I have men to accompany you the rest of the way to the keep," Liam said as he continued to look into the carriage. "Your wife I presume.

She is a very beautiful lady."

"Yes, how far? My wife...she's not well." He said, thankful for the loyal men. In this situation he might not have been able to trust anyone but his childhood friend.

"Two miles," he said. "Can we pick up the pace? With little moonlight it's going to be very dark before we arrive and there are those who would do you and your wife harm."

"I understand we're in peril until we convince my brother he has naught to gain by killing us. No, we cannot go faster, she's pregnant and I fear for her health. Yet she's strong. She's sleeping now."

"All right then, we'll form a shield around the vehicle. At this moment no one knows where your brother or for that matter where Guy is. They could be in route or back in the keep. I fear they are trying to turn some of the clan to their purposes."

A sick feeling swamped him, his heart thundered behind his ribs and every battle instinct kicked into gear. Yet he had to protect his wife first, just as he had always needed to protect Hunter. This was no different.

In those earlier days Hunter had been wild and unpredictable. He didn't care if he lived or died. All Hunter searched for was the money he could gain to buy an estate and so he sold his sword time and again. And in his lust for excitement he'd signed on with his friend, an older brother he'd never had.

As they continued, she slept more soundly and his heart raced faster, fear for her escalating. "Please Lord, give her this chance to survive. We're almost there. I can feel it in my bones."

He bent close to her, whispering in her ear, "You must hang on. I know you've the strength. What I don't know is what is wrong with you other than you've eaten next to nothing these last weeks. I also understand you're exhausted and I've pushed you too hard. This is all my fault."

She had no reply except she snuggled closer to him.

He kissed her forehead, "I love you, Little Fire. I think I did the first time I saw you and couldn't figure out why. Bloody eyes you were only thirteen. How could I, a grown man, love a little girl? You were all arms, legs and wild red hair with the prettiest blue eyes I'd ever seen. I even adored the freckles painted across your nose and cheeks, but I believe your charm came from your innocence and need to be part of everything going on around you. You were in such a hurry to grow up. And soon I also felt that urgency. You were well worth the wait."

The carriage rolled on at what seemed like a snail's pace. He pulled her closer, praying for their arrival to be sooner than later. At this rate though he knew it would be later.

Liam rode up beside him, "We are almost there. The gatehouse is about ten minutes from here. I sent a man ahead to make sure you solar is ready for you and your wife as soon as we arrive. There will be food and wine waiting in the room. Do you want a physician?"

"No, I want Selim. She will know what to do about Aidan or at least will be able to treat her without killing her. She has herbs and ailments that cure things doctors only shake their heads at."

"You sure?" Liam sounded skeptical.

"No, I'm not sure of anything, but there is no other choice," Blade said, wondering at his friend's cautious words. "She has skills that surpass the physicians here." He reiterated impatiently waving his hand in the air. "I've seen her step in and save men who should have died."

"She has always been enamored of you. At one time she thought she would wed you. Are you sure she will treat your wife the way you want?"

"No, I've no idea but I don't think she would... I have to have her at Aidan's side, and I believe I trust her," Blade said terrified of what he was asking. Selim had been his paramour for years. She had been there for him when he needed to talk, when he just needed a woman when he couldn't have Aidan. For all those years he thought she understood she would never be his wife. He'd rescued her from certain death. Selim would have to remember that and come to his aid if he meant anything to her.

"I will send notice that you need her to help your wife but I want you to know I love this woman. I've never acted on my feelings because you remained single. Now I'd like to court Selim. With your permission of course."

"I had no idea you cared for her. Please, I would love to see her happy and you're just the man to accomplish the feat. I thought she always knew I wouldn't wed anyone except Aidan." Of course, he didn't understand how Selim felt. He had always been a bit self-centered and he'd been so focused on Aidan he'd been accused of not seeing what was right in front of his face. "You have my blessing."

"Thank you sir and I'll make sure she is apprised of your wife's situation. She will have the proper medicines for her ready when you arrive," Liam finished then rode off to send the messengers, he promised.

Those minutes to the gatehouse seemed the longest of his life. When they finally passed by the entrance and started down the road to the main keep, he breathed a hesitant sigh of relief. Everything was going to be fine. He would have no more worries. Yet he knew the struggle for power in the MacPherson clan was not yet over.

Anything could still go wrong with the pregnancy. His brother could declare war if he thought he possessed enough power and men. "Aidan." He kissed her forehead in an attempt to wake her. She'd been sleeping since before noon. He should have roused her so she could eat. Then he acknowledged, she would have lost what she put inside her anyway.

"Blade." Her eyes were wide open, gazing at him and the relief he felt sweeping through him he couldn't define. "Is everything alright? You have this strange look on your face."

"How do you feel?" he asked, brushing her hair from her face then placing a light kiss on her forehead. "And I was just worried about you. You've been asleep the entire afternoon."

"Better than before I fell asleep. Maybe I just needed to... "

"What's wrong?"

"I don't know that there is... It's just that..."

"Tell me," he said, trying not to demand too much.

"A cramp, just a small one." She moaned softly as if she tried to keep her pain from him.

"I'm here and I've someone who can help. You won't like it but trust me she understands what women go through in childbirth and I've seen her save at least three babies as well as their mothers when everyone else gave up. I shouldn't have said that but I'm terrified and I don't want you to worry."

"Maybe it's what I didn't eat. It's more in my stomach than..." She blushed seeming unsure of sharing so much.

"You need to talk to your husband." He paused as if to put emphasis on the next statement. "Rather than your womb?" he finished for her, smiling at the first sign of color on her face in what seemed like years. "I do understand a few anatomical facts about women."

"Yes, but it's not hunger pains. It's just cramping." She grabbed her belly, moaning.

"Drink some water." He held the flask to her yet she was shaking her head no.

"I can't." She gasped for air, closing her eyes and seemingly trying to breathe. She struggled for each breath, wheezing in and out.

"Relax," he told her rubbing her back, try to relax. "Just breathe slowly in then out." He strained to breathe for her, and slowly her breaths became more even and regular. "Good girl." He held her close not wanting to let her go, but when the carriage stopped, he had to leave her.

He barked orders as to what to do with the trunks as he helped her from the vehicle and carried her up the steps to the solar. Liam had said there would be food in his chamber and Selim would be there also.

When he pushed the door open with a foot, Selim sat on a chair a mortar and pestle on a bedside table. "Liam told me what you said about your wife. I've seen this condition before. While her disorder is not common, it's perfectly normal. I've mixed a few herbs specific to helping with the constant nausea of pregnancy such as anise and a few others, together and she must drink this every four to six hours. Soon she'll be feeling better."

"I'm in your debt forever. I'd like to repay you." Blade told her watching for any sign she might be angry or hurt but saw nothing that would lead him to believe she would do anything untoward.

"No, I was in yours when you rescued me from a cruel master and slavery. You put your life on the line and risked much to help me. Liam has told me he has your permission to court me. Thank you. I've cared for him for such a long time. He has my heart."

Blade felt several burdens lift from his shoulders with those few words. "So, you like Liam? Why didn't you tell me?"

"He is much like you, strong and gentle too. I've cared for him for a couple of years now but he was so bent on not doing anything until you were wed, he didn't pursue me. Now you must see to your wife. You have enough medicine until the morning. If she begins to feel better, she'll want to eat."

"She's touched barely anything for the last month."

"Don't overfeed her. Just small amounts or she won't be able to keep the food down. She will let you know when she's had enough. Trust her in this. You don't know how she feels and her cure will not come from devouring too much of a good thing." She started from the room then she turned. "Don't force any food on her. I know you Blade MacPherson. You're going to want her to eat the entire platter."

Blade realized just how overbearing he could be. Well he most likely wouldn't change anytime soon. He would try to take Selim's advice.

"You know I heard what she told you. Can I drink what she made so I might stop throwing up?" She held out her hands, waiting and seemingly patient.

Aidan was sitting up, leaning against the headboard when he handed her the drink. "I think you're supposed to drink all of this."

"I'll try." She scrunched her nose. "It smells horrible."

"Trying will have to do. Drink some now then in a little while you can finish. Just remember, as soon as you get some of that inside you, the sooner you'll feel better." He realized how much he trusted Selim.

He wanted to laugh when she closed her eyes and tipped the glass until she finished the entire amount.

"Now I'd like some water." She pushed flyaway strands of hair from her eyes as she stared at him.

"I'm surprised, amazed and pleased that you drank the entire glass," he said looking through the food and drink that had been brought to the room. "Will a little wine work? I can't find water."

"I only need enough to take the bitter taste away," she said excepting the glass and sipping.

He waited eagerly for an announcement that she felt back to

normal and was ready to eat, but to no avail.

The knock on his door surprised him. "Come in."

"Sir." Liam poked his head inside. "Is this a good time to bring in your trunks? Then I'll leave the two of you alone."

"Put them anywhere," Blade said.

The trunks were brought inside and left near the door. He didn't move for the longest time.

"Blade?" Aidan's hand rested on his arm. "I'd like to sleep and you probably want to speak with your father. Really, I'm fine. You can go see him or see to whatever you need to do."

"Father is probably not awake now. It is growing late, but we passed Hunter on our way upstairs. I do need to speak with him. I don't want to leave you though." He was torn with emotions and frustrations.

"You have to. I'll be fine. Strangely I do feel better and I promise that if the urge to eat hits me suddenly, I'll do so."

"I'll go when you fall asleep." He searched through the trunks until he found one of her prim white nightdresses.

She laughed when she saw what he uncovered. "I haven't slept in that since... since that night in the woods before we handfasted."

"Not in those two nights when we were forced to sleep apart?" he asked suddenly curious about those chaste evenings. "Did you sleep naked?" he asked, wishing he'd been there.

"No, my sisters and cousins purchased these filmy negligees from the seamstress in the town. They were for the wedding night and after. I slept in those."

"Why not with me?" he asked, suddenly jealous or angry that he'd not had the pleasure of taking them off her. Seeing through the fabric to her luscious curves would have been more than pleasant.

"Because." She paused, her clear blue eyes penetrating his heart. "You never gave me the chance to put anything on before we made love. You stripped me of my clothing and that was that." She shrugged her tiny shoulders, thinner now that she'd been so ill.

"And even though we haven't been intimate since your sickness, I wanted you naked beside me." He smiled at the thought. "Perhaps I should put this away." He held up the nightdress.

"With the threat of Guy and your brother still hanging over our heads, I do believe that at least while you're not with me I'd feel more comfortable with something on that a person can't see through."

"I would too." Not that clothing would make much of a difference if someone wanted to violate her. His stomach clenched. One more thing he shouldn't blurt out. She had her health to worry about and nothing else should concern her.

Tenderly, he helped her from her clothing before slipping the nightdress over her head.

"Thank you." She smiled, yawning, "my stomach feels normal."

"Good. Good. Normal sounds right. Don't go anywhere," he ordered. "If you need anything, ring this bell and someone will come or they will get me."

"I think I can remember that." She slanted him a flirtatious grin.

He tried to ignore it but his thoughts suddenly turned sensual. He pushed them to the back of his mind, concentrating on the tasks at hand. "When I get back and if you're awake, I want you to try to eat something." He searched the platter for something she might enjoy. "I see strawberries and grapes, two of your favorites. We could start with one strawberry and see if it stays put."

"There is no time like the present." She picked up a strawberry and bit into it then holding the other half out to him. He shook his head. "When you get back, I'll know if I can eat a little more." And she finished the berry.

He placed a kiss on her forehead, craving so much more but willing to wait. Feeling more optimistic than he'd felt an hour ago, he bid her goodbye and strode downstairs to speak with Hunter.

~ * ~

"Little Fire." Selim slowly opened the door. "Are you awake?"

"Yes." She watched curious as to what Selim might want.

Don't mean to keep you from your rest and if you'd rather talk in the morning, I'll come back then, but there are some things you need to be apprised of and I always believe there is no better time than the present."

"Come in. Whatever was in that drink smelled atrocious but it seems to work. I'm not sure I want to know but the information might prove useful. I know many times it's up to the laird's wife to administer to the clan. Maybe you can teach me some of your skills."

She smiled walking the length of the room to sit in a chair beside the bed and laughing said, "I even put an herb in it to make it smell better and yes, I would be pleased to pass on my knowledge. There is a lot of wealth in knowledge."

"Why did you call me Little Fire?" Aidan didn't understand and she doubted Blade would have introduced her to the woman in that manner.

Selim turned to look out the window as if searching for the right words. "Your husband, my good friend, we have shared a lot over the years but I've always understood his love for you. He has never called you by name, only his little fire. I don't even know what others call you."

"My name is Aidan," she said, mulling over Selim's words. "Until recently Blade never called me by his pet name for me. I'm surprised. I believed it was something new."

Selim waved her hand in the air, seemingly impatient. "That is not why I came tonight. I need to ask you how are you feeling. If it proves necessary, there are adjustments to the medicine I can make. We must make you healthy and strong for your sake as well as the baby's. Blade would never forgive himself if you don't thrive."

"Truly my stomach is not in an upheaval for the first time in at least two months. I ate a strawberry and had a sip of wine. And still I'm not running to a bucket. I cannot tell you how thankful I am."

"Good, that is what I want to hear. You will have to keep drinking this for a while or the illness will return. This is not something that will go away anytime soon."

"I'll try plugging my nose next time," Aidan said, laughing and feeling as if she'd known this woman all her life. "And I'll make sure I drink the entire concoction."

"Not a bad idea." Selim looked away again before she turned back. "I don't know how much you heard when I spoke with your husband, but rest assured your pregnancy is normal. You and your child are healthy and will remain so. I promise. Most women suffer some sickness and usually just in the mornings. You, unfortunately, have extreme sickness and it might last more than the three-month mark. Hopefully the nausea will begin to diminish on its own. Then you won't have to take this medicine." She nodded to her morning dose sitting on the table. "You are closing in on two months or more?"

"Blade thinks it's three. He likes to think he got me pregnant the first time he made love to me," she paused, "You said there were a couple of things we needed to speak about?" Aidan asked stifling a yawn.

"Hopefully you should not have to drink this much longer if Blade is right. I see you're tired. I should come back in the morning when you've rested." Selim rose to leave the room.

"No wait." Aidan leaned forward, placing her hand on Selim's arm, hoping she could convince her to stay. "I'll get plenty of sleep tonight. Tell me now."

Selim moistened her lips. "This was over two years ago. I want you to know this and understand the reasons why. I was your husband's paramour when you were younger. I slept with him when he was home and I loved him. He was so kind to me and he rescued me from certain death. He used to speak of you and how beautiful and precocious you were. Even then I understood that he was waiting for you to grow into the beautiful woman that you are now. I would never mean to diminish what there is between you but the people here know we were lovers a long time ago and they will talk."

"I don't know how I feel about meeting one of Blade's lovers. I knew he had them, lovers, but I never thought to meet one or even trust one with my life." She held her breath. "He really never kept anything secret, his lovers, and in the beginning, he tried to flaunt them as if to dissuade me."

"I didn't mean to shock you but you need to know this because there are women here who seek to undermine me. I've heard from Liam they want Blade to believe I mean you harm and my medicines have poison in them. I do not mean you harm. I've loved Liam for the longest time but he never showed any interest in me until tonight. I suppose that's because I was sleeping with his best friend."

"I will tell Blade your story. I'm sure he will see through the lies. He is like that," Aidan said.

"Thank you. You are as kind as you are beautiful." Selim rose. "Sleep now, I'll return tomorrow with more of your drink. You must have that one." She pointed to the one on the table when you wake up then I'll bring your medicine four hours apart."

Aidan rested against the headboard closing her eyes and dozing for a few minutes. She saw herself in a dirty rundown shack, retching but there was nothing in her stomach. She jumped startled by the dream. Fear for her life seized her, her body shaking.

Pushing her sweat-soaked hair away from her face, she looked over Blade's room, trying to rid herself of the dream. The fire danced merrily in the hearth and the platter of food still sat on the end table. She poured herself a small glass of wine, helping herself to piece of cheese and bread.

Hesitantly she ate what she picked out then finished with another strawberry and a few grapes. She felt fine. The wine she drank settled in her stomach and didn't move upwards. Inhaling a deep breath of relief, she smiled.

She rose, walking to the window to stare at the grounds below. The night was pitch-black, a strong wind blowing from the south. The weather was changing. It might well rain tomorrow. Just as Blade had hoped they reached the castle by the end of summer. She strode around the room, picking up various objects then setting them down.

"Who are the women who want to harm me?" Selim had not said and perhaps she didn't know. Selim's life could be in danger also. She'd have to tell Blade all she knew. Which was not much, she admitted ruefully.

She drifted back to the window, putting her hands on the ledge and peering into the blackness. People wandered the grounds below and she wished she could hear what was said. All she could make out were a jumble of words, nothing coherent.

The food on the platter beckoned to her. She'd been told not to eat too much. What had Selim said? Her body would tell her when to stop.

Right now, her stomach was yelling at her to eat something else.

She picked out a piece of meat, paring it with another slice of cheese. Sitting on a chair near the window, she ate it slowly, waiting between bites in order for her belly to tell her what she should do. All was quiet and she inhaled a deep breath of air.

"What are you doing up?"

She jumped startled by Blade's entrance as the door banged open. "I... You scared me." He left her speechless. "I, Selim came to visit me when you left and now, I'm just not as exhausted as I was before. I couldn't sleep without you beside me." She didn't want to tell him about the dream but knew she should.

"So sorry I frightened you." He pulled her into his arms, holding her close. "I see you are eating." He held her slightly away, staring into her eyes then kissed her gently, softly.

When he set her away, she lifted her glass of wine. "And a little wine. My outlook on life has changed suddenly for the better. I feel as if the world has tilted back to the way it was before I became pregnant. I'm no longer feeling as if everything is sideways."

"I'm glad." He sat on the bed, taking each shoe off. "You know this isn't a cure. You have to keep drinking the medicine Selim brings or your stomach will rebel again."

"She explained everything to me. Hopefully I only have a month or less to keep drinking it." She laughed, and kneeling on the bed hugged him from behind, pulling him down on top of her. "Kiss me."

He pulled back for a moment, "I should not." Yet his lips found hers, molded against hers, while he made it clear to Aidan how much he wanted her. When he finished, "That is all, Aidan. You have to get your rest and one drink of the medicine will not cure what ails you."

"Selim explained, only time will do that so do you want to wait another month or possibly more to make love to your wife or do you want to take advantage of my new found health as well as the pleasant fact I'm no longer going to throw up on you?" she asked, unfastening his shirt as she knelt in front of him.

"I will wait as long as it takes," he growled, holding her hands even as they sought to explore the hard planes of his chest. "I will not put your life in jeopardy to feed my base needs."

"You're just afraid I'll lose what I just ate while we..." She couldn't get the rest out as she started laughing. Falling onto her back, she couldn't stop giggling. He fell on top of her then cradling her in his arms he rolled on to his back. She lay against him her breasts pushing against his chest. "Ach lass, I'm not going to jeopardize everything Selim has done to help you, for a few seconds of sweet bliss. We don't know how long this will last. By morning you could be back in the same deplorable condition."

She pushed away from him, straddling him, her hair swirling around her in wild disarray. He ran his fingers through her hair, letting it fall around him. "Silken fire."

"What did you talk about with Hunter?" She moved off him then picked out a few pieces from the platter to eat. "For you." She put the grape on his lips and felt the sultry slide of his tongue against her fingers as he accepted her offering. Even though he refused to make love to her it seemed he couldn't resist teasing and tempting her.

He sat up, "Really nothing. There is little we can do unless they show their hand. We have put guards roaming the halls searching for anyone or anything that might not seem normal."

"You remember how Guy found his way into the McLellan keep?" she asked knowing he most likely did remember.

"An old man and part of a traveling band of performers. That's exactly the kind of perfidy we are looking for but I'm really more worried about my brother. It has not been Guy's way to want someone's leavings. You've clearly and thoroughly been made love to. The only way he'd continue to pursue you would be revenge. At least that is my hope."

"Selim told me there are women and maybe others inside already who seek to undermine her and probably us. They want to convince you her medicine is laced with poison." Aidan watched for his reaction to the words still waiting to tell him about the dream now doubting in its significance.

"It is easy enough to prove one way or another. From here on we will have her drink from the glass she gives you. If there is no poison, she will not have any difficulty drinking it."

"Other than it tastes awful and smells worse," Aidan said, scrunching up her nose to make her point. "But I agree whole heartedly. I wish we would have thought about it with the first drink."

"I did have some reason to be concerned, but Liam disavowed me of that fear. He loves her and hopes she will return that love."

"Selim says she has loved Liam for several years. He is much like you, kind and considerate. She is happy that you gave him permission to court her but she also said she wished he had not waited." It seemed to Aidan, Selim had been cursed by Blade's determination to wait until he considered her a woman grown.

"I believe we know who our true friends are and while I'm sure there are more than the handful we can acknowledge at the moment, we need to remain cautious."

She wavered unsure what to say. It was only a dream after all and couldn't possibly be a premonition. He'd want to know and she wondered if omission was a lie. Yet it bothered her enough to still be on her mind.

"Blade." She ran her hand along his chest. His hand settled over it stopping her.

"Another time, as much as I want you. If you are still feeling well tomorrow night and you've slept at least eight hours, I will do whatever you wish."

"I'll look forward to that but at the moment I think you should know about something that happened tonight." She looked away for an instant as if she could gain courage from waiting that tiny second. "I told you I wouldn't lie to you."

He brought the back of her hand to his lips and kissed her. "What is it? Tell me and the frown lines creasing your forehead will go away."

"And your lines will grow and you will cease to smile. I like your smile and the way it slants up right here." She touched the corner of his lips with a finger. "You haven't smiled in so long.

"I'm waiting and trying to be patient in the process. I can't promise not to frown although I'd like to promise that but the look on your face tells me you most likely spoke true."

"While you were downstairs, I had a dream." She readjusted her position on the bed.

"There is nothing to fear in a dream, unless you have premonitions. Have you ever had one   before?"

"No."

"Then tell me and you can forget about it. At this moment you have piqued my curiosity."

"It was just one thing and it's probably nothing."

"Again, tell me and I can put your fear to rest," Blade said.

"I was alone and in a rundown hut, retching and so sick, just like I have been. Tell me that's not possible."

"It's not possible because you will be protected and inside this keep until all of the danger has passed. I will make sure I double the guards on this room when I'm not with you and perhaps even when I am."

"So, you don't think the dream will come about." She shivered suddenly feeling a whisper of a chill passing through her. With the passage of time it seemed to grow more real.

"I won't let it happen," he said simply, running his hands up and down her back, stopping to massage her shoulders. "You've no need to worry."

His was a gesture meant to reassure and it did somewhat, but the vision had been so real and terrifying she still couldn't get it from the back of her mind, despite his words.

She settled into his arms, closing her eyes and hoping for sleep. Most of the night had passed and she knew sleep would be difficult to find. Next to her, Blade's even breathing gave her confidence.

She must have dozed. Another nightmare vivid and real entered into her. Once again, she was in a tiny hut. She was cold to the marrow of her bones but there were no flames in the fireplace. An old woman hovered over while watching her lose the meager contents of her stomach.

"No," she moaned, wishing the dream would vanish and leave her be.

"Ye are not welcome here. The MacPherson's have caused us nothing but starvation and pain over the years. Now you'll feel the same and know what it is to suffer."

When she looked up the old woman held ropes in her hand, and she realized it wasn't a woman but Blade's brother. She struggled, trying to block it with her arms. Instead she fell to her side. The force of the fall rendered her helpless for a few minutes. He tied her hands and feet then dragged her to a corner of the room.

Then the scene shifted and with strength she didn't know she possessed Aidan pushed herself from the floor and staggered from the dilapidated building. The skies opened, rain sluicing from the heavens above. She slipped in the mud, yet pushed herself up knowing she had to get away, anywhere. Where she was, she didn't know. How she got there she didn't know.

"Blade!" she cried out, terrified but knowing she had to wake up. She needed the dream to end.

"Little Fire, what is it?" He cradled her in his arms, rocking her and smoothing her hair.

"I had another dream." She sobbed in his arms, trembling, trying to fight the premonition that seemed very real.

"Was it the same one?"

"No, I was still in a tiny but your brother tied me up. I've never seen your brother but somehow, I know it was him. He said the MacPherson's had never given them anything but starvation and agony. That I would feel the same hunger and pain."

"Hush now, I will look into this and ask father what he knows about some of the clan who have not prospered. They only number a handful but they could be people who my brother has recruited. He tells lies and they believe everything he says. I've never seen anything like it. And perhaps in my father's failing health all the people have not been seen to properly."

"It is near morning and I pray you can sleep without the dreams. I'm going to have to rise soon. You should drink Selim's medicine now before I leave. I'll ring the bell to get her."

A few minutes later, a servant knocked on the door. "Send Selim here at once. If she is not in her chamber, check Liam's."

"Yes sir."

"What are you going to do now?" She put a hand on his arm, wishing she could keep him from leaving.

"Wait for Selim. When she is here, I'm going to leave her with you so you have someone to keep you company. Then I'm going to work to discover the truth about your dreams."

"Sir, it's Liam and Selim. What do you need?" The knock on the door was not unexpected but the two of them together was a bit of a surprise.

Blade opened for them. "One main thing," Blade began. "It's almost time for the second drink but Aidan has not slept but a few hours. She told me Selim's story. We both thought it prudent if Selim drank from each glass before Aidan does."

"You don't trust her?" Liam sounded outraged.

"It's not that." Aidan put a hand out to stop Blade from replying with more anger. "It is good that you came with her now there is a third witness. Blade trusts Selim with my life. What more can you ask for? Selim has said that there is a conspiracy to undermine her efforts. If we can prove no conspiracy to the people behind this tall tale, then we can put a stop to it. If she also drinks the medicine, isn't that proof it is not poisoned? Think about it."

"Perhaps, you make an excellent point," Liam finally acknowledged. "But only if Selim is willing."

"The only reason I have to refuse doing your bidding is the taste and the smell, but if all of you believe it will clear my name, I'm more than happy to do your bidding. There is nothing in the medicine that would harm anyone, not even a man although it has a woman's needs in mind."

Selim picked up the glass and drank then handed it to Liam who did the same.

"Good, then I've witnessed this as has Liam and Aidan. Go ahead and drink what is left."

Aidan inhaled a long breath of air trying to hold it inside her until she could drink the brew. She closed her nose and gulped the remainder then set it firmly on the table. "There," she said, "water please."

"We must get some water here. Have a tiny bit of wine. Selim, when you get a chance will you bring her a pitcher of water. She shouldn't be drinking wine all day and night."

The loud explosion shook the walls. "What was that?" Blade

looked at Aidan, seemingly horrified. "Stay here."

Liam rushed to the door, "Selim, stay with Aidan."

"Whatever you do, don't open the door," Blade told Aidan. "Put the bolt across. Unless Liam is here or myself don't let anyone inside no matter what they tell you. If they say we're dead or injured don't believe them. We aren't."

Aidan had never heard this side of him. The commander in him showed up replacing the softer gentler part of the man he always showed her. This man terrified her yet gave her confidence at the same time.

He opened the door to leave and looking back, "Promise me Aidan. Don't open the door for anyone except me or Liam."

She was nodding her head, horrified for him, for her. "Of course, I promise."

The two men were gone and Aidan found she was holding her breath while the outside lock turned. Selim seemed to take control, striding quickly to the door and bolting it from the inside.

"Now the only way into this room is through the window and that would be practically impossible to scale that wall," Selim said then it seemed she realized what she'd said. "You need not worry."

"You saw my face pale. I'm more worried about Blade and Liam than I am for us. It's too bad I'm too worked up to sleep. All I seem to be able to do is worry and wonder what will happen in the next moment then the next."

Time crept by as the sun began to rise slowly and the room lightened. The incessant knocking brought Aidan from her trance-like state and she rushed to the door ready to fling the bolt off.

"Stop." Selim's voice brought Aidan back to the reality of the moment. "Remember what they told us."

"Who is it?" Aidan asked, "and what message do you have."

"Blade is hurt and is asking for you. I'll take you to him. Just open the door and I'll lead the way."

"Where is he?" Aidan asked, realizing the man didn't identify himself and she knew Blade would not ask for her after what he told her before he left.

"I'll show you. Just come out."

"No. Blade told me to stay here no matter what." If this was a test, I just passed. "Tell me who you are and I'll pass on your message."

Behind the door she heard his swearing then nothing.

"How did Blade know that would happen?"

"He didn't know. Yet he was smart enough to foresee what might occur. And it was a good thing he gave instructions or we would have followed that man. My heart is in my throat I was so terrified," Selim said. "I do not like waiting and worrying."

"It was a good thing you were here. If not, I would probably be in that hut I dreamt about. Perhaps you stopped my dream from coming true." Aidan felt the sweat break out on her forehead.

"Sit, eat if you want and tell me about this dream of yours," Selim said, choosing something from the platter. "We really need some fresh food but I don't dare call for a servant after what just happened."

"More food? The MacPherson wants you to eat more." The call from the door surprised Aidan but then... She didn't think anything would surprise her anymore.

"We have plenty." She did want some water but knew this wasn't the time. She'd have to make the wine last.

The next explosion sent Aidan to the floor, a little dust from the rafters above sifting in the air. Selim clenched the bedpost to keep from falling. Aidan stood and rushed to the door, her heart pounding.

It seemed Selim anticipated her reaction. She reached the bolt at the same time. "No!"

~ * ~

"If we don't get her now, I don't know what will drive her out." The two men ran from the explosions, taking shelter behind some rocks waiting for the bomb to be discovered. "Guy will not be pleased now will Leod."

"Shouldn't we keep going? Don't know about you, but I don't want to get caught. The MacPherson will hang us for sure if he finds out what we've done and what was planned."

"Keep your bloody trap shut. Watch."

"Here it is." Liam put a hand out to keep Blade from walking into a trap. "See the debris and it's put a small hole in the wall."

"It wasn't meant to do damage just to draw us and the ladies out of the bedroom," Blade said, surveying the area.

"To get Aidan from the room. I can't help but think about her dreams and I pray she followed my instructions," Blade said, realizing he couldn't rush back to see despite the driving need to do just that.

"Selim has a level head. She will make sure Aidan stays where she is supposed to be," Liam said.

From behind the barrier the two men watched and waited. "We'll have to set our second bomb." Don't know if this, I'm frightened...terrified. We should leave now."

"If'n you don't want to get caught take off now," he whispered, watching as the other man left, running.

It didn't take more than a second for Liam to send a man after the garbled conversation. A few minutes later, his men drug the bomber into the area where Liam and Blade waited.

They watched as their men interrogated the bomber.

"Confessed to setting this bomb. Said there was another man and he's right over there. He's given up his co-conspirator to save his life. Says he has a wife and child and the men offered him more money than he could earn in five years."

Chapter Eight

Blade and Liam searched the grounds but failed to find any clues that would lead to Leod or Guy as the main source of the bombing. Another explosion, this time inside the castle, sent them running inside.

Blade wondered if they were pawns in a game of chess being played at his brother's amusement. Once inside they discovered the explosive device had been set close to his chamber but like the other one did little harm.

"I'm going to check on Aidan. Send someone up with water and more food. As soon as you take care of these matters come back. I'll see that Selim stays here with me and my wife." Blade sent Liam away knowing he would want to speak with Selim as soon as he could.

He knocked on the door, his heart thundering and anxious to see his wife. "Aidan, Selim it's me, Blade. You can open the door now."

He heard the bolt slide across the door then slowly open. "Blade!" Aidan wrapped her arms around him, pulling him close. "You're safe. I was so worried about you."

"I am safe. Did you have company when I was gone?" He strode into the room, holding her tightly against him, not wanting to let her go. "And so are you, thank God. I've never been so afraid for you." Well, perhaps he had. Her pregnancy had him terrified at every turn.

"Only because Selim stopped me before I could open the door. They said you were hurt and wanted me to come to you. We had two visitors."

"Well I'm thankful to Selim." He nodded her way.

"They tried to talk us into coming with them, and when I kept refusing, they turned from the door cursing. I don't like this. It reminds

179

me of the time when Guy tried to hurt Hunter. He did awful things and now he's back to torment and terrify us. Wish he'd go away forever."

He sat down with her, holding her on his lap, praying these complications would vanish. It didn't seem to him there had been a moment of normalcy since they handfasted over three months ago.

"Have you slept?" he asked her, lifting her chin so he could look into her eyes.

"A little but I don't want to have any more dreams. They horrified me." She closed her eyes for a moment. "I don't want to think about it."

"That's fair." He kissed her, held her head in his hands and deepened the kiss needing to taste her essence, breathe in her fears and vanquish them.

When he drew away, "I'm going to find my brother. Leod is not going to have any more power over us. This will end so we can find peace in our new home." He needed to leave Aidan to sleep but he also knew his clan would want to see her before the day was over. Courtesy demanded she have an introduction even if there was danger.

"I want harmony and I understand how important it is for your clan to know me. They won't trust me unless I move around them, talk to them," Aidan said softly, touching his chin. "I need to know your people."

"You need rest and that is more important," he said, bringing her head to settle on his chest. Wishing this situation could be different, but he'd known since he left to wed and bring Aidan home this would be waiting for them.

"No," she said, playing with the ties of his shirt. "No, rest right now is not as essential as other things."

He chuckled softly loving her small act of defiance. He'd always be able to count on her to speak her mind, at least he prayed that characteristic would stay part of here nature. "You dare defy your husband."

"I only speak the truth." She appeared smug and self-satisfied and he wanted to kiss her lips, mold them to his. "Someone who means everything to me made me promise to always tell the truth."

He let out a long heart felt sigh, understanding duty called to them both. "I see. So, when you disagree with me you are speaking only the truth." He rested his hand on top of hers, knowing if she continued touching him, he'd give in to what she seemed to be asking him for.

"I believe so." She pushed away and pausing, "I need to get out of this room before I go absolutely crazy. I'm willing to wait only so long for you to say yes. I need to leave just to see a different wall and if I can convince you that I need to breathe fresh air and feel the sun on my face, I know I will feel so much better."

"There is knowing the people then there is going crazy. Perhaps I can manage a short trip to the solar. You can meet father. He usually eats breakfast there before he puts on a brave front and roams the keep for a few minutes."

"I'd like to meet your father, the laird, unless he's already given the title to you," she said, pushing an arm's length away from him.

"Let me get this straight. You don't want to meet him if he's not the laird?" he asked, smiling at the look of horror on her face.

"Of course not." She stood even as he placed his hands on her waist to bring her back to his lap. Defying him again, she pushed his hands away then walked to the window.

He had a moment of apprehension and as she leaned forward a flashback of another time so long ago when she leaned out the window at the McLellan castle whirled in his brain. She might have fallen to her death that day if Eveleen had not pulled her inside. And he also realized she would make an easy target for anyone who wanted her dead.

"You shouldn't do that," he said, his voice tight, trying not to frighten her, yet moving as quickly as possible toward her.

She swirled quickly, her back against one corner of the window, "Why ever not?"

"Two reasons." He wasn't sure if he wanted to frighten her more.

She was tapping her toe, a stern expression on her face and he needed to laugh but the moment was far too dire for humor.

"What are they?" she demanded again, but she'd moved so she was no longer a target.

"I shouldn't have to explain to a grown adult that one could fall out the window," he said, his voice soft yet stern.

She turned a subtle shade of red as if she too remembered that time seven years ago. "I won't fall out now just as I wouldn't have fallen out then." She crossed her arms over her chest.

"You might have then, just as you could now. Accidents are known to happen."

She was walking toward him shaking her head slowly, "Nay, there is something else that concerns you. Out with it."

Suddenly an arrow whizzed by her shoulder. The weapon embedded in the floor near his feet. He thought his heart stopped at that second. He dove for her, sending her toppling to the ground.

"My God it was what had crossed my mind but I truly didn't believe it for a second. Are you   alright?" he asked as he pushed away from her and pulled her to her feet so they were not in line with the window.

"Only a bit bruised where I landed on the floor with your entire weight on top of me," she said, dusting off her skirts and trying, it seemed to Blade, to look indignant while he continued to rest on top of her. With his forearms he braced himself above her.

"I thought you liked this position, my position above you and between your long legs." He laughed despite the tiny projectile that had just entered their room.

"I do," she said, "if you kiss me and do all those other wonderful things you do with your mouth and your fingers."

"Ach lass, if I do what you're asking you won't get to meet my father anytime soon." He felt her hesitation and understood what they'd denied each other for quite a while.

"Then you must be the gentleman and let me up. Remember, I still need to dress."

"What if I don't want that?" He kissed her again, molding his mouth on hers and knowing he had to stop even while she opened for him, accepting a deeper intimacy than he'd been planning.

"I don't either but you were right about meeting my father and our clan. We will continue this tonight then you'll rest and I can do whatever you deem necessary." He trailed kisses down her neck, watching the evocative rise and fall of her breasts and longing to explore her more intimately than an almost chaste kiss allowed.

"Alright then, if you promise, but I need to freshen up a little. Maybe not a bath but a bit of water and a dress instead of this nightdress. I would like to look presentable."

"I see the dilemma."

"Do you think it's safe to stand up if there are arrows flying in window?"

He held out a hand to her to help her to her feet. "We will stay away from the windows and I will send someone out to investigate the surrounding area. All will be fine."

In the trunk they found a pale blue gown that had been quickly made for her in London to accommodate her expanding figure.

"Do you want to be my lady's maid?" She began to undress, seeming to understand what he needed but was not going to entice him further, at least not until tonight when they could have whatever time they craved.

She kept her back to him, when she could have easily seduced him and he wasn't sure how he felt about her sudden compliance to his statements about their lovemaking.

"If you promise to behave yourself," he told her, chuckling inside and realizing what a difficult thing that had always been for her.

She turned slightly looking over her shoulder and smiling. "I don't think I've ever behaved myself. Will you still want me if I change so drastically?"

He ignored her question. He loved her no matter how she acted. "Then I'll have to call for Selim who I'm sure is finding some measure of peace in Liam's arms. Do you want to take that away from her?"

"I want to find harmony and tranquility in your arms," she said, letting the nightdress slip to the floor and pool around her feet.

"I thought you wanted out of the room and to meet father." He loved watching her scramble for words but the site of her naked body sent more outrageous thoughts through him.

"Yes, you're right. I give up. Tonight, I'll try to have some small measure of patience. But I'll be in your arms and it will be so much easier."

He laughed and the lightheartedness felt good. After helping her dress and fix her hair he offered her his arm. "I think you'll like him, my father. He's a lot like David."

"Then I know I'll care for him."

Arm in arm they strolled down the hallways to the solar. Inside, "Father?"

The MacPherson turned, smiling at the pair. "Finally." He rose, "I get to meet my daughter-in-law. Over the years, I've heard so much about you. You realize you've been in my son's heart for ever so long. I wondered when he'd finally wed you."

"All good I hope." She slanted Blade a look that he didn't know how to interpret.

The older man rubbed his chin, "Well, I'm sure it was all true, much of what was said was out of frustration, at least that's what I'm guessing now. You're a very lovely lass and it's about time the two of you are wed. Sit and tell me all about yourself."

They sat down in chairs opposite the Lairds. "Thank you, but there is not a lot to tell."

"Then humor an old man. Why did you run all the way to Baltimore when everyone says you were always in love with my son? Was he so dastardly you had to flee?"

"I don't think you'd like that story." She looked at Blade who cleared his throat.

"Perhaps an abbreviated version," the Laird prompted.

"Would you like coffee or tea?" Blade asked in an attempt to divert the question even while he knew his father would never be distracted by something so lame.

"Tea and all I can say is that he managed to humiliate and embarrass me. I could have run home but I chose to go as far away from him as I was able. At the time, Baltimore seemed the right choice. I knew if I ever saw him again it was because he wanted to be with me. At least I hoped that."

The conversation stopped while servants brought in platters of oatmeal, tomatoes broiled with cheese on top. A rasher of bacon, tattie's and bangers along with sautéed mushrooms, then baked bean and eggs were set on tables.

She paled for a moment at the site of all the food and he prayed the medicine would continue its great work.

"Eat only what you want, Aidan." Blade warned knowing she felt politeness would require her to try something of everything.

"Of course, my dear," the Laird said. "My cook has out done himself today. I sent a message that I hoped Blade and his beautiful wife would come eat with me. Eat only what you want."

"Thank you." She looked to Blade for perhaps a bit of encouragement, "I've not been feeling well but the medicine Selim gave me has made me feel quite a bit better. Unfortunately, my stomach will not hold much these days.

"Blade has told me. You're pregnancy so far has not been an easy one." The Laird sipped his coffee gazing out the solar window seemingly lost in thought.

"Hoped you'd be here." Hunter strode into the room then poured himself a cup of coffee. "Wish I had time to eat some of this."

"Take the time," Blade said. "There is more than enough here. When we finish eating, I'll walk Aidan back to my chamber and we can talk about the bombs. Also, I need to know who in the clan feel as though they've been neglected. Then I want to take a ride through the village and outskirts. Talking to my clan is far too important to leave to chance."

"I'll ride with you," Hunter said, sitting down and dishing up a plate after Aidan and Blade had done the same.

"No, you need to stay here. I want to ride with Liam and get his take on the state of affairs. He knows this land as well as the clan." Blade's gut clenched once again when he mulled over everything he'd been told since arriving. While he hoped Leod would understand he could never inherit and leave, Blade knew his brother well enough to know that would never happen.

"Very well, my men and I will stay here until further notice. Everything so far is fine on McLellan land. Allura has sent a message for me to remain here as long as I'm needed." Hunter rose, his riding glove in his hand, looking a bit as if he wasn't too sure what was expected of him.

Blade inhaled a long deep breath, realizing there was still a great deal Hunter could do here. "An arrow found its way through a window in my solar this morning. I'm hard pressed to keep Aidan safe. She has a penchant for leaning out windows. You probably remember another time. I'd like any possible information on the perpetrator of this incident as well as the explosions that took place last night."

Hunter laughed slapping Blade on the back. "I do remember that day when you nearly died of fright before one of her sisters pulled her from certain death. I will have the best of your men ask questions and report back to me. The men who sided with your brother need to understand the repercussions. They will be dealt with harshly."

"I recall that day also and in that respect she hasn't changed. It isn't just about windows. It seems she searched for ways to throw herself in harm's way." Blade ran both hands through his hair. "Although I must admit, since she has known she carries our child, she has changed somewhat."

"Tell me you're not talking about me again," she said indignantly. "If it's the truth I suppose I can't complain over much. But you told me I'd grown up, married me because of it. So, don't spread rumors about me that no longer exist."

"I did lass, but you are still impetuous and wild. As you said you don't always behave." Blade realized this was not the place for this conversation when he watched her pale, yet he wanted Hunter and even his father to understand she needed to be watched.

"I'm tired." She rose. "Thank you for your kindness. I find that in my condition I need more sleep, sleep which I haven't had." She turned her gaze to him, implying her lack of rest was his fault. Well, in a way it was. Then she spoke to him. "I can see myself to our rooms."

Hunter rose, setting his nearly empty plate on a table. "I'll walk back with her. Perhaps she can shed some light on this escalating situation."

Blade didn't want her to leave him on this note but Liam strode into the solar and he was sure his friend would have news. "Make sure the lock is bolted from the inside." Then he tossed Hunter the key.

Aidan's fiery spirit surfaced. With her brows furrowed he felt as if her eyes shot daggers at him. He knew she wouldn't like his condescending words, but bloody hell he wanted her safe. She didn't say anything and perhaps that was for the best.

Blade stood, welcoming the newcomer and trying to push the thought of Aidan's fury from his mind even though he knew just how to channel her passion. "Another person to help eat this feast cook has worked so hard to prepare. It's good to see you this morning, Liam. Eat then join me downstairs in the main hall."

"Thank you, Sir." Liam dished up a plate then sitting down he ate while he seemed to be waiting for Blade to talk.

Blade watched as his father walked from the room, his back a little straighter and his strides a bit longer than when he arrived. He was alone with Liam and it was time they figured out how to rid the clan of Leod.

A few minutes passed as sunlight increased sending shaft of brightness inside. Blade closed his eyes thinking, trying to remember all the people who lived in the hills and on the outskirts.

They were more needy than those who lived close to the castle and in the village but he always believed they chose the independence and the freedom allotted them because of the distance.

"What's going through that head of yours," Liam asked after finishing the last bite of food.

"Aidan has had two dreams. I'm concerned about them and we need to focus our attention on discovering how much is truth and if they have been derived from the fears of the present."

"You think it's a premonition?" Liam asked, sounding incredulous. "Has she ever had the sight before?"

"Not that I know of and she denies having it now as well." Blade leaned forward, his arms on his legs. "But I don't want to forget what she saw when she slept. The dream could be important and it could lead to the capture of those who plot against the clan."

"Tell me,"

"She saw herself tied up..." Blade continued with the description of the dream, taking note of Liam's features when he mentioned the fact that the old man wanted her to starve and suffer as he had at the hands of the MacPhersons.

"This could be your brother putting falsehoods into the clan's minds. Many of the people are poor but we've always offered food and clothing to those in need," Liam said. "Anyone who lives in this land knows the MacPherson's would never allow anyone to starve."

"And they call it charity, refusing our help," Liam said bitterly. "Yet we have always allowed the men to repay it when they could. I wonder what words your brother is using to sway these people who have always trusted the word of the Laird."

"I want to talk to everyone. It might take a few days but it's necessary and I need you to ride with me. You've been the constant in their lives. They know you and will respect what you have to say, possibly more than me. I have to admit I've been away too much," Blade said.

"And Hunter will stay here?" Liam asked. "To make sure your brother cannot stir up trouble inside the keep."

"Yes, we can start as soon as I say goodbye to Aidan and tell her what we're doing. It's going to take a few days to accomplish this. Let's start in the south and work our way around the perimeter. I'll meet you in the stables."

He passed Hunter in the hallway who gave him back his key. At the door he knocked, "Aidan. Let me in and I'll tell you about our plan."

He heard the bolt slowly slide across. She'd let her hair down and now it fell softly around her shoulders. He pulled her into his arms, kissing her gently. The tiny sounds coming from her nearly had him pushing her into the bedroom and making love to her before he left.

"Ach, Aidan, you are so sweet. I want you lass in the most elemental ways. Be ready for me when I return. I mean to have you beneath me. Liam and I are going to ride the perimeter of our land and search for that tiny one room hut you dreamt about."

"Take care, please," she said, resting her head on his chest while he ran his hands up her back, enjoying the feel of her curves pressing against him.

"I will be home before the sun sets on the western horizon. I promise you and I need you more than I could ever put the need in words. Rest, sleep, take your medicine when Selim comes with it."

"I won't be locked in this room." Her hands fisted at her side he'd never seen her look so determined.

"If I lock it from the outside, you cannot get out." Bloody hell but he needed to keep her safe in this time of peril. Yet he didn't want her to feel a prisoner in her home.

"Would you rather have me shimmy out the window; the bed sheets tied together?" She looked defiant and adamant. "Don't you doubt it for one second that I won't try such a thing if you provoke me."

"It would take more bed sheets than there are in this room," he said softly while she turned her back on him. He placed his hands on her shoulders. "I will leave the door unlocked if you promise to bolt it and send word to Hunter before you step outside the door as I know you will."

"I understand the danger and your fears, mine too. I promise and perhaps Selim will choose to spend some time with me. But I would like to be outside farther than the solar. I need to breathe fresh air, feel the sun on my face."

"Stay inside the castle."

"You are keeping me a prisoner in my new home. You know that. I won't wander outside the gates. I understand the peril of that."

"Ach, lass, I ken it but only for a short time, only until we find my brother." He kissed her softly, "There will be more of this tonight."

He backed from the room and listened while she slid the bolt home, then quickly strode to the stables where Liam waited with two horses. He mounted and they headed toward the southernmost part of the clan's holdings.

~ * ~

Aidan woke and sitting up in bed she stretched, feeling refreshed for the first time in so long she couldn't remember. She rose from the bed, striding to the window even though she understood the potential danger. She couldn't resist the siren's call of the warm summer air and the bright rays slanting toward the earth. The sunshine and heat spoke to her and beckoned. Outside the sun was just descending from its zenith. She figured it must be a little after twelve, time enough to take a stroll around the grounds.

It was time for the medicine. Actually, it was a little past time.

Selim would be knocking at her door soon. She pulled the bell and two servants quickly arrived. "I'd like hot water for a bath and could you find Selim and send her here? Oh, and some fresh fruit, please."

"No need for that." Selim walked around the corner then into the chamber. "I've checked on you every half hour. I've your medicine and food although I heard about your feast in the solar this morning. How did you like the Laird?"

"He seems nice." She didn't know what to say. They'd exchanged so few words but she was sure when she got to know him, she'd like him. In many ways he was like his son, truthful and stoic yet an underlying humor always threatened.

Selim laughed softly. "He's a very nice and caring man. That's why all this trouble seems so absurd. He would never let anyone starve who was under his care. I knew Leod and he lies to get his way. There are some very stupid people who believe the falsehoods he spews. How could anyone be so stupid as to even consider blatant lies as the truth?"

"Even if the Laird was evil, this difficulty is caused by Blade's brother and the Laird most likely has nothing to do with it. No one starves on MacPherson land even visitors."

"Only that it seems in his sickness, he ignored some of the clan. And now that Leod wants to stir up trouble, it's easy to find those in need and pay them to deem in his rhetoric as true," Selim said, shrugging her shoulders as if the knowledge was given.

"Most highlanders don't want charity of any kind. And what Leod seems to be offering is not only a form of charity but disloyalty. Yet I truly believe it's the lies and half-truths that have people questioning the truth as they see it. Somehow he's instilled fear for themselves and their families into them."

"Perhaps these people are not part of the clan," Selim said, pausing before setting the platter of food on the table. "Perhaps they are disgruntled individuals Leod has found to pretend they are part of the MacPherson clan."

"Are we still talking about my dreams?" Aidan asked, wondering at all the scenarios presenting themselves.

"Yes and no, in some ways we are. If Leod has found anyone to help him, your dreams could become reality. You have to stay inside. You cannot become an easy mark."

"I don't intend to make it easy for an enemy to hurt me. Hunter will escort me outside and I do intend to get some fresh air and meet some of my people. I know firsthand how important that is." She smiled and understood the surprise on Selim's face.

"I don't think that is wise and I'm sure Blade will have something to say about it when he returns."

"Of course, he will, but I won't be intimidated and threatened by my husband no matter how well meaning he is. I'm the wife of the man who will become Laird. The people must meet me and learn to trust me," Aidan said, remembering all she and her sisters had done at the McLellan castle.

"It's just your safety..."

"Pshaw," she said waving her hand in the air and using her Aunty's favorite word to tell people it's not the right way to look at the situation. "It is so much more than that. I refuse to cower in my bedchamber when my presence is necessary to help rebuild what has been lost over the years. I truly don't know how to explain how I feel but I've grown up without responsibility, but watching others who have it. I ken what I must do."

"Of course, you are right. I don't understand the responsibilities you shoulder and I never will nor do I want to. I will stay close to your side and introduce you to whoever is about. Everyone will love you. I'm sure of that."

The knock on the door stopped their conversation. "The water is ready."

"My bath." Aidan smiled and watched as the steaming water was brought into the room. "I'll see you back here in about thirty minutes. Go ahead and see to whatever needs you have," she told Selim.

"Slide the bolt behind me and ring the bell when you are ready. Even though I protest your decision, I'll stand by your side and help in every way I can."

Aidan watched as Selim slipped from the room then did as was told. She slid the bolt across the door. Leaning against the wall, she sighed then inhaled a deep and long breath then another. She was terrified of her choices, understanding the danger in front of her but also realizing what was necessary. Blade would be angry. She didn't doubt that fact for one minute but she would find a way to calm his anger.

Straightening her shoulders, she walked slowly to the hot water waiting for her, shedding her clothes on the way. Steam rose from the liquid. She pulled her hair back and wrapped it around itself to secure it in a bun. Slipping into the water she closed her eyes, letting the liquid heat relieve her tense nerves.

Heat soothed sore muscles; muscles it didn't seem she'd used for such a long time. Yet the tension that had been so much a part of her for days and days was created the stress. When this was over, she craved to see Blade's land, her land now.

Closing her eyes, she relaxed. The scene in front of her was different. Blade had never before been part of her dreams, but there he was. He lay on the floor by the hearth in the hut but he was unconscious, bruised and bound hand and foot. She didn't know if he was alive or dead.

The man rose above her and she knew it was Leod a grisly smirk on his face. "You both get what you deserve." Then he vanished.

Her heart pounding desperately in her chest, she tried to rise but could not. Her hands and feet were tied. Struggling to get close to Blade, she needed to know if he lived. She pushed and shoved against the floor, wriggling to get close until she could place her face close to his. He was breathing but barely. A small groan emanated from his chest.

Aidan knew he was hardly alive and needed more help than she could give him but she was all he had. She couldn't give up, not now, not ever. Abruptly she sat up. Water splashing from the tub, her breathing labored and her heart heaving.

"No!" No one heard her cry and no one came to find out what caused her fear. Her body shook while she tried desperately to calm herself with deep breathing all the while imagining Blade's gentle reassuring touch. This could not be true, could not come to pass.

"Blade what has happened to you?" she whispered, hoping to feel his presence but there was nothing, no response. "What can I do to save you?"

"Nothing has happened to me," she answered for him. "I'm here to protect you. I don't need protection. I am fine, everything will be fine."

Tears slid down her cheeks, understanding how precious life was and that he might need help protecting himself but that was Liam's job. She had to get outside and gain some confidence from the clan. There would come a time she might indeed need their help.

"Get yourself together." If anything, she dreamt was true Blade would need her as well as his people. Quickly she finished washing then rose. Searching through her things she found a suitable dress, one she could fasten without help. Then making note of the fact she needed to hire a maid for herself, she grabbed something to eat from the platter.

When she was finished, she rang the bell, calling Selim then waited for her, still determined to find out what was really happening with the family. Yet she knew she couldn't do that but what she could do was make as many friends as possible. She could also listen and observe.

Selim's knock came within in seconds. Aidan slid the bolt again and let her inside. "Are you ready?" she asked, inhaling a breath she understood was for courage.

"If you are." Appearing hesitant, Selim stood aside as Aidan walked from the room, hoping her efforts here would help her husband, not make this difficult situation worse.

Silently they walked down the steps to the main room. Aidan felt the censure from her friend yet somehow knew Selim would stand by her side. She greeted people speaking to them in welcome but not knowing what to say other than small talk that would be meaningless.

Outside, Aidan sat on a bench near a garden redolent with the scent of summer flowers. She inhaled closing her eyes and wishing Blade was sitting beside her sharing the moment and realizing he could be lying in a dirty hut somewhere bound hand and foot. A shiver swept up her spine and she fought back the sudden onslaught of tears.

"Hello."

"What. Oh, excuse me I was lost in thought." Aidan held her hand out in acknowledgment of the young woman standing in front of her. "Who are you? What can I do for you?"

Without answering, the young woman accepted the greeting and held Aidan's hand in hers, seeming to take all of Aidan's soul inside herself.

Her eyes closed for a moment and when she opened them, "You are with child. I've heard the rumors. Congratulations. It is a boy who will look just like his father," the woman said.

"How do you know that?" Aidan was taken aback by the woman's statement sure she made guesses just to unnerve her.

"I have the sight as do you. At least you have it where the MacPherson is concerned." She hesitated, "and of course yourself. What you've dreamed will come true and there is nothing you can do to change that."

"How do you know?" Aidan withdrew her hand, leery of the newcomer and not sure exactly what she should believe. "I would have some proof of what you're telling me."

"You know as well as I do there is no proof."

"Then I cannot put much value on your words," Aidan said indignantly, wishing she had not received confirmation of her worst fears.

"Ah, I see you are suspicious as well you should be. Know that you will also have a girl child. Not now but in the future. Your husband will be enamored of the wee babe just as he is of you."

"Why is that?" Even though she'd seldom seen Blade, if ever, with children she knew he would love their children with all his heart.

"Because your girl child will look just like you." The woman smiled softly, her features changing as she spoke.

"If you know so much, where is my husband now?"

She hesitated looking out the gates and to the south. "You are skeptical as well you should be. I wouldn't have it any other way. Your husband is safe now and on his way home to you. He is, however, hoping to find you barred in the solar and safe. I fear he will not."

"I'm not sure I believe anything you've told me." She looked to the gates as if he would come barreling in as they spoke, but he did not. Relaxing a moment, she then turned her attention back to the woman.

"Of course, skepticism is natural. You must take care. I spoke too quickly before. All of your dreams have a chance to come true. It all depends upon your actions. One's destiny can always be changed."

"You want me to stay locked in my rooms just as my husband wants." Fury and indignation flushed through her body until she was shaking.

The woman placed her hand on her shoulder and the anger dissipated, vanishing as if it had never been. "No, I don't wish that. It is your husband who should lock himself away."

"You're telling me Blade is in danger." She tried to push away the memories of the dream. She could not. This woman confirmed the truth of her worst nightmares. She had hoped it was false and she also knew he would not cave-in to her fears. He would not stay put because of a dream.

"More so than you, but you both will be challenged soon and it will be up to you how this turns out. You must be brave and courageous beyond your wildest imagination." The woman turned and Aidan watched her and before she strode from the keep. She turned to say, "His life is in your hands."

"I'm sorry you had to hear that," Selim said, stepping beside Aidan. "I should have been here to shoo this liar away."

"I'm not. Knowledge gives a person power and foresight. I will need that in the days to come."

"I will take my leave then." The woman turned then seemed to vanish in the milling people of the keep.

"Milady." A woman with a small baby curtsied in front of her. "I hope all is well with you and your husband."

"Thank you, may I hold..." Aidan looked to the woman for an answer. It seemed the lady knew what she was asking.

"Him, of course milady." The woman handed the child to Aidan as if she'd known her forever. "My husband used to play with Blade and Liam. They are of the same age and unbeknownst to their fathers they roamed all of the countryside. They were little hellions if even one of the stories is true."

"And all of them are friends? I assume," Aidan asked, rocking the child and praying the little lad wouldn't begin to cry.

"My husband stands by yours even as we speak. MacPherson took my husband, Liam and three others with him today. There is no need for fear. They will all return safely."

"Then I'm sure they will all protect each other. I will try not to worry over much." Aidan tried to reassure herself even though her hands had begun to shake. Did this lady also have the sight?

"As they have done for at least twenty-five years," the woman said.

"How old is the child?" Aidan asked as she handed the babe to the waiting mother.

"Six months and he is beginning to sit. He is so funny when he tries to push himself along the floor. He looks like a little worm, squirming along."

"He is adorable," Aidan said graciously yet remembering at the same time her dream and how she'd done the same thing when she tried to reach Blade.

Thundering hooves caught their attention. Aidan's breath jammed in her throat when she saw Blade ride through the gates. When his gaze met hers, she let out a tiny, yet terrified shriek.

Picking up her skirts, she turned and ran. She didn't know why she ran understanding all too- well he would catch her. Standing her ground and explaining her actions would have been the most prudent form of action. While she raced toward the front doors, she prayed for time and that he would stable his horse before he came after her.

Yet she knew he would not.

And she was right.

"Liam, take care of my horse."

She didn't have to see him. In her imagination she understood he was leaping from his horse and racing after her. Standing her ground was still an option as was making it up the steps and barring the door before he caught her.

Seconds turned to minutes and still she did not feel his hands upon her body. Her breathing became labored. She was not used to running and had so little food and sleep in the last months, she knew she would not be able to run all the way to their solar.

He would catch her.

Then what?

She stopped bent over at the waist, heaving and trying to suck air into her lungs when she felt his hands upon her. He swept her into his arms then over his shoulder.

"You little fool," he growled.

"No more than you," she whispered, struggling for air, his shoulder pushing into her belly. "You are the one in danger, not me."

"You could have been killed." His voice changed slightly but still held a wealth of anger.

"No more than you."

Then it seemed he had second thoughts. He brought her from his shoulder into his arms where she looked into the cold steel of his eyes. It seemed he was more concerned for her than angry. She supposed he wasn't used to defiance from his wife. Yet he'd known from the first she was not a person to take orders. She had told him so.

Taking the steps two at a time only a few minutes passed before he opened the door and kicked it shut before sliding the bolt home. He strode into the bedroom, his strides long and sure before he placed her on the bed.

"Stay there."

Her mind raced searching for a way to diffuse his anger. Quickly she unfastened her dress and let it slip around her hips then swept her underclothes from her body. Now she sat on the bed naked and waiting for him, trying to smile. It seemed she had no need to hurry. She heard him in the other room, pacing and swearing.

A slow smile crossed her face. She rose from the bed, naked, and walked until she stood framed in the doorway. When he noticed the movement, her hands rose to undo her hair and let it fall around her shoulders.

"You think to seduce my anger away." He walked toward her, stopping inches from her his hands clenching and unclenching.

"I have no other way to change your feelings, so yes. I would like to seduce you but you knew that when you left this morning and when you went to bed with me last night. My yearnings for you have not changed."

"Seduction will not change my mind and will not cease my fear for you." He picked up a long strand of hair before letting it sift through his fingers. When his gaze touched hers, he looked at her with longing and indecision she'd never seen before.

"I never thought it would." She turned away from him walking to the bed where she sat down again. Her heart raced and she tried to keep her breathing even, waiting for him to come to her. She prayed he would.

"I should turn you over my knee."

"But you won't hurt me, never will. So that is not an option for you, for us." Her confidence wavered when he threatened her.

"Bloody hell." He ran his hands through his hair. "Why must you be so obstinate and willful?"

"You wouldn't have married me if I was different, complacent. I excite you and you want me even now, even while you search for some way to teach me some valuable lesson I won't learn at the expense of my freedom. I promise you that."

He turned away again, and she heard him muttering under his breath but she couldn't make out the exact words. She supposed he cursed.

She didn't know if she should go to him or wait but she was beginning to chill, goose bumps forming on her arms. Then he strode into the room, two glasses of wine in hand. When he reached her, he handed her one and set the other on the table.

"You're cold."

She nodded, swallowing the lump in her throat but unable to speak. For several seconds he watched her then turned away only to return with the platter of leftover food.

"I was shocked to see you in the courtyard. Truly, I believed you would stay here but now I understand you will do as you please despite my wishes. I'll have to find a way to curb your impulsiveness. Perhaps I should bind you to the bed so you would always be here and ready for me."

She ignored his comment not believing for a second he would be so cruel. "I told you I would tie sheets together and scale the wall if you locked me in." She wanted to speak of anything else, but it seemed Blade did not.

He sipped his wine seeming to study her, his hand now resting on her leg, tracing lazy circles seducing her when she meant to do the same to him.

"Have some wine. It will relax you." His hand moved higher nearly to the apex of her thighs then lower again.

"I don't want to relax." She sipped but set the glass on the table deciding she would not let him intimidate her. They both wanted the same thing. Becoming the aggressor, she rose on her knees, taking his glass from his hand to place it on the table beside hers.

Her hands rose to his chest before she pulled the fabric of his shirt from his buckskins. When he lifted his arms she tried to tug it off. In her efforts her breast touched his naked body. A tiny mew filled her throat.

When the cloth was finally off and tossed to the floor, he pulled her into his arms. "I only seek to keep you alive."

"I crave the same thing for you." Her fingers fumbled with the fastening of his britches.

Gently he pushed her back on the bed, his legs straddling her. "But you have no understanding of the danger that waits outside these walls."

"And neither do you." She ran her finger down the middle of his chest to just above his arousal, smiling. "I had another dream and I was told by a young woman that I have the sight." Her fingers closed around him, teasing him yet hoping he wouldn't wait to ask questions. She needed him more than she needed her next breath.

He sat, ignoring her for a moment to get rid of his boots before kicking his pants to the floor. "It seems I've waited so long to love my wife again. You're feeling well?"

She ran her hands up his chest, trying to touch him everywhere, even while she spread her legs so he could come inside.

The knock on the door surprised her but it seemed he expected it. "Cover yourself," he said, then naked, strode to the door and opened it.

She had only moments to wrap a blanket around her. Men entered with water it seemed for his bath.

"Blade?" She could barely breathe.

When they finished filling the tub and left, he turned to her. "It is always the custom to bring hot water for a bath when I return from a mission. Care to join me?"

"We won't fit and I'm not sure I want to take a bath with a man who is angry with me." She watched him slip into the water his head and arms resting on the rim, his eyes closed.

"I'm not angry with you, Little Fire, just frustrated, in fear for your life, terrified I might lose you." He sat up. "Should I go on?"

"What makes you think I don't feel the same about you when you leave with only a few men? And I have dreams where you are unconscious, bound hand and foot and breathing so silently one would never know there is breath in your body?"

It seemed he ignored her. She walked to him then, once again trying to take charge of the situation she'd created. The bath was his doing though. She picked up a sponge. "I'll wash your back."

She soaped it then ran the sponge the length of his back as he leaned forward. "My front?" He slanted her a wicked smile.

"I thought you would never ask." She tilted her head sideways and ran the sponge across his chest then lower, until he stopped her.

"Unless you want to join me in here, we will wait until I can give you pleasure too."

"Truly, I don't think we both will fit. You're so big and..." She looked at him pursing her lips then smiling suddenly realizing how he interpreted her words.

He ducked under, soaping his hair before picking up the bucket with the rinse water. He shook his head, droplets spiraling around him and landing on her. His hands wrapped around her waist and suddenly she found herself in the water her legs straddling him. "I thought I already convinced you that I would fit."

"Blade!"

"Ride me, Little Fire."

She understood what he wanted but her legs were cramped with little room. While she tried to take him inside her, "This isn't going to work. I told you there is not enough room for the two of us."

"I'm getting a larger tub," he muttered as he rose from the bath. Holding her in his arms, he strode to the bed.

"Not while we are soaking wet. I don't want to be left with a wet bed when you leave me to do whatever you do downstairs." He must have heard the demand in her voice.

He stopped and while still holding her it seemed he looked for the bath sheets. He set her down and wrapped one around her while he found a second one and dried himself off then he set his attentions to drying her.

"Now?" His lips slanted into a soul-endearing smile.

"Now."

"Tell me about the dream."

"Later." She turned her back to him, her arms crossed in front of her, furious with him and at the same time needing him desperately.

~ * ~

Leod stood in a small, dilapidated hut on the western perimeter of MacPherson land. His two loyal men stood at his side. He knew this was his last chance for revenge and he also had second thoughts. If he left now, he could make a new life for himself in another country. Yet from the depth of his soul and with every breath, he craved revenge. The desire was so intense he would give his life for that one sweet moment.

"Are we ready to proceed?" one man asked. Draping his shoulder was a long coil of rope.

"We must be ready and very careful. Both Liam and my brother are experienced soldiers. They will not be easily surprised." Leod spoke as a chill of foreboding swept down his spine. His jaw twitching, he rubbed his chin in hopes of stopping the telltale sign of his fear.

"If we drop from the trees, they will be taken by surprise," the other man said, grinning and seeming to anticipate the upcoming confrontation. "We will have to lure them to the right spot."

"And if we don't, the fight will be over before it has even begun," Leod said, wishing yet knowing wishes didn't make things happen. The men with him were ruthless and deadly but they were thugs not trained fighters like Liam and his brother.

"Trust me your lordship. That won't happen." His sneering words didn't go unnoticed by Leod.

With a long deep breath driving his courage, "They should be nearby sometime before noon. We need to be prepared and ready. Don't take anything for granted," Leod said, pleased with himself as he looked around the room. Blade would be tied and unable to reach the food and drink he would leave on the hearth. Of course Blade had to survive the beating, and he was going to see to it personally.

"Ah, after what you've planned this will be easy. We'll have him bound and gagged for you before you can blink. Then ye can do whatever your heart desires. I take it you mean to beat him nearly to death."

"I don't want Liam hurt just rendered unconscious. I want him alive so he can lead the Laird's men to this spot." He understood now that he wouldn't inherit, understood too that even if he got rid of Aidan and the brat growing inside her none of this would be his. It wouldn't be Blade's either.

"But not too soon. MacPherson needs to die before he's found." The man stroked the rope as if it was his lover.

"Not too soon." Leod repeated thoughtfully, "However I do want to enjoy my brother's pain. The only thing that would make all this sweeter is if his wife found him and died here with her lover—the brat too. If that were to happen, there would be no true MacPherson heir," Leod said, smiling, knowing no matter what happened to him he would have that pleasure to hold in the dark recesses of his mind.

"Too bad Guy backed out of the scheme. If Guy had stayed loyal, he would have found a way to bring Aidan here. He could have had her. The task would not have been difficult. Her impetuous nature would have made it easy to lure her to this spot. All he would have had to do was send a message about her husband and his possible demise."

"So you promised us one thousand pounds?"

"Two thousand if it goes off without a hitch. I want my brother dead. You can bring me proof in a week and I'll pay you then." Fool, he didn't have one thousand pounds let alone two. In a week he'd be on a ship bound for the States. He meant to try his hand at a business in Baltimore.

"Two thousand? I can build a new home for my family and buy crops to plant and so much more."

"If you spend your money all at once the MacPherson will see and be suspicious. No, you need to be smart and wait to spend the money you've earned. Otherwise you might find yourself in the dungeon waiting for the hanging I'm sure my father will order."

"I understand. I'll be careful."

"Now all we have to do is wait for my brother and his armed guard to arrive. Get your men in place. The sun is higher on the horizon as we speak."

The man turned striding from the room and calling orders. Leod rubbed his hands together, anticipating this last meeting.

"Ah, but it's only an hour or less before Blade is lying on this floor." Leod spoke to himself in anticipation. He inhaled deeply closing his eyes for a moment, remembering all the things Blade did to him while they were children.

This all was Blade's fault.

Chapter Nine

"It's later now, Little Fire. The sun has risen and I'll have to leave in an hour or so." Blade didn't want to believe these dreams might have some truth to them. He put the thoughts from his mind then unable to help himself, he trailed kisses down the back of her neck and across her shoulders.

They lay spooned together, his hand cupping her breast, enjoying the way his touch brought her to instant arousal and wishing he could spend the morning enjoying her luscious curves and delicate softness.

"Only if you'll listen to me and heed what the dream is trying to tell you." She snuggled against him, sighing softly. "I need you to come back to me and I'm tired of worrying about you. Don't like agonizing over your safety."

"You of all people should know I don't take stock in dreams. They can mean anything." He wasn't sure how he felt at the moment, anger, fear, frustration. He had to find the people who joined with Leod in order to prove Aidan wrong. The MacPhersons always gave aide to the people of their clan who required it. This claim was preposterous. His lips traveled down the length of her spine then back.

"Neither did I until recently. Blade..."

"Hmm..." He pulled the tips of her nipples to hard peaks while he slowly pushed into her. "You're so sweet, delicious, delectable."

She gasped for air, moving to take him deeper inside. "Did you or did you not want me to tell   you?" she asked, her head pressing against his chest while her nails dug into his arms.

"Later," he told her, his hands exploring more intimately, massaging the tiny bud that would give her the most pleasure.

A few more minutes spent and she climaxed in his arms while he spilled his seed inside her. Now, he held her closely wishing he didn't have to leave her, praying she would stay safe in his absence.

She turned over, rising slightly above him. "Now?" she asked, her lashes falling across her cheeks for a second. Her eyes were crystal clear and most beautiful shade of blue.

The tips of her breast rested on his chest. He closed his eyes trying for the willpower to keep his hands to himself. "Yes."

He stood, walking to the window, gazing out at the beautiful summer day. The season would change to fall soon. Today was one he would like to spend with his wife. Instead of searching the countryside for his enemies he should take her on a picnic and show her the places he loved in his youth.

"Are you hungry?" He turned then rummaging through his things for a clean pair of pants. He slipped them on then found a shirt before pulling on his boots. "I am."

"I could eat." She sat in the bed sheets around her waist, her hair falling around her, covering most of her, beautiful pink buds peeking out between her wondrous red hair.

"Should I call for your medicine?" he asked, walking into the main room. He didn't wait for an answer but rang the bell. It seemed his needs had been anticipated. Selim was almost instantly at the door with food and water as well as the medicine.

When he returned he found Aidan had donned one of the filmy negligees she'd been given before their wedding. It was the first time she'd worn one and he could see the small baby bump. As she'd told him before, he never gave her a chance to put anything on when he wanted to make love. Single minded in his need, he craved her naked. Now perhaps he thought he should give this option a second chance.

"Here it is." Selim strode into the room with the drink, sipping it before handing it to Aidan.

Aidan set it on the table. "I'm going to drink this later after I eat so it doesn't ruin my food."

Blade brought the platter into the room and set it on the bed. She picked at the assortment Selim had gathered for them. "You really don't want to know about the dream."

"Yes and no," he told her, realizing the less he knew the better he would feel, but he also understood she needed to tell him.

"Which is it?" Her eyes were unwaveringly focused on him.

"You should tell me." He was surprised at the relief he seemed to see sweeping through her.

"Please take grave care today. I saw things in my dreams that shouldn't ever become reality."

"I always do, take care but I see now that you're sincerely worried about me. Tell my why." He never thought a woman, let alone his wife would be so very concerned about his wellbeing. It seemed his heartbeat changed, his soul filled with something he couldn't define.

"I saw you on the floor of the hut." She looked down closing her eyes as if in agony.

"The same hut you were in the first two dreams?" he asked, not having a good feeling about this, suddenly needing to learn more.

"I think so. It was hard to tell but you were unconscious, nearly dead, scarcely breathing. He bound you hand and foot. Your face was bruised and swollen. At first I thought you were dead."

"And were you there, in the hut with me?" he asked.

She bit her lip. She didn't have to say the words he knew the truth.

"I was and I don't know why."

"Leod or Guy must have kidnapped you." He sat down, taking her hands in his. "I ken you would never leave the castle without me or without some kind of protection. Were you also bound?"

"I was but unlike you I was awake and I wasn't hurt. Leod told me he meant to leave us in the shack. He wanted both of us to die, suffering in the process. All I remember after that moment was that I wasn't about to let the events unfold the way he claimed they would but what I've just told you is all I know. There was no more dream."

He brought her hands to his lips and kissed them gently. "This will not come to pass. I promise you with all my heart and soul. Even if it does, I will save you. So you have nothing to worry about." Even to himself he sounded arrogant and too sure of events he might not have any control over.

He watched her struggle with the next words, then said, "In my dream I save you."

"That is hardly possible. You're but a slip of little girl. How could you do such a feat?" He thought her statement ludicrous.

"Woman." The one word held an angry tone. "I'm a woman."

"Aye, lass you are, very much so." He sighed long and deep, remembering their night of lovemaking, then, gazing into her eyes hoping to convince her all would be fine, "I don't want to fight with you or banter over the truth or untruth of your dreams. I swear to you that I'll take every caution. I just wish you'd see how all this transpires so I could be prepared for my brother's perfidy," he said, slowly beginning to take her words as possibility.

"You believe me?"

"Yes, but more so, if I was the one doing the rescuing." He did believe parts of what she told him but not all. He would pass this on to Liam and listen to what his friend thought.

"You cannot conceive that you might need help," she stated, seeming to watch for some form of affirmation from him.

"You should eat more food." He rested his hand on her belly, hoping to feel the child. "Your little baby bump is growing. I find this all very fascinating and having a difficult time waiting to see our child." He bent to kiss her belly. "I really do need to leave so I can return to you."

"Will you still want me when I'm fat and can hardly walk?" she asked him, seeming to grimace at the thought.

He roared with laughter, stopping to give her a gentle kiss on the cheek. "Of course but pregnant is not the same as fat. I want you because of who you are not your size. I believe this pregnancy makes you even more desirable and beautiful. Now that you are no longer sick all the time there is an undeniable glow about you."

For a moment she seemed to watch her hands then she looked at him her eyes filled with moisture. "I suppose you said what I wanted to hear."

He needed to keep her tears as well as her fears at bay and wanted her insecurities to turn to confidence. "It's the god's honest truth. You are the most beautiful woman I've ever known."

"And you've known a lot of women." She laughed softly still looking insecure, her eye wide pools of blue.

"This all true and we both comprehend the reasons why." He didn't want to defend himself yet she did need to admit once more how young she was when he first encountered her.

"Understanding doesn't always make it easier and doesn't change the jealousy I feel every time I think about you with someone else."

"I could not change your age and immaturity any easier than I can change anything else in the past. What we can change is the future as well as make the most of the time we have together in the present."

"I forgive you." She smiled then, sending a bolt of heat to his heart and once again tempting him to put off his mission a little longer.

"Now Little Fire, I really should find Liam and the other men. If I'm to be back before sunset, we need to be on our way. At the most I'll be gone only two more days. If we are lucky today, we will find the man who believes we've starved his family and any others if they exist."

"Or you'll meet up with your brother. I believe he's behind this and he won't stop until you're dead even though he must know he will never inherit. Why can't he just go away and leave us alone?"

"I hope to avoid Leod but if I find him he'll be dealt with accordingly and brought back to the castle for justice," he said.

She was angry again and there was nothing he could do to change that. The critical truth was important. Aidan wasn't a man. What she was telling him simply wasn't possible in the scope of what he understood to be true. She was small and fragile and most of all, she needed his protection not the other way around.

"If I'm late tonight or tomorrow or the next do not leave the keep to find me. Promise. I need your word." He knew his voice assumed a hard edge but he needed her to understand he could take care of himself. "Liam and I will take every precaution and there is no reason to believe my brother is still in the vicinity. No one has reported seeing him. If he has an ounce of common sense, he has left the country."

"Truly, I don't want to defy you, but I cannot give you my word in this matter. Just being late will not have me running after you, but if there is any circumstance that warrants more of a concern for your life, I will do what I deem necessary and prudent. A promise of this nature is not possible." She smoothed her hair back, winding it into a bun. "I did also promise you I wouldn't lie to you."

Once again frustrations filled him, the sigh emanating was long and deep but the helplessness he felt for his wife and child chilled him to the bone. He needed to find a way to change her mind but knew that path was a long and winding one and he didn't have time to explore it now. "I don't understand nor do I accept what you say. It is not just your life you must protect but that of our child. Do not do anything foolish."

He watched her grimace as if soaking in the truth of his words but then her back stiffened in what he was coming to understand as defiance and he knew nothing he said had been accepted by her. In many ways she was much like him, she thought of herself as immortal. Yet throughout his career as a mercenary he'd learned no one lived forever. Now that he had a wife and a child on the way, he wanted to find the peace in life he'd never yearned for before.

"I would never harm my child." Her words hit him deep in his heart sending a shiver of fear sweeping through his veins. "But I know I cannot live without you. If something were to happen..."

"Our child." He needed to make it clear to her he had a say in his son's future. And he was sure she carried a boy. He paused a moment in thought. In a dream he'd seen a dark haired little boy running through the halls of the keep. Perhaps there was more to her dreams than he was willing to believe. He certainly put a lot of stock in his dream.

"This argument is about nothing that has yet come to pass. I see no reason for this fear about a future we truly cannot foresee. Until my dreams felt so real, I took no credence in those who said they had the sight. We must trust in ourselves and the decisions we make as well as the insights into the future god has given us."

"You are trying to take my fears away from you and our child. I appreciate your efforts but as time passes I begin to understand you better each day. I only wish I'd spent more time with you as a young woman instead of trying to avoid you and your machinations all those years. I believe if I had seen you more often, spoken with you, I would understand you better and living with you would be easier."

Her mouth fell open in what he could only interpret as astonishment. "I like that idea but I fear that avoidance was the best choice for you even though I tried desperately to catch your attention. Now we have a life with no regrets unless this situation with your brother escalates. When this is over, we'll live a long happy life."

"I ken what you are saying and I wish we could continue this conversation but I must find Liam and explore the western part of our territory. Already I've tarried too long." He left her and finished dressing then pulled her into his arms for a long slow kiss.

"Please take care," she whispered, while he left the room then waited for her to bolt the door.

Selim appeared. "I will stay by her side. If we remain in the room which I'm sure we will not, I will keep the door bolted."

"Make sure she acts with prudence." He walked away with a heavy heart. His thoughts swirling around all that she told him.

"I always act with prudence." He heard before he was too far away from his chambers.

In the stables Liam waited for him, both horses saddled his other men were also mounted and ready to defend him at any cost. He motioned for the men to gather around him.

"We need to be extra careful. I've heard there might be an ambush. Stay alert and on edge. I don't always believe in premonitions or dreams but these seem all too real to put aside as fantasy."

"Mount up!" Liam called out, his horse sidestepping seemingly eager to be on his way.

The men rode through the gates, Blade and Liam in the lead, side by side. "If anything happens to me, don't let Aidan try to find me. She and the babe must stay safe. My life means nothing if my wife and child die." Blade thought on his words. He'd never expected to care for anyone as much, and he thought on her words as well. *I cannot live without you.*

She would have to carry on for their child's sake, if anything happened to him.

"If you can't stop her, I don't see how I can but I will promise to do everything possible to that end." Liam pushed his mount a bit harder and Blade followed suit.

"Perhaps Selim knows of a potion that would work to that end."

"Selim would never do anything like that." Liam sounded horrified.

"Of course she wouldn't. I was just tossing out an idea." He gritted his teeth together, frustration eating at him.

"Perhaps you should not toss out ideas even around me. Times for our clan are not good right now. No one knows who they can trust."

"I left word with the stable master that we decided to head east instead of west today. Changing our route might prove to keep us both safe. On a better note at least for you, Aidan never saw you in the dream."

Liam laughed, gazing hard at him his lips thinned. "Which means I'm either dead or alive somewhere or perhaps even to unimportant to your wife to play a role in her dreams."

"We cannot speak of our destinations to anyone. I don't trust everyone in the clan. The only way this dream of hers happens is if someone is giving up our plans to Leod." Blade didn't want to think along those lines, but his brother lived here all his life. Leod did not go off to fight wars that had nothing to do with Scotland, deserting the clan. His brother would have friends, people who would help if asked.

"I won't but there is always gossip and rumors. Everyone knows you were planning on searching out the land and they would use common sense to ferret out the destinations."

"I'm sure of it. Did anyone know of our change of plans this morning beside you and me?" Last evening they decided to make the changes, hoping to cause confusion between anyone siding with his brother.

"I've told no one."

"Not even Selim?" he asked, surprised even though he'd said nothing to Aidan. The conversation had not presented itself."

"Not even Selim," Liam said.

The morning wore on, large clouds accumulated in the hills. Blade hoped the thunderstorm brewing in the north would not materialize before they returned home. Only a few hours had passed and he missed Aidan, missed watching the way her eyes danced and sparkled when her thoughts strayed to mischief. The seer had told her they would have a boy then a girl. If that girl was anything like his Little Fire, he'd have his hands full, protecting her from herself.

Good lord but he looked forward to it.

With thoughts of his children who weren't even born yet swirling in his head. He did precisely what he warned everyone about. The yell caught him by surprise and before he had time to react, he was on the ground. He felt the impact to his head as he heard the crack then nothing.

For a few seconds he was in a semi-conscious state. He saw the battle around him and as he tried to pull himself to his feet, staggering slightly he was hit in the back. Pain rushed through him and when he turned to defend himself, he saw, "Leod."

"Blade." The smirk ripped through his heart.

Helplessly he watched as his brother pummeled his face and chest with a board. Someone hit the back of his knees from behind. He crumpled to the ground while his brother hit him again and again relentlessly pummeling his face and chest. Blood flowed down his face while his eyes began to swell.

On the ground, Leod kicked him in the chest and while he tried to curl into a ball, his brother's foot found his face. Truly Leod had one purpose, just as Aidan had told him, to kill him or perhaps just render him helpless so he could watch him die.

"He's powerless now," Leod spoke to his men then kneeling down so he could spit in his face. "Not such a big hero now are you big brother?"

"What now?" one of Leod's men asked.

"Leave Liam where he is. He'll wake up in a few hours and if we have his horse, he'll have to walk back to the castle. No one will find Blade before he dies. Where is Blade's horse?" Blade heard Leod say before darkness descended and the pain vanished.

"Gone."

In the tiny hut, Leod stood over him. Just as Aidan's dreams foretold, he was lying on the dirty floor his hands bound behind his back and his feet also bound. Leod removed the gag but there was nothing Blade wanted or needed to say to the ugly man he once called brother. He wondered if he'd ever had a good thought about this man.

Blade strained to stifle the groan racing through him when he endeavored to sit up. When Leod heard the small sound of pain he laughed. "Got the better of you this time big brother. That's probably the first and will definitely be the last time." He sat down on the hearth. "Don't plan on spending much more time in this godforsaken land."

"I've placed some wine here and a loaf of bread for your enjoyment." Leod chuckled. "But I'm going to make sure I leave you sleeping." He put the toe of his boot on Blades chest and pushed once again, laughing at his groan.

Bloody hell but everything hurt. He didn't think there was one part of him that didn't leave him in agony. Taking stock of his injuries he counted at least two broken ribs and a few that were bruised.

He prayed Aidan wouldn't follow him here. That she would stay put like he'd asked her. She wouldn't but she didn't know they traveled east instead of west. For that matter how did Leod discover the truth or did he just bide his time and wait. He would have guessed they searched the perimeter of the McPherson land.

If Aidan left to find him, it wouldn't be until tomorrow when he didn't return and she would travel west not east. She could get lost in the woods, kidnapped or any host of things. He prayed Liam would wake and perhaps find a horse. Blade needed him to get back to the castle if only to keep Aidan from riding out to find him.

"You thirsty?" Leod asked as he dripped water on his face. The liquid ran down his cheeks missing his mouth even while he tried to catch a few drops with his tongue. Even those small movements hurt.

He closed his eyes trying to force the pain in his body out of his mind. What Leod didn't know is that he'd lived with pain before. A few times as great as the pain his brother inflicted on him now. But what he learned in battle was to rise above the pain, ignore it as if it wasn't there. It was strange what the mind could accomplish.

"Ah, I see you're not. Did you know I'm waiting for your wife to find you? I can't wait too long though. I've a ship to catch but I thought a few hours might bring her to me."

Blade tried to speak but only a garbled sound came from his cut lips and tongue.

Leod laughed again his merriment eating into Blade's soul. "I'll enjoy having her in front of you then leaving her behind to die right alongside you. You'd like that wouldn't you? You, your wife and unborn child all in the same grave on the same day."

He watched Leod walk from the room, heard a few words exchanged between his brother and his men but couldn't understand them. The minutes seemed to tick by and with every shift of his body his bones and muscles screamed out in agony.

Wishing he could warn Aidan he tried to silently tell her to stay at the castle. He would find a way from this place. After so many battle wounds, he wasn't going to die here. Aidan would have to exercise patience and trust him, perhaps trust his men also.

Pushing the pain aside, he tried to reach his knife, which was tucked neatly away in his boot. Bound as he was he couldn't stretch far enough to grasp the handle. Then he searched for another way to cut the bindings but realized he needed to wait until Leod left and he would so on.

Through the tiny window in the shack the light was waning. Leod would need to leave before darkness. Thank God, Aidan wasn't here yet. Hopefully it would mean she wasn't coming today.

The door creaked open and Leod entered with a board in his hand. "Guess she's not going to rescue her husband. Too bad, I had hoped."

Blade watched as his brother raised the board above his head, watched as it fell upon his head then blackness enveloped him again. And he was thoroughly glad Aidan had not arrived to be part of this. Her dream had only been partially right.

~ * ~

"Don't try to dissuade me. I'm going to spend the day in the keep and outside unless the skies open and the rain that threatens makes an appearance." Aidan slipped into the bath water that had been brought in for her. "You can come with me if you want or you can do whatever suits you." In a way she didn't want company today. She craved solitude and to mull over the complications caused by her dreams. Blade issued orders to her today and she wasn't about to obey them if she thought he was in trouble.

"I would spend some time with you. Liam asked me to stay close and I'm not sure why. He usually doesn't say anything before he leaves." Selim fussed around the front room of the chamber.

Aidan could hear her humming and the steps she was taking between the window and the door.

"Are you worried too?" Aidan called out as she rose and wrapped a bath sheet around her. "Do you have that feeling in your gut that makes you think something might be happening to Liam?"

It seemed Selim ignored the question when she hesitated looking from one door to another then, "We really need to get downstairs. I've a bad feeling in the pit of my stomach. It's just as you say. Something horrible is happening."

Aidan knew the same feelings, and it seemed those sensations came upon her quickly. A chill swept down her spine and she felt as if someone had given her a blow to her head. She suffered Blade's pain and it nearly sent her to the ground it was so intense.

"I don't like this either. Even now the sun has disappeared behind the growing clouds," Selim said, gazing out the window now. "Do you know what direction they travelled today?"

"Yesterday Blade told me they were headed East, but I don't believe that's what they did. I don't know why though."

"Leod has become treacherous. I remember the days where he just liked to drink and gamble. He wasn't a threat to anyone," Selim said. "Except perhaps the women he seduced with no thoughts of commitment or complications."

"Help me dress and we'll go to the solar first. Perhaps the Laird has heard some bit of news." Aidan meant to discover all she could before embarking on some impetuous plan. She wasn't going to act impulsively. No, she meant to make decisions based on facts and rational thoughts.

A little later the two walked into an empty solar. Rays of muted light slanted through the windows and a platter of uneaten food sat on a table. It seemed depressing so unlike Aidan's last visit.

"Did you want to eat?" A servant stepped into the solar behind them, surprising her. "I saw the two of you come in. The Laird ate a while ago then left. He wasn't feeling well."

"What was wrong with the MacPherson?" Selim spoke up as if she didn't like this servant any more than she did. "A sick stomach I believe. He left complaining of cramps."

"No, we ate already. Come Selim let's go downstairs." For a reason Aidan couldn't explain she didn't trust or like the servant. She needed to check on the Laird but wondered just how appropriate it would be. Perhaps in a case such as this proper didn't make a difference.

As if reading her mind, Selim said, "We can check with his man. He will know if this is serious. I don't know his name but he always spends the mornings by the fire or with the MacPherson. If they are not together, I'm sure he'll know if there is anything wrong."

Selim and Aidan quickly headed down the steps to the solar. The space was eerily quiet and unnerving, sending shivers throughout her body. Aidan rubbed the goose bumps rising on her arms. "What is wrong here? I feel as if a ghost walked through me."

"Hopefully nothing, yet I feel the frigid sensations also. Wait, look there he is." Selim pointed to a man striding swiftly from the kitchen toward the steps. "We need to talk to him."

"Stop." Aidan held out her hand as if she could physically keep the man from moving. It didn't seem he heard her warning instead he continued.

Selim called out his name and he hesitated whirling in a bit of a frenzy. His eyes wide with shock, he stopped. "What do you want?"

"A word with you about the Laird," Aidan said.

"Selim! I was looking for you. The Laird is ill. I think he was poisoned. You must come quickly and see if there is anything you can do for him." Selim looked to Aidan for advice.

"Go. I'll be in the gardens. I want to walk among the roses and enjoy their sweet scent while I wait not so patiently for Blade's arrival. Summer is almost over. Besides I need a diversion from all this worry and something to take my mind off Blade. When you finish with my father-in-law, come find me."

Aidan watched as Selim hurried upward, hoping there was nothing wrong with Blade's father. When Aidan could no longer see them, she made her way to the rose gardens. Amorica's favorite was the white rose.

All her cousins and sisters had a favorite flower. What was hers? She was pretty sure she loved them all.

She smiled to herself, humming while she walked through the gardens and trying to forget the danger Blade was in. The gardener gave her scissors. She cut the dead flowers and a fresh one of each color for herself, setting them in a flower basket and thinking Blade might like them in one of their rooms.

A rumble of noise then a roar echoed through the keep. Curiosity along with fear drove her to the gates. Chaos took over the scene. People seemed to be running in circles. Everything happened too slowly to comprehend. Men were chasing a horse through the center and as it reared and snorted in fear, she recognized the stallion.

"Tanguy," she whispered, shocked to see Blade's horse without him sitting in the saddle. Her dreams returned vividly to her mind. Terror seized her but she forced the fear aside. "Leave him be!" she cried out, striding toward the big horse and murmuring the few words she remembered from her Celtic ancestors. *Fanacht socair. Ta me anseo.* Stay calm. I'm here."

Her words seemed to quiet the big animal. He nickered and slowly walked toward her. Holding a hand out to him, he bobbed his head. Tears filled her eyes as she waited for him to accept her. When he reached her, she placed a hand on his head, petting him and continuing to speak whatever came to mind.

Then, she asked, "What happed to your master? Is he alive? Why isn't he with you? Can you take me to him?"

As if the stallion understood he nodded his head, snorting, his eyes wide with what Aidan thought was fear or perhaps anguish at his master's pain. She inhaled then let the air out slowly, wishing she knew the answers to her questions.

"Can you take me to him?" she repeated hopefully. "Do you know where he is?" She felt a wave of panic rip through her. Tanguy didn't let anyone except Blade ride him. He was wild and fierce and at times unpredictable, just like Blade. But he was the only living being who knew where Blade was. He had to let her ride him so she could save her husband.

Once again the horse nodded his head, snorting and pawing the ground as if eager to be on his way, his eyes wide. She continued to pet the animal, knowing he would do what he wanted but she also knew there were people who could talk to horses. She wasn't one of them but the urgency of this matter had to count for something.

"Tanguy," she began, "we both love Blade and we want to protect him." She continued to stroke the horse. "Did you know I'm terrified of horses? Not you of course." Of course she was, she shouldn't lie to the animal. "No I'm terrified of you also but you're so big and strong and I believe in you. We have a common purpose. I'm going to trust you not to buck me off."

Tanguy snorted then shook his head. "So, I'm afraid of you and terrified to ride you but you have to take me to Blade. Can you do that?" Lord, she wished this had been a part of her dream. She could have prepared herself. *Fool, nothing could prepare you for riding this stallion.*

Her hands were shaking now as the thought of mounting this huge animal and trying to stay on for miles and who knew how many hours. She had to do just that for Blade's sake. The bigger question was could she vanquish her fears and actually stay on Blade's stallion long enough to find the man she loved?

She called out to a man nearby. "Bring water now." He nodded and raced to the well returning with a bucket of water for the horse. She used her shawl to wipe him down hoping this was enough to soothe the animal, knowing he shouldn't be ridden again today. "You have so much heart, Tanguy. Just as your namesake says, you are a fighter. Together we have to battle the demons threatening to take Blade away from us. If we find Blade I'll bring you an apple every day for the rest of your life."

Again, she reminded herself this horse knew where Blade was. "Are you going to let me ride   you?"

The horse nickered then pawed the air with his forelegs. "Good boy." She took the reins and led him toward the bench she sat on earlier today. Using the extra height to boost herself into the saddle, she now sat astride Tanguy, her body quivering with terror.

She let the breath out she was holding then leaned over Blade's horse so she could whisper in his ear. "Now take me to Blade but don't go too fast or I might fall off. I'd never be able to get back on." Picking up the reins her hands shook but she was determined to do this.

Every bump, every movement of the big animal beneath her stole her breath. She gripped the horse with her thighs until they burned with pain. Leaning over so she could touch the horse's head with her hand. "You are doing well, big guy. I haven't fallen off yet."

He was tired, his breath labored as they moved through the countryside. Tanguy turned east to her surprise. "Are you sure?"

Tanguy snorted as if saying *of course I know where I'm going. Are you crazy? That's where my master is.*

Aidan smiled for a moment. "I trust you. I know my husband as I'm also sure you know Blade. He would be the first to change his destination to throw off his enemies, but in this case it might not have worked." She gave the stallion the lead, watching as she passed through tall trees and bushes, listening to the forest sounds.

As the afternoon moved on and the sun dipped lower in the sky, she grew more concerned. She didn't know where she was or where they were going. No one would look for them in the east. As fear for herself escalated it didn't compare to the terror she felt for Blade. He might be dead by now. No her dreams told her he would be alive when she reached him.

They passed by Liam who was lying on the ground with two other men. She should stop and see if they were alive. But she couldn't. She didn't have time and if she dismounted, she might not be able to mount Tanguy again.

"Liam, I'm so sorry but I can't get off now. I will come back for you. I have to find Blade."

Gusts of wind hit them, stopping their progress as the clouds darkened, threatening. She wished she were curled up on a nice chair watching the growing storm instead of outside in the middle of nowhere feeling the brunt of the tempest. She had not dressed for this kind of weather. Bloody eyes, but she'd not dressed to ride astride a horse.

A small noise caught her attention and it seemed Tanguy noticed also. He stopped, rearing his head but making no sound.

"Hush," she whispered, knowing instinctively Tanguy would

never give away their presence. "Is this where Blade is?"

Tanguy kneeled as if saying *yes, it's time for you to get off.* She awkwardly dismounted, landing on her rear. Standing she dusted herself off then holding on to the reins she walked into the forest.

Men were speaking, so she angled away from the talking, finding a stream and leaving the horse there. "Drink up and rest. I'm hoping I'll return with your master. Will you like that?"

He didn't answer but continued to lap water before turning his attention to the green grass.

Before leaving she stroked his head. "Thank you, for trusting me. You got me here and I will owe you. Now all you have to do is get both of us back to the keep."

Tanguy didn't seem to care. She walked away trying to stay in the shadows even as the wind began to pick up, howling through the thick forest. A flash of lightning lit up the sky. A few drops of rain hit the ground and thunder rolled down the mountains.

The hut suddenly loomed in front of her and her gut told her this was the place of her nightmares and inside she'd find Blade. Holding her breath, she stepped gingerly toward the tiny shack, trying to stay in the shadows. Every tiny sound, every shift of the shadows made her pause.

"Ah, the lass has finally arrived." A hand clamped over her mouth and an arm swept around her waist, pulling her hard against her assailant. Not that it mattered. There was no one to hear her screams, only an exhausted horse and she didn't want to call out to her only means of transportation.

He pushed her toward the shack then once the door was opened he shoved her inside. She landed on her hands and knees, seeing Blade covered in bruises and blood with both hands and feet bound, just as she had seen him in her nightmares.

"Blade..." she whispered, reaching a hand out to him.

A man stepped from the shadows. "You did come. I expected you sooner. Don't you care for your husband?" he sneered then laughed. "This will be so sweet. The two of you will die together and your brat with you."

"Do you want me to tie her or do you want to have your fun first and maybe you will let us have a wee bit of enjoyment with her too. After all she's going to die here. What a pity. Maybe we could take her with us."

"No, don't touch her. It was only a threat to Blade. I've no interest in the red-haired wench especially since my brother won't be able to watch. You're right. He will die as will she. That's all that matters here. Let Hunter inherit this and see if he can rule two keeps."

"Ah, boss..."

"You're not a MacPherson." Aidan said, bristling even while the man held her hands behind her back. "You're a dog." She spit at his feet.

"Nay, I'm an Englishman." He laughed, pulling her against him, running his hands along her body.

"Leave her be," Leod roared angrily. "Bind her and we'll leave them to their torment. The storm is upon us and while I would wish dry weather for our travels, I want to be out of here. I've a ship to Baltimore to catch."

In a matter of minutes she was bound and lying on the floor beside Blade. Leod and his men were gone. Now she had to think hard and figure out how to change this around. Yet even as hope filled her, she lost the contents of her stomach. Everything she ate today spewed from her. She had not taken the medicine.

"No." She moaned, closing her eyes. In this condition, she could not do anything let alone figure a way out of this.

Her stomach lost everything and for too many minutes she rested on the dirt floor of the hut, her body shaking and the weakness within growing. She closed her eyes, stealing each breath she could. Slowly she regained her strength only to lose it to dry heaves.

To the best of her ability she pushed the nausea down swallowing, breathing, frustration at her inabilities. Giving in to her weaknesses would not save him or her. Resting again, she garnered control of her stomach. Then, wriggling she tried to get to the hearth, thinking to rip the ropes apart.

Finding the jagged stones she rubbed the bindings along with her hands on the sharp rocks. She felt the hard edges of the stones bite into her wrists while blood dripped to the floor. Then she remembered the stiletto Blade kept in a sheath around his leg.

Backing up to him, she tried to pull the bottom of his buckskins high enough to grab the knife. Time after time, to no avail her fingers fumbled with the catch. After minutes of trying, she unfastened the knife. More minutes later, her heart racing, she was finally able to slip the dagger from its sheath.

Outside the storm roared to life with bolts of lightning slashing the sky and thunder rolling from the heavens. She cringed at the sounds, still wishing she were anywhere but this tiny shack. She wanted to be in the stone rock wall of the castle, protected from the thunderous elements.

She rested then for a few seconds, holding the knife and turning it so it would slice the bindings. Holding her breath she set her mind on the task at hand. As she tried to cut the ropes, she felt the knife bite into her flesh, felt more blood trickle down her hands until they were slick with it. She pushed the pain away, trying to concentrate on where the blade of the knife was.

Reminding herself no one but herself could do this. She was alone. They were alone. Life or death, it was all up to her. Hours seemed to tick by. She had no idea how long she toiled. Sweat beaded on her forehead, dripping down her cheeks.

Slowly she felt the ropes unraveling but they were so thick. Truly she didn't know if this was working. At times it seemed to her that she was cutting herself more than the cords binding her.

A small amount of sunlight filtered inside. It seemed in the hours she'd been working the storm passed through. Now she labored in a trance, drawing the blade across the ropes, sawing them. Her fingers numb with fatigue and her body chilled to the bone she wondered if she would ever cut through the hefty bindings. Sometime in the middle of the night she stopped throwing up, and her stomach cramped with pain. She closed her eyes, leaning against the hearth, praying for strength.

Suddenly the last thread of rope was slit. The bindings now lose around her hands. Quickly she shook then off, new energy filled her as she turned her attention to the ropes circling her ankles.

Blade moaned, shifting his position then groaned again.

"Blade?" She knelt beside him, brushing his hair from his face then realizing blood dripped from her wrists.

"Aidan..." His voice so raw she could barely hear him. "What are you doing here? You're supposed to be at the keep."

"I'm going to slit the bindings. I have to roll you over. Is that okay?" She understood it would cause him pain she didn't want to inflict but there was no other solution. She tried to maneuver between Blade and the fireplace hearth but he was pushed up flat against it.

He didn't answer just grimaced with the words she spoke. As she pulled him onto his stomach she watched him grit his teeth against what she was sure was excruciating pain.

As quickly as she could she sawed through the ropes around his wrists then tackled those around his ankles.

When she finished she sat back on her knees watching him. "Can you sit up?"

"No, roll me onto my back," he whispered, his voice strained.

"Are you sure?"

"Yes..."

She dabbed at the cut above his eye, only to discover he passed out. "Blade? You need to wake up."

Nothing, she rested her head against his heart. It still beat and she saw the rise and fall of his chest. He was breathing too. "Thank God."

Aidan knew she had to get him back to the castle soon. Even though he was obviously in pain, she had to move him. There would be no way she could get him on top of Tanguy. She had to think of something else.

She strode outside then down to the creek where she left the stallion. "You stayed. Of course you did. You waited for me because you knew I would bring you Blade. Did you find some shelter for the worst of the storm?"

He nickered a greeting as she stroked his head and body. "How are we going to get Blade back to the castle? Hmm..." she asked trying desperately to come up with a tenable plan.

She led the horse to the tiny home and even let him look inside so he could see his master. Blade's stallion pawed the ground as if saying *what are we waiting for? Let's go home.*

"Not so easy but I think I've and idea and I'm glad he's

unconscious. If rolling him over caused him to pass out then this is going to hurt even more when I drag him outside.

Aidan went to work, fashioning a way to carry Blade that she'd read about. She found two long branches then tied them together in the shape of an angle with some of the rope Leod used to bind them. After that she found a way to tie the tip of the carrier to the saddle, she hoped without causing any pain for Tanguy.

With the last of the ropes, she wove them from one pole to the other creating a place for Blade to rest. She stepped back admiring her handiwork.

"Now, all I have to do is get Blade on this thing." No, that wasn't all. She would have to find a way to ride Tanguy again. Perhaps she could walk back. The big stallion was strong but he shouldn't have to carry the weight of two people.

When she stepped inside the hut, Blade still rested on his back. "I'm sorry if I hurt you," she told him, placing her hands under his arms.

He was immovable. She tugged and grunted making little forward progress. Standing up, she stretched her back then began again. Slowly she was able to drag him from the shack and onto the carrier she fashioned. She had just enough rope to bind him to the carrier, wrapping the length around his chest and tying it at each side.

Exhausted she fell to the ground, her head resting on a tree trunk as she sucked in air, sweat slipping between her breasts. Dry heaves suddenly consumed her but it reminded her there was food and water in the hut.

When the episode ended, she slowly walked into the hut. She placed the loaf of bread and container of water on the carrier.

"Are you ready Tanguy?"

He nodded, once again pawing the ground. She held on to the reins and walked alongside the animal. The sun was beginning to rise on a new day. She had about four hours before darkness to get out of the forest and on the main road leading to the castle.

Each step was an effort. When they reached the main road she stumbled, falling to the ground, her eyes closing in exhaustion. She tried, but she couldn't stand. So, this was it. Leod had been wrong. They weren't going to die in the shed but on the road home.

~ * ~

Liam opened his eyes the trees seeming to move. He groaned placing his hand on his head where blood had dried. Pain pumped through his veins. Looking around the clearing, two of Blade's men lay sprawled in front of him.

For a few moments he closed his eyes letting his body rest and hoping when he opened them again, the world wouldn't be turning and spinning wildly. He breathed in a few times then opened his eyes.

"Bloody eyes, what happened here?" He pushed himself to his feet, staggering slightly. Then checking out the men, they were both still alive. He looked to the sky and the growing clouds, remembering the threat of thunderstorms on the horizon.

Not wanting to abandon the men, he knew he would have to leave them. No one knew where they were and if they searched it would be to the west and these men needed help.

His shrill whistle didn't bring his horse to him and he accepted the fact he would have to walk. If there was any luck in this, maybe his stallion found his way home and even now people would be looking for them.

And Blade...

Leod must have taken him, perhaps even killed him. Too confident in themselves they had not proceeded with caution as they planned. They had taken their superior skills for granted not counting on an ambush.

They walked into a trap; one any skilled soldier should have avoided. He strolled, his body aching yet he had learned to push pain aside just as he assumed Blade had. He would not wallow in pity or doom but continue to place one foot in front of the other until he found help. Blade could still be alive out there somewhere, which meant it was his job to put together a rescue party.

Time slipped by as the sun descended. He whistled again hoping their attackers had been sloppy when they got rid of the horses. This time he was rewarded with a shrill whinny he'd recognize anywhere.

"*Nanko*," he whispered then yelled, "*Nanko*! You are my precious gift." Relief swept through him. He knew he couldn't make it back to the castle before the storm reached him if he had to walk.

Before he mounted, he stroked the horse, thanking him for coming to him when he called. Quickly, he prayed he could outrace the storm. The men needed help as well as Blade, but he feared Blade's search and rescue would have to wait until the morning.

As he rode through the gates, the yard was in chaos. People milled around him and the stable boy took the reins of his horse. "Feed him and take care of his needs."

He strode through the keep, calling the names of various men who he knew he could count on then into the main rooms. "Hunter!"

"You're back. Where's Blade and Aidan?"

"We were attacked and I don't know anything about Aidan. Blade was taken. We've men down the road about three miles from here."

"Aidan left early this morning, shortly after you and Blade."

"Dear God, I saw no sign of her. Leod could have both of them," Liam said.

"Or Guy," Hunter muttered.

~ * ~

Selim cautiously followed the Laird's man into his rooms. The MacPherson sat on a couch, head slumped to one side, his face contorted in pain, his breathing labored. She instantly knew what caused his pain and didn't believe it was anything life threatening, just something to keep him out of commission for a while. Surprised the men going after Leod had not ingested some of this stuff but they would not have eaten in the solar.

"I'll be right back." She placed a hand on the Laird's arm. "You'll be just fine in a few minutes. I'm going to mix something to make this go away."

"The pain will be gone?"

She nodded, "You can go to the main room so your clan can see that you are well. I have to gather some herbs first. I'll be back as soon as possible."

"Go then and send Blade to see me. I've got important information."

Selim nodded unsure how much she should tell him. "I'll be right back."

She hurried to the gardens and collected the herbs she needed then in the kitchen she ground the plants before soaking them in boiling water. The aromatic smells emanating from the pot made her smile. Some ailments were easy to cure. She was sure the woman who poisoned the Laird knew little of herbs and their properties.

When she finished she hurried to the chamber where she found the Laird doubled over in pain.

"He is worse, Selim and he heard the news of his son. I'm worried about him," Angus said.

"What news?" she asked curious at what anyone could have said to him.

"Blade has been captured by Leod and he is dead as is Liam." The man said, tears slipping down his face.

Her heart caught in her throat. "No..."

Chapter Ten

The storm hit before Liam and Hunter reached the fallen men. Rain pelted them from the skies above while wind whipped around them. "Bloody eyes but this is one hell of a day," Hunter murmured.

"Thought I was done with all this intrigue after Guy was banished from my land. Never thought I'd have to follow him to MacPherson territory."

Hunter felt the brunt of the tempest and the blackness of the night. Fear for Blade and Aidan catapulted to the pit of his stomach. If Guy had Aidan he wasn't sure where he could look. Guy had resources all over Scotland and people who would hide him and give him aide.

"It was my thought that Guy left MacPherson land a couple of weeks ago. Rumor was that he took a young girl with him," Liam said.

"The question was if she consented or not." Hunter's voice was low and threatening.

The memories of his half-brother and evil emanating from his soul seared in his head. "He tried to take my wife and murder her sisters. We both know he could have returned. There are always those who are willing to do anything for the right price."

"Truly, I don't think Guy is part of this scenario," Liam told him in all sincerity.

"From the man who allowed himself to be ambushed," Hunter said, knowing he shouldn't be so harsh on this man.

"I understand your fears and frustrations along with your anger. Blade was my best friend growing up." Liam reacted to Hunter's words and it seemed he was just as angry at his inadequacies as Hunter was at his inability to prevent this.

"Through all the years I tried to make enough money to buy land, our mercenary years, Blade had my back and I his. I've never met anyone more loyal and Aidan, Aidan is my wife's littlest sister. We cannot lose them. Allura will never forgive me if I fail to protect the youngest McLellan." The sickness in his stomach was born of fear and the inability to pursue Leod. Hunter wanted to ride until they found both his friend and his sister in law.

"No, we cannot and we won't. This storm is a hindrance but Leod and perhaps Guy will be stopped by it also," Liam said, in what seemed to be a feeble attempt to reassure him.

Hunter pulled the hood of his slicker over his head, hunkering down and planning on staying in the saddle until they reached the men Liam left. His thoughts were morose and he tried to uplift them but all he could think of was Blade and possibly Aidan in Leod's hands.

"You say you don't know who ambushed you," Hunter said, searching the length of the road and the surrounding forest for any sign of movement.

"I'm sure it was Blade's brother, Leod, but I can't be sure. I didn't see anyone before my head was bludgeoned with a heavy object. We're on MacPherson land. I don't know anyone else who would be so brazen as to attack the heir apparent," Liam said.

"I don't either but this seems brazen, as you say. Blade's brother knows and I would think he understands he'll never inherit a farthing. Killing Blade will do him no good." Hunter knew reason was not something this man understood. He'd seen it all before when Guy had wanted the McLellan land and title.

"Revenge," Liam said. "He just wants one last parting shot at his father and the MacPherson clan before he leaves. With Blade dead you will inherit this land and you're an Englishman. What better way to seek retribution?"

"Probably none but I would make sure the legal heir would be Scottish. Unfortunately we all, the McLellan's and the McLaren's, have one boy and one girl."

"Your boy could rule both lands. They are not that far apart from each other," Liam suggested.

"It's not my intention to assume Blade is dead. He is alive. My gut is telling me he lives as does Aidan."

"You have the sight?"

"Of course not. Don't believe in that. What I have learned over the years is to heed the hair on the back of my neck and what my gut is telling me. They've never been wrong before." Hunter relied on instinct and for many years instinct kept him alive.

"And neither have mine, but I felt nothing before the ambush. Not sure why but perhaps I let thoughts of Selim into my head instead of focusing on the mission in front of us. We don't have much farther to travel."

"Good because the rain is picking up as is the wind. We need to take shelter before the brunt of the tempest reaches us." Hunter pulled his slicker around his shoulders. Bloody hell but he wanted nothing more than to find his friend and his friend's wife while waiting out the storm in a comfortable place. It wasn't going to happen tonight.

"Do you see a light ahead?" Liam pointed east. "That's about where the ambush took place. "Maybe someone beat us to them."

"Pray it's not Leod or Guy," Hunter muttered. His hand resting on his pistol, he picked up the pace eager for a confrontation or an end to his worry.

The firelight was a welcome site when they drew close enough to recognize the MacPherson plaid.

"Hello," Liam called out relieved that at least one of his men were alive. "How is everyone?" He quickly dismounted, striding to the man who seemed to be keeping the flames alive despite the rain.

"One has a blinding headache the other has a broken arm and a headache to match the other man's and mine. We were lucky."

"Doubt luck had anything to do with this. Leod wanted his brother and didn't have the stomach to kill innocent folk," Liam said.

"You believe it was Leod?" the man asked.

"I do."

Hunter dismounted, striding to the fire and holding his hands out for the heat to relieve the numbing chill. "And perhaps Guy." As yet, he was unwilling to let Guy off the hook for this. "In any case, we should set to work on some shelters. I don't want to spend the night in the pouring rain."

In a matter of minutes the makeshift shelters were set up using tree branches. Hunter sat at the opening of one, tossing pinecones into the fire and watching them sizzle. A guard had been posted and the duty would be changed every couple of hours. He planned on rising at dawn to begin the search for Aidan and Blade.

Hunter knew they were close by and he felt, at times, as if he could walk around the corner and find them. Frustration ate at him, tearing at his gut. If they'd begun this journey sooner, if they'd known the dire trouble Blade and Liam had been in. If... and when had Aidan rushed out of the keep? No one seemed to know the answer to that. Not even Selim could tell him when or why. Selim had left Aidan to tend to the Laird's ailment. Was that a ruse too?

"All we know now is that Aidan is missing," It seemed Hunter spoke to himself.

One of the injured men heard the discussion. "She rode by here earlier in the day. I was half in and half out of consciousness but I heard her apologize for not stopping. She said she had to find Blade."

"Are you sure?" Liam asked.

"Sure as I was hit on the head. Strange, she was riding Blade's stallion and that wild animal doesn't let anyone but Blade ride him."

"Aidan is afraid of horses. You must be mistaken," Hunter said, as he tossed another pinecone into the fire, wishing darkness had not descended so quickly. He craved a few more hours to search.

"No, nobody can mistake that horse or the girl, for that matter," he paused, "all that red hair. She apologized for leaving us. Said she'd send someone to get us as soon as she found her husband."

"Best you get some sleep. We'll be up at first light," Hunter said, mulling over the man's words in his head. Aidan had no business out here alone but he understood the burning need to find Blade. He'd felt the same way about Allura when she had been in trouble, but he was better equipped than Aidan. She was walking into danger.

"I will, but I want you to understand. I wasn't hallucinating." The man tried to defend himself and what he saw.

"Rest assured stranger things have happened. And," he hesitated, "Love has a way of helping people overcome obstacles." Aidan had lusted for and been infatuated by Blade for seven years. Now she loved him, and Hunter didn't doubt she would ride a horse she was terrified of if she believed she could save him. He smiled, laying back, his hands behind his head.

For several hours, dry and inside his lean-to, he listened to the thunder roll across the heavens, prayed Aidan was somewhere sheltered and prayed too they would find her and Blade unharmed. When the storm slowly passed and the rains stopped he supposed he dozed on and off.

He heard the changing of the guards and listened to the chatter as they passed by each other before taking a few hours of sleep. His dreams revolved around visions of Allura and their children. He missed them so much. Since they wed he'd not been away from them at all let alone several months.

Hunter smiled remembering their last trip to the island, making love on the beach before walking to the shelter where they made love again. Maybe they would have a third child or perhaps they wouldn't. Allura had told him she wanted one more now that the others were growing up. He'd give her anything she wanted.

Bright sunlight slanted through the shelter's opening. Liam poked his head inside. "We're ready to ride. Just waiting on you to get up."

"You let me sleep?" Hunter shook the sleep from his head as he climbed from the tent.

"No matter, it's dawn. Men told me you were up most the night. I've sent the wounded back to the keep with one of our men. Don't figure we've got any trouble waiting for them that way. Trouble is ahead of us. Don't you think?"

"You should have roused me. I'm not usually the last to get up." Hunter looked over the camp, buckling his sword and placing his pistol in its holder.

"I did rouse you just now. With a cup of coffee and something to eat, we'll be on our way. I haven't eaten either."

Hunter walked to the fire and a few minutes later men were putting out the fires and getting ready to leave. He sat at the one remaining fire enjoying the cup of coffee Liam poured him and a few slices of cooked ham.

He drew in a long breath, thinking as he stared at the dancing flames. "I don't think they are far from here, and I wish we could have looked for them last night."

"You're probably right but I don't know what direction to go."

Hunter rose and walking around the campsite looked for some sign of passing. MacPherson men had trampled most of the campground but looking at the perimeter he was able to find a trail that had not been demolished by the storm or the men.

"Several horses have passed this way. It seems they are traveling toward the stream." Before Aidan and Blade had arrived, Hunter had spent time surveying MacPherson territory. Most of the time Liam had accompanied him and he was sure there was an old shack close by.

"Liam," Hunter called out. "Is there an old hut near the stream?" He pointed, hoping Liam would confirm his guess.

"I believe so. We passed by it over a month ago while we were surveying the land. Then we're headed in that direction. How long?"

"Most the day. If my memory serves me right it's several hours maybe more."

Hunter thought the same thing, his heart thundering in his chest. He was sure they would find Aidan and Blade. The main question, were they alive? "Then we should ride as soon as possible."

Even with the need for haste taking down the camp and sending the wounded men home took longer than Hunter wished. The sun was beginning to climb into the sky before they were able to start on their way.

Hunter led the way, dismounting every few yards to look for signs of passage. Even if they knew exactly where they were going, it would have been slow. With every passing second, Hunter felt the chance to find them alive lessened.

"I don't like the fact this search is taking so long," Liam said, walking up beside Hunter.

"We can't go any faster. I believe we have one chance, no more. Going off in one wrong direction could mean their lives."

"We both recall the hut." Liam argued, raking his hands through his hair, clearly frustrated with the slowness of the search.

"You're absolutely right and if you also think about it, you'll remember that shack is now behind us. I thought about sending someone there but the trail clearly moves in this direction."

Liam bent over, picking up a piece of fabric that had been caught on a bush. "Perhaps you are right. This could be a piece of Aidan's dress."

"Yes, and there have been other signs." Hunter took the scrap from Liam, turning it over in his hands for a few seconds. "I believe I saw her in something this color yesterday morning. It's a color she has always favored."

Hours drug by while they carefully followed the trail left by Aidan and hopefully Blade. The possibility still existed that they proceeded in the wrong direction. Yet as the sun was slowly moving toward the horizon a tiny hut came into view.

Hunter held his hand up, signaling caution. "Liam," he whispered, motioning him forward. "Come with me. The rest of you stay here."

On the balls of his feet, sword in hand and ready for any surprise, Hunter and Liam approached the shack. He pushed the door open, hearing the creak as he saw into the dark room.

"Blade. Aidan?" There was no reply and he cursed silently afraid he'd made the wrong decision. Striding inside he studied the single room. There was little indication that anyone had been there but on second look, he saw blood and vomit. Ah, Aidan must have run out of medicine.

"They've been here and now they're gone," Liam spoke, his voice tight.

"Don't jump to conclusions," Hunter warned. "From what I know of Leod, he would not take them with him. Hostages would serve only to slow him down."

"Leod wanted Blade dead and if Aidan and their unborn child died too it would please him that much more," Liam said, striding outside.

"So, they found some way to escape or to get away after Leod left them for dead. How? Aidan arrived on the stallion. They must have ridden out of here."

"That's unlikely," Liam said, "Leod would have left Blade bound hand and foot and the only way he could have taken Blade was if he was unconscious."

Blade walked inside again, searching the area where the blood was the thickest. He picked up a piece of severed rope. "Someone must have sliced through this rope."

"And found a way out of here," Liam added.

More determined than ever, Hunter found his way outside, searching the ground for something to help him understand what happened here.

"Look here," one of Liam's men said. "There are twigs and branches here as if they'd been cut."

"Over here there are drag marks and hoof prints, heading toward the main road." Liam said.

"Blade must have used his stiletto to cut through the ropes but why the drag marks?" Hunter said, heart in his throat.

"Perhaps Aidan was hurt enough she couldn't ride," Liam said.

"If I were Blade," Hunter paused. "I would have carried her. I would have needed her close to me, close to my heart so I could tell how she was. I wouldn't drag her along the dirt."

"Then it had to be Blade who was hurt."

"Mount up!" Hunter called out, determined to find them before darkness surrounded them again. "This trail will be easier to follow."

While they didn't dare race through the woods, their speed quickened as the trail was clear and precise, always at a diagonal toward the castle and the road.

"There they are," Hunter pointed to three silhouetted figures on the road. "Aidan, Blade." Hunter's huge stallion reared when he reached the spot before he quickly dismounted.

Tanguy lay on the road, Aidan's head rested on his chest and Blade seemed to be asleep on a makeshift carrier. "Aidan, wake up Aidan. All will be fine."

She moved slightly, looking into his eyes and reaching out to him. "Hunter." She smiled. "You found us. I couldn't take another step."

"You don't have to, little one. I will carry you home."

"Bloody hell," Liam swore, "He still breathes but barely. What did Leod do to you?"

Aidan turned her attention to Liam, "He beat him nearly to death. He woke up once but when I turned him over to cut through the ropes binding his hands he passed out again."

"You cut through the ropes?" Hunter couldn't believe his astonishment.

"I did." Tears slipped from her eyes. "I had to get the knife from the sheath on his leg and cut through mine first." She held up her hands. "I suppose, I didn't do a very good job."

"No, you were wonderful, amazing." Hunter picked up her hands, examining the many cuts. "I'm very proud of you. You would make a remarkable soldier."

"How is Blade?"

"He is hurt badly. I'm afraid he's going to have a long painful recovery but thanks to you, he'll have one."

"Can we make it home tonight?" she asked.

"Too dangerous. We'll make camp here and clean the two of you up a bit so you won't shock everyone when we ride into the keep." Hunter tried to lighten the mood but knew that was nearly impossible.

"He must have a few bruised or broken ribs, two black eyes and who knows what else." Liam took stock of Blade's injuries.

"You over there, get water to clean them up..."

"I will do it," Liam said.

"I've bandages in my saddle bag and liniment which might reduce some of the swelling."

"Be gentle..."

"Blade, you're awake. That's good."

"Aidan?"

"I'm here." Quickly she moved to him," touching him so lightly as if she was afraid to hurt him.

Hunter felt tears form in the back of his throat.

~ * ~

"Aidan, you're safe." Blade touched her face then noticed the blood on her wrists. He tightened his grip. "Aidan? What happened to you?"

It seemed she grimaced, "It's nothing for you to be concerned about. I'm fine."

"I am disturbed. What did Leod do to you?" As he slowly regained consciousness, what he saw bothered him more than anything he'd ever felt before.

"Nothing, not really." She tried to hide her hands from his view. "All he did was tie my hands and feet."

"You're coated in blood."

Aidan shrugged her fine delicate shoulders, "Self-inflicted, I suppose. I was a bit awkward with your stiletto."

Now Blade had more questions than answers. He let his head fall back on the contraption he lay on, closing his eyes. Before he could go on, he inhaled a long breath of air, letting it out slowly then another one all the while his ribs throbbed incessantly.

"This is going to hurt. Try not to pass out again." Liam was beside him, gently cleaning his face and applying cold bandages to the myriad of bruises.

"Not too bad," Blade whispered nearly overcome with the pain that was increasing with each movement.

"Well, I'm going to cut your shirt off. And I'm going to have to get you to sit up so I can bind your ribs tight. It's going to hurt a hell of a lot more by the time I'm finished."

"Bite on this." Hunter handed Liam a piece of willow bark. "I'll make a tea for him to drink."

The next minutes left him grimacing with pain, sweat sliding down his face and chest but when Liam finished he closed his eyes and pushed the agony to the back of his mind, chewing on the bark that he knew would help ease the pain.

"We've a tent set up for them by the fire." A man stopped to tell them. "They should be warm tonight."

When the pain lessened a little, Blade watched Hunter cleaning Aidan's wrists and hands. He needed to have some answers.

"Did someone see to Tanguy?" he asked.

"Your horse has been watered and fed, brushed down and now

he's resting. He helped save your life along with Aidan," Liam said, watching him closely.

He mulled all that over in his head, craving to hear about the time he was unconscious, yet he understood gaining the knowledge would have to wait. Then, Aidan saved his life not the other way around.

Hunter stood by him, "Do you think you can, with some help, make your way to the fire?"

"Is there a choice?"

"Always. You could spend the night here under the stars. It still gets cold at night. Or...you could sleep next to your wife. Platonically of course." Hunter laughed seeming to stare at his wounds. "Doubt if even you can overcome the pain your brother inflicted to make love to your wife."

Blade was able to chuckle but immediately regretted the sensation as pain rushed through him. He understood it would take a few days before he could move or even cough without wrenching agony and longer before he could walk or make love to Aidan.

Supporting him around the waist, Hunter helped Blade to a place beside the fire. The food was typical fare for a night in the woods, but it filled the emptiness in Blade's stomach.

Watching Aidan as she picked at the food, he wondered about her medicine and the last time she'd taken it. He had a flash of recognition that she had been with him in the hut but he didn't know when.

"How are you, Little Fire?"

"Exhausted." She placed her hand on her belly and it didn't seem to Blade she knew she did it.

"And the babe?" He meant to ask about her nausea and hoped she would tell him the truth.

"Fine, I believe." She sucked her lower lip into her mouth, looking away.

"You haven't eaten but a few bites." He tried for a more direct route for an answer.

"I've had no medicine for two days now, if that's what you're asking." She turned away from him as if not wanting to meet his gaze.

"And..."

She turned back, pain seeming etched in her face. "And I've lost everything I've eaten, if you must know. Now I don't want to embarrass myself in front of all these men."

"It's my job to protect you," Blade said, his voice soft, knowing he'd botched that job, all signs seeming to point to the fact she saved him.

"I don't want to lose my food and I don't want the pain it causes when I do. I'm a coward, too afraid to eat even though I know I have to for the sake of our child. In the morning I'll be able to take the medicine again and eat. I'm happy to wait until then."

His heart went out to her. "Try a little bit more." Her soft sigh sent a stabbing bolt of agony into his heart. "I know we'll be back at the keep tomorrow and I also know I won't die if I don't eat tonight."

She picked at the piece of bread and swallowed a tiny piece. "I know what you're going to say." She stood, walking away from him. "So please just don't say anything at all."

He couldn't follow even though he needed to do just that. But he watched her and saw her at the edge of camp, bent over, heaving, losing what little she just ate and drank.

He continued, his gaze focused on her, as she spoke to Hunter and he showed her to a tent. She wouldn't even come back and talk to him. There was nothing for him to do now.

He had no idea what she was going through.

Hunter sat down beside him. "You will never be able to imagine how strong a woman has to be to carry a child. And Aidan has more issues than most. She will be fine but you have to allow her to do this her way."

"She has to eat." He continued on that vein.

"Even if she cannot keep it down? What good will that do her and the child. All she wants is to wait until tomorrow when she can take the medicine."

"I would fix this if I could." Blade looked to the tent. "Perhaps I should apologize."

"If she is still awake when you join her ask her how she saved you. The tale will open your eyes and give you a new perception of your wife."

"She did save me then." Blade had wondered at the last two day's events and what impulse had sent her to find him. All he knew at the moment was that she'd broken a promise and left the keep. If she hadn't acted on her instincts, would he be alive now?

"You could be dead by now if Aidan had followed your orders and stayed put." Hunter walked away a disgusted look on his face.

With a grimace of pain he motioned for Liam, someone who might be a bit more friendly to him.

"What is it?"

"Can you help me to my tent?" he asked, wishing that when he got there he'd be able to pull Aidan into his arms and comfort her. He couldn't even recall the moments with her before he left. He tried but at this second all in his past seemed erased from his mind.

"Come."

Inside the tent, he lay on his back, listening to her breathe and wishing she would turn over and talk to him.

"Are you asleep?"

"No, are you?"

He laughed but stopped himself as pain ricocheted though him. "Tell me how and why you came to rescue me."

"If you won't yell at me."

Her whispered words left a hole inside his soul. "Do I yell at you?"

"No but you will when you hear the story." She turned over. "I was so afraid, Blade. I thought you were dead. Your father had been poisoned and Selim left to give him something that would stop the poison. You must know. He should be fine. I'm sure Selim took remarkable care of him."

"So..."

"When I saw Tanguy race into the keep without you..." She stopped for a breath of air. "He was panicked, rearing and nearly trampling several people. I knew I had to find you."

"You thought to stop him?" He was growing angry and perhaps she was right he would have yelled at her if he hadn't told her he would not.

"No, comfort him."

"Bloody hell, I'm not yelling at you."

"I gather that. I spoke to him in Celtic and it seemed to calm him down. When I asked him to take me to you, he said yes."

"Now you not only have the sight but you can speak to horses?" Somehow he knew his wife would never stop surprising him.

"I think he understood the tone not the words and he needed to rescue you and I was his only way."

"I'm having trouble understanding all of this." His mind cried out telling him no, but she had touched his heart so long ago perhaps she did the same to Tanguy.

"All I want is for you to believe what I say."

"You wouldn't lie to me. What happened next? I know how much you dislike riding, are afraid of horses."

"Tanguy let me ride him. I told him how much I was afraid and he had to make sure I didn't fall off."

Lord but he needed to laugh but knew it would hurt too much. "I assume Tanguy came through for you since I'm not in the shack."

"He took me to your men but how he found the hut I've no idea. Suffice it to say, you're here with me now."

"And there is so much more to the story." He was tired though and she looked exhausted. He decided he'd let it go for the time being. Aidan needed rest also.

"I cut myself when I tried to slice through the ropes binding me," she whispered the words.

A furor of excitement clamored through the campsite. "Liam, Hunter we've found Leod."

Blade recognized the voice of one of his men. He had no idea that Hunter sent men to find Leod and how on earth did they know where to look? A good guess, he supposed. Yet in the blank recesses of his mind, he recalled something about a ship to America.

"I will go find out what has happened," Aidan whispered to him. "I'm exhausted but not sleepy. I would lay here next to you with my eyes wide open for the next few hours."

"Are you sure?"

"I must do this and I am glad your brother will be brought to justice. What will happen to him?" She sat up and started to crawl from the tent.

"Be careful. Just because he has been captured doesn't mean he is no longer dangerous."

"I'll be careful. I promise I won't do something impulsive." She grinned at him, touching his cheek with a fingertip.

"I have second thoughts about this, Little Fire." As long as his brother lived, he'd fear for Aidan.

Grimacing with the pain he followed Aidan from the tent.

~ * ~

With her heart in her throat she watched Leod stumble behind the horse leading him. His hands were bound together and tied to the saddle horn. Her hands fisted at her sides, she had an immediate and incessant urge to hit him, not for her but for Blade.

"He can't hurt you." Blade stood beside her. "Leave it be."

"You shouldn't be out here. Your ribs." She felt his pain, saw it etched in the lines around his eyes.

It seemed he ignored her. "When we get my brother back to the castle, he'll be in the dungeon until we decide if he is to live or die."

"Who will decide?" Her nerves seemed stretched too thin, her body shaking as she watched him.

He stepped up to her and wrapped an arm around her shoulder. Despite the apparent pain, he pulled her close to him. "My father will make the final decision after Leod stands trial."

"Do you think he can be impartial?" She couldn't imagine the objectivity of a parent sentencing his son to death or a life of imprisonment.

"He won't have a choice. He is the ruler of our people, our clan, and he has power of life and death, authority to make recommendations to the crown," he spoke softly.

"There will be a trial." She didn't want to think about that. What if he was found innocent? Leod would forever haunt their lives. "What will happen then?"

"He will be punished. There is no doubt." Then, as if reading her mind, "He will not be found innocent. There is too much evidence against him."

"Until he's locked away, I can't rest. I won't be able to sleep or eat." She watched the men tie him to the wagon and prayed he wasn't as resourceful as his brother then sighed with relief as the men checked him for a weapon that might be concealed.

"He has never fought or defended his country or clan. He would not have any weapons other than a pistol perhaps." As if to give comfort he rubbed her arms, pulling her closer.

Truly she didn't know how he remained upright. "You should rest." She turned trying to guide him to the tent.

"Help me over there."

She heard the pain in his voice. "If I don't you'll find someone else?"

"Or do it by myself."

"Come on then."

He struggled with each step, stifling the impending groans as he moved forward. To Aidan it seemed to take an eternity for him to walk the fifty feet or so to his brother. She didn't know what he was going to say.

He towered above his brother who was now sitting on the ground. "You tried to kill me but worse than that you wanted to kill Aidan as well as our child."

Leod sneered at them. "Almost succeeded too."

"Didn't even come close." Blade said.

"What happened? You wake up?"

"No not until a little while ago. It seems Aidan was more resourceful than you gave her credit for. She untied me, saved me because she loves me unlike you."

Aidan listened to the exchange between them wondering how their relationship had gone so awry. Brothers were supposed to love and support each other.

"She rescued you?" Leod mocked, his eyes, sparking with anger. "That little slip of a woman."

It seemed Blade didn't want to talk about them. "How did they find you?"

Leod shrugged. "Was thirsty. Stopped at a tavern to get a pint and a bite to eat and perhaps a willing woman."

"You stayed too long."

"They got lucky. Your men must have wanted the same thing." He shrugged again, leering at him, "Food. Drink. A willing woman, it's what all men crave."

"Perhaps that's true but maybe they know you and your habits."

Blade turned then, seeming to be finished and with little help and fighting the pain he walked back to the tent. Inside she lay beside him, his big body shaking, his fists clenched at his sides.

She curled in next to him, her head resting on his chest. "Does this hurt?"

"Nay, lass, you give me comfort. I almost lost you today and..." He didn't finish the sentence.

"I couldn't have lived without you," she told him, her hand resting above his heart.

"Do you think you can sleep now?" he asked, placing his hand over hers, enfolding it in his. "Did speaking with Leod give you and closure?"

"Perhaps." She did close her eyes, listening to the sounds of the camp as it quieted for the night. She pulled the covers over them, wishing he wasn't in so much pain.

She recognized the instant he fell asleep, his body relaxing and his breathing slow and even. Needing to hold on to the moment she tried to engrave it in her mind.

Soon all she heard was the chirp of the crickets and croak of the frog then the changing of the guards. Her stomach suddenly feeling more normal than usual, she sat up and found the chunk of bread she'd been eating earlier.

"I'm going to eat now Blade." Gingerly she tried one small piece at a time as she judged the distance between her and the opening. But the food remained where it belonged. She washed it down with a few sips of water then snuggled against Blade again.

"It stayed down," he murmured sleepily. "I'm glad."

She smiled as his arm wrapped around her. The night passed but she slept little. Unable to relax she waited for the morning and the first light. But it seemed she finally fell asleep.

"Time to get up, Little Fire. We're going home," Blade whispered close to her ear.

"How do you feel?" Concern for him encompassed all her thoughts.

"Like I've been stampeded by a hundred horses."

"Is that all?" She tried not to laugh, knowing he would recover and take over their lives once more with his masculine commands.

"And how is your stomach?" His hand rested on her belly, his meaning clear.

"Despite all the excitement of the last few days, our little boy is doing just fine as is my stomach."

"Good, now make sure all your fastenings are fastened before you climb into the open. I couldn't resist you."

"What?" She looked down and found her bodice had been undone.

"I'm surprised you didn't feel the cold air or my fingers exploring," he said.

"I was cuddled up against you and..." She paused searching for the words. "I didn't expect that you would have the energy."

"Where you are concerned I will always have the energy." He smiled touching her bare flesh with a fingertip before tracing the line of her chemise just above the fabric.

"You are incorrigible." She stopped herself just before she hit him in the chest.

"No just a man who craves his wife despite the horrible condition he finds himself in."

Quickly she fastened her dress then smoothed it out to make sure everything was in place. Not trusting herself, she asked. "Is everything where it should be."

He chuckled softly as if he knew a joke she wasn't aware of. "Everything is perfect. You are perfect."

"Well then, since I can't pull you out of this thing, I'll let you get out on your own. If you need help, I'll call Hunter."

Once outside she straightened her skirts and took a quick look at her bodice, even knowing he wouldn't let her leave the privacy of their tiny world for his men to look at her. She stepped aside so he could maneuver himself into the open.

She knew he was in agony, understood that even the smallest movement would send pain shooting through him.

Unable to help herself she gazed at the place where Leod had been tied last night. A cart had rumbled close to him and now men were putting his wrists and ankles in shackles. As he walked to the cart the chains rattled.

"See, he'll never be able to hurt you again. That's the way he'll spend the rest of his life no matter how long it is." Blade rested a hand on her shoulder.

"Lady Aidan," Selim raced toward her. "I've your medicine."

Aidan glanced at Blade asking for advice she was sure he would give. "Thank you but..."

"She might be coming out of this stretch of sickness."

"It has been three months then?"

"I thought a wee bit longer, more like four," Blade answered before she could.

"The food early this morning stayed down. Perhaps we should wait and see how I feel after I have something more to eat." She suddenly felt a burden lifted from her shoulders. In any case she was more than willing to give this experiment a chance.

"Good, good, I'm glad to hear that. The Laird is fine too. He was distressed though to find out Blade was gone from the keep. All will be fine as soon as the both you are inside the walls and Leod is in the dungeon."

"I don't want to see him killed," Blade spoke slowly. "He is my brother and once a very long time ago I loved him."

"Since he didn't succeed in killing us perhaps he won't get the death penalty." Aidan spoke from the heart. She didn't want him to die either.

"If I knew I'd be imprisoned for the rest of my life with no chance of leaving the dungeon, I'd prefer death."

Chapter Eleven

Stifling a groan, Blade pushed himself to a position against the backboard of their bed and watched Aidan brush her hair. She was sitting by the window and the sunlight filtering through the strands caught the highlights of her hair reminding him of all the wondrous colors of a sunset.

"What do you see?" he asked, smiling and remembering the ride back to the keep a little over a week ago.

"You know what I see." She turned, tilting her head slightly.

"I want to see all of you. Take that off and come here." He patted the bed beside him, wishing the week in bed had been because they didn't want to leave it not because he couldn't.

"You're still too weak." She switched her attention back to the gates and the people in the courtyard.

"Let me be the judge of that." He patted the place beside him again unable to give up on his quest to hold his wife.

"It will hurt and I don't want to hear your groans of pain while you're trying to give me pleasure." It seemed she wasn't going to give in to his pleas, either that or she was teasing him.

"I promise you the only groans you hear will be ones of pleasure." He winked at her with what he could only suppose was a silly grin on his face.

She laughed softly and he knew he could never hear that sound enough.

"We can't, at least not right now. Maybe later if you're lucky." She stood and pulled the cord to summon a servant.

"Why ever not?" He thought she might intend to order food or wine. In the last week she gained a small amount of weight and her little baby bump was growing at an amazing pace.

"Company is here."

"Who?" Naked, he strode to the window to peer out.

"I assume it's Allura since Hunter is pacing nervously at the entrance. I hoped she might come for a visit."

With the knock on the door, Blade grabbed a blanket from the bed and wrapped it around him.

"Would you bring water for two baths," Aidan asked when the servant entered. "We'll eat with our company so no need for anything else. Wait, some hot tea would be nice."

When the door closed behind the servant, "I would have preferred one bath."

"Then we would be late and I'm eager to see my sister as well as her children. You can have the larger one. As it is it will take me at least an hour to get ready even if I hurry."

"I will do your hair and that will lessen the time."

"Of course." She looked down for a moment before meeting his gaze. "I will hurry."

"The sooner we greet your sister the sooner we can partake of our carnal pleasures." At the moment he could think of only one thing, making love to his amazing intelligent and strong wife. It seemed to have been an eternity since he had an opportunity to hold her in his arms and explore every bit of her sweet, tender flesh.

"We are spending more than a few seconds with Allura and the rest of the family. You need an introduction to their children If you want to be a real uncle."

"Don't you think she will want to freshen up too?" He knew he had a point and in that case she would retire with her husband.

"I suppose so. How many months have Allura and Hunter been separated?" she asked.

"At least two, possibly three," he told her chuckling. "Hunter is not going to allow her to spend hours in small talk with you even if you are her sister. At least not until he makes sure every delicate inch of her is perfect and just the way he left her."

"I'm sure you're right. And it's very probable that by the time we descend to the main floor, Hunter will have whisked Allura away to have his wicked way with her."

Blade pulled Aidan into his arms, nibbling on her ear. "Is that what you call this? Having my wicked way with you. I should like to do this and more every day for the rest of our lives."

A little while later, Aidan and Blade descended the stairs. Aidan was dressed in a beautiful day dress made from the MacPherson plaid. Belgium lace adorned the corsage and trimmed the edges around the bottom. The low cut bodice left Blade staring at her cleavage and wishing the other men in the room did not get the same view.

He knew though that was all anyone else saw of his wife. He had artfully arranged her hair in a chignon with bright red tendrils of hair curled sweetly framing her face. And, he had waited patiently while she put light touches of powder on her face, tinted her lips with a soft pink then darkened her lashes. As she told him with a smile on her face, it was just for him.

When she blackened her lashes her blue eyes appeared huge and beguiling. They beckoned to him, and perhaps her eyes had been his first attraction to her. "Ach, Little Fire, your eyes drew me to you and kept me by your side waiting for you to mature."

"Your sweet talk will not hasten what you want." They descended the steps.

"A man can try," he whispered close to her ear, delighted when she shivered in response.

Seeming to ignore him, "Allura? Has she been down with her husband?" she asked the McPherson when they reached the hearth where the older man loved to rest and watch his people. With the stress of running the business of the clan gone, his health had gradually improved.

"Hunter barely let the poor woman dismount before he swept her off her feet and to his rooms. They won't be down for a while." He chuckled a glimmer in his eyes. "Hunter has more important things to accomplish with his wife."

More noise from the gates, had her lifting her skirts and rushing to see what was happening, Blade staying close.

"Aunty!"

"Well, I see marriage has not changed your impulsive nature." Charlotte opened her arms wide to catch Aidan in a huge hug.

"No, she has not changed and I pray she never will. She saved my life because of that impulsiveness." Blade said finally acknowledging the truth of his words. He meant to show his appreciation every day for the rest of his life.

"Don't I get a hug too? I am your father after all?"

"Papa, of course." She ran into his arms.

Blade stood back, hands behind his back appreciating how charmed his life had become.

"Charlotte and I would like to freshen up then we'll be down. Could you have someone show us to a room?" David asked, his gaze upon Charlotte looking as if he wanted to devour her.

"Yes, we haven't been away from each other for a couple of months." Charlotte laughed looking fondly at her husband.

They accompanied Charlotte and David inside, chatting along the way before showing them to their room.

Charlotte took Aidan's hands in hers. "You need to have servants prepare enough rooms for all of your sisters and cousins. Everyone is coming to celebrate your marriage and the upcoming birth of your new baby."

"Everyone?"

"Don't look surprised. It is high time we all got together as a family and celebrated our lives. Everyone is wed and happy. You are the last to have a child but I assume in about six months you'll be a mother. There is no better time for a reunion."

"Sooner," Blade said, feeling smug and knowing he did look a bit arrogant, he tried to temper his features. "I'm pretty sure I know when she conceived. At least within a week or two of our marriage if not the wedding night or two days before."

"Amorica, Ravyn and Tira too? When did you all decide this?" Aidan seemed to be ignoring him but he didn't care.

"Yes our American traitors too," Charlotte said laughing and looking younger and more carefree than ever before. "I hope they don't take offense. The plans began after your wedding and were cemented before David and I left. They all came together in one of James' ships."

"I'm..."

"Speechless?" Blade suggested smiling. "When should we expect all of these people?"

"Larena and Gavin could be here this evening but probably late morning tomorrow. After that I can't say. I suppose they'll trickle in keeping us on our toes and ever watchful."

Blade and Aidan left the newlywed McLellans at their door before returning to the main floor where directions were given for the rooms to be prepared for all her sisters, cousins as well as their children.

"We should eat." Blade bent low to whisper in her ear. "I'm famished. We could go to our room to enjoy a pre-dinner meal." He wanted to devour and seduce her just as surely as the McLellan wanted to do the same with Charlotte.

"Surely you jest." She swatted his hand away. "We don't have time for that but eat yes. My stomach is grumbling its displeasure."

They sat in the main dining room where platters of food were beginning to appear on the table in preparation for the coming guests even though no one but Larena and Gavin were expected tonight. She supposed Allura's children, Colby and Nessa, short for Vanessa, would be running wild in a few minutes.

Aidan buttered a scone and put honey in her tea. She broke off a small piece eating it then washing it down with the hot liquid.

"You're still not sure about your stomach." Blade watched her, picking up her hand in an attempt to reassure. "It's been over a week."

"I know but you cannot possibly understand how it is to lose everything you eat and drink."

"No, I cannot ken it and I'm very glad I don't have to go through what you do but it doesn't mean I don't appreciate you and long for all of this to be easier on you. You are so very amazing you steal my breath."

"And I'm not even in labor." She grabbed his hand, holding tight.

"Are you afraid?" As much as he craved to make this easier on her there was nothing he could do.

"Terrified. But I don't want to dwell on it. The birth is months away."

"We have some extra time before the possibility of Larena and Gavin arriving. Would you like a nap with a wee bit of pleasure on the side?"

"Aunty Aidan."

Two little ones, well one was not so little, descended on them.

"Colby. Nessa, you've grown so much. How old are you now?"

Colby puffed up his chest a bright smile on his face. "I'm seven and Nessa is five."

"My the two of you have grown. Has it really been two years since I've seen you?"

"Two and a half," Allura corrected, seeming to float into the room. "Colby, make sure your sister gets something to eat and both of you behave yourselves. I don't want you to act like the little hellions you truly are except when you're sleeping."

"There is plenty of food and more to come. Help yourselves if you are hungry," Aidan said.

"We brought some Maxwell wine. This is from the winery in Tuscany. Logan told me he'd bring a crate of each, maybe two since the entire family will be here to celebrate two weddings. We have to do this right. Might not get a second chance."

"When will they be here?" Blade asked picking up a meat pie to eat while they talked.

"Any time in the next two days. I know this is all a surprise. Everyone will be here by then. The place will be overflowing."

"I suddenly feel like running in the opposite direction," Aidan said, looking to Blade for support. "The thought of all the children running wild in the keep is terrifying."

"We will all help. There is no need for you take on this burden. I want you to have fun," Allura said smiling sweetly. "We are going to celebrate and Aunt Charlotte has some grand ideas."

"Celebrate."

Blade wasn't sure if Aidan was up to celebrating anything. She was recovering from a long bout of horrible morning sickness and he guessed she was exhausted. She had been sleeping longer and seemed to want a nap every day.

"Aidan!" Christel dismounted in the courtyard, racing to Aidan and Allura for hugs.

"Christel, Ryder, welcome," Allura spoke, "And there are the little ones, Kenzie and Tara. We weren't expecting you yet."

Colby saw his younger cousin and it seemed they immediately started more chaos, chasing each other around the courtyard then into the flower gardens. Nessa took Tara's hand and they walked sedately inside chatting as if they spent every waking hour together.

"Oh, my," Aidan's hand went to her chest. "And there are only two families here right now. I feel the pending impact already."

"I told you to rest. With Selim's help, I'll see them to their room and get them settled in. You and Blade go rest. I'm sure you'd like a few moments alone before dinner. Which I will also see to."

"It might be best just to keep food on the main table, wine and Guinness at the ready. Who knows when we will need it? Obviously, no one has decided to keep to a schedule."

"Come, Allura has had the best idea of the entire day. I'm exhausted as I know you are and my ribs are beginning to throb." Earlier all he wanted was a bit of time to be with his wife, now what he craved was a few hours of healing sleep.

With an arm around Aidan's waist he led her upstairs and to their chamber. Inside the main room, Selim had placed a platter of food as well as a couple of opened bottles of wine.

Blade walked into the sleeping chamber, sitting carefully on the bed before leaning against the backboard. "How many people are going to be here, all in two days' time?" He was happy for Aidan but he hoped her family wouldn't make a habit of descending on them whenever the mood hit.

"Not counting the children, twenty-four. Charlotte and David make twenty-six and I suppose Charles might show up."

"Charles?" He'd lost track of the all the names.

Aidan sat down beside him, resting her head on his chest. When he placed his hand on her baby bump, she smiled. "Charles is the father of Ella, Amorica, and the twins, Tavia and Tira."

"I see, and what makes you think he might show up?"

"I've no idea but if everyone else was invited then Aunty would have made sure Charles received an invitation also. The baby hasn't kicked yet if that's what you're trying to feel," Aidan said.

"Yes, but I want to touch you more. If you're willing to wait until tonight then I can live with that."

She sat up, gazing at him seeming overly concerned. "Your ribs?"

"Just like you, that tiny bit of exercise has worn me out. I didn't remember how long it takes to heal after a beating. Never had one this severe before." He started to rise but Aidan stopped him.

"What is it?" she asked.

"I thought to bring the food and wine into the bed chamber. Are you hungry?" He wanted to see to all her needs as well as protect her from the stress that was upon them but he didn't think he could rise from the bed.

"I'll get it and yes I am hungry. Famished." Stretching to reach him, she kissed him then left for the main room, returning a few minutes later carrying a platter, two empty glasses and a bottle of wine under her arm as well as the bottle opener between her teeth.

He laughed then grimaced when his ribs throbbed. "You do that well but I doubt if you can carry anything else."

After setting the platter on the bed along with the glasses and bottle of wine, she removed the bottle opener. She opened the bottle then poured wine into both glasses. "Here." She held her glass in the air. "This is to families and unexpected visits. May they keep us young."

"Very good." He handed her two slices of bread as well as ham and cheese. She sipped her wine, staring at the food.

"You still afraid to eat?" he asked.

"I shouldn't be, but I can't forget quite yet."

"Please." He continued watching as she slowly ate her meal. "Thank you," he told her, trying to understand the constant resistance to food. He didn't want to nag her to eat but she shouldn't be losing weight. Despite her pregnancy and growing belly, her clothes still seemed to hang on her.

"I promise to eat more," she said, playing with the fastenings on his shirt, her head against his chest. "My stomach has shrunk though. And you must remember, the babe is not very big and doesn't require a lot of food."

When he woke, the room was growing dark. Aidan's hand rested on his belly, mere inches above his arousal. The sounds of horns, heralding another arrival boomed through the open window.

"Aidan." He ran his fingers through her hair, reveling in the silken fire he'd come to love so much. He inhaled a long deep breath. "I believe we might be seeing the next round of company."

"I hear it too. Do we have to leave? I feel as if all I want right now is to close my eyes and sleep the night away." She pushed away from him, her fiery hair falling around her and upon him.

"I believe we were given permission to do whatever we wanted by your sisters, Allura and Christel too." He closed his eyes, thinking of the coming excitement as well as the celebration. "You can do what you want. If you want to sleep then we will both stay and sleep."

"I suppose the new arrivals must be Larena and Gavin. I haven't seen her since Ella's wedding. Do you think they have a child?"

"There is one way to find out." He laughed, running strands of her hair through his fingers and wishing they could remain here and make love. "You cannot stay away. I'll fix your hair again, join whoever arrived with drinks and food. Who knows, there may be more arrivals and of course there might have been some when we were sleeping.

When they stepped into the main room, "You were right. I see Hadden and Jarret. That can only mean that Storm and Fayth are here. Storm's girls must be about three and four and Fayth's twins must be almost two years old.

"There is Gavin." She pointed.

"I have a strong feeling you won't be seeing your cousins tonight. With the tiny children they are most likely trying to get them into bed and they will fall asleep exhausted. Children have a way of wearing out parents." He smirked at his prediction.

"And you know this how?" she asked, taking his arm and strolling toward the men who had married her cousins.

"By watching and learning. You are exhausted and the babe is not yet out of the womb. I cannot fathom what it will be like when he is running wild through the keep. We will be hard pressed to keep up with him."

"When the time comes, I will give you that duty. You run faster than me," she whispered as they made their way through the main hall.

"I will do my fatherly duty." He held out his hand in greeting to Gavin, Jarret and Hadden.

"We're honored to be here to celebrate your wedding," Hadden said as he looked to the steps as if hoping to see Storm descending.

"Don't know about Storm and Fayth but I know Larena is fatigued and she will have to rock the baby to sleep after feeding her, sweet little thing."

"I'll have a servant take food and drink to her. Would she like wine?" Aidan asked.

"A glass or two of Logan's Bordeaux would make her smile. He gifts us with his wine every year. Don't see how he can make any money," Gavin said. "He must be giving away all his profits to his in-laws."

"Perhaps you could do the same for Fayth and Storm," Jarret said. "I know with the twins, Fayth will not join us tonight."

"I plan on greeting everyone who is here, then returning to help Storm," Hadden said.

"My goodness, look at who has arrived, three of my favorite suitors. Did I make your lives hard enough?" Charlotte asked as she hugged all three men. "Perhaps we should try again."

"If I recall correctly, you had nothing to do with Storm's and my relationship. She never went to London," Hadden said his voice smug. "But I do think she inherited some of your feistiness. She threatens to hide my golf clubs every time I do something that displeases her."

"You're right about that. Unfortunately for Abigail, Storm's mother, she was weak and gave in to Bradford's demands until she gave up on life and quit." Charlotte waved her hand in the air, "Enough of that, we are not just here to celebrate Blade and Aidan's wedding but to rejoice with our families. We have never had everyone together before and I for one would love to make this a family tradition."

David walked to her side, handing her a glass of wine before placing a protective hand on Charlotte's shoulder.

"Here, here," David said, "To the health of all the clans and the families. May we all live long and prosper."

"Who all do you think will arrive tomorrow?"

"Why everyone who is not here now. They have to because the party begins tonight and they will miss too much if they are any later."

~ * ~

The day of the fete a light mist fell in the morning and when it finally cleared and the sun emerged steam rose from the ground. Sounds of bagpipes tuning filled the air and several dancing troops practiced in the courtyard. Aidan had always loved the sounds of the pipes, which could be happy or sad, depending on the mood.

Early the morning before Amorica and Damian arrived with Jessie and Lyssa Ravyn and Aric with their two boys and all their children immediately joined Allura's children running wild through the grounds as well as the castle. With them Tira held her one year old, who struggled to reach the ground clearly wanting to follow his older cousins in mischief. The baby could walk but not very well.

A bit later the rest of the English contingent rode through the gates. Ella arrived with Drake and a four year old Ashcroft as well as a girl who looked to be about one. Tavia and James with their one year old and Logan and Eveleen with their three year old.

Aidan held her breath as she watched Kenzie and Colby dash by one of the servers and plow into a girl who was practicing her dance steps. She laughed when she saw Allura shoot Hunter a glare. She had to assume it was Hunter's job to keep the children in line and he wasn't paying attention.

She put her hand on her belly then was surprised when Blade stood beside her, both his hands pressed against hers. "I can hardly wait to be part of all this childish chaos," he whispered next to her ear letting his tongue glide around the shell.

"Bite your tongue." She knew he would be just as Hunter. He would tell her he was watching the child but he would be off doing whatever it is men do when they're supposed to be keeping the children out of trouble.

"No, but I'll let you do that. Bite me," he challenged, "as long as you are gentle." He let his teeth graze her ear then down her neck seeming to take delight in the shiver rushing through her that he must have felt.

"You're incorrigible and I'll bet you teach our little boy to be just like you." She didn't know how her father had lived bringing up little girls. If men like Blade chased after a little girl of hers, she'd have to lock them up.

"He will learn to fight and respect the feminine species. He will know how to handle himself in difficult situations. And I pray he will never treat a woman as I did you when you were growing up. But I was under tremendous pressure to do the right thing."

"We're not going to discuss that time in our lives. It is in the past and we shall keep it there where it belongs. No arguments today." She waltzed off, leaving him to talk to Aunt Charlotte who seemed angry with something as she tapped her cane on the ground.

She heard his sigh of what she could only assume as displeasure but she walked away despite it. He needed to learn to deal with Aunty. Charlotte would always have considerable influence in her life.

Closing her eyes for a few seconds and sitting on a bench near the rose gardens, she tried to remember Gracie, her mother. How old had she been when Gracie passed on, four maybe? She just remembered her fiery red hair. She always wanted to touch it, had in truth been mesmerized by the color.

Her mother had the same red hair as hers and freckles. She didn't know why she remembered that. Maybe her father had told her when he reminisced or perhaps at bedtime Allura spoke of their mother. Truly, most was all a murky haze in her mind.

In any case she was pleased her father found happiness with Charlotte. He'd been alone for so long as had Charlotte. They deserved to have someone they loved and trusted to live out the rest of their lives with.

"Are you up to a dance or two, Little Fire?" Blade took her by the hands and swung her around. "Hear pipes? The pipes are calling our names."

"A dance or two for you." *My love.* She said, enjoying the lilting music. She realized she'd been tapping her toe but he'd soon find she had two left feet and could not dance.

He swung her around the dance floor and true to his character into a sheltered corner of the castle.

"At last we are alone." He pulled her close, his mouth descending to meet hers in an intimate kiss. His tongue tracing her lips, easily pushed inside when she opened for him. One hand cupped her breast, teasing the nipple beneath the fabric of her gown.

She couldn't speak, couldn't think, it seemed it had been so long since he touched her intimately. He pulled back smiling at her, trailing a finger down her cheek then across her collarbone.

"Blade." She sighed softly and it seemed he took each word within him. Then she realized he'd been dancing and perhaps that was why he sought relief from the physical activity.

"Nay, lass, I don't hurt, well not very much. The pain is nothing. I can ignore it because it is so inconsequential compared to having you in my arms."

"How about you?" He kissed her eyes closed then the tip of her nose before trailing his lips down her neck.

"If you keep this up, we are going to have to retire to our room before the sun even begins to set."

"I want to tease you all night long then, when we are alone, you'll ravish me." His chuckle as well as his words sent shivers down her spine.

"Tease me..."

"Little Fire, just looking at you has me craving you. That will never change as long as we live."

"Then I shall do the same to you." She slipped her hand between their bodies, touching his pulsing rod. In his arms she felt the jerk and sudden shudder of his body against hers.

"You play with fire," he growled, tugging her gown so his mouth could cover her nipple and suck it deep inside his mouth.

"I'm on fire," she told him, backing away and pulling up her gown. "Be forewarned I intend to tease you mercilessly."

"What are the two of you up to?" Jamie asked as he danced Tira into another corner.

"Only what you want with Tira," Blade whispered laughing before dancing from the alcove and into the rest of the clan, in the process giving Jamie the needed privacy.

They stopped for refreshments and to watch the other revelers. Ashcroft, Ella's little boy stole a cookie from the table and a few seconds later he was covered in chocolate icing.

Lyssa, Amorica's little girl sat next to Nessa, playing with a ball, kicking it back and forth before they headed into the castle. Larena and Gavin were busy with their baby.

"Let us hold him so the two of you can have this dance," Aidan suggested as she and Blade stood beside the harried couple.

"You would do that?"

"Practice." Blade shrugged nonchalantly. "I've never held a baby."

Larena glanced at Gavin then back to Blade, "I'll trust you. I guess. Take advice from Aidan and make sure you don't drop him."

"I've never held a baby either," Aidan said. "Never had time for that sort of thing when Colby and Nessa were born. I don't think Allura would have allowed it anyway and of course Christel's child was taken away from her and Eveleen had her baby when I was in America. So, nope," she shrugged her shoulders. "I've never had any practice and I don't have a clue about what do with one, a baby."

"I suppose you should learn as soon as possible. I didn't know either and neither did Gavin. I suppose it all turned out fine."

The couple handed the infant to Blade and Aidan. Holding the child and instinctively swaying in time to the music, she touched the tiny child's cheek eliciting a tiny gurgle.

"Do you think everyone is enjoying themselves?" Aidan asked while she moved to the music.

"What are you wearing beneath the gown?" Blade asked surprising her.

"Exactly what you are thinking."

Blade groaned softly. "I've married a wicked woman."

"Only if you and your bruised ribs have healed enough to keep up with me." She enjoyed the look on Blades face when she answered.

"Not if I've a thousand tiny buttons to undo before I can give you pleasure." He laughed. "I wonder how I didn't rip the fabric of your wedding gown."

"There weren't a thousand and I don't believe for one minute you don't want pleasure for yourself as much as you do for me."

"How you wound my gentleman's pride."

"It's more your ego."

She was sure she heard him growl but her attention was caught by the other couples dancing then Charlotte tapped her spoon on a glass and called everyone to attention.

She hadn't seen the huge cake arrive from the kitchen.

When it was quiet, Charlotte stood on a chair with David holding her by the waist to keep her from falling.

"As some or most of you know my sole purpose in watching the girls come to London for their seasons was to find suitable matches for them. Well, now all are wed. Some I helped, some I didn't, but there were very few weddings. I actually thought that I would get to plan twelve weddings. Suffice it to say I did not."

"You were wonderful Aunty." One of the cousins called from the crowd.

"Well, thank you," she said. "But tonight this cake is to symbolize everyone's marriages and their happiness. Your mothers, my sisters, would have been so pleased to see you and her grandchildren. I hope to have grandchildren of my own one day. Perhaps my son, Roc will settle down long enough to find a suitable wife.

Epilogue

Aidan and Blade sat on a grassy knoll overlooking a loch near their home. Evan their two year old played with a ball, rolling it along the ground to his father. The little boy stumbled, giggling as his father lifted him the air. Blade tossed him again and again.

"More Papa, more! Do it again." Evan cried out as Blade sat down tickling the little boy.

"You excite him too much and I'll never get him down for a nap in another hour," Aidan said, shaking a finger at her husband.

"I should stop." He gazed at Aidan, understanding if the boy didn't get a nap he wouldn't have a couple of hours alone with his wife. He desperately wanted another child but his wife had asked him to wait at least a year before they tried for a babe. It had been two years now and she'd given her consent a few months before.

"You should, we have things to talk about." She smiled at him while ruffling Evan's dark head of hair.

"We do?"

She looked at her hands in her lap, seeming suddenly shy. His heart jumped into his throat.

"I'm pregnant."

He kissed her soundly, remembering the little boy sitting in his lap." Are you sure?" He'd had business away from home and he couldn't be sure himself.

"I've been sick. So yes."

"I didn't know." She had been able to hide her nausea from him and there could be only one answer to that.

"Selim, I told her."

262

"Before me?" He always wanted to be the first to know. Yet here it was, a woman confiding in another woman before her husband.

"Are you angry?"

"No, a little disappointed you would tell her first. Liam probably knows too."

"Or course he doesn't."

"You cannot be sure." He let his hand rest on her belly.

"You're right but Blade, there is something else."

Now he was worried. "What?"

"It's something I've wanted to tell you since I was thirteen and couldn't leave you alone." Her smile appeared shy and insecure.

"That you actually enjoyed following me around and spying on me when I was with a woman." He chuckled softly. "You did aggravate me and frustrate me. What I intended with those other ladies was not something that a thirteen year old should see."

"No." She was shaking her head then she set her hand on his cheek. "Blade, I love you and I think I always have from the first moment I saw you."

"Why didn't you tell me?"

She moistened her lips, hesitating. "You don't have to say you love me. I'm alright with that."

He set Evan off his lap, "My dearest Aidan I thought I've told you, showed you that I love you and how much."

"No, you have not but like I said..."

He pulled her closer, his lips molding with hers for the longest time before he drew away. "I love you more than life itself, more than I can even imagine and I'm so relieved to finally hear you say the words.

"You love me?"

He kissed her again, his tongue sweeping against hers, inhaling the essence of her heart and soul.

"So much my Little Fire, so much more every day."

"I love you too, with all my heart. You will have to show me tonight."

"Aidan's love, I believe I like the sound of that," he whispered against her lips.

Coming December, 2019
from
Rogue Phoenix Press

Caitlin's Duke

Chapter One

For the third evening Richard Oakes Crandoll Leighton, the Duke of Ravenwood, known to his friends as Roc, relaxed in the Rose & Thorn pub watching the fiddler dance around the room, her long black hair flowing beautifully around her with each motion, her eyes sparkling with enjoyment and raw passion.

Caitlin O'Shea intoxicated him with her beauty. Every night for the last two weeks after she finished work, she shared a Shepard's pie and a pint of Guinness with him. Tonight he meant to walk her home and perhaps steal a kiss and if lucky, two. It seemed every time he took two steps forward with her, she immediately sent him one step back.

He didn't know how she played the fiddle while she danced and twirled around the room, but she did and she was amazing. She finished the last song of the night, sitting flirtatiously on his lap, drawing the last note on her bow. Then she graced him with the smile that sent his heart surging.

Unable to resist this new side to Caitlin, he set his hands on her waist, touching her, enjoying the feeling of her body so close to his while imagining her naked next to him. So far she had eluded him and this simple gesture surprised him. It seemed to Roc she flirted with him tonight, another first. He intended to appreciate every second.

"Cat, do you mean to tease? It might not be wise." He loved spanning her tiny waist with his hands. If things went the way he hoped, she'd return to London with him when it was time for him to go home. To accomplish that he had his work cut out, because she seemed man shy.

She didn't answer right away but set her bow and fiddle on the table then, "Don't know how to tease a man. If that's what I'm doing, my sincere apologies or if you like it I won't apologize." She nodded to her da who stood behind the bar. "Another pie?" she asked.

He let his inhibitions out and roared with laughter. She had a way of switching subjects without blinking. "Another pint too."

She stood, leaving him to go to the bar for the food and drink. When she returned, he'd set her instruments in their case.

He leaned back watching her as he sipped the pint. "Do you want to stay here the rest of your life, here in Portrush? Or would you like to see another part of this vast world?" He'd take her anywhere she wanted to go as long as she would consent.

"Didn't realize there was a choice," she said with her mouth full. "Don't have the means to go anywhere. Don't know where I'd go if I did have the money." Swallowing, she drank her beer then set it on the table, looking thoughtful. "Perhaps I'd go to Africa and take a safari."

"You could go to London or Paris. Switzerland is always fun as is Germany. Safaris are dangerous. He drummed his fingers on the table. Didn't know why he was nervous, but she touched a part of him he thought long dead and he wasn't sure how to react to this slip of a woman who seemed so different from anyone he'd ever known.

She leaned forward, both hands on the table. "Now why would I want to do that? And what would I do there, in London or Paris or those other places you mentioned? Everyone would take one look at me and know I don't belong."

Shrugging, he held his breath thinking about the wisdom of what he was about to say then changed his mind and said something innocuous. "Just curious if those are some places you'd like to see."

"You live in London don't you, Roc? It might be fun but like I said, I don't have the money to travel. Might go to Belfast for a day or two but don't know why I would do that either. The fact is, I don't want to be beholdin' to any man. If you took me somewhere, well then, you'd want something from me."

He tried to ignore her last comment about wanting something from her. "I could help you with that, the money that is. If it's something you want to do." The first night he saw her in the pub, he'd gone home and wrote a message to his solicitor asking him to purchase a townhouse close to his. He knew it was more than presumptive but he didn't mean to return home without her. He also didn't know how to convince her that going with him was the best choice for her.

"Nothings for free," she continued eating and studying him. "Just what would you ask in return?"

He choked, not expecting the straightforwardness of her question. She challenged him, putting him on the defensive. "Only what you're willing to give."

"Now, I know you're a lord of some sort. Heard the rumors running through the town, but I'm a commoner and the only thing I can think you might want me to give you is my body. After all, I've nothing else." She pushed the half eaten food to the middle of the table as if it was no longer palatable. For a few uncertain seconds, she stared at her drink twirling the dark amber liquid in her glass before downing a few gulps. "I'll be no man's mistress."

"I'm not asking," he said, but eventually he would and at this moment he didn't like the direction of his thoughts. All he understood was that he craved her, needed her by his side. It had been years since he felt that kind of elemental and primitive desire. Five years ago he lost the woman he envisioned would remain by his side for the rest of his life. She died in a fire in Tuscany. He put that memory out of his mind for the moment, concentrating on the woman sitting in front of him.

"You're not? Well, I'll believe you for now, but I know that you want me by the look in your eyes. Raw desire, that's what I see and I'll not be givin' myself to you."

He slowly finished the last of his drink then setting his glass on the table, "Just because a man wants a woman doesn't mean he intends to make her his mistress. That's an entirely different proposition," he said, trying to defend himself and found there really was no defense when she spoke such blatant truth, seeming to read his thoughts.

"So you say."

"It's the truth," he told her but not in this case. "You're an amazing fiddler. Don't see how you can dance while you play. What can't you do?" He chose to change the subject instead of drowning in the last one.

Closing her eyes for a second or two and seeming to think, she said, "I'm a terrible house keeper. I spend the mornings cleaning the pub, the evenings playing my fiddle and the last thing I want to do when I get home is clean house. So many times there is dust on the tables and dishes in the sink. It seems I drop my clothes wherever I take them off."

He threw his head back, roaring with laughter, thinking if she were his mistress, she'd have people to do that for her. "I don't like to clean house either, but I suppose I've never really been tested. The chore has never been expected of me."

"What do you want out of life?" She smiled as if she understood the diversion when she asked the question.

"A little peace and quiet," he said quickly, realizing how true that was. He'd travelled most of Europe undertaking different missions directed by the English government. Now all he wanted was to do as he pleased for at least a year, perhaps more. Most of all, he didn't want to feel the need to sleep with one eye open.

"Is that all? I'd think someone of your status would want more, perhaps fame and fortune, perhaps..."

"I've more money than I can spend in a lifetime and because my father was not a wastrel, he was able to pass my title on to me. So no, I need to spend time at White's, find a willing woman who is not afraid of pleasure and perhaps in a few years find a woman I might want to wed and have children with."

"You want to marry." Her face turned a ghostly shade of white.

He couldn't help but wonder why the change in color. "In a few years," he told her, "And you? Do you want to marry?"

"Never," she grit out, turning her face away, seeming to hide from him.

He wanted to see the flicker of emotions over her face, needed to see why she was so adamant in her denial of marital bliss. Perhaps in time she'd tell him. "I thought women wanted to marry and have children. Find someone to take care of them."

She nodded to a well-dressed man at the bar, "See the drunk over there? Da promised him my hand in marriage. He's a mean drunk. His name is Blair O'Connell. I told Da I wouldn't marry him even though he's an Irish lord, but my da insists. Says if I don't he'll kick me out."

Roc felt a moment of anger, which quickly turned to rage as he watched the man, kick a stray dog that had entered the pub. Roc's fists tightened. 'He'll kick you out of where?"

She shrugged her tiny shoulders, shoulders that shouldn't have to bare such a heavy burden. "He owns the small cottage I live in. I pay rent to him so I can be out of his house and by myself. I do value that small bit of independence and it's nice Da allows it. He doesn't have to, you know."

"Is there anywhere else you can go?" *Besides my new townhouse in London.* He knew he was getting ahead of himself. "Can I help?"

"No." She paused, thinking, yet the smile forming on her face gave him a chance to believe he might be part of her thoughts. "I can't afford anything else. He wouldn't ever fire me from the band, but I need to clean the pub if I'm going to pay all my bills."

"I could purchase a cottage and you could pay me rent," he blurted before he realized this was counter to his purposes. Convincing her to come with him in a few days was his priority, not buying a place for her to live in so she could stay in Ireland.

"That is a thought, but I'm sure I'd have to refuse. Everyone would believe the wrong things about me and if I have anything, it's my reputation. Without that there is nothing for me."

Grateful at the moment she refused, "I understand." Deep in his heart he was ecstatic she turned him down, but he still needed to find a way to make her life easier.

"Look, I need to walk home. It's late and I need sleep." She stood then picked up her fiddle case.

"May I?" He took it from her. "Walk you home, that is? A girl shouldn't be out at night alone."

"Chivalry," she murmured, then smiling, "I have to walk home alone every night. I try to leave before the lord O'Connell leaves. I don't want him anywhere near me. He makes my skin crawl and sometimes I think he follows me, watches me in the house."

"So?" He waited patiently for an answer. "May I accompany you home?" he prompted.

"Yes," she smiled at him again, sucking her bottom lip between her teeth, "I think I'd like that, but you have to know that's all. Just a walk home, nothing more."

"I wouldn't have it any other way." He opened the door for Caitlin, stepping out into the cold night air. It was early spring and one never knew what the weather would be like here. Tonight is was cold, nearly frigid because the sky was clear, with stars dotting the blackness.

"Wait," she rushed into the pub then came out with a shawl. "I forgot my wrap. It's a bit chilly. The breeze reminded me." She looked a bit ashamed at her forgetfulness.

"I forget things too." He grinned at her. "Are you warm enough now?" he asked, shifting the case to his other hand before wrapping an arm around her to draw her closer for warmth.

She didn't push away from him and neither did she answer his question. Inwardly he smiled, enjoying the feel of her soft curves next to him. They walked in silence. He knew exactly where she lived. The last three nights and from a distance he made sure she made it to her home safely then set off for his lodgings.

She didn't have to tell him about O'Connell. He'd known the first time he watched the man ogling her there was something more to their relationship, none of it good. Now that he understood what her da had done, he meant to change things. As soon as possible he'd have a long chat with her da as well as Lord O'Connell.

"Here we are." She turned, stepping slightly away from him but now his hand rested at her waist.

He didn't want to let her go, needed to understand her thoughts where he was concerned. "It's dark inside. Do you want me to wait here?" He wondered at the expression flitting across her face. "Are you always afraid to step inside your home when you return at night?"

She was shaking her head even while she stepped closer to him.

Next to him, he felt the fine trembling of her body.

"Was that a yes or a no? I'm a bit confused." He didn't want to laugh. Her fear was real and tangible, and without asking he was pretty sure the terror had something to with O'Connell.

"Both. Yes, when Blair has left before me. I can't know where he is or if he's waiting for me, and no, when he's still in the pub. If he's still in the tavern, he usually sleeps it off on the floor. Da wakes him up in the morning and sends him home."

"My little cat, you shouldn't ever be afraid." He tenderly brushed her flyaway hair behind her ears. The feel was silken and it seemed to be on fire. He wanted to feel the heat surround him and he needed more than anything to run his fingers through the length.

"Believe me, I don't like the feelings." In his arms, she shuddered as if the fear surrounded her.

"May I come in?" he asked, understanding he might very well be overstepping his bounds.

Cat didn't answer but she pulled a key from a pocket in her skirt and fumbled for a few minutes at the door. "I can't seem to..."

"Let me help." He didn't understand the trembling of her hands and he hoped she wasn't afraid of him. He took the key from her.

Seconds later, they stood inside her house. She scurried around the room, sending light into the small cottage. "Would you like a drink? I've tea. Not much else."

He hesitated a moment, unsure of the right answer. He detested tea. "Of course, that would be fine."

She seemed to sense his aversion to tea. "I've whiskey if that's what you would prefer." She stood by the cupboards in the kitchen.

"Whiskey would be nice," he told her and reminded himself he should gift her with a bottle simply because he intended to walk her home every night until they left for London, and he didn't want to deplete her meager supply.

She poured them both a glass, bringing it to him, "Would you like to sit down? I'm not sure what to do, never asked a man into my home before." She fiddled with the glass as if she didn't know whether she should drink it or play with it.

He smiled at her before sitting on the sofa. It was threadbare but must have been nice in another time. She deserved more than this. "I see what you mean about your housekeeping. Doubt if I would make a fuss if no one ever entered where I lived."

With one hand she held the glass and the other she plucked at her skirts, her eyes cast downward. Then she looked up, "Is the whiskey to your liking?"

For some reason he needed to be honest, "I've had better." He laughed. "As I'm sure you guessed."

"Thank you for being truthful. Da gives me the whiskey that no one will order. I'm not sure why."

"He wants you to have something for the man he promised you to if he comes calling." This thought ate at him. He didn't want to think about what that man could do to her in a drunken rage. Men like that were known to beat anyone who disagreed with them.

"I won't let him in," she shot back. "He's not welcome here. Da can promise him the moon but when it comes to me, he has not rights. I'll make decisions that are right for me."

Roc wasn't at all sure how Caitlin would keep the man out if he wanted in and that thought terrified him. Now more than ever, with this added knowledge, he needed to convince her that her best shot at a better life was in London with him.

"You might not be able to stop him. He's a lot stronger than you."

"I know." She ran her tongue around her lips before downing the drink. "Would you like another?" She stood and striding to the bottle of whiskey she poured herself more then seemed to wait for his answer.

He held his glass out and she poured more, setting the bottle on a nearby table. "Why would your father sell you to this man who is nothing more than the town drunk?"

She looked clearly shocked by his expression. "He's not really my father, and the man has money, owns property. Da says he wants more for me than playing my fiddle in the pub."

The answer was short and to the point, "Not your father? Who is he?" now he had many more questions than answers about this young woman he cared for more than he'd cared for anyone his entire adult life.

"I call him my da but he's really my uncle." She closed her eyes then downed the whiskey before pouring another.

"You probably shouldn't have any more."

"Of course, you're right. I have to wake up before six so I can go to the pub." But she sipped again, clearly distraught by their conversation.

"What happened to your mother and father?" The questions surrounding his Cat grew.

She lifted her delicate shoulders slightly, looking at him with tear filled eyes. "My mother died in childbirth and father...some duke or earl...some English lord who didn't care what happened to mother or me. I don't know who he is and neither do I care."

A wave of revulsion at the man who sired Cat swept through him. "Bloody hell," he gritted out unable to think of anything else to say. She was sired by a lord and now groveled in a small hut with nothing to her name.

"It's the god's honest truth. I don't know who my father is but I think Da does, but he won't tell me because I think deep down he hates me for taking his sister's life. And he might be afraid I'd try to find him."

"Then he's not much of a man," Roc said, reevaluating his desires where Cat was concerned as well as his previous behaviors. He'd always taken precautions when he had sex. As far as he knew, there were no bastards, no women he abandoned when he was tired of them. Good God, his mother, The Duchess would have killed him if he did anything like that.

"So you say," she said, standing swaying a bit then steadying herself by placing a hand on the table. "Not used to drinking whiskey. Or so much."

"Perhaps you should have a hot cup of tea before I leave." He found himself in front of the sink not knowing what to do. Bloody hell, it couldn't be that hard to make a cup of tea.

She was laughing and the sound warmed his heart even though he understood she was laughing at him. "I'll just have a glass of water. I'm not drunk, just exhausted and a wee bit tipsy. I'll probably sleep like a babe tonight thanks to you."

"Then I should be leaving so you can get some sleep." He held her hands in his, feeling the callouses on her fingers and wishing he could do something to convince her she would allow him to take her to London. She shouldn't have to work to keep food on her table when he could provide for her.

Yet after the conversations they'd had, he was pretty sure he understood why she told him she'd never be any man's mistress. He vowed though she'd change her mind. He would find a way.

"I like your company," she told him, moving closer to him, her chin tilted upward so he was looking into her blue violet eyes. Tonight they were more violet than blue.

"But you don't want me to stay the night." He watched her expression turn to something he'd never seen before.

"Perhaps what I want is not what I can do." She touched her hand to his cheek, her eyes speaking of desire and passion.

"Just one kiss then I'll go." He rested his hand on hers, feeling the fine trembling, understanding fear had changed to hunger as well as raw passion. "I won't hurt you and nothing we do here, tonight, will damage your reputation."

"Promise?"

He saw the rise of her breasts and felt the pounding of her heartbeat in the pulse at her wrist. "Promise."

She moistened her lips as if in anticipation. "Roc?"

"No time for questions."

His lips met hers, the warmth and softness reached deep into his soul. He needed more yet refused to act on his desires. She opened her mouth, maybe to say something, maybe not, but her tongue swept across his lips, reached inside his mouth.

Her tiny gasp helped him realize she acted on instinct not knowledge. She had no idea what she had done, what she initiated when her tongue met his. But he wasn't about to let this opportunity pass. He deepened the kiss, pulling her closer, exploring every part of her she allowed. His hands held her face so he could have better access while his lips and tongue engaged in as sensual dance with hers.

Minutes later, when he pulled away, her lips were swollen slightly, tempting him even more to pursue this to the natural end. But she'd never forgive him if that was what he did. He didn't want regrets ever in this fledgling relationship.

"Are you working tomorrow?" he asked, hoping she would finally have a day off and he could spend some time alone with her.

"Just cleaning the pub in the morning. I'll be finished by noon. Why?" She moved back from his holding her hand on her chest as if she tried to slow her breathing.

"Good, then I'll pick you up here at one o'clock, if that's alright. We'll go for a carriage ride and perhaps I'll bring a basket of food. Would you like that? And some wine." He craved time alone with her, private time but also understood that for now, he would have to keep his courting to kisses. He laughed to himself, remembering his mother's teaching. "When you are out with a lady, you best think with your head and not your cock." He would have a devil of a time doing that with his Caitlin.

Her hands were under her chin, her eyes bright, "I'd like that, a carriage ride, food and some wine. I've never done anything like that before or been alone with a man."

At her innocent words, Roc's breath caught in his throat. "Goodnight, my little Cat, sleep well and I'll see you tomorrow." Roc left Cat's house, whistling and thinking to himself of ways to help this woman without her knowing. That's all he wanted, to help her and make her life easier. Well, that was not quite all, he wanted her in his bed.

When he stepped inside the home he rented, he sat down, writing another letter to his solicitor and to his mother, The Duchess. What he put in motion, he meant for it to answer the questions to Cat's parentage.

The first letter was meant for his solicitor inquiring as to the progress in purchasing the townhouse. The second one was to his mother.

Mother,

I've met a woman with a very interesting story. She is about eighteen years of age and the most beautiful woman I've ever met. Just looking at her steals my breath. This evening she told me her father was an English lord but she didn't knew who his name and her mother died in childbirth. I'm guessing the mother ran away from the man because Caitlin ended up here in Ireland. This isn't a lot of information to go on, but I will be forever in your debt if you can inquire into her possible

parentage.
   Love, your son
   Roc

~ * ~

   Caitlin watched Roc walk down the road then she slowly closed the door behind her. With the door closed, she leaned against it, her back resting on the wood. She touched a fingertip to her lips, recalling the sweetness of his kiss and longing for more.

   The only other time she'd been kissed was when Blair caught her behind the pub. He'd pressed her hard against the side of the tavern demanding a response she couldn't give him. She shuddered, her skin seeming to crawl.

   Turning quickly, she locked the door. Sometimes when he wasn't too drunk, Blair turned up after she went home, banging on the door until he gave up and left. Before she put her nightdress on, she blew out the lanterns and the candles.

   Darkness surrounded her when she finally pulled back the covers to the bed and slipped beneath the quilt. She turned over, pounding the pillow as if that would help her sleep, but thoughts of Roc's kisses kept her awake.

   To bad Roc was an English lord. Why couldn't he be a commoner like her, someone she could let herself fall in love with? He was handsome, his broad shoulders narrowing to lean hips. His well-muscled legs long, but it was his dark brown eyes that drew her to him, beckoning her and making her feel so hot she wanted to take off all her clothes. But tonight she enjoyed his lips pressed against hers. They were full and warm, soft too, probably the only soft part of him.

   Hours later it seemed she drifted off to an uneasy slumber, dreams of Roc and his kisses haunting her as she pulled and tugged at the bedding. When the clock finally chimed six times, the covers were wrapped around her legs and her body was sweat sheened.

   Rubbing her eyes, she quickly rose and padding to the small kitchen, she took a loaf bread and cheese from the cupboard then heated water on the stove for tea. While she waited for the water to boil, she dressed in a well-worn day dress suitable for cleaning the bar before pulling her hair back and winding it into a tight chignon.

She ate quickly, eager to get the cleaning finished and return to her cottage. They were going for a carriage ride and her fingers shook at the idea of sitting next to him and watching the scenery go by. She wanted another kiss and meant to figure out how to convince him of that. Perhaps she could initiate the kiss. Would he like that?

Winding her fingers around the hot cup, she let the heat warm her hands while she sipped the tea and ate a few bites. She felt a little nauseous, nerves rattling while she thought about spending some special time with Roc.

When she left, she locked the door behind her even though nothing ever happened in the small town of Portrush. She was wary of Blair and what he might do when he had too much to drink and when he discovered she'd let Roc walk her home last night, she didn't know what he might do.

She hoped her da had not let him sleep in the tavern and that she wouldn't find him residing in some dark corner. Waking him so she could clean did not bode well for her. He would ask her about last night because she didn't doubt he saw her walk out of the pub with Roc. It would surprise her if he hadn't followed her.

The tavern was quiet and empty when she stepped through the door. She pulled the curtains apart to let the light of the day inside. No one slept in a corner on the floor. Her breathing seemed to even out as she let the breath she'd been holding from her lungs. Her wishes had been granted.

Grabbing a damp cloth from the back room, she cleaned the tables then put the chairs on top of them so she could mop the floors.

A few hours later she finished her chores and was taking off her apron when a noise in the back caught here attention. She peaked around the corner, "Da? Is that you?"

"It's me, Caitlin. You about finished," he asked walking through the kitchen to meet her and give her a quick hug. "You got a few minutes? I'd like to speak with you about last night." He rubbed his neck, a gesture he used when his nerves were on edge.

Inhaling a long deep breath, she braced herself for a lecture about Roc and why he wasn't good for her and that she shouldn't let him walk her home. She took a quick look at the clock, "I've about thirty minutes."

"Good, put two chairs down for us to sit on." He walked into the main room with two cups of coffee and some freshly made tarts from Ida's place.

"I know what you're going to say, Da." She reached out accepting the hot cup and sipping gingerly.

"I don't think you do." He drank seeming to study her before he bit into the lemon tart.

"Yes, I can already hear you telling me that he's a lord and he's going back to England. All he wants from me is one thing." Her fury escalated as she thought about what she said about herself. Surely she had something more to offer a man than just her body.

Her da was shaking his head, his expression grim. "No, don't need to tell you something you know. Rest assured this is different and it's coming from my heart because I love you."

"Then what?" Impatiently, she ran her finger along the rim of her cup, her mind still on the outing this afternoon with Roc. "Da, I love you too but we rarely agree anymore."

"Your mother." He leaned back in the chair, crossing his well-muscled arms over his chest and tucking his hands under his armpits.

"Mother? You've never said much about her. Why now? Because you think I'm on the verge of making the biggest mistake of my live?"

He leaned forward, bracing his forearms on the table. "Your mother, Fiona, she loved an adventure. It seemed to me she always wanted what she couldn't have. She flitted back and forth from here to Belfast. One day she didn't come home. I got a message from her months later that she was in London and she'd met a man, a marquise, she said or maybe an earl."

"I've heard some of this," she said yet she never tired of stories about the mother she never met. "Nothing you say about my mother can be compared to me. I'm satisfied here in Portrush even though..." She moistened her lips reminding herself Roc was not for her. "There is no one here for me. I'm fine with that."

"I know, bear with me. She returned about a year after she ran off and about ten months after I got the letter from her."

"I'm not going to let that happen. I'm no man's mistress, never will be. If I've learned anything from the stories about Mother, I know what I don't want." Anger simmered deep inside and she understood the simple facts about this. If she didn't know her mother's story, she'd most likely do the same thing. Roc could seduce her if she allowed it, but that scenario would never come to fruition. She would not allow it to happen.

"So you say. I just want you t be careful." He reached for her hands and for a short time he held them in his. "A man such as your lord can be very persuasive to a naïve young woman such as yourself."

"I promise. This," she gestured around the room, "is all I need." But it wasn't. She craved a wonderful man to call husband. There was no one in Portrush and for a moment she understood her mother's need to leave the small village. The move had been necessary for happiness, but it resulted in her death.

"I've pushed you toward Blair because he is a lord, an Irish one. He can take care of you. He has an estate and despite his penchant for drink, is well taken care of."

"He's a drunk and a lecher." She rubbed her arms, wishing her da would find something else to speak of. "The thought of kissing him, or lying in bed with him sends chills up my spine."

"While he's a sloppy drunk, he'll never break your heart." It seemed he gave one last effort to convince her that marrying Blair would be good for her.

"You can't break anything you don't possess. I despise the man and you know as well as I do that he's a mean drunk."

"I don't think he would hurt you." Her da tried to defend Blair to her, but it wasn't going to work.

"He kicked a dog just last night because the poor animal wanted food. You feed the strays leftovers, the animal was just eager." Her words grew more heated and she became more determined as she spoke of Blair and the cruelty that lay just below the surface.

"He would never hurt a woman," he repeated, "especially you. He thinks himself in love with you.

She stood too quickly, knocking over her chair, "He won't hurt me because I don't plan on giving the odious man a chance. A title is not the worth of a man or a woman. Unless you have something else to say, it's time for me to leave. This is discussion is finished."

"What's your hurry? Sit a moment and relax." He reached out again this time to stop her. "You're not working tonight so you've got time."

She didn't want to lie to him, but she didn't see any other recourse. Perhaps leaving out something wasn't a lie. If she didn't come in early this morning the question would have never come up. "I'm tired. I didn't sleep well last night. I need to go home and this discussion with you is exhausting."

"Did your lord stay the night?" His voice turned angry, perhaps accusatory while he glared at her.

"Of course not. Don't you believe me when I tell you I'm not going to sleep with the man. He will not be in my bed because I understand he could never marry a commoner, and I won't be his mistress or his whore." She was very nearly screaming while the frustration of the morning and the lost sleep took over her senses and emotions.

"I'm sorry, dear. I do believe you. It's just that I can no longer protect you and I know that for a fact. I wanted you to have a good man, but it doesn't seem to be happening." He motioned for her to leave. "Go on, get some sleep. I apologize for making you angry."

"Blair O'Connell is not a good man. You need to tell him that you take back what you offered months ago. I'm not ever going to be that man's wife. So tell him I'm unpromised to him."

Her da cleared his throat. "I'll try but it seems he's given me a loan that I would have to pay back if you don't wed him."

She had been on her way out the door, but with those words she whirled on him, fists clenched at her sides. "You sold me? Was the O'Connell the highest bidder? How dare you do such a thing."

With that said she was out the door, slamming it shut behind her. She muttered as she raced to her cottage, needing a hot bath to get the filth of this conversation with the man she'd always trusted to have her best interests at heart off her body. She didn't think she could scrub enough.

Inside she set the pots to boiling then pumped water into buckets to partially fill the tub. Gazing at the clock, she realized she'd have to settle for a tepid bath. Once the water was in the small tub she tore off her clothes, letting them fall on the floor then slipped into the water.

She only had fifteen minutes to bathe and dress. Soaping and rinsing she managed to wash all of her, including her hair. When she stood, she wrapped a bath sheet around her and stepped behind the curtain separating her bed from the main room.

The knocking on the door caught her attention. She turned to look just as Roc opened the door and looked inside.

"Cat, you ready? I know I'm a little early but I wanted to see you." He stepped inside when she didn't answer right away.

She gasped, moving backward and stumbling over the bucket she used to rinse the soap. "No."

"I brought you something..."

A dog jumped on her, licking her face and wagging its huge tale. Desperately, she tried to keep her towel in place. "An Irish Wolf Hound?" She tried to stand but the puppy kept her firmly on the floor.

Roc strode around the corner. "You don't have to take him if you don't..." Quickly he backed from the room. "Sorry, didn't realize you didn't have any clothes on."

She was sure she heard a hint of laughter and maybe a touch of appreciation, and she realized she wasn't very embarrassed. She didn't think he'd seen much except her legs sticking out from beneath the bath towel.

"Just wait out there and take this little guy or he'll never let me get dressed." She laughed as the dog licked her nose again. "Go on, go to your master. Shew."

"You're his master and I can't get him unless I come where you are." He was really laughing now, and if she wasn't completely naked underneath this simple covering, she'd laugh too.

She saw his booted feet, perfectly shined Hessians, below the curtain. "Come get him, but close your eyes."

"Don't think that will work. Don't want to fall into your tub. I'll try to keep from looking at you but it's going to be hard."

"Very well." She let out a long breath of air. "Do your best. I suppose my legs aren't anything you haven't seen before." A sudden and unexpected wave of jealousy washed through her at her very own words.

He stepped around the curtain, and she knew he wasn't looking at her but the dog was practically sitting on her lap. If he were to retrieve the animal, he'd have no recourse but to take a quick look. She pulled the towel higher but as the dog wiggled on her lap, one edge slipped dangerously low. She tugged again.

"There, got him." He now held the squirming puppy in his arms and backed from the room with a devilish grin that set her heart spinning and her mind whirling with so many scenarios she didn't know what direction to take.

"I'll be right out." She dropped the bath sheet before putting on the clothing she'd carefully laid out just a few minutes ago.

"Better be or this little guy is going to be around that corner again. Can't hold this squirming bundle of energy forever."

"Done." She stepped around the curtain, grinning at him, just as the dog wiggled from Roc's arms and made a mad dash for the doorway.

"Oh no," Roc said, racing to take the dog outside but it was too late. The dog stopped and spread legs was doing just what they feared.

"He peed on my floor." She started laughing then laughed harder when Roc joined her, tears sliding down her cheeks.

"I'll clean it up," he volunteered, still laughing. He looked around the room and she pointed to a place by the sink where he found a sponge and soap.

"Tell me why the dog and why do you want to give him to me? Is it one of Ida's dogs?"

In the middle of cleaning up the spill, the dog pranced around him, seeming to think this was some type of game. "Yes, I picked up a basket of food from Ida and she told me the puppies were ready to leave their mama. Thought you could use a good dog for protection."

"I do love dogs and perhaps that's not a bad idea," she told him, scooping the puppy into her arms. Thoughtfully, she rubbed its ears, but he didn't want anything to do with petting. He managed to get out of her arms then found one of her wool socks, worrying it and shaking it as if he meant to kill it. "Now he's got my sock, little rascal."

On hands and knees, Rock grabbed the animal, retrieving the sock without letting the dog put a hole in it. "Got it." He held the sock in the air as if it was a prized possession.

"What am I going to do with him? I can't keep him outside. I've nowhere to put the little devil."

"Let's build a place where you can put him when you're gone. It won't hold him for long, but at least we can go on our outing. Then we can think of something else." He looked for pieces of furniture he could put together to make a pen. "There." He brushed his hands together then picked up the dog, setting him in the new pen. Then he put a bowl of water where the dog could get to it. "You're going to have to think of a name."

She walked toward him, trying to put her damp hair into a manageable do. "I have no idea what to call that beast and in a less than a year, he's going to eat me out of house and home."

"Let me help you with your hair. Can't help you with anything else." She turned her back to him, setting the needed pins on a nearby table. In a matter of seconds, he secured her hair.

"How do you know how to do that? Never mind, I probably don't want to know," she murmured, the same wave of jealousy she felt earlier surfaced. "Do you think he'll still be there when we get back?"

He lifted his shoulders in a gesture that said he didn't know. "I've picked up some of the things you left on the floor just in case he makes a jail break."

"Thank you." She didn't know why she was thanking him. He brought a little adorable nuisance into her home, one she could only feed if Da helped her out with scraps from the pub.

"Do you want a shawl," he asked as he grabbed one from the coat stand as well as her fiddle case. "It appears it might rain a bit."

Outside a breeze ruffled her air and made the leaves on the trees shimmer. A mountain of white clouds billowed on the horizon, but the carriage caught her attention.

"It's huge," she whispered totally in awe.

He let his head fall back, roaring with laughter. "It has nearly all the comforts of home. When I sail on one my ships, I always bring it with me. Come take a look. I had it custom made." He held out his arm for her.

She didn't understand why he laughed at her comment, but she did like laughter; much preferred it over anger and some of the other more depressing emotions. Didn't even care if he laughed at her, she'd try to find a way to laugh with him.

"I would like to see inside."

"Then you shall," he told her, opening the door and helping her inside.

The interior was plush and the seats wide enough to sit three across. "It's beautiful," she said, awestruck, looking to see if he laughed. "Is it as comfortable?"

"Not as much as your sofa at home, and when the carriage is moving one can't get rid of the potholes and rocks on the road but otherwise, yes. It has storage beneath the seats where I keep blankets and other items I've found I like to have handy on trips."

"Did Ida make the basket of food for you?" She sat down, running her hands along the fabric of the seats, soaking in the luxury, thinking if she had something like this to ride in she might like to take a trip to Belfast or perhaps farther to Dublin.

"For us." He corrected then sat across from her. "For long trips I had the man who made this carriage put in pullouts, see." He showed her. "I can sleep, well perhaps relax a bit more than normal."

"Potholes and rocks." She wondered if he ever slept with a woman here.

"No, I haven't," he said grinning again.

"Haven't what?" He couldn't possibly know what she'd been thinking. Why would his mind go there as well unless he was thinking about doing that with her?

"I haven't slept with any woman in this carriage or any other one I own," he told her, holding her hand in his.

"How many do you own?" She didn't understand why she was prying into his life. In a week or so he would leave. He'd told her as much and she'd never see him again.

"Two carriages and four ships." Letting go of her hand he leaned back, spreading his arms across the back of the seat, a smug expression on his handsome and too debonair features. Confidence exuded from him.

"You're very wealthy. What do you see in me?" She wanted to slap herself for asking the question. Didn't she know what he saw in her, an easy conquest and his next mistress? She meant to stay ahead of his game. She wasn't going to be an easy conquest.

"Does that bother you?" He tapped on the roof signaling the driver to start. "And I see a lot in you. You're a beautiful and intelligent woman. I could listen to you play your fiddle all day long."

"He does know where we are going?" She needed to change the subject before she put her foot in her mouth again.

"I certainly hope so," he said, leaning forward and reaching for her hands. "You need to try and relax. You're as stiff as a broomstick. I don't want to make you nervous. This is supposed to an enjoyable outing for you."

"It's just hard when you're so handsome and all I can think about is the kiss last night." She wished she hadn't said that.

His grin sent her heart spinning. "You liked the kiss, does that mean you want another one?" He suddenly drew her to his side of the carriage, settling her on his laps while his lips found hers.

~ * ~

"You've betrayed me," Blair O'Connell, Earl of Glenwild, glared at Sean O'Shea, Caitlin's da, over his pint of Guinness.

Sean pushed the money he borrowed from Blair toward the man, "I didn't meant to betray anyone. The lass doesn't want to marry you. Says she won't."

"You should have done more," Blair insisted, his glare still firmly planted on Sean.

"Did all I could do. If you didn't get drunk every night and right in front of Caitlin, you might have stood a better chance."

"Don't want your money back," Blair pushed it back toward Sean.

"You and I both know you only gave it to me because you thought she'd be your wife. Get it through your thick skull, it's not going to happen." Sean understood most of why Caitlin wanted nothing to do with this man.

"I'm going to find a way to make her say yes." He drank down the beer then pushed the glass toward Sean asking for more.

Sean felt a sick feeling fill his gut. His first thought went to revenge and he recalled Caitlin's words. If he could kick a dog he could certainly do the same to a woman.

"You'll keep your distance where she is concerned," Sean gritted out, his fists tight.

"Or you'll do what? Do you forget who I am? I could have you arrested on some trumped up charge if I wanted to get rid of you."

"You could do that but no matter how smart you think you are or how much power you think you have, the man who is even now courting Caitlin can squish you with his thumb." Sean felt good that he'd done his research on the Duke of Ravenswood. The family was powerful and while the duke had not been present in London for years, it seemed his mother wielded more power than anyone but the prince regent.

"Just why do you think to have such an absurd idea. Who is this man, Roc Leighton, I believe."

"Perhaps I should allow you to find out the hard way by crossing him." Sean liked that idea and the more he thought about it, the better it became. For a time he'd truly harbored the idea of a wedding between Blair and Caitlin, now he sensed what she felt all along. He was a despicable man.

"I'm the most powerful man all the way to Belfast. No one gainsays me." He puffed up a bit with those words.

"Ever heard of The Duchess?" Sean let the question hang for a few seconds while he waited for an answer.

"Never," Blair said but his usually ruddy complexion turned sallow.

Sean knew, just as everyone in these parts knew, who The Duchess was. "The Duchess is Roc's mother, but of course I see you've realized that meager fact. Roc is the Duke of Ravenswood and he commands all the power now."

"Well..." Blair sputtered. "He won't marry her like I would have.

No, he'll take her virginity which was mine to take then he'll turn her into his mistress instead of his wife."

"It was only yours if Caitlin wished to grant it to the likes of you. Now the object of your obsession is out of your reach. I wouldn't even protest if Caitlin chose to become his mistress over becoming your wife" Sean watched for more reactions to the stunning news as well as his insinuations.

"You're just a bitter man because you never found a wife for yourself. You had to take solace in raising Fiona's girl," Blair shot out as if trying to anger him.

He never wanted a wife because he preferred men. He'd always kept a low profile where his desires were concerned. No one in this small village knew of his preference except Ida. She had become his confidant.

"Never had the desire for a wife because I stayed busy with Caitlin. Don't regret one tiny second either." He wiped his hands on the apron he wore. "Clients are starting to come into the pub. I've got work. If you know what's good for you, stay away from Caitlin. It's not a threat from me but one from the duke to you through me."

Blair sauntered to a table after ordering food. He seemed contrite, nursing his beer and staring out the window, his eyes glazed over. Sean had the feeling Blair would be sleeping on the floor tonight unless he could summon one of his servants to bring him home.

He'd be so drunk he wouldn't bother Caitlin, at least Sean prayed that would be the case.

Other Books by Christine Young
Available at Rogue Phoenix Press

Catching Meara
Book One in the McKenna Clan Series

Meara Thorton was a feisty, world-class computer hacker—cornered by the FBI and shockingly given the chance to be their newly acquired technical analyst. Brilliant and intuitive, yet aching with the loss of everyone she has cared about, her restless heart led her to discover a love she fought and a world she didn't know could possibly exist.

Sweet Sexy Sadie
Book Two in the McKenna Clan Series

From the first time Sadie's eyes met those of Brody McKenna in the hot Sierra Madre Mountains, theirs was a potent attraction—not gentle, slow, and easy, but hot, hard, and all-consuming. The daughter of a dysfunctional family, Sadie had dreams no man could wrench from her with hot sex and an all-consuming passion. She'd challenge this alpha male with all the strength she possessed. But her red hair, fiery temperament, and indomitable spirit obsessed Brody...and he knew he had to find a way to show her he was more than he appeared and convince her to make a life with him.

Sweet Misbehavin'
Book Three in the McKenna Clan Series

Cast adrift after fleeing the home of Jokul, the ice demon, Atantsi, a firestarter, grew to womanhood as she moved through time to keep the demon from finding her. Though stubborn and courageous, she was ill prepared to use powers she had not been taught. Her first sight of the intoxicating Carr McKenna left her breathless, and her second encounter gave her hope for a future she never thought she had.

A playboy, a second son and a shifter, a man who thought his life would be carefree, Carr McKenna was shocked to discover the woman he'd paid as an escort is a firestarter who is running for her life. He is the leader of all the McKennas around the world and that he has multiple powers. His passion for Margo and the need to defend her might cost him his life as well as hers.

Sweet Talkin' Sugar
Book Four in the McKenna Clan Series

Lyonesse McKenna, was dreaming or was she? From the instant Lyn saw Deacon McClain across a black jack table in a crowed Las Vegas casino the unmistakable attraction sent Lyn's senses flying into overdrive. Her family of shapeshifters believed in soul mates. She'd always been skeptical yet she couldn't help but question the way her heart sped when he looked at her.

When Deacon appeared in Las Vegas he knew his first job was to save Lyn from a Sea Demon, but the next order of business was to convince her he would someday mean more to her than she'd ever expected. But her stubborn nature and unbendable spirit consumed Deacon...and he had to chase away all the demons real and imagined in order to win her heart.

Sweet Surrender

Book Five in the McKenna Clan Series

Ripped from her family at the top of Infinity Cliff, Kimi McKenna finds herself thrust somewhere into the future. Dark elements threaten to destroy the earth unless Kimi can work together with the white witch to stop the destruction. Confused by her mate's role in the conspiracy, she refuses to acknowledge the connection. But amidst raging fire and attacks on the people she is coming to hold dear, she allows Maska O'keefe into her heart.

Maska O'keefe has loved the beautiful shapeshifter for years. Unable to save her life years ago, he vows to watch over her as he is given a second chance to convince her that even though he is a witch and not a shifter, they are indeed soul mates. Kimi's divided loyalties between her family and the cause she is now a part of will determine their relationship. Only the part she plays as the messiah can bring this to a conclusion in the final battle.

Dakota's Bride
The first book in the Lakota/Pinkerton Series

When Emma St. John received her brother's letter imploring her to escape her stepfather's vengeful scheme and to trust Dakota Barringer with her life, she was willing to chance it. But the handsome, brooding riverboat owner Emma found in Natchez a danger of another kind. For Emma soon found herself surrendering to an unrelenting desire.

Raised by the Sioux when his parents were killed, Dakota had been betrayed once before by a white woman. He wasn't about to trust another, especially one claiming that her stepfather, a powerful U.S. senator, had framed her as a murderess. But he couldn't let Emma's intoxicating effect on him. Now Dakota would risk his very life to protect the innocent beauty who had seduced him with her tender love.

My Angel
The second book in the Lakota/Pinkerton Series

A BEAUTY IN BUCKSKINS
When her father decided to send her to a finishing school back East, Angela Chamberlain refused to be confined to stuffy drawing rooms. Instead, the daring spitfire who could shoot like a man and ride like the wind longed for a life of adventure and romance—and she knew exactly who could give it to her. Devil Blackmoor was a hired gun with a dangerous reputation. But Angela was willing to go to the ends of the earth to capture the handsome devil's heart.

A DEVIL IN DISGUISE
He'd come to America looking for excitement, but Devil Blackmoor got more than he bargained for when he encountered a beautiful rebel who answered his kisses with a wild innocence that touched his very soul. Yet standing between them were more obstacles than either ever dreamed. For Devil had strapped on a gun for the wrong man. And that made Angela his enemy. Now he'll have to choose between his duty and the woman he loves more than life.

The Locket
The third book in the Lakota/Pinkerton Series

The year is 1894. Seeking revenge for crimes against his family, Misha Petrovich follows a path that leads straight to Ariel Cameron's boarding house in Mist Harbor, Oregon. A family heirloom in Ariel's possession leads Misha to believe she is guilty. The locket has been handed down to the oldest girl in the Petrovich family for generations. Ariel is innocent of wrong doing, but her father is not. Misha is torn by his feelings for Ariel and his need for restitution against her father. Knowing that the relationship between them is fragile, Misha does everything in his power to protect Ariel's father. His efforts are to no avail when her father is shot. Ariel comes to realize Misha's steadfast courage and determination to protect her and her father despite what has happened to his family. Ariel's love and devotion heals Misha's heart.

The Talisman
The fourth book in the Lakota/Pinkerton Series

Running from a marriage that lasted one night, Dr. Moriah McKeown discovers the land she has settled on is coveted by determined and lawless men. Yet the proud young woman who once vowed never to abandon her home has second thoughts when her adopted children are threatened. Her only recourse is to enlist the aid of a dark, dangerous gun for hire.

Haunted by the past and a betrayal he will never forgive, Ian Civanovich uses his fast gun and his reckless courage to forget the faithlessness of a woman in his past. He will trust no female—nor will he rest until the threat hovering over Moriah McKeown is put to rest.

Forever His
The fifth book in the Lakota/Pinkerton Series

Struggling to come to terms with the part she played in Jacob St. John's death, Etta Barringer resigns from Pinkerton Agency and seeks peace and solace in a Rocky Mountain Cabin.

Jacob has vowed to discover the reason Etta has betrayed him, sold him out to his enemy and left him for dead.

Isolated in their cabin, they discover their love for each other and learn to trust. But the trust is shattered when Jacob learns she is married to his sworn enemy; the man who left him in the desert to die.

Allura's Secret
Twelve Dancing Princesses Book One

Allura McClellan is horrified by her father's decision to take out an ad in the Times awarding her to the man strong enough and smart enough to win her hand and uncover her secrets. She's an intelligent young woman who takes great delight in the freedom allotted to her by her father. She's well aware that marriage would effectively curtail the adventures she's shared with her sisters and cousins.

Hunter Gray is nothing like the other men who've arrived to vie for Allura's hand in marriage and everything that goes along with it. However, he is the first to refuse to concede defeat and pursue her despite her attempts to disguise her true appearance. It's her temperament that is of more concern to him than her looks. Hunter has worked all his life with the hope of someday owning his own land. Now that it looks like there's a very real possibility that everything he's ever wanted is within reach nothing is going to deter him – including Miss Allura's disagreeable disposition.

Amorica's Wager
Twelve Dancing Princesses Book Two

Amorica Hepburn was sent to London to find a husband. Finding a man was the last item on her agenda. With her two cousins, Amorica wagers she can dissuade her suitor before the others. Despite her efforts she discovers a chemistry that cannot be denied. Suddenly she is the arrogant man's wife, pledged to a marriage neither desire. But swept off to his ancestral home above the Dover cliffs and into his strong embrace, Amorica is soon possessed by a raging passion for the husband she had vowed to despise...

Damian Andrews couldn't afford to trust the emerald-eyed spitfire who happened upon his secret. Amorica's hatred of all men of his kind only inflames the war that rages between them. Still, he can not control the intense desire his stubborn bride inspires, or make her surrender to his will until he has conquered the headstrong beauty on the battlefield of love...

Ravyn's Marriage of Inconvenience
Twelve Dancing Princesses Book Three

A REGAL BEAUTY

When the duchess decides to wed her to a wastrel and a fop, Ravyn Grahm takes matters into her own hands and declares her engagement to another man. Instead of fessing up and telling her great aunt what she has done, she goes through with the pretense. Aric Lakeland is the bastard son of an earl and has a dangerous reputation. But Ravyn is willing to do most anything to keep the duchess from discovering the lie.

A DEVIL-MAY-CARE SMUGGLER

He'd bought land in America, looking to put down roots and end his life of adventure, but Aric Lakeland got more than he bargained for when he encountered a beautiful heiress who made a promise she didn't want to keep. But the promise could not be undone and standing between them were more obstacles than either ever dreamed. Aric had made plans to spend the rest of his life in America and that was at odds with Ravyn's plan of living in England and running her father's estate. Now, he'll have to choose between his dreams and the woman he loves more than life.

Christel's Sunrise
Twelve Dancing Princesses Book Four

He Made Her An Offer...

Life has thrown Christel McClellan some experiences that could have devastated a less determined woman. Beautiful, self-assured and fiercely independent, she is trying to forget the loss of her stillborn child. But is the child alive?

She Couldn't Deny...

Life is carefree for Ryder MacLaren who loves to see what is on the other side of the sunrise. Laird of Clan MacLaren, he is wealthy, handsome and happily unencumbered...until stunning Christel McClellan enters his life. When he hears her story, he believes the child she thought dead has been sold to a wealthy buyer.

Storm's Passion
Twelve Dancing Princesses Book Five

SHE MADE A PROPOSAL...

Life strikes Storm Graham a shattering blow when she learns her father has bartered her to a man she detests. Storm is beautiful, self–assured and fiercely independent, and refuses to be a pawn in her father's schemes, yet she can find no way out of this bargain made in hell. Going on the offensive she asks the wealthiest man on the eastern coast of England to marry her, never believing she might fall in love.

HE TRIED TO REFUSE...

For Hadden Johnston life has provided everything he ever wanted, including a sanctuary for homeless children. He is wealthy, handsome and happily unencumbered...until stunning Storm Graham marches into his life and proposes a marriage of convenience. Yet this type of marriage to a woman who inflames his senses is far from acceptable. If he's going to be tied down, he will move heaven and earth to have this woman warming his bed.

Gotta Have Fayth
Twelve Dancing Princesses Book Six

A regal beauty with raven hair and piercing blue eyes, Fayth Graham is unwilling to parade herself in front of the wealthy Lords of England during the season. Seeking a means to dissuade any man wishing to wed her, she seeks a way to ruin herself for marriage. When she unexpectedly meets a man with sparkling gray eyes and an infectious grin, she decides this is the man who will keep her from agreeing to obey.

He returned from six months at sea, looking for a few nights of pleasure with a willing lass, but Jarret Kinsley got more than he bargained for when he met a beautiful debutant who responded to his kisses with a wild innocence that touched his heart. Yet the obstacles looming between them might rip them apart. Both had vowed never to marry, so when consequences of their dalliances got in the way, Jarret would have to choose between the life he's always desired and the woman he loves more than life.

Ella's Pleasure
Twelve Dancing Princesses Book Seven

A WHISPER OF PLEASURE

Ella Hepburn was an auburn haired debutant from the harsh Scottish coastline—a wild innocent to be seduced and tamed. A spirited beauty, she captivated Drake Montgomerie's jaded heart—while succumbing to the smoldering desire she felt for her unyielding suitor.

A WHISPER OF DANGER

In Drake Montgomerie's glittering world of money and privilege, young Ella discovered passion and desire could overcome everything she'd been taught to resist—entangling Drake, the heir apparent, in a lethal coil of aristocratic family intrigue. But grave peril would only nurse the sparks of a love that knew no limits and a magnificent ecstasy that would not be denied.

Eveleen's Seduction
Twelve Dancing Princesses Book Eight

A WHISPER OF SEDUCTION

A brutal attack on Eveleen Hepburn's cherished island off the Scottish coastline leaves her shattered and bewildered. Learning a man she once trusted can kill as easily as he can breathe even though the deed saves her life, creates questions that need answers. An innocent beauty, she enchants Logan Maxwell's cynical heart—giving in to the raging passion she feels for her mysterious suitor.

A WHISPER OF INTRIGUE

In Logan's Maxwell's world of espionage and privilege, young Eveleen discovers truths about herself she never expected, and a need for passion and love can overcome all her fears if she learns to accept certain truths. She finds herself entangled in a lethal battle for land that was once owned by French nobility, taken from them during the revolution and sold to Maxwell. But grave peril would unleash the flames of love that simmers, creating a magical union that cannot be refuted.

Tavia's Deception
Twelve Dancing Princesses Book Nine

WHISPERS OF DECEPTION

When her father decides to send her to London for her season, Tavia Hepburn resolves to see the world instead. The raven haired beauty decides to disguise herself as a lad and find employment on a ship bound for Barcelona as a cabin boy. But she never bargains on finding passion and love to a red haired sea captain who rescues her from certain death.

WHISPERS OF MURDER

For James Macmurra, the world is black and white until he meets a young debutante, who turns his world upside down. He's unable to deny Tavia's intoxicating effect on him. In a match tense with obstacles, unwillingness to divulge secrets, and unforeseen peril, irresistible desire and passion grows into undeniable love. James would risk his life to shelter and protect the innocent debutante who seduces him with her sweet love.

Larena's Fascination
Twelve Dancing Princesses Book Ten

WHISPERS OF FASCINATION

Fiery, free spirited Larena Graham never wanted to marry a duke. She is thrilled to be in love with the fourth son of an aristocrat, Gavin Broon. But when it seems Gavin ignores her, she set her sights on politics and bettering human life. Unsuspecting intrigue and a plot against her, she continues her dangerous plans despite Gavin's wishes.

WHISPERS OF TRUST

Gavin has every intention of properly courting the beautiful Larena until he must leave the city in order to put his affairs in order. Returning to London, he finds the woman he means to make his own is embroiled in political protests that could lead to a prison ship. Larena must learn to trust the handsome Scotsman whose most pressing mission is to protect her and keep her from harm.

Tira's Eeucation
Twelve Dancing Princesses Book Eleven

WHISPERS OF EDUCATION

Learning how to build ships is Tira Hepburn's only dream until she meets Jamie Lundin and her world is turned upside down. With her raven black hair and vivid green eyes, she tempts Jamie and pushes him to defy his vows. She never bargains on finding an irrevocable love and a passion to a man who cannot fulfill her dreams despite his burning desire for her.

WHISPERS OF A BARGAIN

Arrogant and self-assured Jamie is brought up short when Tira captures his heart. All his carefully made plans are put to the test when he decides to teach her the art of ship building if she will spend a week with him alone on his ship. He is unable to deny Tira's intoxicating effect on him. When Tira leaves him behind unwilling to live with him without the benefit of marriage, he races after her. Jamie will risk everything to shelter and protect the innocent debutante who seduces him with her sweet love.

Twelve Days to Love

When Archer Steele shows up at Calanthe Durand's failing plantation with an alligator over his shoulder, Cali thinks she's never seen a more handsome man. During the war she had to defend herself and her servants from both union and confederate soldiers. Independent and self-sufficient, she vows to never marry.

But Archer Steele has different ideas. The first time Archer sees Cali in town, he feels an instant attraction. He decides he will do everything and anything to convince the beautiful Miss Durand he is worthy of her love. During the weeks leading up to Christmas, he gives her twelve gifts in hopes she will fall in love with him. Yet they are faced with challenges they must overcome before Cali can commit to a marriage.

Door to Heaven

Jessica Lawrence is the stepdaughter of a woman born in the twentieth century transported back in time to the year 1868. An acclaimed suffragette, she raises Jessica to believe in the equality of women. Jess Law believes everything she was taught, and when the time is right she becomes a private investigator. Courageous and impetuous, Jess finds danger in her quest to save all women from white slavery. Her passionate mission results in a wedding to Roc Newman, a man she knows can steal her heart...

Roc can't trust the sapphire-eyed spitfire who invades his home in search of secret papers and knocks him flat with her karate moves. Jessica's refusal to obey his wishes serves to inflame the war between them. Still, he cannot control the intense desire his reluctant bride inspires, or make her surrender her independence, until he has conquered the headstrong beauty on the battlefield of love...

Rebel Heart

HER REBEL SPIRIT DEFIED HIS OUTSIDERS SOUL... She was velvet and silk, eyes the color of a summer storm and amber hair. Victoria DeMontville, because of a promise and a codicil to her father's will, was forced to marry one man to protect her from another. She hated Cameron Savage with a fierce passion. But to hold on to her genetic research and find a cure for the deadly Signe virus, she must pretend to love the enemy at her door, come with weapons of fire to melt her icy heart...

HIS OUTSIDERS TOUCH IGNITED RAGING PASSIONS... He wore a mask, disguised as the Phantom, a true legend come to life. Even as war and debate over new genetic research engulfed them all, he would find his greatest adversary in the beauty who'd branded him an outsider and barbarian, the woman he was born to possess, his soul mate.

Safari Moon

Solo St. John, a wildlife photographer, is preparing for a trip to Alaska. Suddenly, Solo finds women of all sorts invading his privacy, his home and his office, all cooing nonsense words and blatantly throwing themselves at him. Solo doesn't know why, and he has no idea how to rid himself of the persistent women. He finally decides to beg a favor of his best buddy Nyssa Harrington.

In love with Solo for the past ten years and knowing he doesn't return her feelings Nyssa doesn't want to talk to Solo. She knows if she accepts his phone call, she will not be able to resist the temptation to hope again.

Straight to Heaven

Running from demons, Alexandra McMurdie stumbles into Forbidden Ground where up is down and elements of nature are contested. Though a strong independent woman in the twenty-first century' she is unprepared for life in the 1800s. Her first site of the formidable James Lawrence makes her heart skip a beat, giving her cause to reconsider her desperate need to find a way home.

Born with a silver spoon, James' life was torn apart during the War Between the States. Moving west he vows to put the life he once knew in the past. When he discovers a half-frozen woman near Gold Hill, his heart begins to thaw. His love for Alexandra and his need to keep her from a man who has pursued her through time might cost him his life as well as hers.

A Valentine's Anthology

The Lending Library-a fantasy by Christie L. Kraemer

Faeries try to fit into the human world when the forest where they make their home is destroyed by a mysterious enemy.

Chasing Rainbows-a contemporary romance by Genene Valleau

An eccentric aunt, an inventive uncle, a mother who wears poodle skirts, and a brother who wears pearls provide a hilarious backdrop for the courtship of a young woman who yearns for a "normal" family.

The Gift-an historical romance by Christine Young

A man and a woman on opposite sides of the Civil War get a second chance at love after one final battle returns soldiers to their war-torn homes to rebuild their lives.

A St. Patrick's Day Tale
by
Christine Young, C. L. Kraemer, Genene Valleau

Tumble through time…

…to Ireland in 1817, when tensions are high between Protestants and Catholics and faey people guide the fate of villagers. A lovely Catholic lass stumbles upon the weakly ritual fisticuffing between Irish lads. She falls into the lap of a handsome young Protestant. Family ties, grudges, and two conniving faeries threaten their budding love. But the faeries outsmart themselves when they hijack a time machine that has mysteriously appeared in their forest and are whisked to…

…Eugene, Oregon in the 20th century, amid a property feud between the local faeries and night elves. The conniving faeries from Olde Ireland try to stir up more mischief. However, a warrior gnome convinces the magic folk to control their own destiny, and forces the intruding faeries to take refuge in the time machine again, spinning their way toward…

…A modern day castle in western Oregon. An eccentric inventor is determined to reclaim his wayward time machine and save his beloved wife from her latest misadventure. If only they can travel safely past the black hole…

a May Day Anthology
by
Christine Young, C. L. Kraemer, Rosemary Indra, Genene Valleau

Highland Miracle -- Christine Young

HURTLED THROUGH TIME, Sean Michael Sterling, landed in the midst of a May Day celebration he didn't understand, assuming the role of Laird Sterling.
ILLIGITAMATE CHILD OF NOBILITY, Reagan Douglas searches for

a way out of her half brother's house.

Defying the Odds -- C.L. Kraemer

The night elves on the hill aren't happy without their magic. They concoct a plan to punish those who were involved in the act that rendered them almost human. Meanwhile, Uther, the rogue night elf, has returned to woo the Librarian to be his eternal mate.

Love in Bloom -- Rosemary Indra

When childhood friends reunite it takes two fairies and a matchmaking daughter to help them admit their true love for each other.

No More Poodle Skirts -- Genie Gabriel

After drifting for years in the innocent age of the 1950s, a woman struggles to join today's world by finding a career and a new love, with some help from her zany family.

Once Upon a Christmas Moon
by
Christine Young, C. L. Kraemer, Genene Valleau

TWELVE DAYS TO LOVE

When Archer Steele shows up at Calanthe Durand's failing plantation with an alligator over his shoulder, Cali thinks she's never seen a more handsome man. During the war she had to defend herself and her servants from both union and confederate soldiers. Independent and self-sufficient, she vows to never marry. But Archer Steele has different ideas. The first time Archer sees Cali in town, he feels an instant attraction. He decides he will do everything and anything to convince the beautiful Miss Durand he is worthy of her love. During the weeks leading up to Christmas, he gives her twelve gifts in hopes she will fall in love with him.

BOOTS AND BLADES

An ancient evil from the old country has arrived in the high desert of Oregon. Gnome children are vanishing then re-appearing, showing various stages of traumatization. Tiamoon, warrior gnome, will put her skills to use alongside Killian, a handsome warrior, also in need of a cause.

CHRISTMAS PAWSIBILITIES

With their world destroyed and their space ship malfunctioning, the dogizens of Planet Canid have little choice but to crash land on Earth. They face tortuous experiments at the hands of the Geeks in Green...or they can trust an eccentric inventor and his zany family to deliver the Canine Queen's puppies and help them celebrate new lives.

VISIT OUR WEBSITE
FOR THE FULL INVENTORY
OF QUALITY BOOKS:

http://www.roguephoenixpress.com

Rogue Phoenix Press

Representing Excellence in Publishing

Quality trade paperbacks and downloads
in multiple formats,
in genres ranging from historical to contemporary romance,
mystery and science fiction.
Visit the website then bookmark it.
We add new titles each month!

www.ingramcontent.com/pod-product-compliance
Lightning Source LLC
Chambersburg PA
CBHW071446170626
46811CB00007B/2492